Allan Neill was born in Edinburgh and was a wartime evacuee. After National Service he became, in turn, an actor, a verbatim shorthand writer, and a theatre manager, until marriage put an end to the irresponsibility of serial career changing. In 1958 he bought the Royal Hotel in Tighnabruaich, and retained its ownership until he retired in 1997. He now lives with his wife in Argyll. He has a son, a daughter, and three granddaughters. This is his first novel.

FREEWILL
is FORFEIT

Allan
Neill

Argyll
publishing

First published in 2003 by
Argyll Publishing
Glendaruel
Argyll PA22 3AE
Scotland
www.skoobe.biz

The author has asserted his moral rights.

British Library Cataloguing-in-Publication Data.
A catalogue record for this book is available from
the British Library.

ISBN 1 902831 68 3

Origination: Cordfall Ltd, Glasgow

Printing: Bell & Bain Ltd, Glasgow

*This book is dedicated to Maureen
the star without whom I could not navigate.*

Acknowledgements

My sincere thanks to Gray Paterson for his encouragement, and forbearance.
I am grateful also to Ian Williams for technical help, to Lis Durham for editorial advice, and to Joanna Burley for her uncomplaining assistance.

If I should laugh at any mortal thing
'Tis that I should not weep

Byron

Prelude

At the age of seventeen Anna McKay was unhappy. She was suffering from the uncertainties and insecurities of teenage angst. She had come to notice men stared at her. Whilst in her company many of the males encountered often seemed prompted to behave in an odd manner. Curious about this development and rationalising it could be due only to her recent blossoming, she would gaze at her own features.

The exercise did nothing to diminish her confusion. The mirror reflected merely what was already familiar, an unremarkable teenager with dark hair. From a young age Anna had deduced her facial features were too sombre ever to be thought of as pleasing to others. What was it about her that made men stare? It was frightening and unsettling.

In an effort to ease her consternation Anna decided to seek the advice of her Form Mistress. She knew an approach to a teacher would require her to be confessional. She would have to admit she believed men ogled her, deliberately rubbed against her, also that she was confused and apprehensive, and at times felt threatened. She resolved this embarrassment would have to be faced. Unlike most teachers Miss McGregor wouldn't just huff-and-puff and send her away uninformed. Her Italian teacher would try to be supportive. Despite what others might think, Miss McGregor was a person of interesting background, broad in outlook and a good teacher of languages. Anna decided to act on instinct and visit her at the end of a school day.

She found her teacher in the process of tidying up. Anna called from the open door of the room, *'Scusi, permesso?'*

Miss McGregor continued clearing-up and said, 'Hello, Anna. Forgotten something, have you?'

'*Se è possible, vorrei parlare con Lei?*'

'Please Anna,' Miss McGregor responded, 'English, if you don't mind. Italian during class, English when school is out. Okay?' With this matter settled, she asked, 'Well, what's the matter? Boyfriend trouble, is it?'

It was her usual opener. Miss McGregor was often visited by her female charges for advice on matters relating to boys. She had been observing Anna for some time and thought it likely an approach would be made some time during the school year.

When Anna remained silent Miss McGregor stopped tidying and looked over at her pupil. She sensed her casual remark had been presumptious and caused offence and embarrassment.

'Anna, that was gauche of me. Forgive me. Come, sit down.' Anna walked into the room and selected a chair. 'All the conventional courtesies fly out of the window when you become a teacher, it's a common phenomenon,' the teacher soothed, by way of making amends. 'Sod it! It's a fag I need, I haven't had one all day. Want one?' she asked. Anna shook her head. Miss McGregor hitched her skirt, sat down and lit a cigarette. This simple movement put Anna at ease. No longer was she in the presence of a teacher, but in the company of a companion prepared to listen. 'Well young lady, what's troubling you?' Miss McGregor reopened.

'It's not boys who trouble me, it's men.' Anna watched Miss McGregor's eyebrows arch. 'Not one man,' Anna said to quell her teacher's alarm, 'but men: the entire male sex. Their attitudes and deceits confuse me. I feel I need some advice.'

Miss McGregor, to find a foothold, asked, 'Tell me Anna, are you still a virgin?'

'Of course.'

'Why, of course? Don't girls of your age do it anymore?'

'I suppose they do. Yes, all the time, in fact.'

'But you don't?'

'That's right, I don't.'

'Why? No urges? No curiosity?'

'Urges, no. Curiosity, yes.'

Freewill is Forfeit

'Does the thought of the sexual act repel you?'

'Oh! Not at all, I'm sure I'll enjoy it when it happens.'

'But you're happy to postpone it for the moment?'

'Yes. I know it will have to be faced one day. I mean it's inevitable, unavoidable really.'

'You make the prospect sound like a visit to the dentist. Is that how you feel?'

'A little I suppose.'

'You can't conceive that this might be pleasurable?'

'I don't expect it to be unpleasant.'

'Tell me, have you a current boyfriend?'

'Yes, well, I suppose so. He's a boy I've known for ages.'

'And does he ever try to. . . well, get into your panties?' Miss McGregor watched Anna squirm.

'Yes, all the time. Well, for the last two years or so.'

'Is he persistent?'

'Most of the time.'

'And you find this tiresome?'

'A bit.'

'But, you're in control?'

'Yes, but remember he's only a boy. It's men I find intimidating.'

'Examine the situation in reverse. Do you think you intimidate them?'

'How could I? I'm much too timid.'

'It's not your personality we're talking about. It's your physical attributes men find difficult to ignore.'

'My attributes?'

'They're distinctive. Let's just say you have a symmetry that sets you apart.'

'Symmetry? What do you mean?'

Miss McGregor hesitated and looked at the wall behind Anna's head. She seemed unsure what to say. When she looked at Anna once more, she said, 'Life itself will teach you soon enough that men are driven by their sexual appetites. They can't help it. What I am trying to say is all women are targets of these impulses and if the female is young and pretty like you, well . . .'

'Well what?'

'Well, the worst of them will harass you. Some will try to lift your skirt.'

'And I'll see to it they don't,' Anna said with too much vehemence.

Miss McGregor allowed herself to smile at her pupil's naivety. 'One day you'll change your mind.'

'Never.'

'You seem very positive.'

'Yes, I am.'

'You've decided to live a life of chastity, then?' Anna did not respond. 'Listen, my girl, you are made for love, all women are, but you are to be special. Your beauty singles you out.'

'Beauty?'

'You seem alarmed?'

'Yes, I am.'

'Perhaps it's sensible to be apprehensive about the power of beauty. You needn't feel so troubled, everything will work out if you learn to listen to your heart.'

'The trouble is I can't cope with the complication of being me. I'm a schoolgirl in her final year. The atmosphere at home is terrible, I've my Highers to take in a few months and then I'll have to find myself employment. With my luck it will be among leering men driven by their impulses to ravish me.'

'*Stai tranquilla, cara!* Don't be so apprehensive. I've known women to be burdened by beauty, but in each case they've created their own misfortune. Beauty can be your blessing, or your curse, but only you can determine which it is to be.' Anna remained silent. 'You must make a determined resolve it's to be your blessing.'

'I wouldn't know how to do that.'

'From time to time a little guidance wouldn't go amiss.'

'That's why I've come to you.' Anna confessed.

'And why me, young lady?'

'You're the only person I could think of.'

'You chose me from a choice of one.' The teacher smiled.

'You can help by talking to me as you're doing now, share insights from your experience, express opinions, dispense advice,' Anna pleaded.

'In short you want me to act as your mentor?'

'If you could be bothered. I'll try not to take up too much of your time, I promise.'

'Do you trust me?'

'Completely.'

Miss McGregor thought for a moment. 'Very well, but first we must try to become friends. You agree?'

'That's fantastic,' said Anna.

From that moment their friendship flourished. When not at school they met in bookshops, tearooms, museums, theatres, anywhere they considered to be of interest and improving to the mind. Religious attitudes were analysed, current European affairs discussed, politicians demeaned, travel brochures examined, irregular verbs revised, anything thought to be educational, or controversial, were the subjects of conversation. Mostly they spoke of men, of their power and influence, their common weaknesses and vulnerabilities. Anna bloomed as her knowledge of the world increased and Jane took to wearing her hats at a jauntier angle.

Anna's father was first to confront the issue of the new relationship.

'Y'er gettin' tae be a right wee hussy, you.' he complained while watching his daughter apply make-up.

'Just leave me alone father, please?' Anna pleaded.

'Naw, it's about time somethin' was said about what's goin' on. Y'er away traipsin' wae that sophisticated tart aw the 'oors o' the day and half the bloody night sometimes.'

'She's not a tart. She's a cultured woman and a very good friend of mine.'

'She's a lesbian, ya daft bitch. Or dae ye know that already?'

'That's a terrible thing to say. It's disgraceful.'

'Oh! Indignation is it. Eh? Or have I hit the nail on the heid?'

'No, it's straightforward indignation,' Anna spat.

'Now, now, that's enough, young lady.'

'No, it's not enough. You're the last person who should speak with disapproval of other people. You're a drunk, you've broken my mother's heart, you're unemployable and a pathetic example of fatherhood.'

'She loves me. My daughter loves me,' he said using heavy sarcasm. Then, his mood changed. 'Listen you, you know bugger all about anythin'. Y'er a dumb, ignorant wee lassie too gullible tae see that y'er bein' impressed by tripe.'

'You're despicable, but then you must know this.'

'A'll admit a've had ma suspicions, but the way you're headin' is straight tae hell. Dae ye hear what a'm tellin' ye? Straight tae hell.'

'If I'm going to hell it will be an improvement on this midden you call a home.'

'There's nuthin' chainin' ye tae the flair, lassie. If ye feel like that ye've got two legs and there's the door.'

'That's plain enough. I knew it would come to this. Banishment.'

'It's no' about banishment and you know it. This is aw about yer indignation.'

'It's about you making it impossible for me to live here. You've poisoned the atmosphere in this house with your drinking and bad temper.'

'Whit? Aw, I get it now. Y'er forced tae go and live wi' yer fancy woman because yer uncouth faither drove ye tae it. Is that it? Very cosy, but then ye were aye a manipulative wee bisom. Ye realise, of course, the gossip will kill yer mother.'

'What? You destroyed mother with despair years ago. If she had known what was to become of her she'd never have left Sicily. She'll know who's to blame for this debacle.'

'Oh! That's what it is, a debacle, is it? It's a randy wee hoor of a daughter runnin' tae the arms o' her illicit lessie companion, ya disgustin' wee trollup. Ye bring shame on us aw, that's what ye dae. Ye shame us.'

'I'll not be spoken to like this by anyone, including you.'

'Will ye no? Well, away ye go to your pox-ridden future, ya maukit wee harpie.'

This clash had been long in the making but the force and speed of the collision had taken both by surprise. His exaggerated use of the vernacular to richen insult was a standard street-fighting tactic for a Scot. It was recognised that an emphasised guttural added menace. He had wielded a double-edged sword, one edge slashing at the unrealistic pretension of his daughter's new clamour for social improvement, the other cut wounding reminders of her inherited working-class pedigree. He had wanted his words to injure. He was a man weary of life. Misery and depression had erupted to fuel a moment of real passion. Emotion had been given unguarded expression, but had, in consequence, conjured a catastrophic split between father and daughter. He had felt alive during the verbal duel, reintroduced to feeling, but a fracturing of family unity had been the prohibitive cost of his spontaneous vehemence; an extravagant price to pay for a few seconds of emotional intoxication.

Anna had managed to restrain her inclination to respond in the vernacular. It would have been natural to express her indignation in the same tongue her father had used, but her practiced elocution had held fast under onslaught. This self-control marked the scope of her change and reinforced how far she had separated herself from the environment of the home and her father's influence within it.

Anna's father had been wrong to accuse Jane McGregor of lesbianism. Females who followed a freethinking, independent life style often were assumed to be involved in some form of nonconforming sexual activity. Jane McGregor's suspected lesbianism was not an uncommon accusation, it was an assumption based on a type of logic that ran on habitual, but unreliable, rails.

Jane McGregor was a sophisticated woman, cosmopolitan in background and well-educated. While currently enjoying a veneer of respectability, rumour abounded with stories of a bohemian past. That she may have indulged in lesbian liaisons was not inconceivable, rather it was thought to have been highly probable. Such a thought had never entered Anna's head. Her father's slur had intrigued her. The probability of Jane's sexual sophistication excited her. She was infatuated with Jane and the thought triggered an unexpected frisson. It had a mind-twisting fascination.

* * *

Jane was reading in her sitting room awaiting Anna's arrival. It was her favourite place. Books were everywhere. The random mix of coloured spines concocted a comforting pattern in the soft, early evening light. Her volumes dressed the room with a background of tartan: a colourful fabric woven from the threads of human aspiration. Manuals on religion lay beside publications on art. Portfolios of musical scores nestled against familiar blocks of novels. Volumes of favourite authors, given pride of place on brimming shelves, gave the room a reassuring, comforting ambiance. Each publication was an old friend, the attempt of an artist to unravel the ambiguity of human existence. Books were a visible and potent reminder that there was no limit, no boundary, to the collective human imagination. This was her library, cobbled book by book. Over the years she had constructed a monument to knowledge.

Reading, rather than liberating her from cynicism, had reinforced the belief that humankind was flawed and doomed to eventual destruction. Reading had isolated her from society and had, over time, suppressed her gregarious inclinations. She had concluded human creatures were irrational: controlled by passion, smeared by folly and steeped in vice. At times she felt laden with *ennui*. Detachment and she had become common companions. She was not unhappy but greatly changed from the person she once had felt herself to be.

The doorbell rang to interrupt her reverie and she rose in response. She knew it would be Anna and concern creased her brow. She opened the door to the straight, standing figure of her pupil. They stood in silence, neither wishing to speak. Anna broke the gathering tension. 'Did my telephone call upset you?' she asked.

'No it didn't upset me. It surprised me.' Both were unsure of the other's mood.

'I'm sorry, I didn't know what to do.'

They continued to look at one another, until Jane said, 'You had better come in, I suppose.'

Anna's face began to contort and noises came from her throat. 'You don't want me here?' she managed to say, before becoming

Freewill is Forfeit

incoherent. Jane stepped forward and put her arm round the weeping girl's shoulder. Gently she guided her student over the threshold. No further words were exchanged. Jane removed her visitor's coat, settled her in a chair and retreated to the kitchen.

When Jane returned with coffee, she said, 'It's not up to much, the room I mean. In fact, to call it a room is an exaggeration, it's more like a large cupboard. Well, it's a box-room really, but you can have it with pleasure.'

'I don't care what it's like. Anywhere will do.'

'Where are your things?'

'What things?'

'Your belongings, your luggage?'

'This is it, I'm afraid. What I have on my back.'

'What? Not even a toothbrush?'

'It's in my pocket.'

'Well, that's something, I suppose. We can collect your belongings later.'

'No, I want nothing from that house, nothing.'

'A touch cavalier, don't you think?'

'No,' said Anna, using the monosyllabic negative to convey rejection of everything in her past.

The following evening, while sprawled at ease, the two women found their talk returning to the subject of men. At the beginning conversation had been desultory. Anna, quivering still with the memory of the confrontation with her father, became expansive in the manufacture of insult. Seeking relief, she exclaimed, 'He's a pig.' After further thought, aware the insult was insufficient to match her indignation, she concluded, 'All men are pigs. They seem to exist for the sole purpose of visiting misery upon women. They use our tenderness and compassion, to enslave us to their will.'

'*Stai tranquilla, cara.* They're not all bad, but they do seem to share the common fault of insensitivity and be programmed by their genitalia. You must attempt to develop more guile. With guile and patience the female is empowered to bring any man to heel if she is bent on civilising the beast.' Jane was smoking marijuana. It was a habit she acquired while residing in Italy. In Glasgow she continued to satisfy her wont by harvesting a supply of the mild hallucinogenic in her garden. When smoking cannabis she believed complexity unravelled, clarity intensified and thoughts streamlined into simplified order. Words came out to play in her mind. 'A women softens with sex,' she continued, 'reassures with modesty and comforts all hurt with gentleness. That's the given role of a woman in any heterosexual relationship. Also, it's the woman's burden to suffer the multiple infidelities of men, forgive them their transgressions and provide the glue to bind the union if the relationship is to survive.'

'What a stupid, unfair palaver it seems to be,' was all Anna could mutter. What was stupid, or unfair, she failed to mention. Her agitation, however, was being calmed by watching patterns of smoke spiralling in the down lights of the room.

'Marriage can prevail, of course, but what one partner gives up for the other never seems a fair exchange.' Jane was delighted with this remark.

'And homosexuals?' asked Anna.

'If anything they're even more manipulative of each other. Their persistent promiscuity creates a constant liturgy of deceit.' Sweeping statements gave particular pleasure. 'I've yet to meet an un-neurotic queer,' Jane concluded.

Anna was disappointed with this response. It replaced her mood of discontent with sensations of petulance. 'I thought you'd be more sympathetic towards women, especially females who prefer the company of their own sex rather than the usual, predictable, male-female bonding.'

'I'm sure single sex relationships are no more rewarding than conventional couplings,' Jane opined.

'I disagree. Surely sensuality is better understood by women than by the brutish male who comes to love-making half insane with the primal urge to release his sperm.' There, it was out.

Jane's gentle transports were jolted. She sat up and stared at her pupil. '*Santo cielo, tesoro!* You're still a virgin for God's sake. What do you know of men and love? Nothing! Give half the world's population half a chance. You're angry, but don't refuse to accept that men and women are similar creatures. The good, the bad, the sad and the mad, are equally distributed. For every flawed man there's his female counterpart. Neither sex escapes fault.'

The effort of defending mankind had disturbed Jane's tranquillity. She stretched out and relit her reefer, trusting it would re-establish a sense of wellbeing. Anna said nothing. She felt deflated.

'I feel like musing,' Jane said after a period of silence.

'Muse to me on the subject of love, then,' Anna said, still nursing her bout of mild petulance.

'Ah! *Amore*. What could not be said of love?' Jane said. She gazed at the ceiling. 'Aspects of love are endless. Love is the strongest force in the world. The other is lust. The majority of both sexes tend to confuse the latter with the former. One is common, the other rare. Love requires a generosity of spirit, an unselfish soul, and many are incapable, or unwilling, to make the sacrifice of themselves to its mysteries. Those who find love are both blessed and burdened in equal proportion. They belong to an exclusive caste.' Jane stopped and leaned forward to puff at her joint. At the restart of her monologue her tone was lighter, more brisk. 'Lust, however, is the powerful, natural craving we are born with. When nature calls the tune we all have to dance. And what a dance we men and women make of it. Lust can make fools of saints. All the deadly sins are driven by it. It's a distemper without antidote. It's God's bad joke.'

Anna watched Jane stub out the butt of her relit joint and begin to prepare another of her smokes. She was confused, unsure if she should be disapproving of the exotic activity, or pleased with the compliment of being a trusted witness to a bohemian act.

When finished the fidgety process Jane lit the haphazard tube and stretched out once more. Immediately she returned to her monologue. 'Of course, different classes in society deal with the problems of lust in reverse order to expectation. Royalty and the aristocracy, together with those who enjoy high social prestige, accept rutting as their God-given rite. They claim exemption to moral censure. After all, what's the profit in privilege if the most alluring freedom, the freedom to be promiscuous, is forbidden or restricted? The powerful have a tendency to raise two fingers at all the accepted conventions.'

'Lower down the social structure, the upper middle class, let's say, satisfy their carnality in more mannered ways. A religion is made of discretion and deceit becomes their intimate companion. The middle ranks of this class, however, are opportunists. They have to be. They strike when they can, exercising labyrinthine care. Shackled in the chains of their self-appointed responsibility to uphold the imperatives of puritan culture, they pretend to forgo the lure of promiscuity and when they fail, as most do, suffer the tortures of Job on a rack of remorse and guilt.'

Jane liked this. She was warming up, getting in the mood. Rambling conversation when half-stoned was wonderful. She decided another puff wouldn't go amiss and inhaled.

'The lower working-classes,' she continued, 'like their aristocratic brethren, fornicate with enthusiastic indifference to moral law, or state rule. Amid this deluge of depravity, if that's how we wish to describe our responses to a natural urge, exists a type of man, usually seriously rich, who bypasses all the conventions. He's a pragmatist. And what does he do, you ask? I will tell you. He seeks with a fastidious eye the woman of his dreams and when he finds her, exerts the power of his privilege to purchase her perfection with the enticement of luxury. In short, he seeks a courtesan. He's usually a man of taste, a male who has learned to civilise his appetites. He tends to make a fetish of good manners and be a student of sensual hedonism. A Jesuitical voluptuary, if you like.'

She stopped. 'Jesuitical voluptuary'? Where did it come from? Beautiful! Delighted with this oxymoron she continued, 'The contract entered into between this male and female is a triumph of sophistication. Such a veneer enwraps the relationship that its central purpose, the slaking of lust, is hidden in tinsel. This happy idyll is usually sustained until age, the boredom of familiarity, or diminishing inclination, indicates that a severance would be mutually beneficial. All women should aspire to live a life of pampered ease. Only the courtesan succeeds. Perhaps we all should aspire to be courtesans.'

Anna was spellbound. Jane thought the grass she was smoking to be a total knockout.

* * *

Jane entered her bedroom. It was luminous with late afternoon sun. She crossed to her wardrobe, stretched for her green velvet trousers and, with care, selected a matching Mexican-sleeved blouse. In advance she had decided that come this day she would attempt to reacquaint herself with the sensations, and mood, of a bygone period in her life. This adjustment was best prepared for by simple ritual and dress. First, she had bathed and rearranged her hair. As of old she had it drawn back from her face and knotted in a thick plait coiled with a yellow ribbon. It was severe, but elegant. Laid out on the dressing table were the creams, colours and perfumes to assist the transformation. Although many years had passed since last occupied with self-adornment, she was confident her talent to create bewitchment had not become impaired.

Satisfied with her transfiguration, she rose and examined her overall appearance in a full-length mirror. She decided the transition lacked a finishing touch of flamboyance. From her jewellery box, unopened for almost a decade, she selected an emerald choker and completed her preparation by knotting a yellow silk scarf around her waist. Finally, pleased with her reflection, she crossed the room to uncork the champagne. She watched the crystal glass flood with effervescence and subdue to golden pattern of bubbles. She was ready. Lifting the glass she approached the telephone and sat. Without hesitation she started to dial. After a series of connections through various exchanges, ten minutes later, a recognised male voice answered.

'*Pronto, chi parla?*'

Jane inhaled deeply and, with a steady voice, said, 'Hello Charles, this is Jane McGregor.' She fell silent to allow disbelief to dissipate. She waited until she heard his voice say, 'Jane?'

'Yes Charles, it really is me.' Again she gave him time to absorb the shock.

'Jane. This is overwhelming. You've quite knocked the wind out of me. Do you know how long it has been? We'd abandoned all hope of ever seeing you again. Where are you, for God's sake?'

His voice contained the excitement he felt.

'I'm in Scotland, Charles. I came home. I felt I had to have some time to myself at the end of the ordeal. I'm a teacher now. I teach Italian at a Glasgow Grammar School.'

'Oh!' was all he seemed able to say. She had never known him to be lost for words.

'Are you well, Charles?' Jane enquired, to assist him with his temporary difficulty.

'*Si, si, benissimo,*' he said in a rush and then, with more calm said, 'yes, exceedingly well, thank you. All is changed, of course, but at least my health is still intact.' The 'exceedingly' was typical, the hint of cynicism was not. Had world-weariness started to afflict him? A life of privilege, it seemed, had not protected him against the creeping disillusionment of age.

'I should have written, Charles, but I wished to have some time to settle into ordinary life again before resuming contact.'

'Your vanishing caused us great distress. The rejection we felt was terrible.' His bitterness was palpable.

'We all had to suffer and come to terms with the unpleasantness in our own ways.'

'The prison authorities refused to tell us anything other than you had been released. You just disappeared.'

She wanted to change the subject. 'How's Cesare?' she enquired.

'Cesare's in New York.'

'How long will he be there?'

'He lives there now. He's become an American; papers, residence, citizenship, the whole works. He said he wanted to make an irrevocable commitment.'

'Is he still connected?'

'I'm not sure. He's in communications. Runs his own outlet, gossip, fashion, sport, current events, that sort of thing. He seems to like it, but whether it will last I don't know. It's not quite him, I feel.'

'You're probably right. The strangulation of commitment will soon blunt his enthusiasm.'

'Five years, Jane. Five years of silence. Five years of not knowing where you were. That's excessive,' Charles chastised again.

'Yes, I know, Charles. Forgive me. It has taken time to recover.'

'Everything has changed in ways you would not believe.'

'Yes, I read the papers.'

'Have you heard Mussolini signed a Pact with Hitler this morning? Our strutting *Il Duce* occupied Albania last month and if that wasn't enough, he's now in league with war-mongering Germany. The Italian situation is dire.'

'Yes, I heard it on the wireless. Listening to the news prompted me to phone.'

'Do you think it will come to war?'

'Who knows what to think?'

'What's the mood of England at the moment?' He made the common mistake of referring to Britain as England.

'Very calm. Normal. Listening to the news is a little upsetting. Tell me, Charles, did any of my property survive the confiscations?'

'All the businesses had to go, but Cesare made it clear he would tolerate no interference with any of the assets in the Milan portfolio. In the final deliberation his appeal was upheld.'

'And the Villa Bianca, in Lido?'

'That's untouched. Still yours, given and signed. There's also the villa in Sienna, whilst not in your ownership, it's still free for your use.'

'So, Charles, the convulsion, while painful, was not as damaging as first feared?'

'It was devastating. That's why Cesare fled. Never under-estimate the loss of wealth and prestige suffered by us at that terrible time.'

'I'm sorry. It was wrong of me to suggest anything else. Is the villa in Lido being looked after?'

'It's secure and checked regularly, but it's been uninhabited since your disappearance. The gardens will require attention if you're planning to return. It would be a real pleasure to have them tended for you.'

'You're a darling, Charles. That would be splendid. Who knows, all this war nonsense might soon be over. I'd adore to feel the heat of an Italian sun once more, but I think for the moment it would be unwise to plan a visit during all this uncertainty.'

'Of course. Cesare will be delighted when I tell him I've heard from you.'

'Give him my love.'

'He talks of you constantly. You were the one person who brought happiness into his father's life and for that, and the courage you displayed at the end, he will worship you *per sempre.*'

'Don't make me cry, Charles.'

'No. Right.'

'You will look after everything for me?'

'It will give me great pleasure.'

'Grazie, tesoro.'

'Bless you, Jane. Please keep in touch'

'Of course. Until we meet again.'

'Yes, let it be soon.'

'D'accordo. Cioe.'

'Arrivederci.'

* * *

When Anna returned to the flat she was in buoyant mood. The Higher English paper, the examination she had dreaded, had been a gift. Good fortune had left her feeling joyous. All vexation had vanished. The day, her last at school, had been a triumph and better still, never again would she have to tolerate the hated smells of an institutional kitchen, eat the food it produced, or dress in the unflattering style of group conformity. Never again would she have to submit to the verbal excesses of disillusioned academics nursing their collective neuroses. Gone was the fear of failure, the aggravation of scholastic discipline and coping with constant apprehension.

'I'm home,' she yelled to the empty spaces of the hall.

'I'm in my bedroom. Come in,' invited Jane's disembodied voice.

At the first sight of Jane, Anna was speechless. She let her mouth fall open and stared.

'Do you like it?' Jane said, standing to display her metamorphosis.

Freewill is Forfeit

'It's not you, is it? I mean it's more than you. No, what I mean is I'm flabbergasted. Your hair! Your. . . well, everything.'

'Come, have some champagne and bore me with the petty details of your day.'

'Champagne? Crumbs!' said Anna.

'You shouldn't use such childish expressions,' Jane scolded.

'Crikey!' said Anna.

'Are you trying to offend me?' Banter between them had grown common. 'I take it you approve of my transition?'

'It's wonderful. You look untouchable.'

'Would you like to dress up too?'

'You mean get into my russet-coloured number?'

'No, of course not.' Jane placed the flat of her hand on Anna's back and pushed her toward the wardrobe. 'Open it,' she invited.

Anna swung the doors outward and stood back to view the ordered contents. She glanced at Jane to be given further assurance. Jane indicated permission with a nod, strolled to the bed and sat. Anna was confused. What she saw was unreal. The elegance of the garments was intimidating. Jane's possession of this sumptuous collection of clothes was baffling. No indication of its existence had been mentioned. Anna struggled with quandary. To make a choice from such an array of finery was beyond her wit. She decided a random pick might be a sensible solution. Before making a selection, her right hand crossed her body to unfasten the buttons securing the shoulder strap of her tunic. The left side of her school uniform fell away to form the shape of a toga. The bra-less bulge of breast beneath the white cotton blouse drew Jane's attention. Flat-heeled brogues were carelessly kicked off before the toga-shaped tunic was hitched up to assist the discard of dark woollen stockings and school-approved knickers. The tunic fell to the floor, to be followed by the discarded blouse. Slanting shards of sun highlighted the startling sight of the naked female form. The unselfconscious, child-like process of the strip had been an absurd prelude, a clownish preamble, to glimpses of mesmerising femininity.

'Can I try on the red dress?'

'Of course,' replied Jane. It was a low-cut, high-hemmed

confection of chiffon and silk. It had been designed for the singular purpose of enlivening male interest.

Anna stepped into the garment and began to drag it up her body with energetic side-to-side movements. When the top half was hauled into place, she turned to Jane and said, 'Well, what do you think?' Jane examined the dishevel with amusement and said, 'A few finishing touches and it will look fine.'

'I think it's perfect as it is.' Anna pirouetted in front of the mirror, slipped, lost her balance and collapsed into a sitting position on the floor. She laughed and leaned back to support her shoulder against the wall. Her thighs were angled in a position of provocative innocence. Jane stared at a vision of female perfection.

'With a decent hair style, proper shoes, dress adjustment, some facial attention, stockings, a properly fitting bra and an improved hauteur, then, I think, we might begin to make you look half way presentable.'

'Oh! Is that so! And can this be done before or after drinking champagne?'

'During, I think. You will learn it's one thing to be able to turn a few heads in a Barrowland ballroom, quite another to satisfy the standard required to arrest attention in the Piazza San Marco.'

'The Piazza San Marco, in Venice?'

'Where else?' Jane stood, crossed the room and poured the champagne. She carried the glass to Anna's waiting, up-stretched hand and said. 'This is a day for surprises. I've another for you.'

'I know what it is. Or, I think I can guess. You've met a man who interests you?'

'You think a new man has entered my life, do you?'

'That's what all this is about, isn't it?'

'No, you're wrong. What I have to tell you is really a surprise.'

'Okay, tell me.'

'You won't believe me.'

'I promise I'll believe anything you tell me.'

'If I told you I owned a villa in Venice, would you believe that?'

'No.'

'Well, I do.'

Anna sat up and looked bewildered. 'I don't understand.'

'It's true. I own a villa in Venice. It was gift given to me by a boyfriend. I own it lock, stock and barrel. You'll like it, it's on the beach.'

'What type of boyfriend gives his girl a house?'

'A rich one.'

'A rich married one?'

'No, a rich divorced one.'

'My God! You've had an affair. That's incredible.'

'Not an affair, an arrangement.'

'You had an arrangement and he gave you a house?'

'In Venice, yes. He was an Italian.'

'And where is he now?'

'He's dead. He died several years ago. That's when I came home.'

'Did you love him?'

'Yes, very much.'

'Do you miss him still?'

'I do.'

'What was his name?'

'Carlo Visconte, and I think that should end the questions for the moment.' Jane returned to her glass and raised it in the direction of her ex-pupil. '*Alla tua salute, cin-cin*, and here's to our visit to Italy.'

'We're going to Italy? When?'

'Just as soon as this European nonsense subsides.'

'Will we stay at your villa?'

'Yes, but before that, young lady, a transformation from Scottish student to stylish *signorina* has somehow miraculously to be achieved and from your present position of sprawl it inspires little confidence that success can be taken for granted.'

'Do you mean I'm a sloven?'

'Yes, a very beautiful one.'

* * *

One champagne bottle lay empty and discarded on the floor; another, half consumed, stood precariously on the edge of the dressing table. Jane, shoeless and enveloped in a scatter of cushions, lay supine on her bed. She was smoking. It was a Sobranie. A Cocktail Sobranie. She preferred Capstan Full Strength but thought it more fitting, more pleasing to the immediate mood, to smoke a cigarette whose colour matched the yellow of her sash. Anna, cross-legged in a corner, was engrossed choosing and discarding in turn items of jewellery selected from Jane's jewel case. Scattered around her on the carpet lay cameos, lockets, pendants and rings, set with stones of every hue. Minutes had past since either of them had spoken. Jane thought the silence idyllic after the energy-sapping excitements of the day. Anna, entranced, was conscious of nothing other than the beauty of the jewels she caressed.

The doorbell rang. Disappointment pierced the mood of the room. Jane sat up. Anna looked over and made a face. Expressions of enquiry were exchanged. Jane swung her legs from the bed and stood. She walked to the mirror to examine the damage done by four hours of indolence.

'How do I look?' she enquired nervously.

'Perfect.'

Not satisfied with the monosyllabic judgment, Jane turned from the mirror and said, 'No, really?'

'Really! Whoever it is won't wait forever.' The bell rang again. One ring.

'Perhaps they'll think no-one's at home,' said Anna, hoping Jane would choose not to answer the summons.

'Tell me, do I look sober?'

'Completely.'

'Tell me the truth.'

'You look sober.'

Muttering dissatisfactions Jane disappeared into the hall leaving Anna still cross-legged in the corner with the jewel box. Anna heard an exchange of muffled voices, followed by a short silence. The bedroom door opened and Jane entered the room making quick gestures that Anna should rise, then turned and raised her left arm in welcome.

A young man strode into the room. Anna recognised him at

Freewill is Forfeit

once. It was her cousin, Conrad. Many years had gone by since they had last met. He had changed, put on weight, was broader of shoulder and stood at his full adult height, but undoubtedly it was Conrad. He smiled at her across the room as she gawped and struggled to rise.

'Hello, dinkum,' he said.

'Conrad. Where did you come from? What are you doing here?'

'I came to see you.'

'How did you find me?'

'I asked your father.'

'You saw dad?'

'Yes. I was with him half an hour ago.'

'Was he drunk?' It was out before she could stop.

'No, he was sober. He's very upset. He told me he behaved very badly and is ashamed.'

'Oh!'

Jane moved to Conrad's side and invited him to sit. She said, 'Today has been special for us both and, as you can see, we've been celebrating. Your arrival has surprised us. Perhaps you would like to join us in a glass of wine? There's plenty of food if you'd care to eat something?'

As Jane poured the wine, Anna walked from her corner and sat on the edge of the bed. 'My father has sent you to plead with me to return home?'

The young man looked puzzled. He stopped chewing a sandwich and said, 'No, it is you I came to see.' He stopped and turned to Jane, 'Can I have another of those sandwiches, please? They're outstanding.'

'By the way, I'm Jane McGregor,' Jane announced.

Conrad leapt to his feet and said, 'Lance Bennett, Anna's cousin. I do apologise for barging in upon you like this, it was. . .'

'I thought your name was Conrad?' Jane interrupted.

'Only to members of the family. Lance is my middle name.'

'You're an Englishman, Lance?' enquired Jane.

'Truthfully a bit of a mongrel I'd say, but yes, I'm English.' He inclined his head in Anna's direction. 'Our mothers are sisters and they're Sicilian. Our fathers, one English and one Scot, met, married and brought them to live in this country. My family resides in England, not far from London. Probably you had guessed that from my accent?'

'I guessed you were English. No Scot I know would use the word 'outstanding' to describe sandwiches!'

'Categorised by a word. That's amazing.' They exchanged smiles.

'Since you have come to see Anna I'll leave you both. . .'

'No, please stay,' he interrupted. 'What I have to say concerns you both. I believe you're Anna's Italian teacher?'

'I was, when she was at school, yes,' Jane replied.

'But, you're not Italian?'

'No, I'm a Scot.'

'Excellent. What I mean is . . . Look, I may have come here on a wild goose chase, but. . .' he stopped, looked round the room, appeared hesitant and said, 'Just allow me to prattle and it will become clear why I'm here.'

Anna was intrigued. She slipped off the bed and sat on the floor. Jane replenished the glasses and placed the bottle beside Lance. She gestured it was his to finish. They waited.

'Let me start by telling you about myself. Eight months ago I completed my studies at the London Polytechnic and decided to join the Army. I believed then and I am certain now, that war is inevitable. I reasoned, why attempt to settle into civilian employment when conscription was just around the corner. As I was anxious to join the Royal Scots Greys, I knew if I delayed and waited for conscription I would be denied the choice. The Scots Greys tend to be a touch elitist, you see. A conscripted half-breed, like myself, would never have been assigned to such an illustrious regiment. However, to move on, incredible as it may seem, you see sitting in front of you a recently appointed Commissioned Officer in His Majesty's Forces, Second Lieutenant Conrad Lancelot Bennett, Tank Commander, Royal Scots Greys.'

'Oh Conrad, that's wonderful!' purred Anna. Lance put his finger in the air to silence her.

'Last week I was summoned to Whitehall to one of the myriad offices within the Ministry of Defence. I was interviewed by a civil servant who informed me I was to be transferred to the Intelligence Corp.' Lance interrupted his tale and turned to face Anna. 'Before I tell you what transpired, first let me test your knowledge of current affairs. Who was it that stood by Mussolini when he marched into Abyssinia?'

'Hitler,' Anna replied, relieved she could answer.

'What two European dictators collaborated to their mutual benefit in the Spanish Civil War?'

'Hitler and Mussolini.' Simplicity itself.

'Who announced the formation of an Axis Alliance in 1936?'

'Hitler and Mussolini.'

'And who has just transformed that Alliance into what is now called the Pact of Steel?' No one spoke. 'Exactly. When war explodes Italy will join with Germany.' There was further silence. 'However, this official told me my transfer had already been arranged. I protested in the strongest terms and told him if my service with the Scots Greys were to be discontinued I would resign my Commission. We argued. He attempted to persuade me to reconsider by describing the urgency of his need and the importance of the position I was to fill. When I began to understand his dilemma I was relieved. I saw a compromise was possible. It transpired there were not enough trusted Italian-speaking staff to fill the new, and immediate, need for translators, intelligence operatives, liaison officers and other sundry staff. They were desperately seeking suitable people for recruitment. Rashly, I announced I could supply him with dozens of names and it was irrational I should be transferred when so many others could be found to satisfy his needs. In the end he agreed I could return to my Unit if I supplied him with twenty names of people he could safely approach for vetting. I told him he would be hearing from me and left.'

Lance paused. 'So, that's why I'm here. Do I have your permission to submit your names? It will entail an interview and if you don't like what you hear you can walk away, it's as simple as that.' Before either Anna or Jane could respond, Lance once again raised a finger.

'There's another uncomfortable aspect to be addressed. Should the political situation deteriorate all Italians resident in the UK will be forced to register. If the worst occurs many will be interned. The treatment received by these internees will vary. Some, I fear, will be badly treated. Those who are not interned will have other lesser types of restriction imposed upon them. Freedoms that have been taken for granted will be curtailed. By the nature of this exercise many of the judgments made will be arbitrary. Confusion will result. Resentment will fester. It's a gloomy prospect.'

He stopped speaking, picked up the last sandwich. He stared at the wall as he chewed. After a time, he said, 'Anyone who is vetted and becomes involved in Defence work will avoid all this unpleasantness. Give it some thought. Believe me, I'm not here to influence you, merely to prepare you for what looks likely to happen.'

He was subdued. Glances were exchanged. Lance emptied the last of the bottle into his glass. Jane lit a cigarette, another Sobranie. Green this time, it matched her blouse.

1

When the Japanese attacked Pearl Harbour on Sunday 7th December, 1941, Hancock Cornelius Remington was outraged. In common with other bankers he disapproved of war. International strife unhinged stock markets, reduced trade projection to farce and made lunatics of all who laboured in futures. But, holy shit, an unprovoked assault against America, a nation bent on attempting to maintain global stability, was a different kettle of fish altogether. The attack to destroy the American fleet while it lay at anchor went beyond treachery: it was a perfidious act that demanded a retaliatory response of commensurate severity.

After listening to a selection of news broadcasts Hancock came to a decision. He knew what had to be done. The following morning found him sitting in the office of Mr Robert Braithwaite, a senior Board member of the Bank. Without preamble Hancock launched into a diatribe describing what he believed should be the duty of every young man in America.

Mr Braithwaite, inclined to the habit of commencing each meeting with a preamble of exchanged courtesies, was forced, being denied this civilising habit, to listen to Hancock's harangue in a mood of impatient petulance. He thought Hancock's emotional protestations an inexcusable breach of good manners.

When Hancock's sermonising ceased, he concluded by saying, 'So you see, my request is simple.'

Whatever was simple confused the older man. Midway through Hancock's tirade he had allowed his thoughts to stray. Mr Braithwaite had a profound belief that individuals of a subjective disposition should never be allowed anywhere near businesses whose exclusive concern was the management of money. In the paper jungle of finance the possession of a detached temperament was fundamental if multiple rewards were to be reaped. Mr Braithwaite believed Hancock Remington, unlike the boy's father, would never acquire the traits essential for banking success. The young man's manner proclaimed a proclivity for egalitarian concerns. To possess anything other than a dog-eat-dog philosophy was the kiss of death in the arenas of money mongering.

'I'm sorry, but I don't understand what you require of me,' said the confused executive.

'I'd like to be released from the bank in order to enlist in the army,' Hancock replied, surprised by the man's uncertainty.

Mr Braithwaite had difficulty believing his ears. Restraining delight, he said, 'And why make this request of me? Your father is the person you should approach with this proposal.'

'If possible I'd like to avoid unpleasantness. We both know he'd reject my request out-of-hand. Besides, I think it correct I should make this request through your office. You're in charge of Personnel Affairs, after all.'

'You do understand, of course, your father being Chairman of the Board has the power to overrule any agreement you and I may make?'

'He is a stickler for correct procedure. He'd never overrule your decision on this matter.'

'You've given this request for release some thought.' It was an accusation.

'Yes, I have.'

'Your manoeuvre to involve me, although free of fault, will be interpreted by your father as a ploy to circumvent his authority.'

'Yes, it will.'

'It will place me under suspicion of collusion.'

'Yes, I agree.'

'Put me in his bad books, so to speak.'

'Yes, I'm afraid so.'

'I see.' Mr Braithwaite studied the wall behind Hancock's head. Hancock Remington's removal from the bank was the answer to many years of fervent, but impure, prayer. The Good Lord, finally, had delivered into his hands the fate of the brat who stood between him and the coveted position, Chairman Elect of the Remington Bartholemew Bank. Let the executioner's axe fall. Let the bloodline perish. Cast into the broil of war his unwanted presence.

Taking control of facial expression and intonation, Mr Braithwaite said, 'Very well, I cannot think of any reasonable objection why I should refuse your request. Go to your war with my sincere blessing.' He stood to conclude the meeting and stretched out his hand to have it shaken. It was an act of goodbye and good riddance.

'I needn't remind you that your position is assured should you wish to return at the conclusion of the emerging hostilities,' he added, as Hancock was leaving the room. The statement was correct, but the sentiment was insincere.

Two weeks later, on Christmas Eve, Hancock enlisted into the American army. He volunteered to join an Infantry Unit. By this act he was aware his patrician background and natural autocratic manner would expose him to mockery and threat from under-privileged elements. This did not deter him or cause him concern. An expensive boarding school education had been an academic waste of time, but had given him a solid grounding on how to survive in hostile environments. He knew a few energetic fist-fights would convince the ruffian element it was wise he should be excluded from their mischief. As it happened – whether because of height, breadth of shoulder, or just the glint in his eye – the expected intimidation never occurred.

In truth, the manner of his upbringing and regular exercise, had prepared him better than most for the physical rigours of basic military training. He came to revel in the exertions devised to hone the trainee soldier to battleground fitness. To march twenty miles carrying a thirty kilo kitbag; climb a ten metre rope, remain suspended for thirty seconds, and make safe descent; carry a man of commensurate weight one hundred yards, rest for two minutes, then carry him back; negotiate five miles of uneven terrain with kit and weaponry in less than an hour, were all exercises he could complete without too much strain. Sparring with his good friend Jack Dawson and regular games of squash, had kept his fitness up.

Nothing in his civilian life, however, had prepared him for the harsh introduction to military discipline. It did not matter that boots were polished to mirror brilliance, kit presented with impeccable care, hair cut to laughable length, weaponry brought to oily efficiency, nothing he strove to achieve protected him from unfair, explosive, inaccurate denunciations of sloth and shoddiness. He had to learn never to allow his eyes to glaze over with bewilderment during the insult of unfair accusations. Often an invisible reflex was interpreted as silent insolence, a punishable crime in the list of military offences. Following arbitrary accusation a charge of 'Conduct Contrary to Military Discipline' would ensue. This charge was a catch-all trap, applied with enthusiastic regularity. Mere whim was sufficient to provoke accusation and subsequent charge. Hancock concluded that any authority that claimed dictatorial power, the Divine Right of Kings and the infallibility of the Pope, all rolled into one, was a force not to be opposed, but immediately obeyed with mindless obedience.

Hancock further concluded early in his training, or early enough to prevent resentment taking root, that this process of intimidation was part of a devised programme to prepare the soldier for the shock of warfare; a time when the civilised self is required to be abandoned. No matter how bizarre, or outrageous, an order appeared to be, it was the duty of the soldier not to think, or attempt to interpret, but to obey, and to obey with immediate, unquestioning observance. To bring men to this collective condition of reflex is not achieved by friendly persuasion. It requires a degree of brutality, a system of severity to be applied. The army, of course, had evolved such a method.

At the end of three months' training Hancock felt good. Cleansed. Purged. Never had he felt fitter, more alive. Never would he be better prepared to face the fiends of the East who had made him their foe.

During the passing-out parade the Battalion Commander, Lt Col Mattheson, engaged in conducting the final inspection, stopped in front of Hancock. The Colonel stared, leaned forward and said in a conspiratorial whisper, 'What in the name of God are you doing here?'

Freewill is Forfeit

Not knowing how to reply, not knowing if he was allowed to reply, Hancock struggled to suppress disbelief. The Supremo conducting the parade, the hierarchical honcho, he who sat among the immortals, the psychiatrist-in-chief himself, was none other than his mother's brother, his Uncle Matty. Uncle Matty continued to stare at Hancock awaiting an explanation, while Hancock concentrated on maintaining a vacuous expression of obsequious obedience.

The Major accompanying the Colonel incorrectly assumed some mannerism, or small indiscretion, had offended the Colonel. He guessed that Hancock's dress, posture, or demeanour, had caused the Commanding Officer to be displeased and saw it as his expected duty to intervene. He moved forward, placed his mouth close to Hancock's ear and commenced to remonstrate that Hancock was a horrible specimen of humanity who never should have been allowed to step upon the hallowed spaces of a parade ground, that he had better pull himself together in double-quick style, stand up straight, get a haircut and report to the guardroom immediately after parade for punishment.

The Colonel, incensed by this interruption, pulled his gaze from Hancock's stricken features, turned towards his Adjutant and said with cutting weariness, 'Shut-up, Major, *please.*'

The extent of Uncle Matty's dismay became even more apparent when Hancock was marched into his presence later in the day. 'I've just had a telephone conversation with ma sister. She had no idea where you were, or what ya were doin'. D'ya realise how your affectin' the family reputation behavin' in this manner. D'ya think ya were born into privilege so that ya could do just as ya liked? No, sir! For two hundred years, from the moment the family left Scotland to settle in this country, we've bin part of the moral and cultural elite of this nation. We and our like, have brought it to the position of influence it enjoys in world affairs today. Our family has fought and suffered to rise above the common herd to a position of authority and modest wealth, and you, ya take it upon yourself to ignore this and the responsibility it carries, to enlist into a battalion of trained gangsters selected from the gutters of our society. What do ya think ya're playin' at?'

Hancock had listened to this type of subjective claptrap all his life. In truth, the Mattheson family had fled Scotland to avoid being arrested for cattle stealing, a crime punishable by hanging, and in disgrace had settled in Alabama. With blind disregard to moral considerations they proceeded to exploit the indigenous black population by embracing slavery, became enthusiastic activists in the embryo Ku-Klux-Klan and attained a dubious respectability, but high social prominence, by adopting a hypocritical facade of Christian piety. The family history was a tale of poisonous hypocrisy.

'I've decided to have you transferred to Officer Trainin'. Should I ever hear of ya attemptin' to besmirch the family's good name by yar thoughtless and unconventional behaviour, then every servin' member of the Mattheson clan will make it their duty to see ya suffer a befittin' punishment. Do a make maself clear? No, don't answer. Even a cretinous, deluded liberal like yarself can't fail to understand the consequences of ma threat. Yar leavin' this unit immediately. Deliver yar kit to the Quartermaster, collect yar travel documents and be clear of this Battalion by 18.00 hours. Now, get out of my sight.'

As Hancock walked through the company lines for the last time he had the rueful thought that, unlike his parents, Uncle Matty, at least, had sent him on his way with a few words of farewell.

* * *

After suffering a further six months of military indoctrination Hancock – Hank by this time – completed the Officers' Training Course and was promoted to the rank of Lieutenant. At the end of September 1942, he received his first active posting. It was to a Supply and Transport Depot fifty miles southwest of New York. Hank was devastated. After nine months of exposure to brain-numbing preparation for active service he found himself within walking distance of his home and still thousands of miles from the enemy he wished to confront.

His new duties were to depress him even more. He was to assist in executing a major audit of military material. He sensed from the moment he arrived that fate had conspired to consign

Freewill is Forfeit

him to a paper purgatory. The Depot was massive. It stored every item a military unit anywhere could require. There were acres of trucks, mountainsides of the newly designed jeep and tanks lined up as far as the eye could see. Motorcycles, staff cars and autogiros lay strewn about in untidy clusters. There were warehouses of uniforms, factories of foodstuffs, arsenals of weaponry, bivouacs of booze, craters of consumables and subterranean passages of footwear of every size, type and colour. This massive repository of replenishment was managed by a militia of quartermasters, all who appeared to be broad-smiling, overweight and of a hedonistic disposition. Loaded pantechnicons moved ceaselessly in and out of the area, giving the impression that army genius had perfected a foolproof system of inventory control. It was an auditor's nightmare.

After a cursory examination of the inventories that lay heaped on trestle tables, Hank concluded a regiment of mathematical whizz-kids could labour for a lifetime and still not be able to present a record of any worth. This flaw seemed not to affect the ebullience of the man burdened with the responsibility for the accuracy of audit. His name was Major Simon Slant.

At first meeting Major Slant appeared to be a man on the wrong side of fifty. He was thirty-two. A diet of women and alcohol had accelerated his disintegration and now, seemingly deep into his middle years, but with appetites still intact, had developed an ingrained philosophy that life and all its problems, should be challenged with a degree of cavalier insouciance. Hank, on the other hand, plagued as he was with the sedimentary remains of the Protestant ethic, felt compelled by inclination to work with energetic and useful purpose.

After a month of bondage spent in a paper confusion Hank emerged from the dark cavern he had inhabited determined to challenge his officer in charge of Audit Affairs with his discontents.

'Look Simon, the Inventory Systems employed require radical revision. It's impossible to access up-to-date information with accuracy. Until we devise, and adopt, a tighter type of cross-reference system our job cannot be done to any accountable degree of veracity.'

Simon rose from his chair, crossed his office and dispensed two sizeable whiskies. Over his shoulder he caught Hank's eye and pointed to a siphon, then to a jug. Hank sighed, pointed to the siphon and smiled at the man's panache.

When Simon was reseated and had wriggled into a comfortable position, he said, 'In a Depot of this dimension there's bound to be some shortfall; a few pairs of boots here, a side of beef there. At the end of the day it's of little consequence. We're not bankers, you know. Not every last dollar has to be accounted for. The flexibility of our system makes life tolerable, affords us cohorts who work in this unsung sector of the trenches a scintilla of comfort. It takes away the angst, makes life less desperate. I admit the methodology could be improved in parts. I'm aware that our inventory system is not a thing of beauty, rather it's a tool of pragmatic conception.'

'Convenient conception,' Hank interrupted.

'OK, convenient conception and for that we should be grateful.' He smiled and rolled the glass between his palms, then, with a much-practised movement, raised it to his lips and the contents were gone. 'Look Hank, I've been here long enough to know what goes on in a depot of this size. Being the type of creatures we men are a certain amount of pilfering is bound to take place. It's inevitable'.

'It's also avoidable.'

'I daresay, but the cost in manpower and morale might make any proposed reform ill-advised.'

'Nevertheless, the process needs tightening and I intend to make this known.'

'Take it easy, Hank. Why disrupt a system that serves its purpose? I say again, it isn't perfect, but it works, and works well. Take weaponry, for example. Every last bullet. . .'

'I'm sorry, Simon. I know you trust the system more than I and I admit that I bring a banker's eye to scrutinise the work in a manner which might not match with army methods, but I do believe that if I can convince Headquarters to review the methodology, to consider a few suggested improvements, it would make the doing of our work more purposeful.'

'If you believe that, then go ahead. Do it. Make your grand gesture. Be a reformer and the best of Irish luck to you. Another whisky?'

'Okay, but shorter this time.'

By the middle of the following week Hank's report on 'Military Inventory Compiling Procedures and Recommended Revisions' was ready for submission. He was pleased with his work and felt confident not only would his recommendations be accepted, but also implemented. He had no doubt some form of congratulatory recognition would follow and, for a period, he would bask in the reward of due acclaim. The plaudits would be congenial, of course, but he'd attempt to remember throughout his period of minor celebrity to accept the accolades with modesty.

Ten days later he was transferred.

He was posted to Casablanca.

* * *

On arrival at Divisional Headquarters of the 7th Army Executive in Morocco, Hank, in the company of two hundred other arrivals, was informed they had been selected as a vanguard detachment to commence groundwork preparations for a Conference of Allied Commanders planned for the following month. Hank, influenced by strengthening cynicism, guessed his new role would be demeaning, a punishment for his attempt to interfere with traditional Army procedure. He assumed he would be given a duty commensurate to his crime, probably be made a glorified wet nurse to some insufferable, polo-playing Colonel taking a mid-winter sabbatical with privileged cronies. It would be something agonising, for sure.

Hank felt aggrieved. All his well-intentioned labours had been dismissed as irrelevant. He had devised an almost foolproof, cross-indexed, double reference inventory system, but instead of expected reward had been banished to a God-forsaken backwater to dance attendance upon fat-assed geriatrics. It was unbelievable. He would be digging latrines next.

When he reported for duty the following day he received

another shock. He was ordered to report to the Language Laboratory. He learned he was to be given a crash course in Italian. Hank, infused only with a passion for numbers, thought this order preposterous, but by now familiar with the obscure logic of army decision-making knew bewilderment had to be accepted as a normal condition of army life if insanity was to be avoided. He was twenty-five and being sent back to school. He had joined the army to help suppress the traitorous ambitions of the Japanese and instead, found himself in Africa among tribes of Arabs and, if this debacle wasn't confusing enough, ordered to learn the language of a country whose Law, Church and State had gone creepy with centuries of piled-up corruption.

As it transpired, the mental effort of learning a foreign language was reduced to an activity of delight by the serendipity of infatuation. The female teacher assigned to introduce Hank to the fundamentals of the Southern European tongue was a creature of beauty. He was bewitched. The unflattering cut of her British uniform, her flat-heeled, heavy leather shoes, army issue stockings and severe military hair arrangement, did nothing to obliterate the perfection of her form. It was the general agreement within the male area of the barrack compound that the flattening effect of her buttoned-up Sergeant's tunic was a garment of mercy.

Hank, forced by duty into daily contact, had to suffer the sweet agonies of her pulverising presence. Never had he been so overwhelmed, taken over by wonder. The grace of her movements and her soft, deep-throated chuckle held him enthralled. When she spoke he was entranced. When she moved he was spellbound. She was perfect. No, more than perfect, she was sublime.

A hormonal flush drove his brain. He wanted to dazzle this creature of his dreams with feats of memory, convince her of his superior intellect, impress her with the generosity of his spirit, persuade her he possessed all the best traits of a considerate, sensitive, well-educated American gentleman.

For the first time, Hank was in love.

2

New York

On completion of the language course Hank was granted
promotion to the rank of Captain and given a fifteen-day furlough.
Nostalgia motivated him to seek a lift on one of the numerous
aircraft crossing and recrossing the Atlantic with supplies and
personnel. He arrived in New York two days later, missing
Christmas, but in time to attend his father's funeral. His father
had died during his flight home. At the age of fifty, never having
had a day's illness throughout his adult years, a heart attack had
taken his life. He had stopped mid-sentence while making an after
dinner speech and had fallen to the floor. When fellow guests
pulled him from under the table he was dead.

His father had not been a popular man. His death, however,
was an event of some import among Hank's mother's socialite
friends. Items from exclusive wardrobes could be flaunted without
guilt at Memorial Services. The death also had galvanised
speculation among the Board Members of the Remington
Bartholemew Bank. It had been assumed, by tradition, Hank would
inherit his father's position, but the untimely death had thrown
this presumption into question. Hank's age, his absence from
America on military duty and his mistrusted egalitarian inclinations
made him, in the minds of many, an unsuitable successor to his
father's throne.

Pursuit of, and devotion to, money had devoured his father's
life. Nothing else had concerned him. He had been a man fearful
of emotional display, a man of reclusive tendency, aloof and ill-at-
ease while in the company of others. In his later years he had
striven to hide from the world behind a wall of work. By clever
manipulation he had made a fortune early in his career, but the

Freewill is Forfeit   43 possession of wealth had a disgruntling effect and by middle age he had become miserly and melancholy. Disillusioned with riches and querulous with his fellow man, he had passed through life unable to communicate warmth. In consequence he had remained unloved. He would not be missed.

Hank's leave was spent working on his father's papers and answering letters of condolence. It was depressing toil. It encouraged thoughts of mortality. To date Hank's life had been lived by a decree scripted by family tradition. His future had been pre-planned by well-meaning parents. His education had prepared him for a style of life his parents had decided he should follow. He considered this presumption of how *his* life was to be lived a distressing intrusion, and that it had been planned with love, grotesque. Hank knew it was unusual, almost perverse, to have these thoughts. To be born into a position of privilege and to live a preordained life of security was the common, coveted ideal. His father had required and created wealth as a shield against his fear of life, but the bunkers storing his protective, and protected, gold had become his prison and subsequent tomb. Hank's mother, wealthy in her own rite, having inherited a flood of liquidity wrung from the sweat of slaves in the cotton fields of her forbears, was happy to be able to approve her deceased husband's wish that the entire estate be bequeathed to their male offspring. She thought it only right that a son should inherit the father's wealth and position.

When Hank went to see his mother in her room on the afternoon of his departure, he found her employed with the social niceties of bereavement. But she was being diverted from her correctly expressed grief by the task of selecting socially suitable celebrities as guests to her next charity bonanza. In truth this task ranked importance above the inconvenient death of a boorish and replaceable husband. She was now free of all hindrance and could devote her life to the giddy world of East Coast charity events. This high profile, self-imposed social responsibility was not a recent enthusiasm. It was a behavioural addiction which was constantly reinforced by the intoxication of being regarded as a person of inestimable worth dedicated to the selfless duty of overt Christian

Freewill is Forfeit

caring. Although never voiced, it was obvious to all that her charitable work was merely a labour to satisfy her cravings for lavish occasions, uncritical celebrity and self-aggrandisement.

Hank had wanted to hug this frantic lost person that he loved. But she, the principal cupbearer of the Poisoned Chalice, had long since become unhinged from anything Hank could recognise as real. With the bleak thought of having lost both parents, one to death and the other to a consumed life, Hank made his way towards the transport aircraft to return to Morocco and duty.

* * *

Morocco

To the south of Casablanca, outside the semi-circular wall of the old town, lies the residential district of Anfa. It is an area of gracious homes, well-tended gardens and broad avenues. During normal times Anfa is a haven for the well-heeled Jewish community of the town, but on the eve of the 13th January 1943, it was a cordoned off security enclave bristling with threat to unauthorised trespassers. Military delegates had been assembled from all the Allied services. They were awaiting the arrival of the British Prime Minister, Winston Churchill and the President of the United States, Franklin D Roosevelt. Expectation was palpable. As if decreed by God, all normal activity had ceased. A sense of suspension held sway and North Africa held its breath. Roosevelt's pledge to Molotov to clear the German Army from African soil was about to be honoured.

In four months the British 8th Army, following their victory at El Alemein, had advanced westward to Buerat in Libya. This advance had continued until the German forces were driven to the southern borders of Tunisia. This drive of 1,650 miles claimed a military record for the longest continuous advance made by any army in the history of warfare. Rommel's retreat ended when he arrived at the old fortifications of the French Mareth Line. There, with only twenty operational tanks left in his command, he stopped to await reinforcement. When rearmed through the Port of Tunis it was his resolve to launch a counter-offensive.

In a mood to invoke some distracting activity and escape the Spartan interior of his assigned billet, Hank buckled up his uniform, sporting the badges of his new rank and the flashes of the 2nd Corps of the 7th US Army and strolled towards the Officers' Mess. Usually a place of bustle, gambling and loud-voiced exaggeration, he entered a sepulchral silence. The few military personnel present seemed caught in a state of near coma.

'Real spookie evening,' Hank said to the Steward when he ordered his bourbon. The bar attendant, preoccupied and grim-faced, placed the glass on the bar without response.

Hank was toying with his second drink when, without ceremony, a stranger pulled out the adjacent stool and sat. It was twenty-eight years old Major Conrad Lancelot Bennett of the 8th Army.

'Hi Hank! Call me Lance,' he said.

Hank, taken aback by the intimacy of the introduction, felt annoyed that his first meeting with an Englishman should fall so far short of expectation. Good manners, at least, had been expected. Unable to stifle disappointment and disinclined to respond in like manner, he remained silent.

'My name is Conrad, but outside the family circle I'm known as Lance. So, it's Lance to you,' continued the smiling Englishman.

Hank examined the face and allowed his eye to check the badge of rank. One crown. He was a Major, but nothing quite jelled. The face did not match the rank, it was too young, or the rank the demeanour. The battle-dress tunic supported no identification other than a shoulder flash depicting what looked like a black rat. Nothing about the intruder quelled Hank's suspicion that the Englishman was bored and had decided to enliven his evening with a bout of Yank baiting. Hank had heard it had become a prevalent activity. Well not tonight, Josephine! 'That would be improper, Major and you know it,' Hank responded, 'and if you have joined me for the purpose of enjoying some ritualistic sport I should be grateful if you would take your unwanted mockery elsewhere.'

'No impropriety intended Captain, I assure you. When I saw

Freewill is Forfeit

you I thought it would save time and be less tedious if we were to become acquainted without the normal bullshit of military protocol. I've been mistaken. However, now I am here, I'll conclude my introduction and then piss-off. Tomorrow you will receive orders assigning you to my command. You and I are to become comrades-in-arms. Tomorrow evening you will report to me at General Headquarters to be assigned your duties. If you'd prefer we continue to adhere to stiff military propriety, well and good, but the impracticalities of attempting to maintain this correctness will soon become apparent to you. For the moment I will bid you good evening.'

Hank struggled to close his mouth. 'I'm sorry, Major, I completely misconstrued your friendliness. Please forgive my stupidity.'

'Quite understandable, Captain. My attitude was at fault. I've been separated too long from civilised society and have become slipshod in the courtesy department.'

Hank found himself on his feet. 'Sir, I've been a prat. Please allow me to redeem myself. Let me buy you a drink, give you a cigar, lick your boots, kiss your ass, anything to make amends. Just name it.'

Lance smiled and stood. 'Let's start again, shall we?' he said. 'Hi Hank, call me Lance.'

'Hi Lance, I'm Hank. Good to know you.' The two men looked each other in the eye and shook hands.

'Now we find ourselves on our feet, what do you say we get out of this mausoleum and find somewhere more conducive to relaxing the inner man?' suggested Lance.

'Sounds good,' Hank said.

'Let's wander down to the Arab quarter, the old Medina. While we're walking you can bore me with your civilian background and later, much later, I'll satisfy your curiosity about our coming mission. As my old man used to say: Pleasure first, and bugger business. Quite a philosopher was the old boy and crazy with it too. It's difficult to believe, but once he tried to swim the Straits of Messina. Daft bastard! If it hadn't been for observant Sicilian fishermen I wouldn't be here today. He did it to propose to my mother. At the time he was a student studying at Messina University.

He believed his stunted Italian prevented her understanding the depth of his adoration and he thought up this crazy *coraggio* to convince her. It worked, thank God, but it almost killed him.'

'Your mother's Italian?' enquired Hank, attempting to suppress his shock.

'Sicilian. My Sicilian grandfather had two daughters and both married British men, my mother an Englishman, my aunt a Scot. It was their daughter, Anna, who taught you Italian.' Hank was flabbergasted. His pulse rate doubled. He struggled to come to terms with the astounding revelation that his future Commanding Officer was a cousin of his beloved Sgt McKay.

The two men reached the walls of the old town before Hank began to recount some of the events of his own life. After half a dozen sentences he ran out of things to say. There seemed to be so little to tell and, the little he could relate, sounded colourless.

'Your father died a few days ago,' Lance interrupted, 'while you were on leave?'

'Yes, it was sudden, completely unexpected.'

'And how did it affect you?

'It didn't,' Hank admitted. 'Truly, the event left me unmoved. I know it sounds terrible, but not one tear have I shed. Sad, isn't it?'

'Tragic. I'll lay you a wager that within the next few months the impact of his death will induce some type of belated grief.'

'Save your money. In fact money was the only thing that absorbed his life. Money and work.'

'Have you inherited much of it?'

'All of it. I inherited the lot.'

'And how much was that, if you don't mind me asking?'

'To be truthful I'm not sure. It will take a month or two for the lawyers to work out, but, excluding property, in liquid cash somewhere in the region of twelve million dollars, I believe.' Hank heard Lance whistle. 'Don't be impressed. Money can be a corrosive substance. It has a strange quirk of manufacturing misery.'

'Money? Money is paper power. No, it's more, it's paper blood, and a transfusion of a few million is life-enhancing in any currency.'

'To the honest man, yes, I agree. But when it comes in bundles piled high you can be sure some form of criminality, social chicanery, or underhand manipulation has been at work somewhere along the line.'

'Christ! What a cynical bastard you are.'

'No, just a realist.'

'Well, get real. The world belongs to the rich, the rest of us just live in it.'

For the next few minutes they strolled through the narrowing streets in silence, until Lance stopped and said, 'Come with me, Hank'. They turned and began to retrace their steps to the broader avenues of the Medina.

'Have you ever tried smoking opium or hashish Hank?'

'No, a Manhattan is about as dangerous as I get.'

'I thought so. Captain Remington, I'm about to issue my first military order. You will accompany me to a place of my knowing, set yourself upon a couch and take instruction. Is my order clear?'

'Crystal.'

'Do you wish to shape an opinion as to the sanity of this mission?'

'No, sir. You're the boss. If you say piss, I piss.'

'I like my officers to have minds of their own.'

'You'll get used to my little ways. For now, I'm blotting paper in your hands.'

'But are you ready for your staining?'

'I was manufactured for the purpose.'

* * *

'You must do the services required of you. Go, slay thy foe and when thou returnest ye will be delivered into Paradise. Enchanted gardens will be open unto thee. Delights shall embroider thy imagination, and angels shall bear thee into transports of joy.' Abdullah stopped his whispered proclamations and hobbled across the chamber to select some further ingredient for the hookah being prepared. When resettled, his exotic monologue continued.

'May the reward for thy valour be gaiety of spirit. May sybaritic pleasures enchant and refresh thy soul. Voluptuous vacuity be bestowed upon thee to correct thy balance of mind, and when cleansed grant thee resolve to go forth and smite thine enemy again with the vigour of thy righteousness.'

Hank listened to the prayerful muttering of the ritual and watched the old Arab give attention to his quaint employment. He and Lance were in a carpeted, white walled cell, deep within a maze of similar chambers. Lance was stretched out upon a chaise-longue. Hank, sitting on another, faced Lance across a low table upon which two hookahs stood side by side. Stripped of battle-dress and wrapped in silken robes, they listened in a mood of anticipation to the extravagant words being chanted by the old Arab.

'Man is stronger than the steel he hurls, yet his spirit can be tended and refreshed by the humblest plant. Wonderful benefits and rewards, all bequeathed by Allah, are bestowed upon the initiates of wisdom. This you have learned my brother.' Hank experienced a stab of disappointment when he realised the old man's words were being addressed to Lance alone. 'Succour thyself in His reward and may the sacred state of *Kif* be granted unto thee.' The pipe was ready. Lance received the mouthpiece with solemn ceremony and lay back.

The Arab turned his attention to Hank. 'Allah, by His grace, provides bountiful variety. You are, as yet, untested in battle?'

'He is a man in grief for his father, Abdullah,' voiced Lance. 'He requires comfort for a withered spirit.'

The old man examined Hank and said, 'And ye have sought solace in the grape. The vapours are upon thy person. When will the Infidel learn? I will gather from Allah's garden a herb of gentle form. It will grant thee the peace ye desire.'

'Thank you, Abdullah,' said Hank.

* * *

The following afternoon Hank was ordered to appear before Brigadier General 'Cowboy' Thomson.

'Come in ma boy, and sit ye down. I must say you're lookin'

Freewill is Forfeit

tremendously well. I was mortified to hear of your daddy's demise. Your mother must be prostrate with grief of his passin'. She's such a neat and considerate person. I've written ma condolences, of course. I don't know what more I kin do and then I suddenly see you passin' right in front of me in the main hall. Young Hancock himself in the flesh. What in the blue blazes is he doin' here I asked myself'? Then I remembered your uncle Matty tellin' me you'd joined-up off your own bat and he found you, of all places, in a bootcamp sloggin' with the Joes. I see the transfer he fixed has paid you dividends.' Cowboy prodded his shoulder and chuckled.

'Yes sir', replied Hank. Hank knew the General to be a hawkish investor with influential clout in the boardrooms of New York. His family background, and professional Army career, had sprayed his reputation with an essence of trustworthiness, but Hank had met too many businessmen who rued the day they ever shook his hand. Cowboy was the nickname of the trader, not the soldier.

'One day, of course, you'll be takin' ova' your daddy's position and that's a prospect we all look forward to. There'll be dissenters, of course, but we'll soon see them off Hancock, m'boy, have no fear of that.'

'Thank you, sir,' said Hank, knowing it was probable he might never see the bank again if his newfound sense of freedom persisted.

'We've all got to look after each other in this world and protect our mutual interests, otherwise we'd all be castrated before even seein' the knife. What do ya say?'

Hank wanted to say, shut-the-fuck-up, but it was ingrained in him when faced with those who were rich beyond comprehension, yet continued to debase themselves in pursuit of further fortune, to agree with their salivating, self-satisfied, self-seeking opinions. After all, these were the individuals who constituted the backbone of the bank's business. But when was enough, enough? How enormous did their obscene hoards have to become before they began to question their mind-disturbed greed? Never, it seemed. It was a common conundrum.

'And that's why I think you should listen now to what I have to say. I see you've been selected to serve with a Major Bennett, one of Monty's boys?'

Hank's interest revived at the mention of Lance's name. 'Yes, sir. I was told this last night.'

'Have ya met him?'

'Only socially.'

'Did you form any impression of the man?'

Had the old bastard got word of last night's visit to Abdullah's? 'Yes I did. He is an officer of the first water, I'd say.'

'He's an I-tie,' Cowboy protested.

Was the pathetic man accusing Lance of being untrustworthy? 'Yes, he did tell me he was of Southern European stock.'

'This does not alarm you?'

'Not in the slightest. From the little I know I'm relieved he's on our side and not opposing us.'

'The naivety of the young,' the General said, excusing Hank his generous opinion. 'Blood will out, you know.'

The old fart now was resorting to cliché to reinforce bigotry. 'So I've heard it said, sir.'

'And have you heard he's a critter inclined to insubordination?'

Hank also had reached the point where the luxury of being insubordinate was irresistible. 'No, I've not, but you make him sound similar to our Commander-in-Chief, General Patton.'

'Our Commanding Officer would be distressed to hear ya say that, Hancock. However, we'll let that steer remain unbranded, eh?'

'Whatever you say, sir.'

The General's eyes narrowed. 'What I say is I think this mission they're sendin' you on with this Italian guy, frankly, is an escapade not to ma likin'. I think it's foolhardy. It does not fit with proper army ways.'

'I wouldn't know sir. I won't know until I see the Major.'

'Without revealin' details ya would be well advised to allow me to use ma influence to have you withdrawn from this suggested how-dee-do. I could have ya reassigned to ma outfit where I could keep an eye on ya. You can regard it as a small favour for past support.'

Hank knew his suggestion had nothing to do with past support, it was future advantage Cowboy had his eye on. 'Thank you, sir, mother will be grateful when I tell her of your thoughtfulness, but I'm sorry I can't accept your offer. Major Bennett and I shook hands on the assignment last night. For me it's now a matter of honour.' Stick that in your pipe Cowboy. A honourable handshake, you shit, not one of your slimey con-jobs.

'Without knowing what the mission is to be?'

Hank decided to go out on a limb.

'Without my initial infantry training I feel sure I wouldn't have been selected.'

'You'll be mixin' with the scum of the earth. Assassins, criminals and. . .'

'Sir,' Hank interrupted. 'With respect, I would prefer Major Bennett to brief me. I'm attending the briefing this evening before his arranged dinner date.'

'Dinner date?'

Caught you, you pompous old fart. 'He's dining with Winston Churchill at 22.00 hours.'

The whiff of mockery made the General's nose twitch. He stood up, walked round the desk and put his hands in the air. 'You always were different, always rubbed against the grain. Well, m'boy, good luck. I hope we all come through this war and get back to normal times before too long. Remember me to your mother. Fine woman. Dismiss now.'

'Thank you, sir. Goodbye, sir,' said Hank, cock-a-hoop with his small triumph.

'Goodbye, Hancock,' said the General without his usual mock-friendly expression.

* * *

It took Hank a few minutes of searching among the corridors of the basement in the GHQ building before he located the room assigned for the briefing. He found Lance and two unrecognised men awaiting his arrival. One, a Corporal, was small and thin, the other, a Sergeant, was tall and had a girth to match his height. A large illuminated map of North East Africa, Sicily and Southern Italy, hung on one wall of the chamber. It was streaked with coloured arrows. It looked like an impressionist painting gone awry midway through conception. There were two trestle tables. One was covered with a scatter of loose documents and communication paraphernalia, the other bore the weight of, and glistened with, a selection of small arms and light weaponry. No chairs were visible.

Lance, standing by an easel, was spurred and booted in the chain-mail regalia of cavalry blues, dressed for his dinner. Hank marched to the centre of the room and saluted. It was an American salute, a slack-handed, formal gesture of politeness. Lance, bareheaded, acknowledged the courtesy by inclining his head in correct formal response.

'Good evening, Captain Remington,' Lance said, in welcome. 'Allow me to introduce you to the other members of our mission. This mess of humanity,' he said, pointing at the smaller of the two men, 'is Corporal Gianluca Fazzi, my batman. Throughout many regions of North Africa he is known as 'Fuck-up'. Believe me, it's a deserved and well-earned *nom-de-guerre*. Joe, as he is conveniently called in ordinary society, speaks little English and having been brought up in poor peasant circumstances garbles a form of Italian recognised only by a few of us familiar with the complexities of obscure Sicilian dialect. His English, when he is forced to attempt our language, is equally indecipherable. This need not cause you concern, however, as his presence will be kept as far away from your person as circumstances will allow.'

Hank smiled and said, 'Hi!' The small man returned the smile showing the loss of several front teeth. As an afterthought, remembering to adhere to military etiquette, he stood erect and saluted. It resembled a haphazard wave. During its execution he muttered the words '*Piacere Capitano*'.

'This Canadian colossus,' said Lance, pointing to the other man, 'is Sergeant Robert Lambert. From his size you might deduce he is to be our protector against the threat of belligerence from nasty Nazi bullies, but no, he is released to us from his indolent life with the 8th Army to advise us on all matters technical. Despite

Freewill is Forfeit

his expertise in modern weaponry he is inclined towards the belief that the claymore is the most honourable weapon for the battlefield and believes battles should be fought with chivalry. In short, he's a latter day knight. Robert and I know each other well and fought side by side at El Alamein. We remained with the 8th Army until relieved from front line service to be sent to Scotland. There we were recruited into the service of the SOE, the Special Operations Executive and introduced to the nether world of skullduggery. This is our first mission under SOE jurisdiction. Robert, say hello to Captain Remington.' The Canadian stood to attention, pulled his arms to his sides, brought his heels together and executed a textbook salute. Hank shaped an American equivalent in return.

Lance broke from the introductions and crossed the room to take up a position beside the map. He turned and waited until he was sure he had their attention. 'First of all let me announce the momentous news confirmed to me this afternoon. Supreme Command Allied Forces have agreed, after months of indecision, the next major war operation to be mounted will be the invasion of Sicily.' Lance stopped and turned to his batman. *'Capisci, Joe?'*

'Si Signore. Ho capito,' said the small man, visibly shaken by the news. *'Scusi,'* he muttered and leaned forward to cover his face. Lance walked forward and touched the man's head. *'Ok, Joe. Fra poco vedrai le colline della tua casa di nuove. Ma, primo, abbiamo alcune cose di fare. Adesso, fai attenzione.'* ('Okay, Joe. Soon you will see the hills of your home again. But first, we have several things to do. Now, pay attention.')

Hank was grateful for the emotional interruption. He had been astounded by the news and was relieved to have time to stabilise the shock of disbelief. Surely this was nonsense, merely an espionage ruse, a hoax to deceive the enemy, a calculated diversionary ploy? If Supreme Allied Command intended to invade Sicily those responsible for the decision aught to be certified en-bloc on proof of collective insanity.

As Lance returned to the map, Hank struggled to recollect his composure. 'Many Allied Commands will be astonished, some even incensed, by this decision. They will argue all available manpower and resources first should be utilised in an effort to free France.

By this unexpected Allied decision we establish the advantage of surprise and also benefit by keeping German divisions inactively pinned-down in French positions they dare not evacuate for fear, and in expectation, of invasion.' He paused for effect. Operation Husky is the codename selected for the invasion of Sicily and should all go according to plan, it will be launched on the 10th July. It will involve the largest amphibian force ever to be assembled in the history of warfare.' Lance altered his position to give a clear view of Sicily on the map.

'First of all,' he continued, 'before the invasion of Sicily, the Allied forces have the small matter of removing the occupying German Army from Tunisia. At the moment the existing defensive German Divisions are being reinforced through the Port of Tunis. New Divisions of Waffen SS are arriving as we speak. How effective these new troops will be is, as yet, unknown. What we do know, however, is the existing forces on the ground consist of battle-hardened veterans. These crack Panzer Divisions are itching to confront the untried rookies of the American 2nd Corps. Reason? They'll want to show the Yanks they have committed a fatal error by interfering in European affairs. Since the two armies have never met in battle the Germans will want to seize the opportunity to establish military superiority and deliver the spanking they think the Yanks deserve. The two armies could not be more different in mood and experience. The Germans would appear to have the advantage, but in warfare it's never wise to predict anything.

'So you see, this matter of clearing Tunisia will be a bloody affair, but without military control of the country the invasion of Sicily is up shit creek. However, we must not allow ourselves the indulgence of cynicism, or speculate on matters that should not concern us. We must guard against making negative assumptions. We have much to do in five months. 'Let's get on with it' is the attitude to be adopted.

'And now, I come to our mission. We are to be parachuted into Sicily to establish contact with the Cosa Nostra.' Lance paused for the news to be absorbed. 'When contact is established and we're fortunate enough to meet with a non-belligerent reception, it will be our purpose to extract a promise of co-operation during the

Freewill is Forfeit

pre- and post-invasion periods. By recruiting their services we will harness the power to create minor havoc as a forerunner to invasion.'

Lance stopped speaking and looked at each man in turn. When he spoke again his voice was lower in tone. 'In other words we are going in to turn them round. Trade with them. Make them allies. They are pragmatic men and they know the tide is turning. They won't reject us out of hand. The hard rules of their brotherhood demand they give full concentration to their own self-protection and profit. I realise our mission appears alarming, but I've no intention of leading you like sacrificial lambs to slaughter. We are fortunate. We have Joe. He is our golden key and remember I also have a maternal grandfather already imbedded in the nest.' He stopped and smiled at Joe.

'At this juncture let me make a brief comment about each of you in turn and why you have been selected to serve on this mission. First, Captain Remington. Belatedly, for reasons that remain unclear, the Yanks insist this Operation should be a joint Allied affair and Captain Remington has been assigned to join us. They could have sent us someone unsuitable and, for one terrible moment, I thought they had. But, I was wrong. By happy coincidence Hank is exactly the man we need. Hank is a professional dealmaker, an infantry trained soldier, proficient with small arms, a wizard with figures and a trained negotiator to boot. It is rumoured, also, he has earned a reputation for possessing an uncooperative disposition. Perfect. Hank squares our circle.' To Hank's surprise polite noises of appreciation were made.

'Sergeant Lambert, our Canadian colossus, is with us because I made a personal request that he be part of the team. Why? Because there's no other man I'd rather be with when things get bumpy. Robert epitomises the ideal soldier, the warrior poet. Disciplined, unemotional in crisis and, when his blood is up, mighty in battle.' Lance stopped and smiled. 'Recognise yourself, Robert?'

Robert grinned, 'You should know, Major. Maybe, it takes one to know one.'

'When Robert enlisted he did his training with a British Commando Unit. He is a trained SOE operative and, in consequence, an efficient saboteur. He can make himself understood in three languages, French, Italian, and when persuaded to utter anything at all, which is seldom since he seems to do nothing more than read books and scribble notes, is inclined to express opinions in a strange form of Victorian English. I often feel that a prefrontal lobotomy might be helpful in this regard.'

Joe looked confused, Robert guffawed and Hank smiled in polite silence. 'However, to continue. Since his sojourn to Arisaig, a small village in the Highlands of Scotland and the SOE training centre for the insane, he appears to have become imbued with a fascination for causing explosions. Be warned, he plays a mean hand of poker, thinks the monarchy a splendid institution, farts a lot – apt for an explosive expert, don't you think? – but doesn't snore.' There was further laughter.

'That's a black-hearted lie,' Robert protested in mock affront. 'The truth is the boot is on the other foot.'

When the merriment subsided, Lance continued. 'Joe, on the other hand, as already mentioned, you forget at your peril. He has a habit of testing his mortality to the limit by feats of ineptitude. To enjoy a relaxed relationship with Joe is something to be avoided like fear and hope. He is unique in that he has devised a foolproof survival technique: fight for both sides during conflict. Joe was a serving corporal in the Italian army, but decided to detach himself from that defeated and disillusioned assemblage and volunteered to disrupt the Allied war effort by offering his dubious fighting skills to the British Army. By special dispensation and freakish circumstance, he has become a serving soldier in His Majesty's Forces at the same rank attained while fighting for the Fascist cause. It has been my suspicion that Mussolini personally ordered the transfer as an overt act of sabotage.' Joe, all smiles, clapped with delight, Robert made noises of agreement and Hank grinned.

Lance's mood changed. He switched from being jocular to become solemn. 'Quaint as it may appear Joe is to be burdened with the duty of acting as our Intelligence. He will act as our go-between. It is he who will bear the responsibility for our collective fates. With his knowledge of important Cosa Nostra families and having been a member of that organisation from early youth, his

Freewill is Forfeit

knowledge and the trust he commands amongst its members, will be invaluable if we are to succeed. For reassurance I should tell you that Joe was employed as a courier between the families until he volunteered himself into the Italian army. Joe will make our contacts, arrange meetings and negotiate our safe conduct while trespassing on enemy territory. I have no fear on this escapade, if only to redeem his tarnished reputation, he will execute his duties with an unaccustomed lack of alarm. We must look after Joe and see to it he is afforded our best protection. He risks much on our behalf and it's not for us to question his fidelity, or entertain negative thoughts about his commitment. That he has volunteered for this mission puts his courage beyond doubt. That he has earned my trust is obvious.' Lance turned to face the small figure of his batman and said, 'Welcome aboard, Joe.' Joe's eyes glistened. Hank and Robert applauded.

Lance nodded to indicate the initial part of the briefing was at an end. He crossed the floor to the trestle table holding the weight of light arms. 'Now,' he said, 'we'll turn our attention to examining the weapons available for personal selection, but before we settle to make our choices there is one thing I omitted to tell you. The codename for this mission is to be called Operation Sleekit Beastie.'

3

From a window on the second floor of the German High Command (Headquarters) building in Tunis, thirty-three year old Lt Colonel Baron Gustav von Hauptmann watched a convoy of tanks rumble through the main thoroughfare of the town. The noise of the grinding machinery was irritating rather than reassuring. Armaments, munitions and men had been pouring through the streets for three days. Tunis had become a river of steel. Did these straight-backed, rigid-bodied tank Commanders ever stop to think what they were doing in Tunisia?

During the Army's advance through Czechoslovakia, Poland and Russia, the indiscriminate slaughter of civilian nationals had been soul-searing to witness. The mindless brutality had been an affront to Gustav's Christian sensibilities. It had given him his first insight into the insanity that lurked at the centre of the Nazi philosophy. Stalingrad had been the last straw.

His release from the naked savagery of the Eastern Front had been a merciful answer to many prayers. He knew from what he had witnessed that neither side now would sue for peace. The conflicts of ideology had been allowed to escalate into principles of attrition. It was a fight to the finish. One culture had to destroy the other to survive.

When America entered the war there had been a moment when sense might have prevailed but, instead of initiating pragmatic negotiations to sue for the cessation of conflict, Nazi fanaticism had intensified to stiffen the German resolve.

Gustav had taken to prayer. He found it a comfort. But to date, the spiritual peace he craved had been withheld. Perhaps the

Almighty judged it sinful, or cowardly, that he should continue to conceal his opinions, but when life expectancy was reduced to whim, discretion had to be nursed with care, not only for himself, but also for the continuing safety and security of his wife, Lisa, in Berlin. Just to know she was alive and well was reason enough for some thanksgiving.

He had not seen his darling Lisa for three years and pined for her presence. If he should survive his Tunisian posting then, surely, leave could no longer be denied him. The battle for the last North African foothold would not be a protracted affair.

It was a sad day for Gustav when the British declared war in response to Germany's invasion of Poland. The first two years of his architectural training had been spent in Scotland studying at Edinburgh University. He had made many friends in that small, egalitarian country and was aggrieved by the thought he would now be regarded by many of them as an enemy.

His minor aristocratic title had gone unnoticed in Scotland. It was not until his studies had taken him to the Universita di Lecce, in the Puglia district of Southern Italy, that he began to regard its minor advantage as an encumbrance. His title had isolated him from his fellow students to such a degree he had considered dispensing with the social adornment. He was grateful he had resisted the temptation. Anything generating respect among the corporal-brained Generals in the ranks of the unspeakable SS was to be coveted. The aura the title bestowed protected him from the worst of their uncivilised enthusiasms.

The clatter of boots on marble sounded in the corridor. Gustav turned to face the double doors of the room. They swung open and Major General Hans Olbricht entered. He remained with his back pressed against the door, arms behind his body, hands clutching at the handles. He looked ashen and appeared to be locked in a struggle to maintain a veneer of emotional control. Gustav waited in respectful silence.

'Forgive me Gustav. You will not yet have heard. There has been terrible news. Freidrich's 6th Army has been overrun. Marshall Voronov has broken the German resistance. Twenty-one German Divisions have been destroyed or immobilised. The estimated number of prisoners taken is in excess of ninety thousand. Do you understand what this means?'

Gustav decided the General's question was rhetorical. He understood more than the General would ever know. Until ten days ago he had served under Field Marshal Friedrich von Paulus and would have been among those freezing in the hell of a Russian detention camp, or worse, had it not been for General Rommel's request that he be transferred to Tunisia to assist in the planned counter offensive. In Russia the conditions had been unendurable. The cold had been intense, food and ammunition scarce and an outbreak of typhus had destroyed the last vestiges of morale at every operational level. Despite incessant pleading Berlin had been adamant that under no circumstances would a withdrawal to a position of relief be countenanced. When retreat was rejected as an option, the inevitable happened. Hitler's refusal to allow his Generals to control their Divisions had lost the German army the victory within its grasp. Hitler's rigid order should have been opposed by the *Wehrmacht* hierarchy, but no one dared defy the will of the *Führer*. The Vatican itself genuflected in obsequious approval of his insane dictums. Compliance to his every inclination was sacrosanct.

'Our beloved Fatherland is being brought to its knees,' continued the General, still rooted at the door. Following a long pause the General shuffled into the room and took up a position behind his desk.

From his stance at the window Gustav crossed the room and waited for his ranking superior to sit. 'Do you have any family serving with the 6th Army, sir?' asked Gustav, with careful intonation.

'Yes, Gustav. I have a daughter with them. She's a nursing sister. Her mother will be distraught when she hears the news.' The General bowed his head and shook it from side to side, then, as if he could no longer tolerate the weight of his body, slumped into his chair. After a further period of silence, he straightened, fumbled with documents on his desk and looked up.

'All of Germany will be grief-stricken by the enormity of this defeat. It's a catastrophe. There will hardly be a family unaffected by this tragedy. The nation's mourning will be excessive.'

'Would it be better that I left you to recover from the shock of this terrible news, General?' Gustav suggested.

'No, that won't be necessary, Gustav. It's a kind thought. I shall recover in a few minutes.' It was self-deceit; never would he recover. He was aware Germany had not only lost a battle, but now was in grave danger of losing the war. It was the termination of all his past dreams and future hopes. Russia had turned the tide and in righteous anger would resolve to reduce the Fatherland to rubble. Complete humiliation of the German nation would be the least of the punishments demanded by the Russians for the sufferings they had endured. To date, thirteen million of their number had perished in a conflict that had taken the meaning of indiscriminate slaughter to new levels of disbelief. Russia's revenge would be terrible in its purpose.

'Is there any news of the Field Marshal?' Gustav asked.

'He was taken prisoner three days ago. I wonder if we will ever see dear Friedrich again?'

'You and he were friends?' Gustav enquired.

'We first met in 1930 and have been friends since. He never did like Hitler, you know.' Again he shook his head as if the movement gave him comfort. 'They never did see eye to eye. It's all so. . .' He stopped to search for an appropriate word.

'Unfortunate?' suggested Gustav.

'Much more than that, Colonel. Much more than that,' he repeated and took to shaking his head again in disbelief that events of such enormity could happen. It was worse than any conceived nightmare. There was a brooding silence.

'I believe you have my orders, General?' Gustav suggested after a respectful period.

'What? Oh! Yes, of course.' The General looked around the room as if to take his bearings. He sighed and wearily raised his right arm to indicate his resignation to the noise of the passing tanks. 'Our task in Tunisia is about to begin,' he said, without hiding the exhaustion he felt. 'I suppose in the light of present events we'll have to see our duty is done with customary resolve.' His tone made a mockery of his words.

Gustav felt alarm. He was certain the old soldier was about to utter some dangerous indiscretion. It had become obvious he had lost the ability to function with the detachment expected of a *Wehrmacht* General. Gustav had no wish to witness his superior officer's further disintegration.

'You are very tired, sir and we are both suffering from the shock of the terrible news. Could I respectfully suggest, for both our sakes, that we postpone this briefing for a few hours?'

The General looked up and nodded. 'Thank you, Gustav,' he said, 'I think that would be wise.'

* * *

Days of warmth in the North African sun and regular meals of nourishing food, reintroduced Gustav to a sense of wellbeing. The weight loss suffered in Russia was no longer a concern and the chafes and festers common to flesh when exposed to extreme cold finally had disappeared from the surfaces of his body. In a few more weeks his appearance would not alarm Lisa. Had she seen him on his return from Russia she would have been shocked at his appearance. He had lost one fifth of his body weight, but in the last three weeks, since his withdrawal from front line duty, he had regained almost half the loss. The skeletal wreck that had stared at him from his shaving mirror now appeared less daunting. Weight loss had been traumatising. He had become lethargic and prone to depression. Good food and rest were returning mind and body to recognisable normality.

Following a two-day delay he finally received his orders to join the 10th Panzer Division. Gustav's first reaction to the news was relief. He would have been heartbroken had he been selected to serve with one of the newly formed Waffen SS Divisions. What pleased him more was the serendipity his new Battalion Commander was to be Colonel Count Klaus von Stauffenberg, a man admired for gallantry. Gustav had met von Stauffenberg during his months as an Officer Cadet. They had been students together and had formed a friendship. The thought of meeting him again and to serve under his command was a pleasing prospect. Gustav

Freewill is Forfeit

knew von Stauffenberg would be relentless in battle, but would insist his troops adhere to the Articles of War. The shooting of prisoners, or the mindless slaughter of civilians, would be forbidden. Gustav felt fortunate to have been chosen to serve alongside battle experienced men, who, like himself, had seen too much of war to have retained an appetite to inflict unnecessary suffering. At least, in his new posting, he would be able to wear his battle scarf with a degree of renewed pride.

* * *

On arrival at the barracks of the 10th Panzer Division Gustav met von Stauffenberg in the central corridor of the Headquarter's Building. They recognised each other and stopped. They shook hands making noises of mutual pleasure. Following the initial polite exchanges von Stauffenberg made a simple plea. 'Let's not talk of Russia, Gustav.'

'Fine by me.'

'Not unless you harbour some burning desire to express revulsion.'

'It would be a pointless exercise.'

'Quite! You're not yet back to normal functioning, I suspect?'

'I'm fine. Much better now, thank you, sir.'

'Please,' von Stauffenberg muttered in objection to the formality. 'All's well at home?' he enquired.

'Lisa's fine. She sends her regards.'

'Wild cherry wine,' von Stauffenberg said.

'Pardon?'

'If I remember correctly the last time we met Lisa's wild cherry wine reduced us to babbling idiocy.'

'One very dangerous draught, if I recall,' Gustav agreed.

'We had no choice but to drink it. It was either Lisa's jungle juice, or nothing,' von Stauffenberg complained.

'I'm convinced to this day she hid the brandy on purpose. She has this odd determination everyone should enjoy her wine making skills.'

'Light and refreshing is how she described it. 'Lemonade with a cheering edge' she said at the time.'

'And it was true, until we discovered we couldn't stand up.'

'You became hysterical with laughter as I remember. Completely lost control of your physical faculties.'

'I did?' questioned Gustav. 'I remember thinking how beautiful everything looked, how perfect the world was. I admit I may have allowed myself a few chortles of appreciation in celebration of that fact.'

'Nonsense. You were reduced to a state of legless lunacy. Bacchus had claimed you. Happy days', von Stauffenberg sighed. 'The laughter of innocence, how sweet it was. Something we'll never recapture, Gustav.' There was silence for a few seconds.

Gustav noted von Stauffenberg's war experiences had failed to roughen his thoroughbred mien, but somewhere in evidence there was a new characteristic. Was it detachment? Whilst his conversation was animated it was as if his thoughts were engaged in attempting to solve some far away riddle.

'Have you been allocated your quarters?' asked Stauffenberg.

'Not yet. I arrived only seconds ago.'

'You have yet to unpack?'

'I've yet to report my arrival.'

'In that case our meeting has been timely.'

'I don't understand.'

There was a hint of hesitation before von Stauffenberg spoke. 'I do believe, Gustav, you might be exactly the man I seek for an unusual mission. I think I would like you to execute a reconn-aissance for me. It's not a hazardous duty, more a jaunt I would say: an adventurous excursion. You might not need to unpack, after all. Come with me to the Map-room and prepare to be surprised.'

4

Tunisia

From a plateau, near the summit of Jabal ash Sha'nabi, an Arab, mounted on a camel, watched two streamers of dust mark a line on the desert floor. One dust trail approached from the south, the other from the west. The trails had miles to travel before they would converge. If the vehicles had a rendezvous it was simple to guess where they would meet. It would be on the lower slopes near to, or at, the south entrance to the pass. Were they travellers on separate missions? It mattered not. They were the enemy. The purpose of their journeys was irrelevant. Whoever they were a reception party was making ready to extend them a rude welcome. If they should be taken alive they would be made hostage. Perhaps the triumph of a capture would reintroduce the fire of new resolve and reverse the ill fortune that dogged the Arab Brotherhood.

The mounted man ceased his musing and gave his attention to the noise of preparation floating up from the area of the caves below. Prolonged motionless posture had stiffened the sinews of his back. He flexed the muscles of his buttocks to ease the discomfort. The robes draped over the flanks of his animal remained undisturbed by the movement. Man and beast were as one, a timeless picture in a timeless scene.

The Arab's father, and grandfather, had watched the surrounding landscape from the same position. When alive, they too had been initiates sworn by oath to hold secret the existence of the caves. The caves were a gift from Allah, a bequeathed citadel for the shelter of the Berber. It was a proud boast that no army of occupation had ever discovered the secret existence of the caves. Constant vigilance had prevented discovery.

It was rumoured the caves once had been found, and occupied, early in the 10th century by the Almohad from Morocco. Records confirmed the Almohad, under the leadership of Caliph Abd-al-Mumin, had invaded Tunisia during that period, but there was little proof to support the hearsay the caves had been discovered. The rumour was discounted as myth, a fable to be recounted and enjoyed, during evenings of communal hilarity.

Around campfires many tales were told of conflict. Voices often could be heard relating remembered ancient indignities. Many of the stories were embroidered with flamboyant inaccuracies, but men, when at leisure, were given to fanciful exaggeration. At the kernel of all the tales, an eternal truth was proclaimed: 'Man would walk the earth of his homeland in freedom, or perish in protest'.

The men who told these tales were the inheritors of oppression. Never had their lands been free of an invader. For centuries marauders had come, one race following upon another. The Romans, the Carthaginians, the Moroccans, the Turks and the French. Now, adversaries in a global struggle had emerged to infest their territories. The infidel had come again to do battle upon the holy soil of the Arab. Contestants in a bloodbath to possess what they could never own.

From the numbered enemies of the Arab the Christians were the most hated. They killed with relish, and were indifferent to pain inflicted. Now they had taken to fighting their own kind, Allah be blessed! May their blood deepen rivers! May Allah grant them the vigour to assure their mutual destruction! May they go to their eternal torments taking with them their myths and common brutalities, and then, in the lands of the Muslim, herds may safely graze and peace forever reign. But time would have to pass, wrongs made right and battles fought before the Berber could seek rest.

For the present Habib Bourguiba – his name as leader be forever revered – without trial, was forced to suffer the indignity of imprisonment in Rome. Retaliation was required to challenge the injustice. To salt the wound the traitorous bey al Munsif consorts with the Teuton. He quaffs their wine and carouses in German salons of luxury. Treachery was everywhere. Villainy was the infidel's constant companion. Their Christian smiles of viper charm hypnotised sense, separated reason and beguiled the

Freewill is Forfeit

intellect. Bending the bey al Munsif's resolve would have been a simple task to such men. Only Bourguiba had the strength to defy their deceptions. Behind bars he would remain defiant. His release demanded action. Was there a passage, a footway, some method to release him from captivity? Allah would provide the answer in response to the supplications of the devout. Let the enemy multiply a hundred fold. Numbers were of little consequence. To the crack of doom the sworn duty of the chosen would be to rid the lands of the Arab from the curse of Christian pestilence.

The Arab looked at the sun. It was time to make descent and prepare his horse. The men below would be impatient to leave. They would not be kept waiting. Discipline was not an attribute given much attention among the freedom fighters of the Neo Destour.

* * *

The jeep, driven by Robert, was making its way through the rocky scrublands of the border area between Algeria and Tunisia. Earlier in the day the squad had flown from Casablanca and had landed at Tbessa. They were on the last leg of their land journey to the Allied airstrip at Kasserine. From there they were to be flown to Sicily the following day.

'*Fai attenzione,*' Joe said to Robert. In response to the warning Robert applied the brakes. In the rear Hank and Lance were jerked to consciousness by the sudden deceleration.

'There,' said Joe, pointing between a break in the ground giving a narrow view of the valley below. A trail of dust could be seen.

'Well, well! What do we have here? A wee look-see might be in order. What do you think, Major?' enquired Robert.

Lance, reclaimed from a doze, made a guttural noise in his throat. The indecipherable response was sufficient for Robert. He turned the ignition key to kill the engine. They stepped out of the jeep, stretched their limbs and together commenced to scramble up a mound of loose scree to the top of a rise. Their new position opened up the sweep of the desert floor. In the foreground a vehicle was patrolling the open spaces.

Hank was first to speak. 'Holy shit!' he said, 'they're Germans.' The others said nothing. Silence followed, until Lance said, 'What's a German patrol vehicle doing so far behind the Allied front line?'

'It looks as if they're here to reconnoitre the area,' said Robert, giving everyone's thought a voice.

Lance passed his binoculars to Hank and said, 'Take a look and tell me what you think.'

Following examination, Hank said, 'It's an unusual vehicle. It's neither one thing nor the other. I'm familiar with most of the Nazi transport, but I've never seen anything quite like it. It looks like a cross between a weapon carrier and a reconnaissance vehicle. It's a battle-wagon of sorts,' he concluded.

'Fancy transport to be so far from home,' Robert said with unhidden relish.

'Vengono del sud,' Joe continued.

'Correct, Joe, they came from the south,' Lance confirmed. 'They're on reconnaissance, but why?'

'Should we make it our business to find out?' smiled Robert.

'Control your impulse, Sergeant,' Lance chastised. 'We're not getting involved, so don't get yourself all whipped up in expectation. We've other fish to fry.'

'They stop,' Joe interrupted. 'See!' he implored.

The German vehicle had come to rest beside a patch of vegetation scattering the area.

'Isn't that just dandy,' said Robert, with intended mischief. 'If they stay we'll have to make a detour, or wait until they decide to leave. They're practically camping on our route.'

'Okay,' said Lance. 'Let's examine what might be happening down there. We assume they're on reconnaissance. Why?'

'To examine the terrain,' said Robert.

'If that's correct, why?' persisted Lance.

'Tanks,' answered Robert.

'We know they came from the south. Could the Germans be contemplating mounting a pincer movement to out-flank the US 2nd Corps?' This was the crucial question and they knew it. No one spoke. They wanted to listen to Lance develop his thoughts. 'It would be logistical madness. If action became protracted the supply line would fracture leaving their rear exposed and vulnerable. It would be a desperate gamble. If the venture failed their loss would be catastrophic.'

'But, should they succeed the prize would be Tunisia itself,' insisted Robert.

'We're speculating on a hypothesis, don't forget,' said Lance, exercising restraint.

'But can we risk not knowing?' Robert pushed.

'It's only one bloody vehicle, Sergeant. Don't let's get carried away on imagined flights of fancy,' snapped Lance.

'Captain Remington has pointed out this is no ordinary vehicle.' Robert persisted.

'Okay, Captain,' Lance said, turning to face Hank,

'Let's have your thoughts on the matter.'

Hank agreed with Robert. 'If we believe they're testing the terrain for a proposed tank offensive, then I think we're duty bound to attempt to confirm the assumption. It will cause delay and inconvenience, but it's too important a matter to ignore.'

'Information such as that can be secured only by capture and successful interrogation. Let me remind you we're not here as an infantry unit. I can't allow extra curricular action to jeopardise our primary mission. I agree there's something afoot requiring closer examination. Since it seems we're to be delayed we can employ our time by collecting as much information as we can, but I'll permit observation only. Anything we might glean can be passed on to Intelligence when we reach Kasserine. I want no engagement with the enemy. Is that clearly understood?' He looked at each man in turn. They responded to his gaze with a nod. 'Very well, Joe will proceed over the ridge to observe from the best position he can find. *Capisce?*'

'*Si, signore, ho capito.*'

'Hank, Robert and I will skirt around the base of the hill until we find concealed viewing positions. Robert will cover the southwest, Hank and I the northeast. Any questions?' The men remained silent. 'Right,' he said, looking at his watch, 'we'll conceal the jeep and be ready to move at 1330 hours. I want everyone back here by 1600 hours at the latest. Anything else?'

Weapons? asked Hank.

'Side arms should be sufficient.' They looked at one another, nodded and rose to return to the jeep.

* * *

'There, over there, that's the place for us, Hans,' Gustav said to his driver. He was pointing to a patch of vegetation near to a track that led to the hills. 'If they're unaware of our presence they will drive to within two hundred metres of us.'

'I can't believe we've not been spotted,' said Corporal Hans Stumpff.

'We'll soon find out, Hans. If they don't arrive within the next hour then we'll know they have us under observation,' Gustav replied

'A jeep shouldn't present too much trouble to this Italian abortion, but to tell the truth I'd prefer to be sitting in a tank,' added Hans.

The third member of the crew, Lt Herman Kurt, sitting beside an open hatch highlighted by the mid-afternoon sun, threw down his pencil.

'You should try to relax more, Herman. You'll be given ample time to conclude the paper work when we return to the Battalion.'

'And when is that to be, sir?' Although angst-ridden, the question sounded casual. Herman was a Cartographer, a conscript fresh from university and military training. This was his first taste of active duty. Apart from confirming existing data there had been little for him to do. The maps had contained a few inaccuracies, but nothing of serious note. He had found the ground to be perfect for tank movement, flat and firm. Water and fuel presented a problem, but a reliable supply line would eradicate the difficulty.

Herman had not enjoyed his desert trip. Three days of uninterrupted field duty had reduced him to a state of mental derangement. The heat, the stench of unwashed bodies, near rancid rations, insects, boredom and lack of privacy, had engendered in him a condition near to incipient hysteria. A return to the order and comfort of barrack-room life was all he craved. Instead, he had

Freewill is Forfeit

overheard it was the intention of the Colonel to lie in wait for an enemy vehicle to appear. This was an action beyond their remit, a provocative act exposing their small mission to unnecessary risk. He considered this to be irresponsible, quite unpardonable.

'Who knows, Herman,' answered Gustav. 'War tends to disrupt the wishes of those who seek certainty. Be thankful you have been assigned to serve your country without having to endure the trauma of frontline combat. This is a picnic detail, so don't be in such a hurry to have it end.'

Philosophy and platitudes! The question asked had remained unanswered, but what else could one expect from a senior officer who allowed his Corporal to address him by his Christian name. 'I feel it's my duty, sir, to suggest if we wish to avoid trouble we should leave this area as soon as possible.'

'And the trouble you expect?'

'Your proposal to confront an enemy vehicle. Unnecessary provocation could place our mission in danger. I believe it's our responsibility to deliver our findings to Headquarters as quickly as possible. Now our survey is complete, we should withdraw. If we made tracks for home we could be back in barracks by tomorrow morning. Besides, we're not equipped to take prisoners, nor do we have the provisions to sustain them.' Herman knew he was babbling and forced himself to stop speaking.

'Congratulations, Herman, we've not had the pleasure of hearing much from you during our desert sojourn. We were beginning to wonder if you had lost the power of speech. Your objection is noted and will be mentioned in Report.' It was a novelty for Gustav to find he was sharing a duty with someone who possessed nothing of the warrior spirit. Waging war outside office hours would be an inconvenience to Herman. Before Hitlermania flourished, it had been common among servicemen to get through each day by doing just enough to avoid being charged with indolence. It was reassuring, despite the present ubiquitous triumphalism, with all its militaristic fervour and heroic resolve, that the old tradition of duty avoidance had not entirely been eradicated.

It was the last duty Herman would attempt to avoid. Gustav

watched Herman's facial expression contort to one of surprised complaint, then set in motionless grimace. He was dead. A bullet had punctured a neat hole in his left brow.

Gustav leapt to the machine gun turret and yelled at Hans, 'Drive man, drive. Get us out of here. Anywhere, but drive.' Gustav reached for the securing pin that held the machine gun turret in the locked position and pulled. It jammed. He thrust his finger deeper into the ring and pulled with all his strength. It released and propelled him backward bringing his head into contact with the bulkhead. His unconscious body fell to the side and jack-knifed over the central seat. His head came to rest three inches above the boot on Herman's splayed and lifeless, leg.

Hans continued to hear bullets strike the armour plating of the vehicle. He thrust the gear lever into its forward position. The machine lurched as if unwilling to respond. At once Hans knew the tyres had been shot away. The time for heroics was over. He grabbed the white towel, placed over the engine cover to dry and thrust it through the nearest aperture. He heard the cheers of his triumphant captors.

* * *

When Lance heard the single shot his first thought was Joe had been spotted and had drawn German fire.

'Get down,' he said to Hank. When certain it was safe he stretched his neck and peered down the slope. Boulders and scrub obscured his view. Nothing of the activity unfolding below was visible. When a renewed period of fire commenced, he rose and ran to a position he hoped would give him some sight of what was happening. Hank remained stationary. The shots ceased. The sound of cheering came up from the desert floor. The noise echoed faintly in the hills. Lance motioned to Hank to remain still and crawled forward to vanish from sight. Hank's excitement was electric. He experienced an overwhelming desire to move, to do something physical, to become involved in activity.

In the following silence Hank's mental agitation produced paranoia. He felt straitjacketed, held in limbo, locked in isolation.

Typical, he thought, left in the middle of an unknown desert while others were cavorting here and there, responding to impulse, satisfying curiosity, moving and making active decisions, while he, as usual, was left slouched behind a rock, hidden like a small boy at one of his mother's soirees. Was he fated to spend his entire army career in a state of useless inactivity? Holy shit! This was probably the precursor to another fuck-up, a big one this time, and what was he doing? Nothing. Sitting on his butt, waiting until some other activity came along to insult his sense of usefulness and further sully the sorry affair that had been his army career to date.

Lance reappeared and, from a distance of twenty metres, gestured Hank should make his way up the slope by the same route they had come down. In the process of the climb they moved towards one another and, when together, collapsed in breathless relief.

'Arabs,' Lance said, as he gulped for air. He raised his hand to indicate he would continue to explain as soon as he was able. 'About twenty of them, some on horseback,' he said, still struggling for breath. 'I'm buggered if I know who they can be, or where they've come from.'

'Horses?' Hank questioned.

'Some were on horseback,' he repeated, as if he had witnessed the unbelievable. 'Not a camel in sight. They must have a hideout somewhere nearby. That means they know we're here. Christ! This is all we bloody-well need, a rogue group of fucking bandits.' His disbelief was palpable.

'You've no idea who they might be?' asked Hank.

'Not the faintest.'

'Could they be allies?'

Lance made a noise in his throat. 'I wouldn't bet on it. I've an ugly feeling these bastards would murder you for your boots.'

Hank felt the grip of fear. It was a paralyzing sensation. 'How many of them are down there?' he asked, attempting to hide the panic in his voice.

'One thing is certain, we're soon to find out.' Lance's breathing had returned to normal. 'Let's go,' he said, springing to life to restart the climb. They ascended in single file, taking care to remain hidden, until they were almost at the location where they first observed the German vehicle. They lay flat until the heat of the ground forced them to seek the shade of a rock. Lance crawled up the final few yards of the slope to overlook the pass. The roadway was clear. He returned to his position beside Hank. 'Not a sausage,' he said.

'Translate, please.'

'Nothing, nobody, empty.'

'I see. What did you expect, the 7th Cavalry?'

'It's too quiet,' Lance said with irritation. 'Where have Robert and Joe got to?'

'Your order was to assemble at the jeep. They'll be making their way to where it's concealed.'

'That would entail crossing the open territory of the road. They won't do that. Well, Robert won't, Joe might try. They're both to the south of us, so we know roughly where they are. My guess is they'll wait until it's dark before they attempt to make the crossing.'

In the distance, the sound of sporadic gunfire was heard. Shots were being discharged in celebration. The festive reports mingled with the whoops of carousing men. The noises thickened the tranquil air with menace.

Hank's moment of terror had passed. His self-control had returned. He now felt imbued with feelings of intense excitement. He resolved throughout the coming trial never again would he allow the indiscipline of terror to besmirch his resolution. The time had come for his courage to be examined, when his derring-do was to be put to the test. He determined not to be found wanting.

Deciding that he was to die with chivalrous aplomb made him feel better. What was life, after all? It was an existence fraught with struggle, pain and constant multi-layered discomfort: a merry-go-round of endless and repetitive function, unavoidable boredom, frustration and constant misunderstanding. Was it worth the candle? And what of those whose lives were less privileged? Those who had to struggle in ill-paid employment merely to exist? The millions on the earth who were locked into a conspiracy of universal enslavement, held in thrall by the edicts of religion, manipulated by commercial imperatives and political chicanery. Each power structure pontificating its own interpretation of what is right and proper for the obedience of the common throng: preaching duty, demanding conformity, suppressing hedonism, manipulating and sterilising human behaviour to patterns of unrealistic norms.

Hank broke the settled silence. 'What now, Lance?'

'Water, weapons, food and transport are more than a mile away. We'll have to secure the jeep.'

'I agree, and secure it before it's found by one of our unfriendly nomads. Do you want me to attempt to reclaim it?'

'With respect, Hank, the man for that job is Robert. His experience makes his selection automatic.'

Hank felt aggrieved. His offer had not been given due consideration. He stiffened his tone and said, 'Time's wasting, Lance and Robert isn't here. He might not appear until it's too late, until all initiative is lost.'

Lance, scanning the slopes to the south, lowered the binoculars and when focused on Hank said, 'I can't risk you getting lost. Desert areas are peculiar places. The topography tends to be disorientating to the unaccustomed eye, especially after daylight. Your desert experience is zilch, so forget it.'

'I know where the jeep is and I don't need desert experience to find it.'

'Hank,' Lance said, with new firmness, 'we'll wait here until we're all assembled and when that is accomplished we'll move together as one body. Where one goes, we all go. So, hush yor mouff.'

Hank couldn't believe his ears. 'Hush yor mouff?' he queried.

'Good, ain't it?' Lance said, grinning with satisfaction.

'Oh, please!' Hank protested.

'What?'

'It's lamentable.'

'It's an authentic American quotation,' protested Lance.

'Oh! Yeah?'

'Yeah.'

'No American I know would use it.'

'It's a direct quote from the classic 'Uncle Tom's Cabin' you cretin. You've heard of *it*, I suppose?' An ironic snort ended the conversation.

Lance resumed his scrutiny of the slopes. The gunfire had ceased. There was silence. They lay upon the high slope and looked out over a panorama of emptiness. Neither spoke, nor moved. After timeless moments the silence deepened.

Hank's spell was interrupted when Lance gripped his arm and pointed. Joe had appeared from behind a rock some fifty metres below and was waving his arms. He disappeared and moments later, by some affront to natural law, reappeared from behind a boulder at Hank's left hand. His face was covered with blood. Blackish streaks, powdered with dust, had encrusted a design fashioned in nightmare. He presented a spectacle of someone who had weathered hardship, suffered pain and endured tribulation.

'Christ Almighty, Joe. Are you okay?' enquired Lance, with alarm.

'*Sì,*' said the Sicilian and rearranged the pattern of disfiguring streaks by adopting an expression revealing his urgent need of dentistry. Hank assumed it was an intended smile. '*Sì*, but I glad I find you. No good alone. I no like it. *Troppo pericoloso.* Now I here, I better.' There was dignity in his simple words. Hank thought his small comrade both inspiring and tragic. To tolerate adversity with such cheerfulness was exemplary.

'How badly are you wounded, Joe?' asked Lance, with concern.

'Wounded?' Joe looked confused. '*Non ho capito.*'

'*La testa,*' said Lance, pointing at his head.

Lines of embroidered blood contorted to a new design of uncertain meaning and reassembled to form a configuration that Hank could only assume was a display of pleasure. 'I not hurt,' Joe said. 'I fall, yes. I. . .' he paused, 'How you say?' He looked at the sky for inspiration, then removed his cap and pointed to the crown of his head. 'I run, and I fall. I. . .' still he had not found the word he sought. Then, with a smile of triumph, exclaimed, 'Bump! I bump head. *Non è niente di grave.*'

'Of course,' Lance said, as if he should have guessed from the

Freewill is Forfeit

first sight of his bloodstained batman. 'Well, your 'bump' has leaked. Wipe your face, it looks frightening.'

Joe gripped the cuffs of his dust-plastered uniform by making movements with his shoulders. He tightened the material of the sleeves and rubbed both sides of his face with his arms. When satisfied he had removed the evidence of the unsightly staining, he looked up to reveal a full-faced mask of red, black and yellow grotesquery. 'Okay?' he enquired. He looked like a fiendish clown.

'Okay,' replied Lance, unable to conceal weary humour. 'Where's Robert? Did you see Robert?' he asked.

'No, I no see Robert.'

Lance began to question Joe in Italian. Hank ignored the conversation. Thirst was becoming a concern. He looked down at his uniform. It was crumpled, blackened with sweat and congealed with dust. He was filthy. Never had he been more in need of a bath, and yet, had water been available not one drop would he have wasted on cleanliness. Washing was a no-no activity from now on, or until he was a thousand miles away from any known desert. Until then, water was for drinking. He knew Lance and Joe would be suffering similar pangs and determined not to be the first to complain.

Lance directly addressed the issue. 'Soon we'll be unable to function coherently without water. Time is becoming our enemy and further inaction is no longer an option. We'll have to gamble. Joe and I will search for Robert and, when we find him, make our way to a position directly north of here to where the road almost joins the desert floor. Do you know the place I mean, Hank?'

'Yeah, about a mile east of the German's parking site.'

'Correct. You get the duty you want. Secure the jeep and drive it to that area. With luck, we'll be already there, concealed and waiting. If not, you'll wait for us no more than two hours before hot-footing it to Kasserine to recruit assistance. Any questions?'

'I'll wait as long as it takes for you all to arrive.'

'No, Hank. My order is to wait no longer than two hours. Understand?'

'I hear you. Two hours and then I blow.'

'Anything else?'

'Assuming I make it, how will you find me? It will be dark by that time.'

'Don't worry, we'll not be stumbling around in a blackout. For good or ill the moon is in its second quarter and that will give us more than sufficient light to manoeuvre. If you make it we'll find you.'

'With respect, Lance, your orders are too inflexible. Why not set an exact time? Restricting me to wait two hours after an unknown arrival time is too imprecise for my liking.'

'What do you suggest?'

'I suggest midnight. If you're not there by midnight, I leave.'

'And, if you're not there by midnight we'll know you won't be coming.'

'That's about it.' There was an awkward pause. 'In that case I'll take my leave,' Hank said. He stood and with military formality said, 'With your permission, sir.'

'Carry on, Captain and good luck.' The military propriety covered the emotional awkwardness of the moment.

Hank nodded to Joe and slipped down the slope on his buttocks. Before moving off, he stopped in the sitting position, turned and said, 'This is one occasion when having millions in the bank is no help at all, Lance.' With that he smiled and disappeared from view.

5

Robert had learned throughout his travels that every geographical position had its own smell. Tunisia was no exception. The air had a distinctive spiciness; it was a mixture of hot dust and distant shit. He had read once that a pinch of shit was the last, and secret, ingredient added to perfumes by famous French perfumiers. They had deduced it gave their essences an irresistible appeal. When was it last he had been transported by the fragrance of perfume? How long had it been since he had inhaled the soul-nudging scents of a woman's body? How long since he had luxuriated in the sweet, sharp fragrance of the nature-sweetened air of Canada? Too long! It was best not to think of these things. Best to keep the mind occupied with tasks. Time passed more quickly.

Interference had forced this unnecessary duty on the squad. He had been out of order, unmilitary. Lance, always cool, had tried to restrain him, but no, as usual he hadn't been prepared to listen. He should remember had it not been for Lance's restraining good sense he would never have survived in Egypt. His impetuosity, once again, had landed them all in a duty of unnecessary discomfort. In the full heat of the day, here they were, scattered around the hills of a God-forsaken area observing a group of Germans enjoying their unconcerned ease within a vehicular oddity designed by a maladjusted intelligence. They should have waited for the Germans to move on, found some suitable shaded area and relaxed, instead of sitting in sweaty discomfort two hundred yards from Nazis who had the insolent confidence to act as if they were on holiday. Blissfully unconcerned the lieutenant was, writing up his journals, or whatever. Normal duty was to shoot the bastards, not to ogle them while they sat scratching platitudes on paper.

For as long as Robert could remember impatience had been

his Achilles heel. It was a trait he should have learned to control. Instead, it had become an ingrained part of his personality. Many people remarked on how placid he appeared. They knew nothing of the struggle he had to restrain impulse. He had a need always to push forward, gain the next objective, to do what had to be done in a rush. Why? What was the hurry? Was it an impatience to be done with everything, an impatience for death perhaps? Or was it simply a genetic inheritance from his father? His father had been a big-boned, quiet-natured man. During his life as a lumberjack he had been renowned for his capacity for work. To watch him fell trees had been an impressive sight. He could drop growing timber like skittles. Was it compulsion that drove him, an irrepressible impetus not to stop until finished what he was doing? Get on with it. There's a forest to clear and, after that, another. Impatience must have been his driving force.

He had watched his father exert himself beyond sense to see tasks finished. When was anything ever finished, until the final exit? Even in death he had had an axe in his hand. Chopping wood for his evening fire at the back door of his cabin. No doubt he had been doing that too with customary haste.

The only time he saw his father truly at peace was when he had his head buried in a book. By the light of a paraffin lamp he would sit late into the night and devour publications selected for him by his mobile-library friend. Dickens and DH Lawrence were the authors he most admired.

His backwoodsman father had been judged to be a simple man. He had been assessed by outward appearance, the austerity of his home and the simplicity of his trade. He had appeared to all as an unlettered man. Never had he minded. He had chosen to live a life of obscurity and had a dislike of those who sought celebrity. People were more comfortable with companions of their own type and like. They were less self-conscious and more unguardedly friendly. Why trouble good neighbours with the unnecessary knowledge of his interest in literature and language. They would have thought it pretentious. It would have separated him from their society, disturbed the balanced reputation he had earned as an easily accepted and unremarkable neighbour.

During the long stretches of the night his father had inhabited another world. In his private life he had kept company with artists of intellect. At his fire he had sat entranced and silent as he was escorted on explorations of human frailty, nobility and inspiring achievement. Through the magic of language all knowledge and human thought was made available to him for examination and private discernment.

Interest in language was yet another trait he had inherited from his father. Written language assisted him to better understand the confusions of the world. But unlike his father he had developed a need to express thoughts on paper. He found it helpful when affected by wonder, or confused by the anomalies of existence, to commit private feelings to the pages of a notebook. Often the exercise would produce revelatory, poetic results.

Lance had a habit of describing this creative activity of Robert's as odd. He regularly used the term 'warrior poet' during descriptive assessments. It had been mentioned at the briefing. It was true. There was no denying it. When the blood was up fear was forgotten. But, at other times, his other self had a need to unravel uncertainties.

Robert's poems did not seek to be profound. They were no more than personal reflections written as an exercise on the daily anomalies of life. Merely notes to interpret thoughts and emotions. The act of writing often clarified disordered thinking and, at times, generated a chemistry that produced unexpected and revealing script.

Robert raised his binoculars and focused on the German lieutenant. The man appeared to be distressed by some on-going conversation. He adjusted the focus and re-examined his enemy's face. He was a mere boy. His appearance suggested he should still have been at school canoodling with girls instead of dressed up like a soldier-boy playing bang-bang with dangerous toys.

Robert heard a single shot. He watched his schoolboy enemy stiffen and fall forward. Robert checked his cover and looked down to his right. What he saw galvanised his actions.

He turned and started to scramble up the slope. The loose consistency of the sand compounded his difficulty. He reached within himself for energy. A ludicrous, involuntary, verbal utterance came from his mouth to match the exertion and rhythm of his frantic climb. 'Fifty ferocious Tuareg appeared from a nowhere place'. It repeated in his head like a mantra. It helped him to put one leg up, take the strain and push, again and again, time after time, until the movement became as automatic as the idiotic chant in his head. The secret was not to stop, to forbid his conscious to register the pain of effort. He slipped on loose scree and to prevent sliding he twisted his body to fall on his back. His field implements jarred his spine and caused him to grimace. Unable to continue he lay back, ignored the discomfort of the equipment digging into his spine and gulped air into his lungs. He looked down to where he had been. He knew he was lucky to have escaped notice.

Robert surmised that Lance would immediately attempt to secure the jeep. On the strength of this hunch he decided what he should do. He would continue to climb, cross the pass and attempt to secure a position that would afford effective covering fire for the jeep's retrieval. Thereafter, he would accept whatever fate decreed. He checked his water bottle. It was almost full. He remembered the rest of the squad hadn't bothered to burden their observational duties with the weight of water bottles. Stupid! If all went well he would torment Lance with this carelessness for the rest of the war. Robert knew he had insufficient ammunition should action become necessary, but three grenades, a sten with a few clips and a loaded revolver, if used with thought and not enthusiasm, could be enough to disrupt attention for long enough to allow the safe withdrawal of the jeep.

He sat up, turned and recommenced the climb. The mantra started to repeat in his head, but it lacked its original effect. The mysterious appearance of the marauders was now less puzzling. They hadn't appeared from a fairyland, or any other magical place. They had been here, sitting in wait for the arrival of convenient and easy prey. Interlopers to the territory, obviously, were regarded as game to be hunted down. For what purpose he never wanted to discover.

After the ascent Robert crossed the open space of the pass. It was a risk that had to be taken. It meant breaking the cardinal rule

'Never allow the enemy an opportunity to know your position until ready to engage in combat.' Lance would dine out on the indiscretion, if ever he should find out. The only defence would be to state that rules should never be carved in stone and conclude the test of a good precept should be judged on its capacity to be flexible. Robert knew this statement wouldn't protect him from mockery.

Robert guessed the Arabs would split into groups to cover the area. There could be as many as one hundred of them within the parameters of the hills. How well armed was immaterial. A hundred men constituted a fighting force of considerable power, even if armed with clubs.

The plateau Robert selected as his redoubt gave him a good view of the area. He could see where the jeep lay undisturbed, camouflaged under its canopy of scrub. All he had to do was wait.

Within minutes Robert became aware of a movement east of the position where the jeep was concealed. He raised his binoculars and picked out the figure of Hank. He was advancing at speed. There was no sign of Lance, or Joe. Robert swept the area surrounding Hank's position to check if an Arab hunting group was within threatening distance. Reassured, he refocused on Hank to watch his progress. To Robert's surprise Hank's concealment and field techniques were impressive. He covered the ground with care and agility. It was evident he was a well-trained soldier. Robert wondered why he had difficulty in acknowledging this fact and smiled at his own deceit. He still had to become acquainted with Hank's military efficiency, but watching him manoeuvre while in murderous territory was a reassuring confirmation of his courage.

Robert scanned the area again and saw nothing to distress his eye. Circumstances, although bleak, were better than he had dared hope. If current progress continued uninterrupted the squad could be free and clear within the hour. If not, it would be an ironic conclusion to his military career should he fall victim to a band of undisciplined Tuaregs.

Recently the thought of death had been troubling him. At night his dreams had been filled with images of the dead. Ghosts of slain men had become recurring visitors to his sleeping mind. The phantom figures appeared free of wounds and mutilations. Their bodies were whole, but their expressions were fixed with the shock of being violently wrenched from life. The malevolent moment of death was frozen on each face. It gave them the appearance of open-mouthed outrage; affronted disbelief. The spectral intruders were allies and enemies, war-afflicted men who had shared the common fate of a violent removal from existence. They appeared together, friend and foe, sometimes hand-in-hand, mouthing their accusations in silent protest, as if pleading from behind a wall of glass. Were they demanding the killing had to stop? If so, they were preaching to the already converted. God knows! He had seen enough of death. Graveyards-full too much of it, but if it meant filling several more to succeed in exterminating a rule of tyranny from the world, so be it. Until that time the killing would continue. There was no going home until the return to native soil was free of threat. The land of a country is sacred to those who dwell upon it, but only worth its nourishment and care if inhabited by people free of bondage. Without freedom the territory of a homeland becomes a mocking burden, a slavish inheritance.

Robert observed Hank was within fifty metres of his objective. He had stopped moving forward and had gone to ground. He was taking his time before making his final move, resting, or perhaps checking his progress had not been observed. Robert's interest intensified as Hank stood upright to sprint over the final distance. On arrival at the jeep he watched Hank make a bound to land on the bonnet and, in a single movement, start to strip away the camouflaging scrub.

While Hank was involved in his furious labour Robert readjusted his position to scan the rim of the hills overlooking the pass. Nothing. Empty landscape filled his view, except to the east. Over the outline of the hills, on the far horizon, a dark line had formed. It caused Robert to frown. His standard issue 7x35s were not powerful enough to give him the definition required, but he could see what he thought to be evidence of some growing military activity. Could it be the vanguard of German units taking up their positions to mount their pincer movement? He dismissed the thought as unlikely and returned his attention to Hank's endeavours. He witnessed Hank propel himself into the driving seat. When the engine fired the shock of the noise made Robert cringe, he knew the sound would carry for miles in the desert silence.

Once again he tore his gaze from Hank and refocused on the rim of the hills. What he saw sickened him. Along each side of the pass there was Arab movement. Men were positioning to blockade the exit from the territory. Hank was to be made to run a gauntlet of rifle fire.

Robert again fixed his attention on the jeep as it bounded its way towards the road. On the flat surface of the pass its progress became less alarming to watch. Robert concentrated his attention as Hank entered the area of danger. Several volleys of single shots rang out. The jeep swerved to the left, leapt in the air, plunged forward and smashed into the upward slope skirting the side of the road. On impact Hank was thrown clear. He was catapulted forward and propelled with force against the face of the bank. The vehicle remained suspended, held by the indentation of the impact, then crashed to the ground to rest beside Hank's fallen body.

When Robert regained control of his emotions he refocused on the crash site and witnessed a band of men scrambling towards the wreckage. He watched two Arabs haul Hank's body clear and carry him to the edge of the road. As they placed him on the ground they threw their arms in the air and executed a dance of pleasure. Robert turned his gaze from the rituals of their delight. To exhibit such triumph over the body of a slain enemy was an inexcusable barbarity, a testament to the inhumanity of their kind.

During the Arab celebration Robert decided to abandon his place of safety and recross the pass. He knew where Lance and Joe would be waiting, if still not captured. They would return to the original place of departure. The sun was beginning to set. In a short time the light would fail and a cloak of darkness would afford protective cover. Freakishly, everything had gone wrong. Their operation was in ruins, all smashed by incredible misfortune and probable tragic death.

Two hours later Robert met up with Lance and Joe. Robert's appearance was accepted as unremarkable. The greetings were subdued. Robert unhitched his water bottle and handed it to Lance. It was accepted in silence. Lance took a deep draught and handed the bottle into the up-raised, waiting hands of Joe.

Lance was first to speak. He said, 'Hank?'

'I think he might have been killed.'

'I see,' was all Lance said. There was silence. After a few moments Lance spoke again. 'I have to tell you our troubles are not at an end.' Robert raised an eyebrow in question. 'I think the German pincer movement is a reality. It's probable this place will be swarming with Krauts before daybreak. A large force is approaching this area as I speak. There's nothing more we can do. It looks like our war is over.'

'In that case I think we should try to get some sleep,' Robert suggested. 'Tomorrow might be a busy day. What do you say, Major?'

Lance nodded agreement. There was no desire for further conversation. Both stood in soundless companionship before they broke off to whatever slumber the cold of the desert night, and the torment of their thoughts, would allow.

At dawn they lay and listened to the creak and grind of tanks rumbling through the pass. The familiar sound had an eerie overlay in the half-light. Joe was first to move and scrambled up the slope to look over the ridge. Within seconds of his peering down, he stood and started waving his arms. Alarmed that stress had affected his reason Lance and Robert rushed to restrain him. On reaching Joe's position they looked down to see the flutter of an American flag on the aerial of a passing tank. It was the US 2nd Corps in full retreat from Kasserine. As Lance had predicted the American Army's first confrontation with the battle-tested Germans had come to grief. In despond the Yanks were dragging slowly westward to the safety of other Allied forces.

Three men stared down at the scene with mixed emotions. They had to face the unsettling truth that their escape from capture, or worse, was at the cost of an ally losing a crucial battle.

Freewill is Forfeit

6

Tunisia

An American Captain emerged at the top of the rise. He ignored the unconscious figure of his Master Sergeant lying on the ground and approached the Corporal in charge of armed soldiers encircling three men.'Okay, Pete, what's the story?' he asked.

'Who knows?'

'Jis' tell me what y' know.'

'Nuthin'. A come up here followin' Brutus an' a sees this guy lay one on 'im.' He gestured in the direction of Robert. The Captain didn't look round.

'Who are they?' the Captain enquired.

'Don't know.'

'Okay, you guys, bring them down and stick them in a transport. We'll sort it out later down the line. Keep them under guard. Attend to Brutus and don't let him anywhere near the guy who attacked him. Let's go. Move it.'

* * *

It was almost noon when an orderly from Battalion Headquarters awakened Lance from a fitful sleep. 'Come with me, Major, please,' he whispered, before disappearing from view. The orderly had been careful not to disturb the sleeping figures of Robert and Joe. When Lance jumped from the tailgate he staggered and fell. He allowed the young American to assist him to his feet. His feeling of weakness surprised him. His movements seemed to lack co-ordination. He experienced a condition of unreality as he followed his guide through the temporary Company lines.

The chaos of a hurried retreat was everywhere in evidence. It was a piteous sight. Disorder and confusion lay on either side. Tanks had been parked without thought, or care. Artillery was scattered untidily amongst arsenals of dumped ammunition. The higgledy-piggledy nature of the armour was reminiscent of an unkempt scrap yard. Desolation and disillusion hung in the air. It was quiet. The lack of activity reminded Lance of Sunday mornings at home.

The escort turned, pointed to an arrow nailed to a slab of wood and walked on without a backward glance.

'Bn.HQ' was a tent. Lance approached the makeshift Head-quarters, drew back the flap and entered.

'Excuse me?' he said to a group of officers gathered around a trestle table. The men, annoyed by the interruption, looked up and stared.

'Major Bennett reporting, as instructed,' Lance said and waited.

'Next tent, buster,' said one of the group and eyes returned to a collection of maps. Lance dragged his body along a line of shabby canvas and walked uninvited through the open side of the adjacent tent. A voice called out as he crossed the threshold. 'The British officer is here, sir.' The duty NCO pointed to a flap and indicated Lance should enter.

The Battalion CO, Lt Colonel Flynn, was standing peering into a mirror mounted at head height on a tent pole. He was stripped to the waist and in the process of shaving. He had the slim, wiry body of a long distance runner. Without interrupting his concentrated activity he said, 'Park yourself anywhere you can find a space, Major and tell me your story.' Lance chose to sit on a foldaway canvas chair. He slumped into it with relief. Fighting his weariness he related the events that had overwhelmed them during their journey from Tbessa to their intended destination of Kasserine. When finished his tale the Colonel, still peering at the mirror, enquired, 'Have you had breakfast, m'boy?'

'No, sir.'

'There are some doughnuts and coffee on the far table. Help yourself.'

'Thank you, sir, but if you don't mind I'll wait and eat with my men.'

The Colonel stopped shaving and, for the first time, turned to look at Lance. He wiped his face with a towel and snapped his fingers. An orderly entered and, without instruction, set about tidying-up the shaving accoutrements, then left. Lance was aware during the short interruption he was being assessed.

'Where are your men at this moment, Major?

'Asleep in the back of one of your transports, sir.'

'And are they British too?'

'One is Canadian, the other Sicilian, but both now serve in the British army. As I've already explained we're on a special assignment.'

'Yes, Major, I was paying attention. You omitted to tell me, however, what that special assignment might be.'

'Yes, and with respect, sir, you have no authority to demand to know.'

'That may be the case, Major, but since, by your own admission an American, a serving officer of this Corps, no less, having disappeared in mysterious circumstances, gives me the right to harbour some curiosity.'

'You've the right to refer to Allied Command for confirmation of our probity.'

'True, and I'm sure the circumstances of your unfortunate misadventure can be confirmed to our satisfaction without too much delay,' he drawled. 'In the meantime, Major, you look completely done in?'

'Merely lack of sleep, nothing more, I assure you.'

The CO snapped his fingers again and the same orderly appeared. 'Find Captain Rogers of 'C' Company and tell him to locate the British troops picked up this morning and order them to Battalion Headquarters, at once. That's all. Go.' His attention returned to Lance. 'You've had an interestin' time of it, Major Bennett.'

'The usual unexpected fuck-up, yes.' Both men allowed themselves the hint of a smile.

'And you were bound for Kasserine? Well, Kasserine, as doubtless you have surmised by now, is temporarily out-of-bounds. It has become *terra incognita*. We smart-assed, rookie Yanks were expelled from its precincts by force.' His bitterness was tangible.

'You were up against the cream of the German army, sir. There's no disgrace in your defeat, I assure you.'

He looked steadily at Lance before he said, 'Your words are appreciated, Major, but we Yanks seem not to take too kindly to the word defeat. I often think it should be struck from our dictionaries as a redundant word. For us, forged in a democracy of our own devising, defeat is a revelatory concept, a phenomenon strange to our senses, a word we cannot properly understand or fully accept. It is a condition we find difficult to tolerate.' He made a sweep of his arm to acknowledge the surrounding turmoil of his Battalion. 'For the moment the guns are silent, our graves are dug and our dead buried. The survivors of our ordeal rest in tormented sleep. When they rise, then tell them that the battle for Kasserine is lost and they will laugh.' He turned away to struggle with submerged emotion. He walked over to a chair behind a construction used as a desk and sat. 'You'll be pleased to hear that our counter-offensive is imminent. It is being planned as we speak.'

'Your resolve is commendable, Colonel.'

'You better believe it,' he said with aggression. 'In the meantime you and your men will be our guests. Rest, and we'll have you in Kasserine within a week. That's a guarantee.' He raised his arm and snapped his fingers. Once again the orderly's appearance was instantaneous. 'See to it that the Major and his men are given access to hot water, clean clothes and food. Until further notice billet them in the supernumerary tent adjacent to the Officers' Mess and if they require any medical attention have the sick-bay staff attend to it.' He waved his right hand in dismissal and turned his attention to Lance. 'Should you require anything further, Major Bennett, make your requests known to Captain Rogers. He will attend to all your needs from now on. Dismiss.'

Lance rose to leave and saluted. The Colonel nodded and returned to examine his face in the mirror.

While Lance waited at the side of Bn.HQ's tent for Robert and Joe's arrival, he listened to the conversations emanating from the interior of the canvas. For a while the talk centred on recommended citations, new field promotions and the preparation of work lists, until the Colonel instructed a clerk to prepare a Report on the circumstances surrounding the arrest of British troops.

'That limey Major sure looked in need of a good scrubbin'. Who are these guys, sir, if you don't mind me askin'?' enquired the orderly.

'Frankly, I don't give a damn. They could be anybody, Ali Baba and his two thieves, for all I care. One thing I do know, their story stinks. It needs checkin' out. See to it that Captain Rogers gets a written Report from that mysterious Major. Something screwy was goin' on out there when we happened along and it involved one of our own boys. Get Security to keep an eye on them. Tell them try not to make it too obvious, but if they start being troublesome to stick them in the slammer.'

Lance felt a sharp pain of frustration. The account of their misfortune had been disbelieved. A reassuring mask of trust had concealed the reality of active suspicion. Their fidelity was under question. They had escaped the threatening attentions of Arabs only to become prisoners of untrusting allies.

* * *

Despite everything, he had to admit he was feelin' good. Pity about the Company CO. buyin' one like that at Kasserine, but that's war. Some guys are lucky and get through it all without a scratch, others are made to pay the ultimate price. War was nuthin' more than a game of roulette. Many lost; a few gained. There was no denyin', so far, he was makin' out as one of the winners. Good fortune jist kept on smilin'. It wasn't often that an ordinary Joe from the Bronx made Major, especially in a tank outfit. Of course, he had gained by the misfortune of others. But, what-the-hell, luck was a fickle lady. She had to be wooed with care. You had to be smart, keep your eye on the game, put yourself about and be in positions where noticed. The recipe for success was to pretend to work hard, smile a lot and keep a careful tongue in your mouth.

It had been the same back home in the Club. He had gone from sweeper-up to head croupier in four years. The army was different, of course, harder, but the same rules applied. Now, he was a Company Commander, a guy with clout, somebody to be reckoned with. The promotion had to be confirmed, of course, but that was a formality. Full fuckin' Major! Could it be believed? It would take some time to sink in. The reality was too much. But, by keeping a clean nose, he had earned it. Done everything by the book. Bin careful not to put a foot wrong and had applied himself when under observation. At Christmas he had bin a nowhere, no hope, two-bit Corporal and then bin lucky enough to wangle a Commission'– another story concernin' small deceits – and now he was King Kong, top-of-the-heap, big-time fuckin' medicine. It sure was a funny old world. Other people's bad luck jist seemed to push success his way. Yep, the Army and the Casino had a lot in common. With a few tweaks here, and a bit of manipulation there, he would have 'C' Company shaped to his likin' in no time diddly-squat. The first problem was to whip the Master Sergeant into line. He was nuthin' but a two hundred and fifty pound mountain of trouble. There were hundreds like him in the Bronx. They had to be out-foxed, kept in place, or they could make life a misery. The guy had called the shots for too long. He was soon to learn things were gonna be different from now on. 'C' Company was under new management. A guy from the Bronx had arrived, not an Ivy League, polo-playin', fat-assed fucker, who didn't give a shit because all the authority he ever needed was his by birthright and fancy education. A streetwise guy now was in command. The days of Master Sergeant fuckin' Brutus, stridin' around spreadin' grief and causin' unnecessary aggro, were at an end. Finito. Yes, sir, it was move ova' time, big boy, Major Buck Rogers has arrived and was takin' a grip of the reigns.

His thoughts were interrupted when a Corporal's head appeared through the flap in the tent. He said, 'The limey Sergeant is jist passin'. You said you wanted to speak to the guy. Will I give him a holler?'

'Yeah, yeah. Wheel him in, if he's there. Is he alone?'

'Yeah, on his ownsome.'

'Ok, do it.'

'Sure, Captain, or is it Major now?'

'Captain will do for the moment. Go, man, haul his ass in here.'

This was gonna be interestin'. Three guys appear at the top of a hill from nowhere and wham-o, Brutus is out cold. Somethin' never bin known to happen in the history of the Battalion. Smart-ass, big-shot, Master Sergeant had met his match and bin flattened. No doubt about it, lyin' stretched out cold he was. Brutus for Chris'sake! Jees-sus! This was somethin' else, big-time.

The Corporal's head popped through the flap. 'He's here, sir.'

'Well, bring him in, dummy.'

Robert marched into the makeshift office in British military fashion. He came to a halt slamming his right heel into the ground, turned left and again brought his heel down with practised thunder. He threw up a drill instructor's salute to complete his entrance.

The intended mockery was not lost on the American. He chortled and said, 'Yeah, yeah, that's very good, very impressive, very fuckin' British Army. Now you're gonna tell me how ya did it.' The Captain looked up at Robert and waited.

'Did what, sir?' asked Robert, confused.

'Lay out Brutus, of course.'

Robert wondered if he had heard correctly. 'I don't understand your question, sir.'

'Brutus, my top Sergeant. Brutus, the guy you walloped yesterday morning.'

'I see,' said Robert pretending to understand, while hoping soon all would be revealed.

'Well, how? Spill the beans, man.'

'He tried to disarm me.' Robert said, hoping it might have some relevance.

'He was arrestin' you guys.'

'With respect, sir, you don't barge around arresting allies and you don't insult them by attempting to disarm them while in a theatre of war.'

'Yeah, yeah, yeah. So you say. But, how did you do it?'

It was the same idiot question; little wonder the whole caboodle of them were in retreat. Good God! ALLIES! 'I asked him to desist and he became abusive.'

'And?'

'He told me if I didn't comply he would knock the shit out of me.' Robert heard the officer chuckle.

'What next?'

'He laid hands on me and I resisted.'

'In what way?'

'In the normal manner. I pushed him away.'

'Oh boy! And then what happened?'

'He lost his temper and decided to assault me, so, I hit him. It was a simple act of self-defence, an unfortunate incident, a complete misunderstanding.'

'How many times? How many times did you hit him?'

'Just the once.'

'He was unconscious for ten minutes.'

'So I heard.'

'So, how did you do it?'

By now Robert was convinced he was speaking to a mentally retarded officer. 'I've told you, sir.'

The newly promoted Major sat back in his chair and grinned. 'Well, well. Son-of-a-bitch! Did it really happen? One punch?'

'Yes, just one punch,' Robert said wearily. 'I can assure you.'

'I believe you, Sergeant. Believe me, I believe you.' The Captain stood, walked round to where Robert was standing and thrust out his hand. Robert extended his own to have it shaken. He attempted a smile to hide confusion.

'What you did made a lotta guys in 'C' Company very happy. Hittin' him, you hit the jackpot in the popularity stakes. The morale of ma men jist soared.'

Robert was stunned. Only two days had passed since they had suffered defeat in battle and this commissioned cretin was salivating with pleasure over a minor aspect of morale.

The Captain returned to his chair. He was smiling when he said, 'A don't suppose you'd like to do it again?'

'Do what again, exactly?'

'Well, 'exactly', lay him out, flatten him, but this time in front of the entire Battalion.'

'And why would I want to do that?' Robert asked, convinced he was conversing with a battle-scarred soldier. The trauma of defeat had detached him from reality. Robert had seen it happen before.

Men started focusing on trivia when all around was falling apart.

'Because the guy's a bully and a bullshittin' motherfucker who's badly in need of a good lickin'.'

At last Robert found himself on firm ground. 'I wear this uniform to fight enemy soldiers not fellow Sergeants who happen to have psychopathic personalities.'

'Neat,' said the new Major, taking no offence. 'The guy is goin' around bad-mouthin' you, sayin' you hit him with a weapon.'

'The man can say what he likes. He believes he was hit with a weapon. In this case the weapon was my right fist.' Robert said with force.

'Cool it, man. We all know that now, so relax. I say again, there's not a man in this outfit who wouldn't give a week's pay to see you do it again.'

'I'm not a brawler, Captain and, with respect, I think your request is offensive.'

'Back off, Sergeant.'

Robert, never one to back off, whether right or wrong, said, 'If your Sergeant uses inadmissible force in the execution of his duties it's your responsibility to discipline his behaviour, not mine. Your request that I fight your Sergeant in order that, somehow, he may be brought into line, besmirches your rank and your uniform.'

The Captain glared at Robert in disbelief. He struggled for control. 'If that's the way you feel about things, Sergeant, there's nothin' more to be said, except I think all you limeys are so tight-assed it's no surprise you're so full of shit. Jist forget this conversation eva' happened. Dismiss.'

Robert, who had been standing to attention throughout, took one foot-banging pace to his rear, flourished a salute and yelled 'Sir' in traditional style. He turned to the left and marched out of the tent to the whistled strains of 'Colonel Bogey' sounding in his ear.

7

The Caves, Tunisia

Somewhere in Hank's unconscious he became aware of a nagging discomfort. Slowly he surfaced to a distressing wakefulness. He was forced to struggle against some invisible restraint. The discomfort was not localised; it was an uncentred ache, an all-enveloping malaise. His physical structure seemed fractured, held in a vice of uncomfortable paralysis. His brain seemed unwilling to function. He was confused, disorientated. He told himself these mysterious effects were manifestations of semi-consciousness. Control of mental and physical faculties would return when complete wakefulness was achieved. When fully conscious the sensations of helplessness and disorientation would disappear and be forgotten.

With a concentrated effort he forced his eyelids to blink open. He stared at a glimmering darkness. It was weird and peaceful. Sufficient light from somewhere far away made it possible for his eyes to discern shape. In the gloom, above his head, a ceiling of jagged rock was visible. He was in a cave. His eyes moved in a downward sweep to reveal the sight of a man crouched upon his knees on a floor of sand. The stranger was facing the source of the cave's dim light. In the gloom his blond hair shone with an ethereal luminosity. He watched the man with interest. It did not seem strange that the figure appeared to be at prayer. Beneath a bowed head the stranger's lips shaped unheard words. It was fascinating. The man was wearing the uniform of a German officer. It was a phantom, a hallucination. The brain had gone askew. What was witnessed was a manifestation of what was wanted to be seen, merely a wish-fulfilling spectre, the vision of a contrite German soldier, a bowed and beaten enemy confessing to the guilt of his race. Hank closed his eyes. He was tired. Very tired. It was all a muddle of visions and mysterious pain. Sleep would remedy everything.

* * *

When consciousness was regained he discovered a German officer peering down at him. How he came to be lying immobilised in a cave was beyond his understanding. The last thing recalled was a vague memory of examining Joe's blood-streaked face. Had some unremembered incident occurred during which he had sustained injury? The kneeling man at his side drew a cloth from his uniform. It was shaken and allowed to drop somewhere out of sight. When it reappeared it was saturated with water. Hank watched as it was held above his head and allowed to drip. This peculiar ritual was repeated, over and over, before the cloth was laid aside. The stranger then commenced to massage his throat. He stared up at the man in wonderment. Stabs of pain were experienced throughout his body as strong arms raised his shoulders to cradle his head. A metal mug was placed at his lips. For an inordinate time acute discomfort had to be tolerated.

Throughout, his mysterious attendant had chosen to remain silent. Only grunts of encouragement and sympathy were made. When finished the man sat back on his haunches and wiped his hands. 'You have been lucky,' he said, in well-modulated English. 'No bones are broken, but you have incurred extensive bruising, suffer from dehydration and your tongue is in a state of tumefaction.' A quiet half-smile concluded the mysterious administrations. 'You must rest now. Be at peace. You are no longer in danger.'

* * *

Hank had no idea how long he had been lying in the cave. Pain and sleep had knitted a tangle of timelessness. Sometimes he had woken to a darkness dimly lit with tinges of colour and at other times to a sepulchral light. On several occasions he had been awakened by his self-appointed nurse to be sponged and have ointments applied to his body. When last awake he had crapped himself. He had almost wept with helplessness, but the embarrassing evacuation had been attended to without grimace or signs of displeasure. Instead, his male Florence Nightingale had smiled throughout the entire clean-up procedure. He was a mysterious guy. He had a strange devotional air. It was spooky. He seemed to be the type who took comfort from assisting the helpless. It was as if some deep conviction required him to be saintly. Who was he? Who might this man be? Was he a German officer? By his demeanour he was a man of culture, someone who had been expensively educated. How had he described the condition of the tongue? It had been by some unpronounceable word that had scared him shitless. Not entirely true, as time had proved.

Since then his guardian angel had chosen to remain silent. Only eye contact had been maintained. Food had been offered, but refused. Apart from having no appetite, swallowing would have proved difficult. When the pain had been at its worst he would have assigned his soul to the Devil for a spell of relief. Now that the condition of the tongue had improved and the pain bearable, he felt relieved that a pact with 'Old Nick' had proved impossible to bargain.

To divert the mind from pain he had concentrated his thoughts on Anna, the effect her beauty had wrought in his consciousness: the mystery evoked, when unbeknown to her, he had allowed his gaze to rest upon her features. It had been a type of enchantment never before experienced. Never once had he called her Anna. While at dinner, on the occasion of their arranged end-of-the-course date, even then he had called her Sergeant McKay. Somehow it had not seemed strange. Different, or what? To the life he had led in New York – very different!

For five years he had lived the life of a sexual hooligan. He had not been alone. In common with other young men in his group the sole purpose of attending any social event was to achieve sexual fulfilment with as many of the young fillies as opportunity, or energy, would permit. In consequence, they had run riot through numerous ranks of nubile debutantes.

Now he was enthralled by a different type of feminine beauty; a beauty that imbued the spirit and laid claim to the heart. Anna's grace shone from within and had illuminated his life. Her perfection was embedded in parts of him that, until now, he had never known existed. The memory of her serenity had had the power to ease the agony of his pain and had bequeathed him the will to endure the timeless torture of recovery. Anna had kissed him when saying their goodbyes. She had stretched up and had placed her lips gently against his left cheek. It had been a peck, no more than a politeness. The touch of Anna's lips was a moment his memory would cherish until his dying day. He would seek out Anna after the war. She would not be difficult to find. She was Lance's cousin, after all.

Holy shit, LANCE! His mind was in such a confused condition the existence of his comrades had been forgotten. What had happened to them? Were they still alive? Had they been captured? Good God Almighty! He knew nothing about anything. Nightingale probably would know. He of all perfection, the comforter of all alarms, he would know. It only required the question to be asked, but there remained the irritation of not being able to shape coherent sound. Why was life so prone to continual frustration, or was this observation peculiar only to those who had insight enough to be aware of its annoying, permanent, overlaying presence? Perhaps Nightingale would know the answer to that question too, if ever he were asked. A deep weariness overwhelmed him and once again, he fell asleep.

8

Glasgow

The man confronting Jane McGregor was from the War Office, or so she thought. They had met before. It had been prior to the outbreak of war when he had travelled to Scotland to vet and recruit personnel for the war effort. As a result, Anna had been enlisted into the Education Corps and she in turn had been persuaded to accept a term of temporary duty at Bletchley Park. After three years he had reappeared, out of the blue, with no more formality than a knock on her door. Without an introductory rigmarole, except the muttering of his name, which she did not hear and had forgotten, he flashed an identity document and entered her flat.

He placed his hat on the hall table, discarded his coat and gas mask on her antique settle and without invitation or need of direction, wandered into her sitting room to deposit himself on the chair that any sensitive stranger would have surmised as her own exclusive territory.

She did not know whether to be amazed at his lack of courtesy, or impressed by his nonchalance. Since his visit had some official purpose she decided not to offer him refreshment. Without preamble he placed a black briefcase, embossed with the gold insignia of State, at his feet, and began to examine the contents. He produced a file, placed it securely upon his knee, sat back and said, 'While assisting at Bletchley Park you signed a document restricting you to secrecy. It's my official duty to inform you the information to be exchanged between us today will be treated within the strictures and conditions of that oath.'

He opened the file, waved a sheet of foolscap in the air and returned it to a bundle of papers without offering it for examination. She did not doubt its authenticity. This man did not play games. He was a committed agent of the State, objective and efficient.

She had met many like him while working at Bletchley Park and had grown to admire the singular dedication they brought to their exertions. Unfortunately, she recalled, many were unable to leave their grim intensity at her bedroom door. Among those she had allowed to share her bed, mainly as a reward for the mental slavery they were forced to endure, many had suffered the affliction of premature ejaculation. During the six months she had served in that high intensity enclave only once did she experience full orgasm and that had been with an engineer sent in to repair the central heating. She recalled on that occasion she had allowed herself to behave shamelessly. Promiscuity had marked her behaviour during her short tour of duty at Bletchley. The charged atmosphere of the place had upset her normal balance. In fact, everybody had rutted like goats in season and nobody had given this departure from the norm a second thought.

The intellectual coterie assembled at Bletchley Park to crack the codes of the German Enigma machine were challenged to solve what was thought to be unsolvable. The unique categories of men who were recruited for the task waged their war in cardigans and fought with pipes in their mouths. In their determination to achieve the impossible they peered at paper marked with what appeared to be indecipherable twaddle and at sequences of words and figures that were rearranged at irregular intervals by random code. Patterns of nonsense assailed their days. Absurdity became their constant companion. They fought their battles in the trenches of the mind. Was it any wonder these men craved comforting arms and the release and solace of sex? To have denied them this small comfort would have been prudish and prudence never had been her strong suit. During the quiet watches of the night she had suffered their groans with genuine sympathy and their unfortunate inadequacies with tenderness and uncharacteristic patience.

'Before coming to the main point of my visit I would like you to confirm some of the biographical data held on file.' There was more perusal of paper. 'You were born in Edinburgh in 1907.' He looked up at her. 'You are currently thirty-six years of age. You look younger, if I may say so.'

'That's kind of you,' she muttered, wondering if it was to be the opening shot of a man who intended making a pass.

'You are the only child of Scottish parents. Your father was an engineer who worked for a shipping line and your mother a Music Hall artiste. Both are still alive and presently live in Perth, Australia?'

'Yes. They left about ten years ago.'

'Quite,' he said, as if he suspected their emigration had not been a simple matter of choice. 'You received your primary education in Edinburgh, at Stockbridge School and from there, in 1919, you were awarded a bursary to study at James Gillespie's School for Girls. You left there in 1925 with the Scottish Higher Leaving Certificate. Following a short period of unemployment you were successful in securing a job with an import and export company in Milan, Italy. There you worked as a secretary in the general office attending to run-of-the-mill duties?' He looked up and said in a conversational tone, 'I take it that consisted of doing things like filing, typing, making translations and the like?'

'Yes, exactly that.'

'Thank you,' he said and reverted to his official voice. 'After two years you were promoted to a position of power within the company. Can you explain how this dramatic rise came about?'

'Yes. I was good at my job.'

'Was it not that you had caught the eye of *Il Capo,* or should I say, the Managing Director Signor Carlo Visconte?'

'By that time we had become lovers, yes.'

'The affair triggered off a divorce from his wife and caused bad blood?'

'Yes, unfairly, I thought. The marriage had been on the rocks for years. Long before my appearance in Italy.'

'But your relationship with Visconte caused friction?'

'Only between his wife's family and him.'

'You were threatened by them, were you not?'

'It was bluster, mainly.'

'I see.' Again he used an inflexion to suggest what he was hearing was only half true. 'Tell me about the business.'

'We imported goods from the Far East. Silks, hardwoods, bronzes, furniture, agricultural. . .'

'By the time of your promotion had you become aware that the legitimate side of the business was merely a front to obscure illegal activity?'

'Within days of my arrival I was aware the agricultural imports far-and-away outstripped the other traded commodities.'

'The firm was importing forbidden produce. The truth is the company was the fulcrum of an international drugs ring masterminded by your employer and lover, Don Carlo?'

'As far as I was concerned the shiploads of hemp arriving from Thailand were processed to produce ropes, sacking, linoleum, sailcloth. . .'

'Yes, yes, yes, you're trying to avoid admitting you found yourself up to the neck in the production and distribution of cannabis.'

'If you're trying to. . .'

'No. Please. I want you to understand I've no interest in either the morality, or legality, of your previous life. I wish only to confirm the information held on file. There's no reason for you to be coy or evasive. Now, shall we continue?'

'Very well. Carlo was a member of the Cosa Nostra. Your files are correct. He was a Don. The company took regular delivery of high-grade grasses from Thailand. In 1929, without thought, or consultation, the Thais increased their supplies and what had been a safe and clandestine operation became difficult to control. In order to resolve the problem Carlo and I embarked on a round trip of the families. We travelled throughout Italy and Sicily to reorganise distribution methods. It was agreed our allocation system be reformed by the simple expedient of increasing the quotas to our most efficient outlets. This caused trouble among some of the smaller families and disagreements broke out. Arguments became more heated and unreasonable and no doubt you know the rest. It's strange to recall now, but abundance generated greed, greed led to violence and the whole sorry affair cost Carlo his life.'

'And your arrest.'

'Yes.'

'You were charged with murder and drug-trafficking.'

'These charges were reduced.'

'The drug trafficking charge was dropped against you due to lack of evidence and murder was reduced to manslaughter.'

'Yes.'

'You shot Carlo Visconte's assassin.'

'I did. I've never denied it.'

'And in consequence became a mythical figure within mafia circles.'

'Notorious, perhaps, but hardly mythical.'

'At the time, *Il Corriere* reported your behaviour as heroic. Your name was eulogised as the avenger of a slain Don. Your stock within the international compass of the Cosa Nostra soared. It was reported you had bigger balls than Mussolini.' He was pleased with this item of research and smiled.

'Yes, I heard that while in prison.'

'You were sentenced by the Court to eight years imprisonment?'

'I served five of them before being released.'

'Following further legal proceedings the company was closed down and a large proportion of the assets were confiscated?'

'I've no knowledge of that. I had no shares in the company. I was an employee. When released from prison I came directly to Scotland and I've been here ever since.'

'Yes, that ties in pretty well with everything on file. Thank you.' He tidied the batch of papers, replaced them in a file, put it in his briefcase and snapped the lock. He readjusted his sitting angle to a more comfortable position, cleared his throat and said, 'Now that's out of the way, I'd like to have a chat with you about your ex-student, Anna McKay.'

'Anna's very well. She's in Casablanca at the moment.'

'Yes, I know. Her superiors speak highly of her. As I remember she joined our Service at a time of great need. You, also, co-operated by volunteering to assist at Bletchley Park when at its beginning we were having trouble forming a backbone of permanent staff. As I recall you arranged to take a sabbatical from your teaching post?'

'I took French leave.'

'Your help was greatly appreciated and did not go unnoticed.'

'Well, thank you.'

'No, sincerely. You were very popular among the boffins. They still talk of you fondly.'

Jane wondered whether he was being facetious and quickly decided he was not. 'It's kind of you to say so.'

'You met Anna's cousin, Conrad Bennett, only the once, I believe?'

'Yes, but he was Conrad only to his family. Everyone else called him Lance. It was he who persuaded both Anna and me to volunteer our services to the Crown.'

'Exactly. Well, he's a Major now and I'm sorry to tell you he has been reported missing. He was on a mission, en-route to Kasserine in Tunisia, when he vanished. From there he was to have been parachuted into Sicily with three others to make contact with your friends.'

Jane looked confused for a second, then felt the force of his meaning. 'Ouch!' was all she said.

'No slight intended, quite the contrary, I assure you. While in Sicily it was his intention to use his grandfather's house as a refuge. The old man, of course, is Anna's grandpa too.'

'Anna will be distraught when she hears the news.'

'Of course. If the missing men do not appear, it will force us hurriedly to train and prepare a replacement team. As you can imagine suitable personnel for this type of mission are not easily found. You, however, would be perfect. The purpose of my visit is to attempt to persuade you to volunteer.'

Jane wondered whether she had heard correctly. When she realised he was serious, she exploded. 'You're joking!'

He shook his head and said, 'Just think how perfect an emissary you would make.'

'That's all very well, but unless I am mistaken Sicily at the moment is an enemy country saturated with Germans.'

'True. That inconvenience can be overcome, however, with care, planning and a little good fortune.'

'How reassuring. And tell me, exactly how do you plan to get me there? By one of Mr Cook's organised Adventure Itineraries?'

'By parachute.'

'Me,' she yelled, 'me, parachute into Sicily! Have you lost your reason?'

'You'll be given proper training and instruction, of course. You might find it extremely exhilarating.'

'What!' she screamed. 'Exhilarating? I can't walk down a flight of stairs without feeling nervous. The condition is called vertigo. I'm in a panic just thinking about it. I've never heard anything so terrifying.'

'Trust me,' he said. 'We have developed methods of counter-acting panic of that type.'

'No method on earth could ever induce me to jump out of an aeroplane.'

'We could, of course, go by submarine and land by sea, but that would entail the hazard of an overland journey through occupied territory.'

'Stop! I'm having difficulty believing this is happening. You arrive from London unannounced; interrogate me about confidential events from my past; soften me with a compliment or two; venture to give me some terrible news of a friend; invite me to volunteer to jump out of an aircraft to land in an occupied country swarming with enemy and other known groups who would not hesitate to garrotte their grandmothers for the price of a whore; invite me to become enmeshed in espionage and I don't even know your name.'

'David Hardie,' he said without ceremony. 'Friends call me Dave.'

'Well, Mr Hardie, you do understand why I feel I'm conversing with a madman?'

He didn't answer. Instead, he rose and walked to a side table upon which stood several bottles, an ice bucket, a jug of water and a siphon. He examined the cluster and said, 'It's been a long day. Do you mind?'

'An aperitif before an expected meal, perhaps?' she stung.

'I could nibble a morsel, now that you mention it.'

'You Londoners will have heard of rationing, I suppose?'

'Naturally. We Southerners have had to adjust to imposed deprivation as well as you Scots and have learned to make allowances for meagre provisions,' he beamed. 'A biscuit would suffice, but I'd be grateful for a glass of whisky. I haven't seen a malt for centuries.'

She didn't attempt to rise. Co-ordinated movement was beyond her. She implied her consent with a wave of her arm.

'Will you join me?' he invited.

'No, thank you. I need something more calming than a glass of whisky. You wouldn't happen to have some chloroform in that fancy bag you carry?'

'Would an aspirin help?'

'Only if you have a lethal supply.'

He resettled into *her* chair and began to caress the surfaces of the crystal glass. When the foreplay was complete, he raised it to his lips and sipped the contents. With eyes closed, he muttered, 'Nectar'. Then, he said, 'You will have a personal bodyguard and also be accompanied by a trusted companion of your acquaintance,' still with his eyes closed.

Jane, in shock, gaped at him in disbelief. She wondered what he could mean. Then, suddenly, she knew. 'You mean Anna?' she screamed. When there was no reply she realised her guess was accurate. 'You mean Anna,' she shrieked again.

'Three of us will make up the team.'

'You intend coming too?' she spluttered.

'Only to see the pair of you come to no harm. You can look upon me as being nothing more than a glorified chaperone.'

Anna had had enough. 'I'm sorry, this is all too bizarre, too incredible for me to absorb.'

'Yes,' he muttered in sympathy, 'war does make strange bedfellows of us all.'

'What, exactly, do you want me to do, should we ever get there?'

'Merely make contact with old friends and converse with them.'

'About what?'

'Mutual interests, but you will receive a full briefing if you agree to participate. It is nothing they won't want to hear and it will do wonders for your already exalted reputation within their ranks.' He was smiling again.

'And you're to be my bodyguard, you say?' He nodded. 'Forgive me, but you hardly seem the type.'

'Whatever can you mean?' His face was expressionless.

'Well,' she said, looking into her lap, 'you're not big enough to be frightening.' She looked up. 'Usually, bodyguards look intimidating. They're big, brutal men with psychopathic eyes.'

'I'm five nine and weigh twelve stones. That's not too bad, surely?' he said, struggling to keep a straight face. 'But, you're right, I probably don't look frightening enough for the task. I admit it, I don't match the stereotype and that's the truth of it.'

'Have I offended you?'

'Why should I feel offended? Surely it's a compliment to be told one's features look un-psychopathic.'

It dawned on her he had been enjoying gentle fun at her expense. It gave her a warm feeling. 'Tell me, did you volunteer for this mission?'

When the original parachute drop was known to have failed, radio communication had been re-established with the Sicilian underground. During the transmission a fourteen-day postponement was agreed. It was thought the revised arrangement would afford sufficient time to resolve matters. It had been a miscalculation. It had taken three days to find Jane McGregor, another two days to have Sergeant McKay posted home, leaving only nine days to meet the new deadline. Restricted by time and unable to find a suitable Italian-speaking operative to train and escort two female agents, David decided he had no other choice but to volunteer for the duty.

'Yes, I did,' he said. 'When I heard the men of 'Sleekit Beastie' were missing I made a request to serve on the replacement team. Contrary to your opinion, I thought I might just fit the bill. If I've been egotistical, I apologise.'

'You must try not to be so sensitive. What's a sleekit beastie when it's at home?'

'Sleekit Beastie? By tradition all operations are given codenames. That's the given name for this caper.'

Freewill is Forfeit

'Very apt,' said Jane.

'The Head of the Department is a Scot and has the habit of selecting weird Scottish utterances for missions. The last raid on Norway was called 'Operation Snell Wind'. 'Snell', what does that mean?' he asked.

'It means bitter-cold,' Jane explained. Have you any other examples?'

'Yes, a few. There was 'Operation Glaikit Grievance', 'Operation Gallas Laddie'. There are hundreds of them. What's a malky, by the way? One was called the 'Glasgow Malky'.'

'I'm not sure, but I think it means a head-butt.'

'I thought the head-butt was affectionately known as the Glasgow kiss.'

'As the Eskimo uses a hundred words to describe snow, we Glaswegians use a variety of expressions to eulogise our quaint social rituals.' Jane was pleased with this explanation and favoured him with a smile. He laughed.

'The operation name I liked best was one he was forbidden to use because of a suspected sexual connotation.'

'Well?'

'Operation Channering Badger'. Some other Scot thought it was too near 'tadger' for military adoption.' This time they both laughed.

'What made you think you were a suitable person to lead this mission?' Jane asked.

'I'm a cautious, unimpulsive, low-profile sort of individual. All the qualities required for a mission of this type. I am aware these traits often attract a pejorative interpretation among the more gregarious. But, there you are!'

'When we last met you were in uniform. An army uniform.'

'I'd forgotten that.'

'The Military Cross is not usually awarded to cowards, at least not in my experience.'

'So, you noticed. That was observant of you.'

'You know a great deal about me and I know nothing about you. Since you're to be my bodyguard don't you think I should be indulged with a few biographical details?'

He grinned. 'Sounds reasonable. Well, I'm forty years of age and a professional soldier. I joined the Army straight from school in 1921 and presently hold the rank of Lieutenant Colonel. In 1935 I was seconded to serve in Counter-Intelligence. Apart from making a few trips abroad, Whitehall has been my base ever since.'

'You're a desk jockey?'

'More or less.'

'And the medal?'

'The higher the rank the easier they are to obtain.'

'Family?'

He didn't answer. He looked at something above her head, lifted his glass and sniffed the contents. In one movement he finished the remaining half-inch of whisky and laid his glass on the side-table. 'My parents are both dead. My wife and three-year old daughter were killed in an air raid. It happened in 1940, at the height of the blitz.'

A single chime broke the short silence. It was four-thirty in the afternoon. An early evening February gloom had formed unnoticed. The glow from the fire tinged the sitting room with the colours of tranquillity. It enclosed them in a cocoon of intimacy. After a respectful period Jane said, 'How's your Italian?'

'Pretty good,' he said. 'I lived in Milan for a while.'

'And Anna? When do you propose to tell her?'

'She already knows. She has confirmed should you volunteer she will be willing to join the party.'

'You have spoken to her?'

'Yes.'

'She knows Lance is missing?'

'Yes.'

'And if Lance should reappear?'

'Then our little adventure would be cancelled and he and his squad would continue as originally planned. In the meantime we must prepare in the belief that their reappearance is unlikely.'

Jane rose from her chair and stretched out her arm. 'Have another glass of whisky,' she said. David smiled and placed the empty glass into her waiting hand. 'You take it neat, I suppose?'

'Is there any other way?'

'Some youngsters prefer it with ginger ale.'

'Sacrilegious ingrates. Will you join me this time?'

'No. I drink alcohol less and less these days. I'm an Aldous Huxley devotee. He predicts alcohol will have fallen from fashion by the year 2000 and by that time will have become the drug of the uneducated, unsophisticated underclass. I'm ahead of my time. I prefer to smoke cannabis to unwind.'

'I must try it sometime.'

'Good,' was all she said and walked to the table. She returned with the replenished glass, together with the bottle and placed them by his side. 'Help yourself,' she said and sat. She reached for her handbag, opened it and searched for her cigarette case. It was her favourite possession. Carlo had given it to her the week before he was murdered. She sprung it open and selected one of her special smokes from a pre-made layer.

'I take it you've never smoked cannabis, Colonel Hardie?'

'No, never, and please call me David.'

'You should, David. No side affects, no hangovers, no queasy stomachs and a much nicer high than alcohol.' She leaned back, tucked her legs beneath her and lit her joint. She was aware of his attention. 'If for some reason we're betrayed and end up in German hands, will we be shot as spies?'

Her question took him by surprise. 'We must see to it that it never happens,' he replied, before quickly adding 'It's such a remote possibility it's hardly worth considering. It's an aspect of the mission that's best not contemplated. After all, it wouldn't do to have a heroine of the Mafia, in Sicily of all places, betrayed and shot in cold blood by Germans. It would be dynamite. The Sicilians would never allow it to happen. The families would never live it down. The loss of face would destroy them.'

'Yes,' she agreed and then asked, 'when did you last have a meal, Colonel? Would you like a little something to eat?'

'David, please. I had toast and tea at six this morning.'

'You must be hungry?'

'A little something to eat would be most welcome.'

She rose, placed her joint in the ashtray knowing it would extinguish itself and moved towards the door.

Instead of going to the kitchen to make her guest some food, she entered her bedroom, moved to her dressing table and sat. She gazed at her reflection in the mirror. The high cheekbones, the strawberry-blonde hair, the light green eyes, were all familiar. The mirror, however, reflected nothing of her internal turmoil, the confused mix of emotions that assailed her. The recounting of past events had reintroduced feelings of long forgotten trauma. Emotions that had been suppressed for years had been disturbed and given new life. She had promised never to have any further association with the Cosa Nostra. Not that she had disliked Carlo's friends. They had been kind, generous and loyal. The Colonel's assessment had been accurate. They would never see her harmed. But, successful contact might be difficult to establish. Sicily swarmed with Germans. Undeniably, she was the ideal replacement. She liked David. She had been unsure when he arrived, but his translucent integrity and the manner with which he bore his grief, had impressed her. His attention to detail, his modesty and non-judgmental disposition were traits in his character she admired. But, to become involved in espionage was not a decision to be decided by likes or dislikes, no matter how pressing, or convincing, the reason. The thought of violence re-entering her life was a terrifying prospect. Fear of its mindless force had already made her reclusive and cowardly. Out-of-the-blue, her sheltered, uneventful existence, the style of life she lived, had striven to establish, was under threat of being blown to smithereens by an urgent petition, that she agree to participate in an adventure that was, at best, outrageous in conception.

The entreaty, however, required a response. There was a decision to be made. Did she have a choice? Could she choose to say no? Could she refuse and continue to live an unaffected life with the memory of a refusal, when all around sacrifices were everywhere to be marvelled at? A refusal to participate would be regarded as unpatriotic. It would declare an unwillingness to assist the war effort at a time when the survival of the nation was being menaced by a barbaric, rapacious regime. To refuse would be a self-protecting, demeaning act. The poison of self-approach would despoil all possible future contentment. The knowledge of a refusal

Freewill is Forfeit

would remain embedded in her psyche and follow her to the grave. There was no choice. Freewill was forfeit in war.

She refocused her eyes and without awareness began to brush her hair. She sighed and selected a lipstick. She applied it without usual care. She placed two hands on the dressing table and pressed down to rise. Standing, she again examined the solemn reflection staring back at her. It was not fear she saw but weary resignation.

She left the bedroom and made her way to the kitchen. Somehow a meal had to be prepared from the scraps left over from her weekly ration.

* * *

Casablanca

Anna had become adept at distancing herself from the sexual demons that afflicted her pupils. Young men in uniform were far from home, lonely and condemned to an existence without the comfort of female companionship but it hardly excused the behaviour of those who grabbed at her and attempted to smother her in a frenzy of groping. Not all of them resorted to this type of imbroglio but when it happened, and in truth it was happening too often, it forced protest.

Subsequent embarrassment then had to be endured and thereafter, often it was impossible to re-establish a proper pupil/ teacher relationship. Other pupils, less bold in their approaches, but equally determined to manipulate intimacy, would manufacture a pantomime of manoeuvres to adopt positions that made it impossible to avoid physical contact. These were the sneaky ones. Their underhand methods to gain intimacy were more reprehensible than their octopus-like comrades. Open protest was avoided but distaste lingered.

Her American lieutenant had fallen into neither of these categories. During the month she had known him his conduct had been exemplary. So polite had he been, it had almost been too good to be true. He was intelligent, dedicated to study and blessed with a fabulous memory. He had been, by far, the best pupil she had been assigned. Handsome, too, but then most Americans were. They were a good-looking race. It was odd that never once had he mentioned his family during their many tea breaks. Often he had spoken of his job at a bank and of his dislike of some of the people who worked there, but never about anything more personal. He had been cheerful and witty, but, best of all, whilst in his company she had felt free from the threat that he might make unwelcome advances. He had been attracted to her and she to him, but his restraint had been admirable. His expressive hands had fascinated her. She had found herself studying them from time to time when she knew he was unaware of being scrutinised. During class exercises, while practising the sounds and rhythms of language, he had behaved without inhibition. His pronunciation of the vowel-saturated sounds of the Italian language, for a beginner, had been excellent, for an American, miraculous. Yet another oddity was the painstaking care he had taken when compiling study notes. Every detail of his work material was indexed and the memory aids he had concocted had been works of art.

In the third week of the course, when he suggested they dine together at its completion, she had been correct to break her promise never to date a pupil. Despite it being his final night his ingrained self-control had triumphed over his amatory inclinations. So impressed had she been with his behaviour, in the end, it had been she, rather than he, who had taken the initiative. Her goodnight kiss had stunned him.

She had not seen him since. Conrad had mentioned him in his letters and she had been delighted fate had conspired they were to serve together. Now he, Conrad and two others, had disappeared. Nothing was known of their whereabouts. They had vanished. Since being told her feelings had been confused and somewhat puzzling. It was strange that her thoughts had dwelt more on Hank than on Conrad. She was apprehensive for both, of course, but uppermost in her mind was her almost singular concern for Hank. She could not remove the thought of him from her head. It was weird. She constantly could hear his voice in her ear. 'Sergeant McKay', it repeated, time and time again. He had never called her by any other name. Never once had he called her by her Christian name. It had been one of his quaint idiosyncrasies, another of his distinctive touches of gallantry. What a lovely man he had been.

Why had she not realised this glaring truth when he had been with her every day for a whole month? Why had she not cut free from the Presbyterian restraints of a Scottish upbringing and allowed herself, just once, to loosen up and act like an ordinary young woman with normal desires? The anxieties that had afflicted her youth had long since evaporated. It seemed her past fear of men had been replaced by something worse. She had become an ice-maiden, a cold, unresponsive, insouciant, controller of male behaviour.

Hank had been different. He had caught her eye and she had suppressed the truth of this miracle. He had displayed gallantry, intelligence, consideration, wit and she, in turn, had responded as if he were just another run-of-the-mill student. Her reserve had ruined an opportunity to share a relationship of greater depth. On the present behavioural curve by the age of twenty-five she would be, at best, a spinsterish freak, or worse, be thought of as a lesbian icon. Jane, at her age, had kissed goodbye to her hymen by several years. Jane, of course, revelled in male company. She was unafraid of her sexuality and indulged freely in affairs. She had taken and given pleasure in equal measure and, in consequence, was a person of unjudgmental and happy disposition and not a shrivelled, suspicious, emotional cripple like herself.

War had changed everything. Nothing would ever be the same. It was ironic that the first visit to her mother's homeland was to be made in circumstances so far removed from what she had once imagined. It would be by parachute, as an enemy agent and not as a spurious debutante bent on pleasuring the senses.

It was strange that coincidence had decreed she and Jane should be selected to replace the missing men. The operation was to be led by Colonel Hardie, the same officer who, at the beginning of the war, had recruited them for military service. So, it was goodbye Casablanca, hello London, then off to Sicily.

The daily drudgery of having to cope with desert life, of having to eat food infinitely less appealing than the worst of the school dinners and forced to teach disinterested soldiers the principles of basic grammar, was finally over. She was tired of attending Mess functions only to be exposed to the depressing sight of men drinking with mirthless abandon. The flies, the heat and the lack of jollity had become mind-numbing encumbrances. The entire environment was boring beyond belief. But, life was about to change. Tomorrow she was flying home. She and Jane were to embark on an adventure of risk and danger. It was inexplicable, but instead of feeling apprehensive she felt invigorated. She would meet her grandfather. Speak to him in his own language. She would meet many of Jane's old friends, acquaintances from her colourful past, but most important of all, be involved in a war mission of danger, daring and risk. She couldn't wait. It was exactly what she needed, life-enhancing adventure to shatter the self-protective shields that had inhibited her life.

When at home she would make an effort to repair the broken relationship with her father. Time and absence had made her realise how thoughtless and cruel she had been, they both had been, during their final, terrible confrontation. He had implored her always to remember her working class beginnings and never allow herself in her struggle for betterment to abandon the solid ethics of her upbringing. In his broken condition he had sensed her impatience to escape into a world where he feared the egalitarian philosophies, those by which he had lived his life, would be forgotten and mocked. His daughter, his little girl, the perfect creature he had adored as a child, was abandoning him, his home and his life. Not only had she spurned him for his persistent drinking but, as a final act of cruelty, had accused him of the uselessness of his ideals, of his failure as a man, as a father and decent human being. She had lashed out at a damaged loved one at a time when he had been most in need of sympathy. She had failed to understand his fury.

Emotional illiteracy had scrambled understanding. But, his perverse fit of temper had sprung only from fatherly apprehension. She had not understood this at the time. His acrimony had been motivated by concern for her and her alone. It had been an

Freewill is Forfeit

inarticulate plea, an incoherent outburst of anxiety for her future and how she should strive to live it. In turn she had made him feel worthless. Little wonder that he had fallen into despair and been forced to submit to treatments of electro-convulsive-therapy. Her poor daddy, so unhappy he no longer wished to live and she had contributed mightily to his misery through her own thoughtlessness and self-concern.

9

As the sun rose to herald the dawn on 25th February, 1943, it illuminated a world engulfed in internecine slaughter. As millions roused themselves they could only guess if this would be the day their lives would swell the toll of the already countless dead.

In the Far East, naval and land battles raged between American and Japanese forces with hitherto unimagined ferocity. In Russia, the Red Army had reached the outskirts of Kharkov in their quickening purpose to evict the German invader from their soil. In New Guinea, defeated Japanese forces chose to commit mass suicide rather than surrender to the victorious Australians. In India, Wingate, in valorous mood, prepared an elite band of marauders to penetrate Burma. In Europe, major cities were being reduced to rubble by opposing air forces, each determined to break the will of the civilian inhabitants. In Africa, Montgomery stood ready to penetrate the Mareth Line in his determination to remove the German and Italian Armies from Tunisia. On the oceans and seas battleships vied for strategic advantage. Aircraft carriers and cruisers hunted prey with murderous intent. Destroyers, frigates and torpedo boats, manoeuvred with piratical purpose. Submarines skulked for victims. Kamikaze pilots hunted their targets. War was global and total. Godlessness could no longer be denied.

On this morning Gustav's concern was how best to move a bucket. Should he haul it, push it, or attempt to carry it? He was involved in his daily chore of carrying water from the wells to replenish the tubs scattered around the public areas of the caves and to refill the vessels placed at points within the sleeping areas of the redoubt. It was a task made difficult only by the shape and size of the half-barrel given him to accomplish the task. It was too broad. When full of water its weight made forward movement

Freewill is Forfeit

difficult. His lower legs were bruised and cut with attempts to carry the tub in conventional bucket-carrying fashion. When it was held at arm's length progress could be made only a few steps at a time, but at the risk of muscle strain. There was also the indignity of resembling an uncoordinated cretin as the lift, stagger and lay procedure constantly had to be repeated. Soft sand did not help matters.

He was comforted with the thought that these hardships were nothing compared with those he had had to endure in Russia. He was reminded he must pray with more urgency to be relieved of the memory of his recent past. Nothing could change what had been done, but some soothing balm was required to quieten the torture of recall. He knew if anger was not controlled it would sap him of sensible balance, divorce him from dignity and eventually separate him from self-esteem. Like the water-bucket, negative emotions were too corrosive to carry without inflicting some eventual personal damage.

Two more lifts and he would rest. He would ignore the derision he would attract. Insults would be loudly voiced. The Arabs enjoyed displaying their disrespect of him in the public arena. Curses had an approving audience when expressed in the precincts of the main cavern.

It was a misnomer to call it a cavern. It was a cathedral of rock, a geological phenomenon. When his blindfold had been removed and he had been given his first sight of the natural wonder, he had gazed at its splendour with his architect's eye. He had thought at the time human hand had assisted nature in creating the vaulted design. After further inspection, however, he became convinced that volcanic forces alone had designed the architectural masterpiece. He reasoned that the rock canopy, the pyroclastic layer, must have been supported by a gaseous pressure which had dissipated, or explosively erupted, from the shell of the cooling magma when it had firmed enough to be a self-supporting structure. What would have taken man hundreds of years to construct had been accomplished by one simple expulsion of God's ferocious breath. It was an awesome edifice.

Within the interior the air was sweet and the temperature was a pleasant constant both day and night. Jagged cracks in the rock canopy allowed sufficient sunlight to enter and filter a mystical visibility throughout. The solfatura, the vents that once had emitted the sulphurous gases during the primordial conflagration, now served as natural chimneys to dispel the smoke of the campfires at night. From two wells within the precinct water was in plentiful supply. The latrines were situated in an interior alcove, a split of rock, which allowed privacy, a throughput of fresh air and the efficient disposal of waste material into the subterranean bowels of the desert. The largest of the interior rock indentations was used as a stable area for the animals.

At the dark far end of the main cavern there was a zone given over to what looked like a small cemetery. To the left of this corral could be discerned the shapes of the captured Italian transport and the wreckage of the American jeep, parked side by side. This area was forbidden to him. Contact with Hans was also forbidden. They saw each other daily across the expanse of the interior, but neither, as yet, had waved in acknowledgement of the other.

Hans had been put to work in the stables. He appeared to be in good health, if one could make such a judgement by observing him as he groomed and fed the animals. Hans, he knew, would enjoy labouring amongst the horses and tending the few goats that were tethered, but the camels would give him pause for thought, spitting, horrible beasts that they could be when in recalcitrant mood. Gustav wondered if he should risk waving his hand to greet his old corporal. It would be a small gesture, a silent hello, nothing more. He decided against the inclination. It would be making a contact, breaking the spirit of the order they had been given. It was better not to assume too much. Why risk causing unnecessary annoyance to captors who had proved to be humane?

The Arabs had shown no kindness, but they had not been cruel. What had most impressed Gustav was the observation that within the confines of the caves all men appeared to be of equal rank, money had no relevance and food was shared from a common pot. The sick and wounded were tended with consideration and each man was free to express opinion without fear or favour. It was as if the Arabs, without the benefit of education and ignorant of Christian admonition, had structured a Utopian template for future societies.

The American Captain's survival was now assured. It had been feared for a time dehydration and extensive bruising would have proved fatal. The first few days had been concerning. Dehydration and prodigious bruising were dangerous afflictions to be twinned. During the healing process deep bruising requires to draw liquid from the body. A dehydrated body requires that same reservoir of fluid to sustain life. Re-hydration solves both problems, but this simple course of action had been impeded by the condition of the tongue. An inability to swallow had made the contest for his life a close run thing. In the end, attention and patience had prevailed, although it was not until the third day of careful nursing that survival could be taken for granted. A bowel movement had indicated he would live. Had he still been suffering from life-threatening dehydration he would have been unable to defecate. The fouling had announced the crisis was over.

Being a prisoner had given Gustav time to think. Several confusions remained unresolved. He knew now that von Stauffenberg had deliberately sent him on a wild goose chase with an elderly corporal and a schoolboy lieutenant. The assigned reconnaissance had had a purpose other than the reason given. During the mock briefing Stauffenberg was aware that any military action initiated from the south would have entailed unacceptable risk. The hastily conducted briefing had been nothing more than theatrical farce. Stauffenberg, knowingly, had sent him on a fool's errand. Why? Was it to protect those he wished to save from the trauma and danger of the coming battle? Were the rumours true? Had his purpose been to withdraw *Wehrmacht* officers from battle duty and have them replaced with officers from the Waffen SS and other convinced acolytes of the Gestapo philosophy? Had he launched a personal crusade to protect the remnants of the *Wehrmacht's* Officer Corps? It seemed likely. If so, his manoeuvrings were misguided. There was now nowhere free from danger. Lives no longer could be protected. Death lurked everywhere. It came out of a clear blue sky. Young Lieutenant Kurt became aware of this truth in the last second of his otherwise safe and protected life.

A letter would have to be written to the young man's mother. It was a perplexing task of rank, but until writing material was made available there was nothing he could do to fulfil this dismal and hated responsibility. It was unlikely the Arabs would allow such a communication to be sent. Perhaps, for the moment, it was merciful those at home be left in ignorance of what had befallen. Denied communication concealed a grievous reality.

* * *

Wrapped in robes against the chill of the night two Arabs sat by one of the many fires giving light and warmth to the men gathered within the confines of their secret stockade. They spoke in the guttural tones of the Arabic language; a language designed by poets and utilised by scholars; the linguistic tool employed to lead mankind out of the darkness of ignorance to the enlightenments of the Middle Ages. These men spoke of mutual concerns and of riddles that afflict the wise.

'Has it come to this that now we are involved in cowardly acts of murder and hostage taking?' the Hadji questioned.

'Quieten your spirit, Hadji, too long have we laboured in the vineyards of the oppressed. The moderation you advise no longer can prevail. Our young men grow impatient. They become convinced cunning and cruelty are the instruments to unfetter our lands of the Christian invader.'

'To be cunning and cruel are the ways of the Infidel. Beware the genius they have for convenient interpretation of Scripture, ben Youseff. It benefits few and delivers many to misery.'

'Your words are wise.'

'When the ancient wisdoms are ignored the evils of men multiply.'

'True, but to sustain righteousness while tyranny reigns is a tribulation beyond sufferance. Violence begets violence. It is the way of nature.'

'As I grow older weariness begins to afflict me. Middle-age brings bitter thoughts to burden my days.'

'Tell me, Hadji, what news do you bring from Tunis?'

Freewill is Forfeit

'Little of good. Our coffers are empty, our demands ignored and our influence has atrophied to the level of insult.'

'We exist in unfortunate days, but let us bear our afflictions with courage.'

'I come amongst you as a harbinger of doom. My cynicism would indicate I am now a man weakened by the weight of his heart.'

'Be comforted, Hadji, the strong are as many as seeds at harvest, but men of wisdom scarce as salt.'

'You attempt to ease my woe with words of flattery. Wisdom is bequeathed to all of contrite heart. The texts of our forefathers proclaim this truth. Their knowledge is written on tablets of stone. The Koran, the beatitudes of Jesus, the holy books of the Hindu, all instruct men on the pathways to probity. Ambitious men close their eyes to wise discernment. They choose instead to follow dogmas of dissension.'

'The wickedness of men always will be a tragic concern. Tell me, wise one, how fares the struggle between our foes?'

'Axis power has the grip of a hunting dog. From Faid to Gasfa the Teutons move westward with wagons of iron. Sheitla, Kasserine and Fariana are all within their unholy sway.'

'And what news of Bourguiba?'

'Our leader now lays his head on the wooden pillows of a foreign prison.'

'It is said he languishes at the French Fortress?'

'No longer. Now the Swastika flaps in triumph atop the Eiffel Tower the new masters of France have transported him to Rome.'

'Our French oppressors, in turn, now are oppressed by the Hun?'

'It is so. Strange are the ways of Allah. The Germans hold our leader in the Vatican dungeons under the feet of their Pope. Bourguiba suppurates in Rome a forgotten man.'

'But, he remains defiant?'

'His defiance is the inspiration that saves us from despair.'

'Be at peace, his suffering is soon to end. The instrument of his release is bequeathed to us by fate.'

'You speak of the hostage? The German Colonel?'

'I do. He is to be bartered. His freedom, for the release of our leader.'

'You risk much when you attempt to bargain with a tyrant power.'

'We would have you employ your skills in this matter.'

'You wish me to act as a go-between, pretend to be a man of authority, while in truth I am a representative of a scorned race stripped of all diplomatic relevance?'

'But, you are wise in the understanding of men's motivations. Your comprehension of the human heart knows no equal.'

'What of the American?'

'He is a catch of unknown value. His worth will be discovered only when his capture is reported to the American army authorities.'

'This also is a duty you wish me to accept?'

'Our respect for you is boundless.'

'To condone kidnap grieves me, but on this occasion I will compromise my ideals for the greater good, but let it be known that these favours will be at the cost of my self-respect.'

* * *

It was still and silent. Hank lay examining the rock canopy above his head. His physical discomfort was bearable and his tongue had reduced in size to allow him to wiggle it in his mouth without pain. Memory, however, remained defective. Recall was vague and uncertain; a jigsaw of disconnected happenings. A swirl of haphazard images made it difficult to discern what was dream and what was real. It was strange, but memory of life in New York was remembered with clarity. During the lonely, silent period of recovery some trick of mind had granted vivid recall of young adult years. Past friends had reinvaded his mind. He remembered them all with fresh and sentimental relish.

Hank became aware of an ache in his right leg. Unreality unravelled in a rush. He emerged from daydream to discover Nightingale was tending his wounds. When the therapeutic activities ceased, Nightingale removed the soiled linen from the cave. He reappeared in the company of two Arabs. One was in his late twenties, the other middle-aged. The Arabs approached and looked down. They conversed in French. Hank felt no alarm. He watched the younger Arab kneel and bend forward. While his body was being examined Hank could smell his captor's breath. It was not unpleasant. The Arab straightened and produced a knife to cut the leather thong encircling his neck. The removed identification discs were handed to the older man. The Arab remained on his knees to make further examination of his body. When the inspection was complete, the Arab rose and spoke to his companion in an unrecognised tongue. They both nodded and left the chamber.

When sure the Arabs were out of earshot, Nightingale spoke. 'Nod your head if you can hear me?'

Hank thought the request stupid, until he realised Nightingale had little idea how impeding his injuries might be. Dutifully, he nodded his head.

'Good. Are you hungry?' This time Hank shook his head.

'Fine. Do you know who you are?'

Hank thought quickly. It hadn't occurred to him advantage might be gained by pretending to have lost his memory. A deceitful bout of post-traumatic amnesia might be a self-protective expedient? He rejected the idea. Nightingale didn't deserve to be lied to. For the first time in a week, Hank spoke.

'Yeah, a fucked-up, confused, American soldier.' His voice had a husk, but his tongue, while still awkward in his mouth, had regained sufficient flexibility to enunciate words.

Gustav allowed a brief smile to flicker on his face. It was the type of initial remark he should have known to expect from his fellow prisoner. 'In that case we are much alike,' he said. 'The only difference separating us is one of nationality.'

'You were in the armed land-wagon? Hank asked to fix Nightingale's identity.

'Correct, and you were on jeep patrol. While watching each other we both fell victim to a third force, a force that neither of us knew existed.'

'We are prisoners?' Hank enquired.

'Yes. There are three of us. My Corporal, myself and you.'

'And the rest of my squad?'

'Nothing is known of them. It must be presumed that somehow they avoided capture.' Gustav watched his patient frown and decided to change the subject. 'Are you still suffering pain?'

'No, the pain is over. I feel weak, very weak and vulnerable.'

'Perhaps this would be a good time to introduce ourselves?'

'No need,' said Hank, to Gustav's surprise. 'We both know each other. Uniforms no longer matter. To me you're Nightingale. That's the name I've given you.'

'It doesn't trouble you that we are enemies?'

'Don't let's get into that. It's too complicated.'

'That's fine by me. Why Nightingale?' Gustav asked.

'You nursed me back to health, thus, Nightingale. Get it?'

'Gustav looked confused. 'No, I'm afraid not.'

Hank didn't explain, instead, he said, 'I joined the Army to fight the Japanese. It's very confusing I find myself here. The war has become unreal to me. I've lost all sense of reality.' He stopped and, after a silence, asked, 'What are we doing here?' His mood was almost childlike.

'Thousands of soldiers daily ask that same question.'

'Do you think so?'

'I know I do.'

'Yes, me too, now.' They were quiet for a moment. 'You seem to pray regularly. I've watched you. Were you praying for me?'

'Your recovery was given a mention. I pray for people in distress. I must confess lately I've allowed myself to become a little too self-absorbed. I'm not a very good Christian, I'm afraid.'

'Where are we, Nightingale and who are these Arabs?'

'I'm not sure, but I can make an educated guess.'

'Frighten me with it.'

'We're being held in caves not far from where we were attacked. I think we're prisoners of a gang of Tuareg who have seized us for ransom.'

'You're kidding. You think we've been kidnapped? Is this what all this nonsense is about, a few lousy dollars?'

'The frightening proposition is they don't yet realise there's no one prepared to pay for our release.'

'I will.'

'I don't understand?'

'I'll give them the dough to get us out of here, if that's what they want.'

'Are you rich?'

'Rich enough to pay a ransom.'

'I don't think the process works like that.'

'I don't see why not. Surely, we're allowed to negotiate for our own lives.'

'Our capture may have some political motive.'

'Politics is about power and power is about wealth. QED.'

'True, but hostage-taking is not always a straightforward matter of a ransom being paid. Usually some issue other than money is involved.'

'And, as yet, we don't know?'

'Correct.'

'Don't worry, Nightingale, I'll get us out of this mess just as soon as we're allowed to know what demands they're making for our release.'

'We?'

'I'm not leaving without you. I owe you that small debt of gratitude.'

'That's reassuring, but impractical. We're wearing different uniforms. A war continues outside these caves and we are on opposing sides. We're seen to be enemies. Your fanciful prediction of being able to negotiate our release, if successful, would return us to our separate fighting units.'

'One step at a time, Nightingale. Fursht, let's get ourselves out of where-ever-the-hell we are, then we can deshide.'

'Your tongue is not quite back to normal.'

'Jush about.'

'You're beginning to slur your words.'

'Don't change the shubject. What da ya say?'

'What I'm moved to say might surprise you.'

'Sho, shurprise me.'

'To my eternal discredit I'd rather die here than be returned to a fighting unit. I'm finished with killing. I can do no more of it.'

Hank looked up at his nurse and fixed him in the eye. In some pain he struggled on to his elbows. When settled, he said, 'Tell me, Nightingale, who is Lisa?'

Gustav smiled. He let his head slump to his chest. A period of silence followed while an attempt was made to choke back waves of sudden emotion. He failed. Tears began to stream from his eyes. Out of nowhere her spoken name had wounded his heart. He wept. When recovered he shook his head from side to side in a brain-clearing motion and looked at Hank. Still glistening with grief, he smiled and with genuine curiosity, said, 'More to the point, who is Sergeant McKay? Last night you kept me awake with your first coherent utterances. Her name was repeated *ad nauseum*. Who is this Sergeant McKay person who denied me a restful night?

10

A duty clerk knocked and entered the office. Brigadier General Thomson didn't look up. He seldom did. 'Well, what do ya want?' he enquired.

'These are the casualty lists you asked for, sir.'

'Put them down.'

The clerk hesitated, 'I'm sorry, sir. Where, sir?'

'Here, man,' Cowboy said, directing him with a nod to the one clear space on the desk. When the clerk failed to move the Brigadier General finally looked up. 'Well, what now?' The clerk seemed transfixed. 'What's the matter, man?'

'Look, sir,' the clerk said and pointed.

Cowboy rose and turned to look out of the window. What he saw was a strange sight. An Arab robed in colourful ceremonial was undulating his way through Headquarters lines mounted on a camel. The animal was draped in a cloth of gold. It was an eye-catching sight.

'Go and find out who this guy is and come back and tell me.' Cowboy addressed this to the window.

'Yes, sir,' said the clerk and left the room.

Cowboy continued to watch the Arab's progress. The vivid colours were mesmeric against the drab tints of the military enclosure. He watched as the Arab went through the dismount procedure and walk forward to meet a waiting orderly. They spoke. The orderly shrugged and made a gesture he should be followed. In a bout of mixed impatience and curiosity Cowboy left his office and took up a position in the corridor where he knew he would be able to overhear anything said. What he heard was spoken in French. *'Je suis un envoye diplomatique representant les interets de l'armee Nationaliste des Neo Destour.'*

The man was a diplomatic envoy of sorts, but whom he represented remained unclear. The final part of the introduction had been lost in a jumble of vowels and echo. No doubt, he was some local dignitary come to gripe about grazing restrictions. Bloody wogs! This posting was turning out to be a real bitch. Tunisia? No, thank you!

Disappointed, Cowboy re-entered his office and returned to his desk. As he sat he felt his uniform tighten around his waist. Having to eat lousy foreign food was playing havoc with his weight. He had been to the tailor twice in the past month for adjustments to be made. So what! Weight gain was common in his age group. Corpulence and middle age went together. Nevertheless, he would have to take better care of himself. If he allowed his weight to get out of hand polo might have to be scratched from the social agenda. Without the input of information from the guys at the Chukka Club he'd be finished. To be denied their valuable inside revelations would be a disaster, might as well retire.

He once had presumed while in retirement he would cavort with the legion of bored wives at the Golf Club. Now, there would be no point. Women no longer were of interest to him. The doctor told him this recent disinclination was due to an over-indulgent lifestyle. Tough titty! A well-rolled cigar always had been preferred to a well-rolled woman as far as he was concerned. No, it had to be polo. Polo was the essential requirement in his life. Polo was the open sesame, the magic carpet to Eldorado. The international money markets were manipulated by these guys; they who wielded the mallets, wielded the power.

Taking exercise was a bind, another of his disinclinations, but it was essential, soon, that he buckle down to fight the gathering flab. He would start riding again. He would start immediately. Tomorrow. He stretched for the telephone. 'Tell Sergeant Worthington to have Tabbie ready for mounting at 0730 hours tomorrow. Tell him to bring the horse to the Mess. What? Yes, I'll have breakfast when I return. What? No, I've no idea. Say nine o'clock.' He replaced the receiver. Immediately it rang again. He grabbed at the receiver and yelled 'Yes'. He stiffened when he heard the voice. It was the Divisional Commander.

'I have an Envoy here I think you should see. How's your French?'

'Somewhere between crap and terrible.'

'I'll send an interpreter along. I think this one will interest you. Good luck.'

Odd, thought Cowboy, he could have sworn there had been a hint of a chuckle in the voice. There was a knock on the door and the orderly strode into the room. 'Sir, the Arab is a Diplomat and has been taken to the OC.'

'Dismiss,' Cowboy said, making no effort to keep weariness from his voice.

The orderly left the room, only to knock again and re-enter. 'Sir, there's a delegation here to see you.' He stood aside. Cowboy rose. The camel-riding Arab entered with the sergeant interpreter. Cowboy circled his desk and stood in the centre of the room to greet his guest. The sergeant stepped forward. 'Sir, this is the Hadji Tahar ben Ammar, Noble Member of the Tunisian Grand Conceil. His credentials have been verified. He has come on a mission of mercy representing the interests of the Neo Destour.'

'And who the hell might they be?'

'Sir, the Neo Destour is the Tunisian Army of Liberation.'

'Terrorists?'

'Freedom fighters, sir.'

'That's what I said, terrorists.'

The sergeant turned to face the Hadji and said, 'This is Brigadier General Thomson,' and stepped back.

Cowboy gestured to his guest to sit and returned to his chair. 'Okay, sergeant, let's hear what he has to say.'

The Arab shifted his position and fumbled among the folds of his jellaba. He withdrew a leather thong. Hank's identification discs glinted in the sunlight as they were handed over to the sergeant, who in turn placed them into the outstretched, waiting hand of his superior. Cowboy looked at them long and hard. He could hardly believe his eyes. Straining to control his excitement he looked at the sergeant and said, 'How did these dog-tags come into his possession? No, ask him first if this soldier is still alive?'

While the two men spoke Cowboy attempted to follow the

conversation, but failed. If young Remington had been killed the information would be dynamite. The news of his demise would rock the balance of the Board at the Remington Bartholomew Bank. That this information should have landed on his desk was nothing short of a miracle. He would contact Bobby Braithwaite immediately. With Hancock Remington out of the way it would clear Bobby's path and give impetus to his claim for the still disputed Chairmanship of the Bank. Bobby's gratitude would assure future, limitless reward.

'Sir?'

Cowboy struggled to refocus his thoughts. 'Yes, get on with it, man.'

'It transpires that Captain Remington has been apprehended by the forces of the Neo Destour. During his arrest he suffered injury. At present he is recuperating and should be fully recovered within half a mo. . ., sorry, two weeks. The Neo Destour is prepared to release their prisoner on condition compensation for his life be paid into the funds of their movement.'

Cowboy concealed his disappointment. Remington was alive, but there was the comfort he was being held by a bunch of cut-throats. The Army would never agree to pay a penny to a rabble of bandits for the release of a prisoner. The official policy was to allow hostages to rot rather than be blackmailed into paying ransom. In effect, Remington was as good as dead. 'They're holdin' him hostage. Is that the message?'

'No, sir. The Ambassador is quite adamant on this point. Germans are being held hostage, but not so Captain Remington.'

But not so? Why not, but not Captain Remington? What kind of Army did America have these days? 'Ask him, how much.'

'Pardon, sir?'

'Ask him how much for Remington's release.'

'With respect, sir, perhaps a diplomat would find. . .'

'Ask him,' Cowboy demanded. 'How much do they want?' When did sergeants start giving Generals advice? Christ-all-bloody-mighty! What type of initial training were recruits given these days? Cowboy leaned forward and scribbled a memo. It stated 'Review Training Manuals'. When he looked up the men were still conversing. 'Well,' he said with open impatience, 'what does he say?'

The Arab stopped talking and the sergeant straightened from his slouched position. 'I'm having a little difficulty with this passage of conversation, sir. I fear the philosophical force of his reply will be reduced and, perhaps, lost in translation.'

'Passage of conversation', 'philosophical force', 'lost in translation', where in the name of God did they find these specimens? Was this Sergeant taking the piss? 'Just give me a precis. A rough outline will do.'

'It comes down to what is the life of a man worth? Some cultures, mainly in the Northern Hemisphere, argue that life is beyond price. It is also posited. . .'

'Stop,' yelled Cowboy. 'Ask him the simple question how much money do they expect to receive from us for the release of our soldier. Ask him in those words, those exact words.'

'Permission to speak, sir?' Cowboy nodded consent. 'I was about to say, sir, the Envoy mistrusts haste in these matters and advises against making an impulsive agreement. He humbly submits that a measured consideration of the matter would reap mutual benefit. He suggests, with your consent, that he return in a week. In the meantime he pledges the American officer will continue to receive medical care and suffer no further harm.'

Events were improving at every turn. Should it become judicious Hancock Remington's incarceration could be engineered to last a decade.

* * *

Lance stood at the side of his allocated tent and looked out on a scene of military preparedness. Neat lines of M3 Grant tanks stretched out before him. The American disarray had been transformed. By the alchemy of determination and hard work the scrap yard shambles of the previous week had converted chaos into visible evidence of battle-readiness, a feat of industry Lance would have found difficult to believe had he not witnessed the transition with his own eyes. The endeavour had reassured him Britain had an ally of energetic resolve. American battle know-how might be undeveloped, but given time their fighting techniques would mature to shape a formidable fighting force. The Yanks had a good tank in the M3. Not as impressive as the recently designed M4 – the Sherman – at present rolling off the assembly lines, but nevertheless, a sturdy, well-prepared design for tank warfare. It possessed some unusual features. The 37mm gun in the turret supported by the larger 75mm gun in the hull was an odd innovation. It gave the tank a distinctive identity, an unmistakable silhouette, but its real worth would only be revealed by its battlefield performance. Would the M3's speed and firepower be sufficient to engage successfully with the German *Panzerkampf-wagen* 111? Lance struggled to suppress doubt.

It had to be confessed, from a British point of view, American military methods, in many respects, were distinctly unorthodox. They lacked the British Army's strict disciplines. Colonel Flynn's inappropriate intransigence indicated trust between the Allies had not yet been fully established. The Colonel's refusal to inform British Army Command of the circumstances of their disappearance amounted to a breach of military protocol. On three occasions he had pleaded with Colonel Flynn to comply with the reasonable request that their fate be made known at Allied Headquarters, only to be rebuffed with refusal and reminded no procedure would be initiated until the fate of their American Captain was known. It seemed the Yanks were prepared to remain inflexible while the destiny of one of their soldiers was in question.

If Col Flynn was stubborn and found wanting on the one hand, his industry could not be faulted on the other. His dedication to the task of repairing, rearming and reforming his Battalion had been an impressive feat of energy. Perhaps the ignominy of defeat and his single-minded preoccupation to quickly make amends, had reduced every other consideration of his command responsibility to a level of niggling unimportance. That, at least, would give some credence to the obstinacy he had shown. Their non-arrival at Kasserine would, of course, have been noted at British Headquarters, but having received no further news they would know only that, unaccountably, the entire squad had vanished without trace.

Freewill is Forfeit

After release it would take more than a week to remount the Operation. Doubts were beginning to sprout whether the enforced delay was an ominous precursor to failure. Robert had been in a strange mood throughout the enforced detention. Was it his concern for the mission, or was it the loss of Hank that still troubled him? He would talk with Robert, attempt to break into his brooding silence; reassure him they were going to Sicily, come what may. A month's delay was not an insurmountable problem. In truth the hold-up may have intervened to their advantage. The Sicilians would be monitoring the battle for Tunisia with interest. They, more than most, knew the significance of the outcome.

Lance became aware of a young lieutenant approaching. The American officer came to a halt and executed a salute. With polite formality Lance was informed Col Flynn wished to see him and would be grateful if he would present himself at his earliest convenience. Having become familiar with little more than grunted and monosyllabic utterances the studied courtesy of the young officer seemed almost unreal. Lance dismissed the gracious messenger with a returned salute and a nod of approval. The man beamed with pleasure and left. Lance checked his uniform for irregularity, straightened his cap and commenced to walk the short distance to the Bn.HQ.

Without military palaver Lance was greeted with open camaraderie. 'Major Bennett, I have the sincere pleasure to inform you Captain Remington is alive and well. The information is he suffered injury during the process of his capture, but now is out of danger and well on his way to recovery. He is being held hostage by a dissident group of political agitators.'

Lance experienced a weakness at his knees. He removed his cap and rubbed each side of his head. The Colonel nodded his permission to sit. When settled Lance became aware Col Flynn had more to relate and strove to refocus his thoughts.

'I've been wrong about you, Major and wish to apologise for my mistrust.'

'You've had other more pressing preoccupations to deal with during the time we've been with you. Your mistrust has been frustrating, I admit, but under the circumstances, understandable.'

'I've had Divisional HQ deliver their disapproval in no uncertain fashion. They're jumpin' mad at neglect of correct Allied procedure. However, all that's behind us. Brigadier General Thomson gave me instructions to re-equip your depleted squad to assist your forward mission.' Col Flynn said this with a smile. He was a tough field officer who regarded desk-bound gold braid with healthy cynicism. 'So, there you are, Major. At least you have one high rankin' Yank prepared to acknowledge the celebrity of your military importance. It must be reassuring to have your worth appreciated by such an elevated authority.'

Lance refused to rise to the bait. Instead, he said, 'He's commonly referred to as Cowboy.'

'You know him?'

'He's a friend of Captain Remington's family.'

'Is he, indeed? You should have mentioned this.'

'Would it have made a difference?'

'No. None, at all.' Both men laughed. 'I've instructed Major Rogers to see to it you are given all the supplies and equipment you require. I would suggest you attend to this matter immediately. My battalion is ready to move east. We leave tomorrow to retake Kasserine.'

* * *

Lance entered the tent and stood. It was irrational, but he wanted Robert and Joe to be on their feet when they heard the news. He waited. To voice an order seemed inappropriate. Joe, quick to realise Lance's wish, rose from a slouched position on his bed. Robert, who was scribbling in a notebook, looked up, sensed something unusual in the air, sighed, threw down his pencil and lumbered to his feet. When Lance was assured he had their attention, he said, 'He's alive. Hank is alive.'

The reaction was soundless. Joe beamed and bowed his head as if in prayer. His relief was obvious. They heard him begin to sob and accepted this reaction as an expected response to the news. They had become used to his bouts of tearfulness. Robert's reaction was unexpected. He remained impassive, seemingly unmoved. He

Freewill is Forfeit

then strode forward and hugged Lance. Lance knew Robert had been affected by the uncertainty of Hank's fate, but to have him display his relief in such an unprecedented manner confirmed his apprehension that Robert's present emotional disposition had become unbalanced. Lance had seen him in all his moods and could predict his reaction to most events, but never had he seen Robert behave in such a peculiar manner. To prevent his rib cage from collapsing he managed to splutter 'If you could put me down I'll tell you the rest of the good news.'

Robert released his grip and stood back. He was smiling. His face shone with unselfconscious relief. He bent forward and dusted Lance's battledress with flicks of his hand. Lance remained stoical and ignored the odd reaction. It was too un-Robert-like to be recognisable.

'We've been given our freedom,' he heard himself say.

'Today we are to be supplied with everything we require for our departure.' Why, he wondered, was he talking like an officious schoolteacher? Why was everything so unreal?

'We're going back for Hank,' Robert declared. They stared at him as if unsure they had heard correctly. 'We're going back to reclaim Hank from these bastards holding him. That's the first thing we have to do. It must be done.' Robert's jaw was set, his eyes fixed. The atmosphere crackled with emotion. 'Can't you see?' It was Robert again. 'If we can't fight for friends, why fight for anything?'

'You're thinking with your heart not your head, Robert. Do you understand the predicaments we could trigger by interfering with political processes we know nothing about? Our interference could unbalance settlements that might already be in place.'

'I understand only one fact, Hank is being held to ransom by a bunch of murderous brigands.'

'By the Tunisian Army of Liberation. They call themselves the Neo-Destour.'

'Murdering bastards, all of them and we know where they are. They're to be found in the rocks and crannies of the pass. It's fantasy to believe Hank will be released by negotiation. The threat of having cold steel rammed up their jacksies is the only type of negotiation these sub-humans will understand. If they don't play ball we'll threaten to blow their happy little hunting ground to dust.'

'We can't just walk in to their territory and simply demand Hank's release by muttering a few threats. Be sensible, Robert.'

'That's exactly what we can do. The Americans have offered us what we need in the way of transport, explosives and weapons. Let's take everything we can carry and put these bastards to siege. We could show these Neanderthals some real fireworks if they're of a mind to be uncooperative.'

'You're talking like a crazy man, Robert. We would require a two-and-a half tonner stuffed with dynamite. . .'

'Yes,' Robert interrupted, 'and a few other fancy weapons that come easily to mind. We'll gear up with everything we can carry. Let them see we mean business. A show of strength will be persuasive should their simple minds develop a reluctance to agree with our uncomplicated request. If push should come to shove, the three of us, if properly equipped, could make their lives a misery.'

Lance felt his day becoming stranger by the minute. Was it only fifteen minutes ago he had stood mindlessly daydreaming? Now, he was faced with the problem of having to solve an immoveable obsession. Robert had become fixated; his dependable, steadfast sergeant had flipped. No longer was he a functioning individual whose behaviour could be predicted or recognised. But what Robert said was true. There was a danger Hank could be left to rot. Also, there was the possibility he could be shot. It was not uncommon following negotiation failure for hostages to be executed. Perhaps a deal could be negotiated? Perhaps Robert's desperate suggestion offered the only feasible solution? It would depend upon how generous the Americans were prepared to be. 'Major Rogers will never agree to release the amount of military equipment we would need to mount an effective threat.'

'Major Rogers?'

'Yes. He's been given instructions to supply us with our needs.'

'Major Rogers of 'C' Company?'

'Why? Do you know him?'

'I know him.' Robert turned to Joe and said, 'Well, Joe, what do you think? Should we go back for Hank or forget him?'

'We go back for Hank. Then we all go to Sicily together.'

'What do you say, Lance? You're the boss. If I can extract all we need from Major Rogers will you agree to sanction our extra curricular activity?'

'You haven't a hope in hell of extracting half of what we need.'

'But, if I can?'

'Then, I would agree. If we can secure the tools to do the job then, and only then, would your suggestion be marginally feasible.'

Robert smiled the smile of a happy man.

* * *

It was a strange sight to see Robert and Joe walk through Company lines. They made an odd couple. One was not half the size of the other.

'Hey, Sicilian! Come to inspect what we're gonna ram up the asses of yer Kraut pals next time we meet?' This was shouted from the turret of a passing tank. The tanks were being positioned for the following morning's departure. From another tank a voice yelled, 'Limey, yeah you, big boy! Where have ya bin hidin'? Big, bad Brutus bin bustin' his gut lookin' everywhere for ya.'

Robert looked down at Joe. Joe was oblivious to the shouted insults. He had difficulty understanding American drawl. Robert continued to examine Joe. He was healthier, cleaner and brighter-eyed than at any time Robert had known him. The man was a walking tribute to Lance's charity. The story of how they met often was recounted in idle conversation. It was a strange tale.

Lance had been on reconnaissance. It was a duty he enjoyed. Observation and curiosity suited his temperament. He spotted a crumpled heap and went to investigate. It was the body of a wounded Italian soldier. It was Joe. Lance transported what he thought to be a mortally wounded enemy soldier to a medical unit and left. Three months later when all memory of the incident had been forgotten and over a thousand miles from where the rescue had taken place, Joe re-appeared in British lines. It transpired after receiving treatment for his wound, dressed as an Arab, he had walked out of the Allied hospital and, with dog-like instinct, set out on a mission to find the man who had saved his life. Joe never spoke of his journey or how he had managed to locate Lance, only of his certainty that one day he would find his saviour. The single-minded determination and spirit of the small Sicilian impressed all who heard his tale, including Headquarter's staff. After much head scratching it was decided he could stay. He was issued a uniform and assigned to Lance as his batman.

Why he had been found in a condition of near death, miles from any habitation, remained a mystery for some time. Embarrassed by the event Joe had chosen to remain silent. One night, when drunk, it all came tumbling out. He had become detached from his Army unit following an Allied advance. Most of his comrades had been taken prisoner or were dead. Lost and wandering about in confusion, he met with another victim of the battle. It was a woman, one of the camp followers. She had travelled with the Italian Army throughout its desert campaign. In the confusion of retreat she too had become separated from the main body of troops and, like Joe, had become lost. She harboured a dark resentment she had been abandoned on purpose. Had she not been conscientious in giving comfort to all soldiers, irrespective of rank? For a period of two years had she not given solace to thousands? Her generosity had been heroic, her dedication more than ample confirmation of her patriotism. For all her conscientious toil the perfidious Army had conspired she be banished from their ranks. They had left her in a featureless country, far from home, frightened, confused and impoverished. *'Tutti u'omini sono maiale,'* (All men are pigs) she would endlessly mutter as she wandered the trackless wastes. This chant sustained her strength and gave comfort to the bitterness she felt.

She was half-mad with resentment and hunger when fate decreed she should stumble across Joe's meandering path. Immediately she offered him jiggy-jig in return for a slice of bread. Stunned by his sudden good fortune he agreed to the trade. Without hesitation she spread-eagled on the stony ground and

Freewill is Forfeit

lifted the rags she wore to cover her nakedness. Joe, forever compliant, first allowed himself to gaze with enchantment at her scrawny form, then, in a state of simpering lust, threw himself down upon her waiting, disinterested and unresponsive body. During the hapless intercourse she withdrew Joe's knife and stabbed him. How long he had lain before found by Lance, never would be known.

Now, after many months, Joe had lost his pallor and was showing signs of having regained full health. It was good to see. Robert liked his tiny companion, he was a courageous little fellow, dangerous to be around and unpredictable, but brave and uncomplaining. They had a good team for the Sicilian escapade. Doubts harboured at the beginning of the mission were yesterday's thoughts. The squad chosen was almost faultless and Hank's release would re-establish the perfect balance.

When Robert and Joe arrived at the Company orderly room their request to see Major Rogers was refused. 'Return later,' they were told.

Robert leaned forward to speak into the ear of the seated clerk. In a conspiratorial voice, he said, 'Go and tell Major Rogers I think his top sergeant is a crock of shit. Say that to him. I'm sure he'll understand why I must speak to him immediately.'

The smiling orderly disappeared and returned within a few seconds. 'Walk right in, Sergeant, you're correct, he'll see you, immediately.'

Robert indicated to Joe he wished to enter alone. Joe shrugged and looked around for somewhere to sit. To his surprise a chair was offered by a smiling orderly.

* * *

Robert strolled into the ex-croupier's office. He ignored the Major, crossed the floor of the tent and selected a chair. He sat, stretched out his legs, put his hands in his pockets and leaned back. When settled he looked across at the man from the Bronx and said, 'I think it might be a good idea we take a walk, Major. It's a fine day, we've a lot to discuss and I'd hate us to be overheard. I've come to prove we limeys are not so full of shit as you surmise. We Brits can boogie too, you know, only we tend to have more sense of occasion, more propriety. The last time we met I was a little hasty in my judgement. However, I've given your suggestion further thought and I think you and I might be able to agree a deal. What do you say, Major, shall we take a stroll?'

The news went round the Battalion with the force of a forest fire. It didn't require the posters prepared by Major Rogers to publicise the event, nevertheless, scattered groups of animated men encircled the areas where the notices were displayed. It was reassuring to have an anticipated event confirmed. It took it out of the realms of rumour. The happening had the weight of official approval. Announcement wrapped it in certainty.

Unlike clipped military notices the bulletin read like a promotional tract. It proclaimed that Major Rogers, in his concern for the morale of the troops, had concocted a special treat, a spectacular entertainment for the eve of departure to front line duty. A boxing bout of explosive interest had been arranged. Not an ordinary, run-of-the-mill boxing match between two lack-lustre opponents, no! This was the genuine article, a fight to the finish between two famous sergeants renowned for size and strength, an inter-allied contest, an international event between contestants who made no secret of their dislike of one another. It had every-thing. It would be a blaster, a sensational event. It was requested that all attending should be seated in the dining tent by 20.00 hours. The small print at the bottom of the bulletin announced that Major Rogers, in response to popular demand, had volun-teered to organise a betting service to enhance the evening's entertainment.

Buck strode around the orderly room rubbing his hands in gleeful self-satisfaction. What a sensational day it had turned out to be. Would continuing good fortune never cease? The guy just walked in as cool as you like. Who would have thought behind all that pompous, Limey shit, after all that I'm-a-better-guy-than-you crap, he was nuthin' more than a dude straight from the poker tables at home. Just another con-artist. Jeeesus! the world was a complicated place. You never knew if anything said was kosher, or not. At first, to clinch the deal he'd wanted a tank. A fuckin' TANK, for Chris'sake! Reminded me of the Colonel's order that I'd a duty to supply him with all the military gear he needed. Did he think we Yanks were nuts? No way, José! Argued for ten minutes before he quit. In the end had to bargain him down to acceptin' an old lorry, a pile of dynamite and, to compensate for his disappointment, an allowance of artillery. Had a list already prepared. He and his Italian monkey had it loaded and removed not half an hour after the deal was struck. Yeah, and what a deal! Suggests as a betting scam if the odds were set high enough to assure heavy betting on Brutus it would take a month to count the winnings. When asked if certain he could handle Brutus, jist snorted and asked which round did I want him put away, but not to make it too early in the fight as he wanted first to give Brutus a good smackin'. But, best of all, had wanted not one bent dime of the betting proceeds. Said he didn't need the money where he was goin'. They were on some kinda secret operation. Nobody knew. Wherever they were goin' it was sure gonna be noisy.

Robert, too, was pleased with his day. The difficult part was over. He had managed to secure the explosives he had hoped for, been given a two-and-a-half tonner to transport it and a Jeep crammed with weaponry. More than sufficient to reassure Lance it was feasible to return for Hank.

Like most things in life it had its price. The remainder of the day would be spent squaring accounts. First, he owed Sergeant Brutus an apology. Never should he have raised his hands to the man. It had shocked Lance. He had shocked himself. His military indiscipline had been inexcusable. Would he forever be a slave to impulse? Tonight the American would be repaid for this lapse of military protocol. Payback time had arrived. True, Sergeant Brutus was not a well-liked man, but that was irrelevant. Victory tonight over a Limey Sergeant, plus the substantial rewards to be reaped by those having the good sense to take advantage of the generous odds being offered, would obliterate all bad memory and current unpopularity. After the fight the atmosphere in 'C' Company would be transformed. Brutus, when popular, might even become a likeable person. Who knows? What was known, however, after the fight the American troops would leave for battle buoyed up with new morale and have five dollars more in their pockets for every dollar punted on their own sergeant. The indignity of brief humiliation was a small price to pay to compensate for an inexcusable, unmilitary, impulsive act of aggression.

Major Rogers, on the other hand, was about to receive his comeuppance. His dream world was about to come crashing down around his ears. Financial ruination and deserved loss of face, hopefully, would go some way to correcting his inadequate attitude to rank and responsibility. It would be a salutary lesson, but deserved

Robert determined that tonight he would steel himself to do his theatrical best. During the build-up and the usual razz-a-ma-tazz, he would present himself as an arrogant thug. He would prance around, punch the air with aggressive intent and look mean and threatening. He would attempt to put on a show of unattractive confidence and make an effort to appear un-sportsmanlike. At the bell, he would lunge to the centre of the ring, spar with intent and wait patiently for the big punch to end the contest. If it was the first punch Brutus delivered, well and good. The performance could be over in less than five minutes. All debt paid, all duty done, all inappropriate action judiciously solved and the first steps taken in the resolve to have Hank released.

Freewill is Forfeit

11

London

David Hardie was untruthful when he agreed with Jane's suggestion he was little more than a desk-jockey. In 1935 he was seconded to Whitehall to work in Counter Intelligence. At the time his task had been to train agents in the use of weapons. It was neither taxing, nor dangerous. As a freshly promoted Lieutenant, with a young wife pregnant with their first child, he felt fortunate to have been given a posting in London. Whitehall employment afforded the luxury to return each evening to their small Highgate apartment. Nadine, his wife, was French. They had met, and courted, in Paris during an earlier period of his military service. Nadine's English was poor and her lack of fluency embarrassed her. Her stunted English left her with little desire to socialise and, when required to mix with David's friends, she complained of feeling alienated.

During their first two years in London seldom did Nadine leave the flat. David, at her insistence, did the shopping and took responsibility for the domestic duties she claimed she was unable to perform. He believed her social reticence was a passing phase caused by cultural and environmental change. As time passed they found they had little need of company. They had each other and it was all they desired. When Elise was born their social sterility intensified.

It was not until Elise was eighteen months old they were forced by courtesy to attend one of David's regimental dinners. It was a Mess function where formal dress was *de rigueur*. They enjoyed the occasion and decided never to miss another. Nadine, comfortable now with her command of English, had allowed herself to unbend. The relaxed conviviality and the roistering good nature of David's fellow officers, had enthralled her. During the evening champagne had been quaffed with flourish, she had danced with sensuous *éclat* and flirted with French flair. Her presence was declared to have transformed a run-of-the-mill dinner into a memorable occasion. Male friends admitted their jealousy of David's great good fortune to have married a woman of such vivacious beauty. David smiled at the compliments. The young woman he married was beginning to emerge from the shell that had held her enclosed for three years.

During the months leading up to the war uncertainty and increasing national nervousness, stimulated a need for escapism. Whitehall party-making reached a new zenith of popularity. Young officers could disport themselves at a ball, or dinner, a reunion, or whatever function took their fancy, on each night of the week, if it was their desire to seek entertainment. They knew their presence would be made welcome. To be a known functionary within the Whitehall structure was all that was required for admission to the multiplying social events. Wives and girlfriends were made especially welcome.

When this parasitic idiosyncrasy became obvious to Nadine, her party-going hunger became unassuageable. Her delight at being accepted into the swirl of London nightlife gave David warm pleasure. The admiration she attracted confirmed what David had known for years: Nadine was a woman apart, a creature capable of inspiring devotion.

Shopping ceased to be an avoided chore. The once resisted activity became an enthusiasm, almost an addiction. Nadine's voice was now heard in the clothing salons of West-end stores. If a particular shade of blue did not match her fickle requirement, the complaint would be strident. 'Please, take it away and bring me the correct colour, and while you're at it, something lower cut at the bust.' From being abstemious, she became a regular imbiber. Her appetite for sex became more voracious. She began to complain that David should pay more attention to his dress and would he please, please, get himself fitted out in new Dress Blues before the rags he wore in pretence of a uniform fell off his back at some important function. David, although somewhat mystified,

Freewill is Forfeit

nevertheless, remained overjoyed by her transition. Funds in the family bankbook plummeted to a precarious level, but the re-emergence of Nadine's lust for life was worth more than any concern he had for money.

More often than not David was left in charge of Elise. He became proficient at providing to her every need. Elise was approaching the age of three, the perfect age for a female child. His attention was devoured by happy hours of attending to the routines of bathing and feeding his daughter, unaware that the mother of his child was enmeshed in a bout of alcohol-induced affairs. Nadine had fallen victim to the hedonism of the time and was lost in a giddy world where the casual liaison had become the norm.

David remained unaware of his wife's infidelities, not because he was easily deceived, but rather he was disinclined by nature to believe she would ever be unfaithful. Further, as a soldier, he was preoccupied by the deterioration in the political atmosphere.

Each evening on his return from work his little girl banished the frustrations of his day. The therapy of tending to his child never failed to eradicate the disquiet he felt. Ten minutes in the company of his treasured Elise was sufficient to banish all apprehension. Worries vanished in a concentration of love. He was amazed that a helpless child could endow his life with such joy. The simple action of putting Elise to bed, tucking her up and reading to her the tales of bunny rabbits and fairy Princesses, was a ritual of utter happiness. He thought Nadine's unselfish attitude to the father and daughter bonding was admirable. That she should be willing to stand aside and allow him these joys was ample proof of her thoughtful and unselfish concern for his happiness.

On the day war was declared everything changed. Lethargy was transformed into a bustle of energy. When Winston Churchill replaced Neville Chamberlain as Premier on the 10th of May, 1940, Whitehall became galvanised with new purpose.

One of Churchill's first decisions was to set-up an organisation to specialise in sabotage. This resolution was opposed with howls of protest. It was argued underhand methods of waging war did not match with the reputation of British fair play. Churchill's response was immediate. He instructed his Minister of Economic Warfare, Hugh Dalton, to 'Set Europe Ablaze'. This order gave birth to the Special Operations Executive with a given responsibility to spread sabotage, create subversive activity, activate black propaganda and promote espionage behind enemy lines. Churchill knew war was a dirty business and was prepared to sup with the devil to obtain advantage over a detested tyrant.

On 1st July, 1940, David was promoted to the rank of Captain and transferred to the SOE as a Training Operative for secret operations in Europe. His life of uneventful domesticity changed. His existence became charged with risk. Acts of violence and deceit became his new employment.

The week following his transfer and only two weeks after Germany's occupation of France, David was parachuted into the enemy territory of his wife's homeland. His duty was to organise an underground resistance cell through which future subversive action could be organised against the enemy. His mission was a disaster. An informer betrayed his presence in Paris. He evaded capture, but those involved in organising his escape were discovered, arrested and shot.

Two weeks later he was in France, again. On this occasion he posed as a bereaved Frenchman with German sympathies. His story was the British, in their uncaring haste to evacuate troops at Dunkirk, had killed his wife in a road accident. The deceit was successful. He obtained employment as a farm labourer and within a period of a month, despite his anti-British proclamations, gathered around him a trusted group of patriots. When recalled to London, although he felt he had done little to deserve the honour, he was decorated with the Military Cross and promoted to Major.

During David's absence in France Nadine had left the family home in Highgate and had moved to Chelsea. Without communication, or explanation, she had taken up residence with one of her lovers, a middle-aged Naval Commander. David was on his return journey to the UK when he heard the news of Nadine's desertion. He was informed of her infidelity aboard a submarine returning from France. The young midshipman, the bearer of the heart stopping news, was none other than the son of the man who had enticed Nadine to leave. David was certain Nadine's decision to abandon home and marriage had been made while in a haze of drunken lust. But what did that matter now? The happiness of two families was destroyed. He was further informed that the young man's mother was in hospital recovering from a suicide attempt. The midshipman was distraught and begged David, with tear-stained pleas, to strive to repair the tragedy that had befallen both homes.

David was numbed by the shock of the news. Much as he loved Nadine he feared the uncertainty of not being able to forgive her. Concern for Elise flooded his thoughts. Was she being looked after with proper care? He didn't know. He knew only one thing, nothing would ever separate him from his daughter, his little girl: his own flesh and blood.

On his arrival in London he returned to an empty home. He stood in the sitting room and listened to silent echoes. There was a letter. It sat waiting his attention in the middle of a mantelpiece stripped of usual clutter. He opened the envelope and read its contents. She had fallen in love with another man. He must try to forgive and forget. It continued with the blah-blah of how sorry she was to have caused him pain and hoped he soon would recover from the shock and suddenness of her decision. Not one word in the letter referred to Elise.

He experienced, for the first time, the full force of Nadine's calculated cruelty. She would have known the pain she would inflict by her sudden departure, but to compound the misery she had chosen, by an incomprehensible act of vicious omission, to ignore the existence of his daughter. How could she have failed to mention Elise when she knew of his adoration for the child? The omission was the callous action of a heartless woman. At that moment he decided he would sue Nadine for the custody of Elise. He was heartbroken.

Never did he see Nadine or his beloved child again. On September 15th, 1940, one week after his return from France, during an air raid that involved 230 bombers, large areas of London were smashed to fragments. Both Nadine and Elise were killed in the carnage. The home-wrecking Naval Commander survived the ordeal. He lay under rubble for two days before his unconscious body was discovered. His injuries were severe enough to be life-threatening, but he survived and following medical care was returned to the bosom of his family.

David's grief for his child was terrible. For days he stumbled around the spaces of the house that once had been their home. He decided there was no purpose in continuing to live. In a void of grief his compassionate leave passed with mystifying rapidity. His return to active service required him to shave, take regular meals, dress correctly and make conversation under the pretence that a modicum of normality somehow had been retained. A painful drag of days enveloped him.

In time he emerged from the crucible of grief and made two resolutions: to extract revenge on those who had killed his daughter and never again to allow the emotion of love to sully his sanity. The pain of lost love was too terrible to bear.

* * *

'Go on, jump'. David yelled up at Jane who was standing thirty feet above him. She was on the lowest of the platforms scattered around the training area.

'I'm sorry, David, I can't. It's impossible. I'm too terrified,' Jane shouted down at him.

'Okay,' he replied, 'come down and we'll see if something can be worked out.' Jane unclipped from the harness and attached the loose end to the pulley. She made her descent and walked over to join him. His head was bent. He continued to stare at the ground. She wanted to make some noises of apology, but knew it would be pointless. She hated when David went into one of his strong, silent, broody moods. 'Let's face it David, I'll never be able to do it,' Jane protested.

'Extreme problems sometimes require extreme solutions,' he said without looking up.

'What's that supposed to mean?'

'Nothing, really,' he said. David was worried. If Jane refused to parachute into Sicily the mission would be in jeopardy. A Lysander could be employed to land in some secluded spot, but suitable areas of flat ground were difficult to locate in the mountainous centre of the island. Besides, Lysanders had been used in France for infiltration purposes with disastrous results. Too many agents had been arrested at the landing zones. Those who chose to enter enemy territory by parachute had the best chance of avoiding unwanted attention. A submarine could be employed to land them almost anywhere on the shore, but it would entail a subsequent trek that would daunt a Commando Unit. Jane would never survive the trauma of the trudge across the rough terrain and, if she survived the ordeal, would be too unfit to be effective. The parachute it had to be. David raised his head and said, 'Come with me,' and strode off.

When Jane caught up, she asked, 'Where are we going?'

'To the Medical Unit.'

'Why, for God's sake?'

'To ask them to give you something to solve your problem.'

'What on earth are you talking about? No elixir on earth will remove my fear of heights.'

'We'll see,' he said and quickened his pace.

When she caught up with him again, she asked, 'Are we in a hurry?'

'In a great hurry. The time wasted by indecision makes haste essential. Time is of the essence.' He stopped and swung round to face Jane. 'I'm asking you to do one last thing for me.' His plea was earnest. 'Will you do it?' He stood waiting for her answer. 'Well?'

'I'm not promising to do anything until I know what it is you want me to do.'

'It's a small matter.'

'How small?'

'So small you'll hardly notice. It will take only a second of your time, believe me.'

'It's not to jump off that platform, is it?'

'No, nothing like that.'

'And it's not dangerous?'

'It's not dangerous.'

'Okay, I'll do it, whatever it is.'

'Good girl,' he said and strode off.

Jane went into a trot to follow. 'Well, tell me. What do you want me to do?'

'Have an injection.'

'Have a what?'

'An injection. You know, a small jab in the arm.'

'Why?'

'It will relax you. Make you more', he hesitated, 'amenable.'

'You want to drug me in the hope that while in a state of induced befuddlement I'll throw myself off thirty foot platforms. Well, no thank you! Forget it and think again.'

'You agreed to have the injection. It won't induce inebriation, in fact, quite the opposite. Your faculties will feel very alive. Please trust me. What I'm asking you to do is not abnormal procedure.'

'What is this drug?'

'Dexedrine.'

'Have you ever taken it?'

'On many occasions.'

'What are the effects?'

'It will make you feel euphoric.'

'And the side effects?'

'None to my knowledge. It's an amphetamine.'

'A pain killer?'

'A confidence booster.'

'Okay, let's give it a try.'

* * *

They were aboard an American DC3 somewhere over mid-England. The conditions outside the aircraft were unpleasant. Anna, slumped on the floor of the stripped-out main cabin, was conscious of the wind and rain buffeting the fuselage. The roar of the engines inhibited conversation. Communication had to be shouted over the tumult. The cacophony isolated those on board to their own thoughts. Anna looked over at Jane and smiled. Never had she

Freewill is Forfeit

seen Jane look so unfeminine. Military combat gear gave her a sexless identity. She was a bundle of misshapen camouflage, a well-stuffed scarecrow wearing a bonnet of steel. When Jane returned the smile it was cheerful and assured, full of 'isn't this wonderful' enthusiasm.

Anna thought it strange that Jane had lost her fear of heights. Throughout the entire period of the training programme her mood had been nothing less than ebullient. Her energy levels had been startling. Had Jane, like herself, craved release from a humdrum life and become intoxicated by the thought of being involved in an adventure brimming with risk? Had the excitement of the enterprise refreshed and galvanised her energy? Something in her had changed. It was difficult to pinpoint. Perhaps it was David's influence in her life? Lover and military mentor was an exotic mix. Was David the sorcerer who had transformed her spirit? Had his wizardry evoked a dramatic rejuvenation? Whatever the reason there was no doubting she had adapted to military life, the constant activity, the discipline and the general rough and tumble, with untroubled ease.

It almost had defied comprehension. Small arms training, parachute practice, fitness regimes, equipment parades, lectures on the dos and don'ts of espionage, all had been tackled with a competence that mocked both her natural inclinations and age. Travelling from place to place had been exhausting: lectures at the British Museum, parachute training at Ringway, weapon training at Catterick Barracks and an overnight exercise on Salisbury Plain. The frenetic movement had been enervating enough to diminish the enthusiasm of the most dedicated trainee, but Jane had taken all inconvenience and hardship in her stride. Now, at three o'clock in the morning, strapped into parachutes, they were flying north in a storm to God knows where. Soon they were to throw themselves into the night, into the foul weather, hopefully to float to earth and arrive in a physically undamaged condition. Mental damage was another matter. The army had little concern with the mental condition of combatants.

This was the final exercise in the training programme. If completed without a hitch the next twenty-four hours would be spent preparing for departure. In three days Anna would be in the company of her maternal grandfather in enemy-occupied territory. It was a stomach-churning thought.

The intensity of the training programme had prevented the planned visit to Glasgow, but she had found sufficient time to write a letter to both parents. The letter to her mother had been to reassure all was well, that promotion beckoned and how fortunate she was to be in a posting far from any theatre of war, or threatening danger. The letter to her father had been a straightforward plea for understanding and forgiveness. She wrote of her love for him and of her regret that she had caused him distress. During the writing of both letters she had wept.

There was still no news of the missing men. Each day that passed the mystery of their disappearance became more disturbing. The recent news from Tunisia was good. The Americans first having suffered defeat had re-engaged the enemy and secured victory. In the south the Mareth Line was disintegrating under the pressure of Montgomery's forces. The Allied Divisions now held large areas of Tunisia and still a silence persisted as to their whereabouts. Had they been taken prisoner? Had they been caught in the initial German thrust? It was surmise, but possible. It was known they had been in the vicinity of battle action when they disappeared. Just to know they were alive would be a mercy.

Should it transpire they had been captured it would eradicate any hope of ever meeting Hank again. By the end of the war any memory he retained of an admiring Italian tutor would have faded from his mind. After release he would return home to celebrate his fresh sense of freedom in the arms of beautiful, responsive, adoring women and all recollection of her, and previous army life, would evaporate in a merry-go-round of well-deserved amatory relationships. It was all so predictable.

She decided she would do all in her power to prevent her prediction becoming true. If Hank had been captured she would make it her business to discover where he was being held and write to him. She would tell him of the mystery of her attraction, confess her affection, admit he invaded her thoughts more than she cared to confess. She would write him daily, comfort his loneliness with words of support, make him realise his importance in her life. She would win his heart by determined effort.

A red light started to flash in the gloom. David stood and steadied himself against the bulkhead. 'Get ready, ladies, we're here,' he said, as if arriving at a local bus station. Anna felt her body tense.

'Ready, Anna?' David asked.

'We're going to be soaked to the skin by the time we land,' Anna heard herself say.

David smiled. 'You'll be picked up immediately. Within the hour you'll be in a warm bath.' He turned to Jane. His face was smeared with concern. 'Okay, Jane?'

'You said this would be fun. Let's see if it is,' Jane said and waddled to her station. She had volunteered to jump first. Anna fell in behind and, in an attempt to empty her mind, studied the black metal gleam of the floor. The light turned to green.

'Number one.' David barked above the noise. Anna watched Jane's feet shuffle forward, heard her clip on, observed her knees as they flexed for balance and she was gone.

'Number two.'

In a trance Anna walked to the black, swirling hole and in a few unremembered seconds was floating in space. Everything was fine. Everything was as she had been told it would be. While drifting to earth no one heard her hysterical laughter.

* * *

Tunisia

Hank had been alone throughout the day. He felt well and was in no pain. Weakness and boredom were the afflictions he now had to bear. The long hours of his convalescence had given him time to think. Mostly he thought about the type of individual he had become. Had his disposition towards women been overtly chauvinistic? Irrefutably. Had he got it wrong about religion? After observing Nightingale, he wondered. Was his attitude to money illogical? Was it not some perverse, subconscious reaction to the guilt of possessing wealth in an otherwise impoverished society? Why did he cleave to, even cherish, his many resentments? He had resented a dead father for his life-long miserly proclivities. He resented the double standards at play in his mother's life. He resented the multiple hypocrisies that bedevilled society. He resented the imbedded narcissism of parents who presumed to mastermind the future lives of their offspring. He resented the arrogance of institutional religion, institutional government, institutionalised corporations and every other type of self-feeding organisation created to restrain and control human endeavour. Why was it, he wondered, that he alone was tormented with the growing suspicion that all professions were merely conspiracies against the common laity? Had his cynicism spun out of control? Had he become an oddball, an outsider, a social freak?

His friend Jack had accused him of having a predisposition to dangerous and bewildering idealism. Often he would shout, 'Here comes our demented iconoclast, the last free thinker on Wall Street'. Had Jack meant it, or was it just his usual humour at play? Why were most of his sincere predilections mocked? Were they too Utopian to be thought valid? Did his friends secretly regard him as a class traitor?

His main rebellion was against the stricture that had bound him to a type of life he was unsure he wanted to live. His life had been hijacked at birth. All he was expected to do was dutifully follow a track already prepared. A return to an elevated position at the bank would be the acceptance of a pre-planned lifestyle of scripted predictability. It would dictate friendships; the type of girl he would marry; the manner in which his children would be reared; the style of house lived in; the model of car driven; the holiday resorts visited; the restaurants, the parties, the clubs, the clothes, even the shoes on his feet would have to match current, fashionable expectation. All the fickle idiosyncratic palaver of class would have to be adhered to. It was expected. Keeping up appearances was an integral part of the job. To deviate would be regarded as infra-dig.

Holy shit, it was no life at all. It was painting by numbers, a scripted performance; a grotesque farce. He wanted life to be

Freewill is Forfeit

fulfilling, a challenge to energy, to have freedom of choice and movement. He had observed, too often, individuals who had devoted their lives to the acquisition of wealth, only to find, at the end of their successful quest, loneliness and bitter disillusion.

Gustav entered the cave. He removed his tunic and walked over to where Hank was lying. 'How are you feeling?'

'I think I'm well enough to start taking a little exercise, but there's a problem?'

'And what's that?'

'Clothes, where are my clothes?'

'They were cut from your body and burned.'

'Burned? How considerate.'

'They were blood soaked.'

'How unusual, just imagine, a blood-soaked army uniform.' Both smiled at the sarcasm.

'Allow me to remind you when first you were stretchered into this Arab Care Centre you were more dead than alive. Had it been rock instead of soil you hit your uniform would have been your shroud. However, if you feel strong enough to take a little exercise, I'll see to it you're given a garment to cover your nakedness.'

'How kind.'

'I can't vouch for fit or colour, but the jellaba, I'm told, can be worn with enjoyment after some initial discomfort. They say it's very practical apparel.'

'I'll take your word.'

'Are you hungry, Hank?'

'Famished.'

'Then I'll try to find you something to eat.' He left the cave and returned ten minutes later carrying a flat board spread with pieces of chopped meat. 'Tonight's menu,' he announced, 'is stewed horse. You may have it all. *Buon appetito.*'

When Hank was picking at the last scraps, Gustav said, 'You've just demolished a double ration of carrion. You must be feeling better.'

'I am and that was delicious. Thank you Gustav, you're a gentleman. To me you're the best.'

The compliment caught Gustav off guard. He had received

many in his time and had accepted them without undue self-regard, but Hank's casual utterance hit a warm centre. Seldom had a compliment sounded sweeter. Gustav said, 'I'd rather be thought of as a good Christian.'

'What is it with you and Christianity? Hank asked. 'You make me feel I'm missing out on a big deal. Everything you do appears to be woven with some mystical motive. Your humility is beginning to give me a complex.'

'We Christians set ourselves high standards. They're imposs-ible to achieve, but you mustn't blame us for trying.'

'As I understand it, the big deal is, you commit to suffer and serve today to inherit eternal paradise tomorrow? Is that it?'

Gustav was surprised at the sudden change of subject. He was caught on the wrong foot and was annoyed he should feel defensive. 'There's much more to it than that, I assure you,' he said.

'But, that's the base line, or am I wrong?'

Gustav began to experience sensations of *déja vu*. You're not a Christian, Hank?' he asked.

'No.'

'You sound as if you don't approve?'

'I feel it would be gauche of me to disapprove. Had it not been for you, a man acting and believing as you do, I wouldn't be here to question the mystery of religious conviction.'

'Were you brought up to believe in God?'

'Everybody in America is brought up to believe in God.'

'But you doubt the international wisdom of the teaching?'

'We're also taught that we have evolved from the great apes. Is there a dichotomy at play here?'

'I've never thought so.'

'For myself I've never given the matter much thought, that is until I met you,' Hank complained.

'Belief in God requires a leap of faith to be made.'

'That's not true. Most individuals accept belief in the Almighty without making this leap of faith. The majority of people accept God's reality as a matter of popular belief and not by any sincere conviction.'

'And why do you think that should be?'

'Because God is a Being beyond ordinary imagination and the man-in-the-street, baffled by myth and complexity, bows to the societal conformity. They believe God's existence is beyond argument. Our social conventions almost demand a belief in God. You can't bury a friend, marry a blonde, break the law, attend a ceremonial, do anything of any significance, without paying some obeisance to His Earthly Kingship.'

'That's very well reasoned, Hank. And true. I've no argument with that.'

Hank looked up and said, 'I'll never understand dedication to faith. The punishment and self-denial willingly suffered for your belief is beyond my understanding. It's so gracious on the one hand and so pathetically naïve on the other. It's admirable, yes, but perhaps also self-deceiving. But, who am I, the recipient of your Christian attentions to carp at and question your convinced philosophy.'

'Who better?'

'I've come to the conclusion you're involved in making reparation for some past sin.'

'That's partly true. My religion has never seemed more important to me. In fact, of late, it's been my only comfort. I can't make sense of life without the crutch of Christianity. Without faith madness would have claimed me months ago. If you understand nothing else, accept that fact?'

'I'm not criticising you, Nightingale, to me you're a real first-class, top drawer guy.

* * *

They crossed the moonlit desert travelling in convoy. Lance and Joe were in the jeep, with Robert following behind in the truck. Their plans were made. Each man knew what had to be done. It was crucial everything be ready and in position before dawn. Lance and Joe travelled in silence. Both were preoccupied. Apprehension was tangible. The plan was bold and if it were to succeed they would require more than a share of good fortune.

It had been agreed to attempt a forthright deceit. It was Robert's idea. It was a simple, up-front, concept. The truck, bedecked with a flag of truce, was to be driven to, and parked at, the narrow point in the pass. It was hoped to dupe the Arabs by the deceit of false ambush. On arrival at the chosen spot Robert's duties were to select the position of and plant and prepare the explosive devices to be detonatated and return to the vehicle in time to await first light and the arrival of a curious enemy.

In the same two-hour period Lance and Joe had to transfer weapons from jeep to truck, conceal the jeep, find suitable machinegun positions on both sides of the pass and make preparations to expedite safe withdrawal should the intrigue blunder.

If the stratagem failed Robert's life would be in danger, but during the planning phase all consideration for his safety had been given scant consideration. While analysing the operation doubt had been expressed as to the wisdom of Robert's plan, but in the end, his will had prevailed. He had argued, and convinced, with blind disregard for self-preservation. During the discussions Lance had witnessed the re-emergence of the recognised soldier. When battle beckoned Robert became charged with wild purpose. His confidence banished doubt and uncertainty.

Lance remembered being told by Robert of a painting that had hung in his father's cabin. It was of a clean-cut young man, dressed in chain mail, kneeing at the feet of a beautiful princess. The supplicant, in reward for noble deeds, was being dubbed with silver sword a Knight in her Service. The picture inflamed the imagination. Robert had thought it quite magnificent. It explained much about Robert's out-dated, unfashionable, poetic conceptions. During his boyhood he had been confronted with a painting both chivalrous and romantic in theme. Unknowingly, he had identified with, and become a disciple of, the young man portrayed. By the mystery of osmosis the notion had formed that while war was brutal, nevertheless, it should be conducted by chivalric rules of combat. Soldier should fight soldier in honourable, straightforward fashion.

Ten minutes in the presence of Winston Churchill would have

disabused him of this odd ideal. Modern war was total war. No longer was concern given to the niceties of ancient codes of chivalry. They were gone forever. They belonged to a time when gallantry was the essential attribute of the knightly class.

War, now, enmeshed everyone in its maul. Soldier and civilian alike had to tolerate its fury. Suffering and loss were ubiquitous conditions. Everyone was made to suffer front line danger. The old and young were not excluded. 'Civilian' had become a redundant word, 'Non-combatant' a meaningless term. War had moved with the times. Robert's idea of war had not.

Lance looked at his watch. They were ten minutes from E.T.A.

* * *

Brigadier General Thomson replaced the receiver and beamed with delight. The news from home could not be better. Bobby Braithwaite had broken cover and made his bid to secure the position he coveted. Armed with the information that Hancock Remington's release would take years to resolve, Bobby had made his move to secure the post of Chairman. For the first time in the history of the Remington Bartholomew Bank an individual outside the founding families would be in control of the trading philosophy of the Board. The financial pages of the New York Times would buzz with comment for months.

It had been astute of Bobby to act before news of the capture was announced. If he had delayed it would have drawn accusations of underhand, unfair and unpatriotic manoeuvring. Inside knowledge, once again, was bearing fruit. Nothing now prevented the delayed communiqué from being released. It could be announced without further stonewalling. When the news of Remington's fate hit New York pragmatism would over-ride old loyalties and propel Bobby Braithwaite into the vacant Chair. It would end the internecine conflict that had bedevilled the Board for too long.

Cowboy sat back in his chair and let his eyes wonder around his office. It was big, comfortable and safe. Life was good. He felt good. All and all, when viewed in the round, his entire life had been good. Good family, good school, good career and, above all, he had managed to establish good relationships with the most important money managers in America. Yep! What more could a man ask for, other than good health to enjoy it all. Even the war, to a degree, had been tolerable. He had developed the happy knack of befriending the right people. The old adage was accurate. It wasn't what you knew, but whom.

He had been more fortunate than most to have met and kept company with the best people. Not many men were on first name terms with the President. Victory at Kasserine had helped, of course, and had reflected glory on the entire Division, but when the Old-boy phoned to say how proud he had been to hear the news, it was time to party.

At tonight's celebration the young officers, as usual, would make fools of themselves. The occasion would be an exercise in over-indulgence. Free nights in the Mess were rare and tended to disintegrate into boisterous chaos. One uncomfortable aspect was, as the night progressed, rank began to be ignored. During the merrymaking discipline was forgotten. The antidote to the problem, of course, was to get thoroughly pissed and remain semi-comatose throughout. It made the event tolerable.

It had been days since he last had allowed himself an unrestrained binge. It was time for another. It was to be a special occasion, after all, a festivity in celebration of Victory. Tonight, he decided, he would over-indulge on the best champagne the Quartermaster could provide.

12

Tunisia

Robert slithered down the last of the incline and walked to the side of the truck. He looked up at the sky. It was dark grey. It would be daylight in half an hour, perhaps less. The preparation had gone well. Lance and Joe were settled in their positions and there was nothing more to do, except wait. It seemed to him his entire life had been spent waiting. As a youngster he had waited to grow up. As a youth he had waited for his first experience of sex. As a soldier he had spent an inordinate time just waiting between bursts of intensive action. His first conscious childhood memory was one of waiting. Sitting in a strange room, in a frightening building, waiting for his mother to die. Perhaps life itself was just one long wait for death. He thought it strange such a thought should enter his head. This was not the time to be thinking morbid thoughts. He must stay alert and not allow his mind to wander.

He walked to the rear of the truck to check the ties were loose on the canvas flaps. Satisfied, he strolled round to the cabin door, opened it and stretched in to remove the key from the ignition. He closed the door and rearranged the drape of the white flag. It was important that it be conspicuous. Assured all was in place he wandered to the front of the vehicle, sat on the bumper and stared into a grey gloom. Nothing could be seen. He stopped his breathing to listen. Not a sound could be heard. He was enclosed in silence. He pulled up the collar of his battledress against the cold of the morning, crossed his arms and settled to his wait.

It was the animals he heard first. He calculated they were coming up the pass heading directly towards him. It was time to screw his courage to the sticking place. He uncrossed his arms and reached into his pocket to withdraw cigarettes and matches. He put an unlit cigarette in his mouth and gripped the matchbox in his left hand. When he looked up he saw approaching camels in the distance. They were trotting. It was difficult to judge distance in the early morning light. He decided at the count of twenty he would strike a match and light the cigarette. By that time they would be close enough to have sight of him. At the count of fifteen he took three steps forward and sat cross-legged on the ground. He ignored their approach and with a cupped hand lit the cigarette. He exhaled, tossed the match aside and turned his head to watch their final approach. There were eleven of them. Ten mounted on camels led by a single horseman. The camel riders were armed with rifles, the horseman wore a sword. Twenty yards from where he sat the camels stopped. The horseman rode forward and dismounted. As he approached Robert discarded the cigarette by flicking it with thumb and forefinger and rose from his sitting position to come face to face with his adversary. He saw a tall, gaunt, solemn-faced man.

'Who are you and what are you doing here? the horseman enquired. He spoke in English. Robert was delighted and struggled not to show relief. It had been assumed the Arabs would speak French. On this assumption it had been decided that he, rather than Lance, should conduct the negotiations. Like most Canadians his French was adequate, but he had feared his fluency would be found wanting. This worry was now behind him, he was off to a running start.

'I'm a sergeant in the service of His Imperial Majesty King George the sixth. I come in peace as a benefactor bearing gifts.' Robert felt he sounded like Errol Flynn on a bad day.

The horseman said nothing. He made a sweeping gesture with his right arm. The camels walked forward and surrounded the truck. The horseman removed his gaze from Robert's face, drew his sword and commenced to make a circular tour of the vehicle. Robert watched as the Arab flicked at the flaps with his weapon to peer into the interior spaces of the truck. During the inspection Robert grinned up at the encircling group of grim-faced men.

When the horseman was satisfied Robert was alone he returned

Freewill is Forfeit

to the front of the vehicle. 'We do not welcome those who come among us wearing the military garb of a colonial power. You say you come in peace? Your transport speaks of belligerent intent. It groans under the weight of arms.'

'The vehicle, and all it contains, is a gift from His Majesty King George. It is given to your freedom fighters to assist in your struggle against forces of oppression.'

'Why would a foreign King regard the men of the Neo Destour worthy of such beneficence?' The horseman's lip curled as he asked the question.

'He is a wise and far-seeing King. His great arsenal is open to all who fight against tyranny.'

'Your King is a colonial despot. Millions bend the knee and pay obeisance to his power. An Imperialist does not reward those who would oppose colonial authority?'

'Be assured, his intention is righteous. His wish is to provide succour to those forced to live in serfdom under the heel of undemocratic rule.' Robert listened to the Arab make noises of amusement.

'Amuse me more, funny man. Tell me, why are you here?'

'To deliver the gift and to ask you to extend a small kindness in return.'

'And that would be?'

'To have released from your custody the American officer, Captain Remington.'

The horseman's face lost its smile. 'And if we were to refuse and cut off your head instead?'

'Your will be done,' said Robert, humbly. 'But, I think your refusal would be ill-advised.'

'Tell me why, funny man?' the Arab sneered.

'It would force me to obey my orders.'

'And they would be?'

'To destroy your garrison and slaughter all therein.' There, it was out. He had practiced the line over and over in French. He had had a fear it sounded too biblical. But fine, it had sounded just fine. English had given it balance, the correct gravitas.

The horseman's first reaction was disbelief. Then he laughed.

To share his amusement he shouted Robert's threat in Arabic to the surrounding men. The collective merriment was genuine.

'And how do you expect to accomplish this miraculous deed? By thunderbolt conjured by magic?' The horseman asked, tingeing his amusement with mockery.

'In a sense, but not by magic. Dynamite.'

The horseman's eyes narrowed. After a thoughtful pause, he said, 'You're not a funny man. You're a crazy man.'

'So I've heard it said.' Robert sensed the horseman's patience was spent. His next act would be to strike with his sword, or have him seized. To surprise the Arab he took a forward step and said, 'We have not come to trade insults or give offence, only to negotiate the release of an illegally held soldier.'

'We?' asked the horseman.

'Robert made a circular motion with the fore-finger of his right hand. The Arab understood the gesture and looked up at the surrounding slopes. There was nothing to see. Reassured, he said again, 'We?'

'A British Army unit.'

'This unit appears to be well concealed.'

'A precautionary ploy of well-trained soldiers.'

The Arab let his eyes make another scan of the hills. 'You appear under a flag of truce with intention to threaten. Be advised, crazy one, we are many and you are few.'

'But we are strong and you are weak. We know your number and have come prepared to take our soldier by force should you choose to remain stubborn.'

'Captain Remington must be a man of rare worth to have you risk your life on his behalf.'

'He is a comrade-in-arms. We would be prepared to do the same for any of our number. You should be informed we are of a determined disposition on this matter. We have no fight with you, or your ideals. We're all soldiers in a struggle to claim liberty and freedom from regimes of despotic power. Return our comrade and we are prepared to increase the strength and fighting capability of your small force to a level you can only have dreamed of.'

'And you should be made aware negotiations with the Americans for his release are almost concluded.'

'Terms have been agreed?'

'Not precisely.'

'How imprecise, exactly?'

'Compensation is being considered.'

'Compensation? Is that a euphemism for ransom?'

The Arab's eyes flashed with anger. 'Be advised to control your tongue.'

'And you be advised the American Army will never pay a renegade gang of men 'compensation' for the release of a prisoner already categorised as having been illegally apprehended and held hostage. They are scrupulous in this matter. We on the other hand are not burdened by scruple.'

'Enough.' said the horseman. He turned to the Arab on his right and indicated with his sword that Robert be seized.

Robert raised his right arm. Immediately the terrain of the adjacent land was transformed by a huge explosion. Robert stood erect as he watched the ensuing chaos. Showers of debris and desert dust darkened the morning sun. Camels dismounted their riders and sprinted in every direction. Others bolted with men clinging to whatever part of their animal they could hold. When the disarray subsided Robert raised his hand once more. Machine gun fire threw up spurts of sand on either side of the remaining group of men. Robert strolled forward and, in a manner as if nothing had happened, said to the electrified horseman, 'The deal is this. You see behind me an army vehicle, it's yours with all it contains. The truck is loaded with modern armoury: machine guns, ammunition, hand grenades, rifles, light mortar, dynamite, landmines, in short, enough fire power and explosive to equip a small army. All this is yours to assist in your on-going struggle for self-determination. And more, we will train your men in the use of these arms, drill them in modern warfare techniques and discipline them to a level above that of marauding bandits. It will transform your small army into an effective fighting force, improve their morale and bring them to an condition they will have no further need to resort to primitive methods of hostage taking. Well, do we have a deal, or do we both perish?'

'How can I accept the word of a Christian?'

'I'm not a Christian, I'm an atheist. We atheists are moral men. Our morality is our accepted orthodoxy. More to the point can a Muslim be trusted?'

'The word of a Muslim is sacrosanct.'

'Trust is irrelevant. Should you break your word large areas of your homeland will be obliterated by timed explosive. If our simple request is met the explosives will be defused on our departure.'

'You are a very impressive soldier.'

'You can skip the flattery. Go, now and fetch Captain Remington and bring him here. You have until noon.'

'You speak as if a bargain has been struck.'

'Well?' Robert challenged, locking eyes with the gaunt man.

'Yes,' he said, 'we'll make the trade.'

'Swear it in the name of Allah.'

'I swear it in the name of Allah.' He bowed and turned to leave. His horse was nowhere to be seen. He walked to a clutch of riderless camels, selected one and when mounted made a screech of command to his men that he should be followed. He trotted off in the direction from whence he came.

* * *

'He spoke the truth. The Americans will never pay for his release.' This opinion was expressed by ben Yousseff. He was speaking to the Hadji.

'Did you agree to the bargain, Yousseff?'

'I was forced to agree. I was ordered to have him delivered by midday.'

'Well, are we to deliver him, or fight?'

'Why fight? By opposing them we have nothing to gain and put ourselves at risk of losing everything. By avoiding battle we can unburden ourselves of a worthless man and in turn reap a rich reward.'

'But, was it a rich reward? Was it not a collection of redundant weaponry and old swords?'

'It was a mini arsenal of modern arms.'

'You saw it?'

'Yes, with my own eyes. It was as he described, a veritable arsenal.'

'Then it is a profitable trade?'

'In every consideration.'

'I like the sound of this soldier. He is correct to criticise our hostage taking. Against my better judgment I have listened to your counsel on this matter. I was wrong to do so. It is an unworthy act, an unbecoming activity. Order your men that it stop.'

'The fighting men will object. It pays a handsome reward and we are in need of funds.'

'Impoverished we may be, but remember why we fight. Our struggle is to reclaim title of our land. When this is achieved and the history of the Neo Destour is written, our actions will be remembered and judged. Let it not be for cowardly deeds and demeaning acts. Let it be more glorious. At the new birth of our nation let our story be an inspiration to our future children and not an embarrassment to be forgotten.'

'Your words always are well considered.'

'Now, go. Take the American and deliver him to this soldier and be noble in demeanour.'

'Before I leave there is one matter I would mention. It is a concern that distresses me.'

'Give it voice, Yousseff.'

'When the British are amongst us there is a danger our caves will be found.'

'True.'

'We have the responsibility to protect our ancient secret.'

'We must adhere to that, above all. Accept their gift of arms and reject the offer of training. It is a duty they will be pleased to relinquish.'

'So be it.'

* * *

Gustav's work was less onerous. He had been given two normal-sized buckets. When an Arab had stopped to enquire after the condition of Hank's health, Gustav had taken the risk to mention the unsuitability of the vessel he had been given. The next day he was presented with two easily carried water buckets with rope handles. Contrary to expectation he found the Arabs to be fair-minded and pragmatic. Despite their primitive life style and their penchant for marauding, within the confines of the caves they adhered to codes of consideration and decency.

Gustav had grown to enjoy his assignment as water carrier. Although it was a simple task, it had integrated him into the communal fabric of cave life. He had learned if he executed his task with thoroughness nothing more was expected of him. As time passed the habit of cursing him had stopped. The once fashionable sport had lost its original appeal. His presence now tended to be greeted with grunts and nods of recognition. He had become a familiar, a conscientious, uncomplaining labourer in their service. He had integrated himself into their routines. Apart from the torment of not knowing what was happening in the outside world and his constant worry over Lisa, the slow passing of peaceful days was a merciful relief from the madness of the world he had escaped.

Gustav was refilling the buckets at the well when he became aware of a riderless horse galloping unattended around the area of the central precinct. It was snorting and bucking, as if in fear. When it was gathered and taken to the stables, the incident was forgotten.

Shortly after, Gustav began to witness the arrival of complaining men and stray camels. He stopped to watch as screaming, stick-wielding men struggled to herd the animals. It was at this point he saw Hank. He was blindfolded and being escorted towards a group of waiting men.

Driven by curiosity to discover something of what was happening, Gustav abandoned his buckets and went to cross the floor of the cavern. All around men appeared to be preoccupied with urgent tasks. When midway across the open arena eight horsemen emerged from the stable area. Hank was at the centre of the group as they rode off in the direction of the exit from the caves.

Gustav became aware Hans had been watching his movements.

When assured it was safe he made a pointing gesture in the direction of the latrines and turned to walk away. Two minutes later they greeted each other with an embrace.

'How are you, Hans?'

'I'm okay, sir, and you?'

'I'm fine. Are they treating you well?'

'Well enough. Loneliness is the worst thing, it's doing funny things to my head, but physically I'm fine.'

'Loneliness and depression are difficult conditions to tolerate. Are you being overworked?'

'No.' Hans wagged his head from side to side. 'It's just that I'm a little worried.'

'Tell me.'

'I think I'm beginning to hallucinate.'

'How strange. Are you seeing things, or hearing things?'

'Both. Well, yes both. A British soldier appears at night and has become my companion.'

'I don't understand.'

'Neither do I.'

'You're having vivid dreams. It happens when you're lonely. The mind compensates for the lack of stimulation.'

'No, they're not dreams. When he's present, he is very real. I can even smell his breath. To be honest, sir, I think I'm going nuts.'

'Does he talk to you in English?'

'Fluent German.'

'Leave it to me. I'll see that something is done about this. Now, tell me what is happening? Why is everything in confusion? What's all the kerfuffle about?'

'I don't know.'

'You must know something, you're in the thick of the activity.'

'I don't know. I can't understand one syllable of their bloody awful language.'

'Okay, Hans. Calm down. Tell me what you have seen.'

'After I've just told you I'm hallucinating? Even I don't trust what I've seen.'

'Please, Hans, tell me.'

'Before dawn I was wakened and told to go to the stables. When I got there about a dozen men were readying themselves to leave on some raid. Two hours later the boss-man returned alone. The odd thing is he left on a horse and returned on a camel. He had a conversation with the man who sometimes struts around in a multi-coloured cloak. About fifteen minutes later, during further confusion, another group of men appeared. They ignored the disorder and mounted horses. In the chaos a blindfolded Arab was placed on a horse and they rode off.'

'The man in the blindfold was an American soldier. We share the same cave.'

'That's quaint.'

'What is?'

'For company you have a Yank and I have a Tommie. At least you know your companion is real.'

'Was real. It seems he has been taken away.'

'That's about all I can tell you.'

'Thank you, Hans, it's enough. Believe me, it's enough. We had better return to our posts before we're discovered. Fear not, Hans, we are not being held by barbarians. They will listen to my pleas on your behalf. Now that the American appears to have left I will make the request we share a cell. I'm sure they will agree, so take heart.'

'They will know we have spoken.'

'Don't worry. I'll quote them the Geneva Convention and my rights as your Commanding Officer.'

'Thank you, sir.'

'Now, go, and take care.'

Gustav returned to his employment in a mood of despond. He liked Hank Remington. Although he was a Godless man burdened with naïve ideals, he possessed the rare quality of transparent honesty. Go well, and go safely Hank. We met as enemies and parted brothers. One day may we meet again!

With a heavy heart Gustav lifted his buckets.

* * *

When Hank was awakened, he was ordered to dress, blindfolded and hoisted on to a horse. When the animal started to trot the pain from the wound in his right thigh caused him to wince. Every step increased the discomfort until the jolting became unbearable. He soon was past the point of caring where he was being taken, or for what reason. To have the horse stop juddering beneath him was his only concern.

He had lost track of how far they had travelled, when a shout brought an end to his misery. It was a shout of anger. He heard it again. The voice was familiar. He forced himself to listen. 'Get that bloody blindfold off. Now, you bastards, take it off.' It was Robert's voice. It was impossible. Pain was playing havoc with his mind. 'Stop, now, all of you, and remove that fucking excrescence from his face.' It *was* Robert. Robert was the only man in the world who would use 'excrescence' to describe something unsightly. Hank felt light-headed. His pain disappeared. He felt hands on his head as the blindfold was removed. The light of the midday sun blinded him more completely than the cloth binding. For days he had lived in filtered light and the glare seared his eyes. He heard Robert's voice again.

'Hank?' It was a question of alarmed concern. Sightless, Hank groped down in the direction of the voice and felt for Robert's face. He found it. Robert was real.

'What's up, Hank? Are you blind?

'No, Robert. It's the light. I'm not used to the light. It has blinded me.'

'Can I help you dismount, Captain?'

'That might not be a good idea. I can't walk very well, you see.'

Robert's voice changed. 'Have these bastards been abusing you?'

'No. I'm not at my tap-dancing best, that's all.'

'Well, you just sit there for a moment, let your eyes adjust to the light and I'll get help.' Robert made a high-pitched whistle. In explanation to the encircling Arabs, he said, 'Don't be alarmed, I'm bringing down two of my men to assist with the Captain.'

Through half-shut eyes Hank could see he was surrounded by

Arabs on horseback. Robert was in the middle of the group, standing by his side, staring up at him. A thousand questions filled his mind. Before he could speak, Robert said, 'Sit there, don't move, I'll be back before you can spit. Okay, Captain?'

'Right on, Sergeant.' He watched Robert and a tall Arab walk towards a truck parked at the side of the pass. They stopped at the front of the vehicle and spoke. He observed both men nod in agreement. Hank looked at the mounted men surrounding him and made a gesture he wished to join the conversing duo. The Arabs merely shrugged. Interpreting this as permission he broke ranks and nudged his horse forward. 'Would you like to tell me what's happening here?' he asked Robert.

Robert looked up at him. 'You're free, Captain. We've struck a deal for your release. We're tying up the loose ends now.'

'What's the deal?'

'The truck, odd equipment and a collection of weapons in exchange for your release. Everything is settled. I'll fill in the details later.'

'I'm not the only prisoner. There are two Germans being held. If you're making a deal let's also try and negotiate their release.' Robert and the Arab looked up at him in confusion. 'It's important to me they're given their freedom,' he explained.

'With respect, sir, *stazitto*.' Robert used the colloquial Italian for 'shut-up' to prevent the Arab understanding the reprimand. Robert was fearful Hank would persist and upset what had already been arranged.

Hank looked down at Robert and nodded. He knew nothing of what had been agreed and was in danger of wrecking whatever bargain had been struck. Impulse had to be controlled. Would he be doing Nightingale a favour by insisting on his freedom? Had Nightingale not voiced many times he was happier in captivity than having to serve in a disintegrating Army? Release would only ensnare him in a harsher form of detention. Hank decided to take Robert's advice and shut-up.

'That would be impossible to arrange,' the Arab announced. 'The German Colonel is being held to bargain the release of our leader, Bourguiba.'

Robert looked up at Hank. 'Is that clear enough for you, Captain?'

'Right,' said Hank.

Robert returned his attention to the Arab. 'If not used with care some of this equipment may expose your men to risk.'

'Your concern does you credit, but your offer to train our men must be declined'

'In that case, let me point out items that must be handled with caution.' The men walked to the rear of the truck. Hank nudged his horse to follow. Robert loosened the side bolts and allowed the back flap to fall with a crash. The two men scrambled on to the platform and disappeared into the interior of the vehicle. Hank heard Robert begin to explain the advantages and disadvantages of the weaponry. After several minutes Hank decided to interrupt. 'Robert,' he called through the canvas.

'Yeah?' he heard Robert's voice answer.

'Can I speak with you?' There was silence. 'Just for a minute?' Hank requested, again.

'Okay, Captain,' replied a weary voice. Robert jumped down from the transport and squinted up at Hank. 'What is it?'

'The Arab hasn't a clue what you're talking about.'

Robert looked at the truck and returned his attention to Hank. He pointed to his mouth and soundlessly shaped, 'I know. Who cares?'

'I have a suggestion,' Hank said, loud and clear. 'Tell the Arabs to use the Germans to instruct them in the use of the material you're supplying.'

Robert was confused. Hank seemed obsessed with the fate of enemy prisoners instead of his own release. If he continued in this vein the Arabs could lose patience and the deal fall apart.

The tall Arab jumped down from the truck and looked up at Hank. 'You reason well, Captain,' he said, 'but the German officer may refuse to assist.'

'Give him some status while he is with you. Begin to treat him with respect, not as a common servant. You are fortunate to have in your custody a respected *Wehrmacht* officer and if you recruit his help you will find he can do more than just show you how to use a few weapons, he will be able to instruct you on how to improve your entire military efficiency. Treat him with the respect he's due and he will repay your consideration with invaluable military advice.'

Robert looked at the Arab to gage his reaction. The Arab merely inclined his head and looked into the distance.

'I have more to say.' It was Hank, again. 'If, as I suspect, the German High Command refuse to release your leader, what do you intend to do with your prisoners? Execute them? Hold them for ever?'

'That is a matter for our Conseil to decide.'

'Do they realise the Germans will reject your demand out of hand?'

'I know this in my heart. Our leader Bourguiba never will be released until this war you wage in our territory is over.'

'Even then they may hold him. Go back to your Conseil and tell them I intend to deposit one million dollars in a Swiss Bank with the instruction the money is paid to the Neo Desour when the two prisoners you hold are granted their freedom. The Proviso for payment will state only two conditions. One, that the prisoners must not be released, I repeat, *must not be released* from your custody until the cessation of hostilities between the Allied and Axis powers, and two, upon release proof must be furnished as to identity and a statement received to confirm their reasonable treatment throughout the period of captivity. You will receive confirmation of this offer through existing diplomatic channels. When the million dollars is deposited for transfer a Promissory Note will be sent to your Headquarters. This should be in your possession within a month. Its arrival will be proof of my probity.'

The Arab was thunderstruck. Robert was stunned. Neither man could believe what they had heard.

Robert was first to explode. 'Two hundred and fifty thousand quid! Have you gone mad? Take it easy, Hank, you're disorientated. What you're suggesting is preposterous.'

'I've never been more serious. I owe my life to a German soldier. This is the only way I have of repaying my debt to him.'

'You're overreacting, Hank.'

'You're wrong, Robert. I know exactly what I'm doing. It must seem nuts to you, I know, but I'll explain everything later.'

The tall Arab stepped forward. 'You must be very rich that you can afford to dispense such largess on a whim?'

'I am,' said Hank.

'I believe you. You have the look of an honest man.'

'Thank you. It's an essential requirement for a banker in New York to have an honest face. American bankers strive to develop the look early in their careers.' Hank's humour broke the tension. They laughed.

When the mirth subsided the Arab unbuckled his sword and stretched to present it to Hank. 'I give you this as a token of trust and admiration. Your advice has uncovered my eyes and your generosity refreshed my spirit. Be assured, the men of the Neo Destour will tell their children of your nobility. You have given Tunisia new hope by an act of benevolence of historic significance. You are a man of true Praetorian spirit and your name forever will be revered within our ranks. I swear to obey and fulfil, your every desire.' He bowed his head as he presented the sword.

'Thank you,' said Hank, as he accepted the memento. Feeling awkward and sensing some correct, formal gesture was lacking, he thrust out his right hand and said, 'Let's shake on it.'

Hank and the Arab solemnly shook hands.

Robert scratched his head.

* * *

It was late afternoon when fatigue and hunger persuaded them to interrupt their journey to Kasserine. A shaded indent of land was selected as a suitable spot to camp for the night. Safe from the attentions of the Neo Destour and the threat of German forces, they relaxed with exchanges of noisy humour. A fire was lit from collected brushwood and with the luxury of unaccustomed hot water they washed, shaved and unhurriedly settled to a meal of US field rations. The mood was celebratory and charged with self-satisfaction. After a while the caressing warmth of the evening sun settled them into mood of somnolent inactivity. The chatter became more desultory and Hank was first to fall asleep.

Joe had never been happier. The relaxed company and the friendly banter, reminded him of a long-ago time spent among his family in the isolated, sun-scorched regions of his homeland. He listened to the *sotto voce* conversations between Lance and Robert. Lance was explaining he had entertained serious doubts about whether to comply when he had heard Robert's whistle to break cover and come down from the hill.

'If you were honest you would admit to having had doubts about the entire exercise,' Robert chided. 'Admit it, all along you thought it was too dangerous to attempt.'

'Dangerous, yes, but when did that ever stop us?' They shared a smile.

'Success in everything is in the preparation,' explained Robert.

'So you say, but it meant taking one hell of a risk.'

'We were never in any real danger.'

'Oh, no? It didn't look like that from where I was watching,' Lance exclaimed.

'But then you always were a calculating, careful, sod.'

'Sensible, rounded and pragmatic, that's me. Impulsive, impatient and certifiable, that's you,' Lance proclaimed. A snort of derision ended the conversation.

'You did well, Joe,' Robert said, turning his attention from Lance.

Joe beamed. He was wallowing in a mood of hero-worship. To be thought of, and accepted, as a comrade to men he venerated was an honour beyond his comprehension. 'My hand not shake once, Robert,' he said with genuine pride. 'When I hear the whistle I come down at once.'

'By the time you both arrived everything had been stitched-up. Hank's private agenda was the real clincher.'

'I no let you down no more,' Joe blurted. 'Before I always too frightened. Watching you both, I get brave. Now, I be a better soldier.'

'That's good, Joe,' Robert said, in quick sympathy. 'Just remember that promise when we get to Sicily, if ever we get there that is.'

'Hank won't be coming with us,' Lance announced. 'He's no longer in a fit state for active service.'

'Why not wait and see what the Medics have to say before jumping to conclusions,' Robert suggested.

'If he come I look after him,' volunteered Joe.

'We must take him,' Robert said, 'even if we have to carry him. I tell you, Lance, this guy's a blitzkrieg negotiator. He'll have the Sicilians eating out of our hands in no time.' He turned to Joe. 'We'll see to it he's pampered, won't we, Joe?'

Joe was in his seventh heaven. He was so happy he was near to tears. 'We look after him,' he said.

'It's not for us to decide,' Lance said. 'Tomorrow we'll deliver Hank to the Field Hospital in Kasserine and if they see fit to release him he can come, if not, too bad. It's as simple as that. We'll also have to report our whereabouts and the reason for our delay. Our landing in Sicily will have to be rescheduled, weapons and gear reissued and contacts renewed. The whole bloody palaver will have to be rejigged and that's going to take a couple of days, at least.'

'By that time Hank might be tap-dancing like Fred Astaire,' Robert remarked.

The phrase was strange to Joe's ear. The remark contained unfamiliar words, words he had never heard before. He wondered what they could mean? He decided he would never know. Despite this, he clapped his hands in agreement.

* * *

It had been a boring morning at Divisional Headquarters. In the unaccustomed slack atmosphere Cowboy had settled to the dreary necessity of clearing the clutter of paper covering his desk. It was a task for secretaries and minions, but had the usefulness of keeping at bay the anger felt after reading the news from home. The communiqué announcing Captain Hancock Remington's kidnap had caused an outbreak of adverse comment to appear in the columns of the New York Times. What else could be expected from the 'stay-at-home' scribblers of the American journalist fraternity? Already the rumourmongers were grovelling in a mud of futility in their attempts to uncover chicanery. Bastards! The expected front-page news of the kidnap had been demoted to a demeaning mention on page five. Page five! What an insult.

In the column 'Reports from the Fronts' uncertainty was expressed as to the authenticity of the news that Hancock Remington, Chairman Elect of the Remington Bartholemew Bank, was being held hostage by a group of hostile Tunisian terrorists. The journalist had written, 'If true, how timely and convenient for one aspiring banker in New York.' Mercifully, he had not mentioned Bobby's name. The article continued, 'If this rumour is proved false, then a new type of anti-democratic ethic is at work in the higher echelons of finance.' The columnist 'Jack' had signed off with the sentence, 'Watch this space'. Well, confirmation of Remington's incarceration will put your pipe in a peep 'Jack', whoever you are. Cowboy made a mental note to remember the name and resolved on return to New York to arrange this smart-ass 'Jack' suffer some suitable comeuppance. 'Jack' indeed, never heard of the swine. Probably he'd be a jumped-up social crony of the Remington family, or a contented shareholder loyal to the Remington dynasty.

There was no denying in the past the Remingtons had been good for the Bank. For over a hundred years the family had toiled to build a business of unmatchable fidelity. Old grandfather Hamish had been a solemn-faced swine, but had ruled during a period when banking had required men of dour integrity, men of strict probity, mirthless men of undeviating, Presbyterian incorruptibility. Banking had changed. Daddy Remington had recognised this phenomenon. He, also, had been a miserable sod, but had been far-seeing enough to move with the times. Neither had he been averse to putting his own interests before that of the depositors. In an underhand manner, but legally, he had manipulated his position to acquire a personal fortune. Clever man, never openly dishonest, but, nevertheless, had been a foxy, acquisitive, anti-social creep of the first water. Had his son, the young pretender, not rebelled and volunteered himself into the Army his elevation would have been secure. It would have been a disaster for the Bank.

Freewill is Forfeit

Young Remington's attitude to the wealthier client did not recommend him as the right type of material for high position. His social life, too, left much to be desired. His attitudes offended the respectable, ambitious, Republican depositor.

There was one loose end, however, still to be concluded, the satisfying business of issuing a principled refusal to the terrorists holding the Remington brat. Cowboy pressed a button to summon his orderly. When he arrived Cowboy asked, 'When is the camel-riding Arab due to make an appearance?

'He should have been here yesterday, sir, according to your diary.'

'Strange,' said Cowboy. 'That's all, dismiss.'

'Will you lunch at the Mess today, sir?' asked the orderly before leaving.

'Only if the menu is half-way decent.'

'I'll bring it in, sir.'

'And the wine list.'

The Arab's non-appearance was annoying. Usually men who held diplomatic rank made a fetish of honouring appointments. Etiquette was part of their meticulous code. Even a two-bit nig-nog like Ben whatever-his-name-was should have had the courtesy to apologise for absence. But, Bobby Braithwaite had nothing to fear. He would have little trouble securing the support to usurp the inherited rights of an imprisoned mediocrity The Remington demise, finally, was nigh. *Quod erat demonstrandum.*

The telephone rang. He lifted the receiver. 'Sir, there's an Arab asking to see you,' a voice informed him.

'Is it the expected envoy?'

'No, sir.'

'Well, who is he?'

'I don't know, sir. He's accompanied by three soldiers.'

'What kind of soldiers?'

'British Army soldiers.'

'What rank, man?'

'A Major, a Sergeant and a Corporal, sir.'

'Ask them why they need to see me.' He waited.

'On a matter of some urgency, sir,' the voice declared.

'What type of urgency?' Exasperation loomed. He waited, again. 'A secret type, sir.'

This was the last straw. 'Tell them to report to the Officer-of-the-day and don't trouble me again with idle requests.' He slammed the receiver into its cradle.

The telephone rang again. He heard a terrified voice say, 'I'm sorry, sir, but the Arab insists I tell you his name is Remington.'

* * *

Hank stopped at the door marked 'Brigadier General Thomson'. Before he knocked he turned to face the others.

'Well, here we go,' he said and took a deep breath.

'Good luck,' said Lance. Robert gave the thumbs-up sign and Joe smiled his broken toothed support.

'I'll do my best,' Hank muttered and knocked on the door. A voice called 'Enter'. When they obeyed they saw a portly figure stride towards them with outstretched hand.

'Come in, come in, and a thousand welcomes,' the General said and shook Hank's hand. He ignored the presence of the others. No remark was made about Hank's strange attire, or the general dishevelment of the squad.

Hank thought the General looked agitated. Perhaps the old boy had been hitting the bottle. He had a reputation of going off the rails now and again. He looked twitchy and his complexion was florid. He appeared ill-at-ease.

'It's very good of you to see us, sir.' Hank knew Cowboy approved of the standard courtesies. Cowboy believed politeness was the measure that distinguished the gentleman from those who lacked breeding.

'Think nuthin' of it, ma boy. It's a real pleasure to see ya again.' As an afterthought, he turned and nodded at the ramrod figures of Lance, Robert and Joe. 'Sir,' they responded in unison. Cowboy struggled to hide his disapproval of the British military correctness, but failed. That he should have to entertain such low rank soldiers, who resembled a troupe from a circus rather than a troop of serving men-at-arms, put a strain on his tolerance. He returned his

Freewill is Forfeit

attention to Hank. 'Heard you men had gone missin',' he said.

'It's a long story, sir. We were delayed by. . .'

'I know what you're about to say,' Cowboy interrupted. 'You were apprehended by a mob of terrorists. I have ma ear pretty close to the ground, ya know. I like to keep a check on all ma boys. It's only befittin'.'

'It's behind us now, sir,' Hank cut in. 'The vexation is, the delay has endangered our mission.'

'Vexation'? Had the Army become a breeding ground for clever-dicks? 'And no bad thing in my opinion,' Cowboy managed to say. 'As ya already know I've never bin a wholehearted supporter of your military escapade.'

'The plain fact is, sir, we need your help to get us back on track,' Hank announced.

'I don't think I understand. You want me to assist you to remount your operation knowin' I disapprove of the whole shmozzle. Is that it?'

'I would remind you, sir, it is an approved Allied venture under the auspices of the Special Operations Executive.' Hank saw an expression on Cowboy's face he couldn't quite decipher. Was it uncertainty? He appeared worried, hesitant. Perhaps it was nothing more than annoyance at being disturbed. Something was causing discomfort.

The General turned and walked to his desk. Before sitting he gestured to his subordinates they had his permission to be seated. Hank looked over at his three comrades and reassured them with a wink.

When settled the General looked up from a thoughtful pose and asked with neutral formality, 'When were you released, Captain Remington?'

'Yesterday, sir.'

'And by what means?'

'By the forceful persuasions of Major Bennett, sir.' Hank gave the General a broad smile.

Cowboy looked over at Lance. 'No doubt by unorthodox methods, knowin' your reputation, Major.' There was no smile.

'In this instance it's our Sergeant who must take the credit for

Captain Remington's release. When motivated he can be quite persuasive,' contributed Lance. Robert squirmed while suffering the disapproving stare of the General.

'We're a team, sir,' Robert said in explanation. 'We look after each other's interests.'

'Indeed,' said Cowboy, sniffing at the scene of collective satisfaction. He was never fully at ease with non-commissioned ranks. He returned his attention to Hank. 'And in what manner do ya' think I might be able to assist?'

'By arranging our immediate dispatch to Sicily,' Hank stated.

The request took Cowboy by surprise. It was not beyond his remit to organise air transport and have this comic assembly dispatched to their dubious task, but if he were to implement their request he would place himself in danger of being accused of manipulation by elements of the smart-Alex watchdogs of the American press. Hancock Remington was alive, well and free. The news, when it reached New York, would destroy Bobby Braithwaite's ambition of ever claiming the coveted position of Chairman. It might even destroy his entire future career. The gamble had come to grief. It was time to change horses mid-stream, or face the danger of being swept away on the same tide of derision soon to engulf his erstwhile conspirator. Self-protection had to be exercised. 'As already mentioned your operation is under the control of the Special Operations Executive and I would advise before ya' hot-footed off to Sicily that contact be re-established with London. Under present circumstances they may wish to abort the operation.'

'I agree under normal circumstances that would be the correct procedure, but in this instance, in order to avoid the risk of cancellation, or possible recall, we considered the alternative of making representation to you. It has the advantage of eliminating the frustration of further delay,' Hank pleaded.

The time had come for Cowboy to make his move. He hardened his tone. 'Let's face it, ya've made a balls-up of the operation entrusted to yer collective responsibility. It will take weeks to reorganise this mission, but rather than face the inconvenience of proper procedure ya've come to me in the hope I'll agree to re-

Freewill is Forfeit

implement a military operation I've considered from the outset to be a degenerate exercise. No, I'll not assist you in this matter. Instead,' he swivelled in his chair to face Lance, 'you, Major, are ordered to report to British Command Headquarters and make them aware of your incompetence. Further, you will make contact with the SOE and await their further instructions.' He swivelled to face Hank. 'As reported, you have bin wounded and have suffered the trauma of imprisonment. It may be judged you are now unfit for duty. You will report to the Medical Centre for examination and inform them I want the results on ma desk by six o'clock tomorrow night.' Cowboy sat back in his chair and looked at each man in turn. 'Now, dismiss, all of ya.'

The four men stood in unison, came to attention, turned to their right and commenced to march towards the door. As they were about to exit the room Cowboy called out to Hank, 'Remember to send ma regards to your mother, Hancock. A sterlin' woman who should be praised for all the work she does for the boys at the front.'

'I'll remember to do that, sir,' Hank lied, knowing his mother hadn't done a day's work in her entire life.

13

The night was warm and windless. A full moon cast its light over a landscape of mystical shapes. Enrico Verga looked out at the scene from a slumped position against a wall. He was unaware of the surrounding beauty. He was depressed. He had no funds, property, prospects or sustaining employment. At twenty-three he felt himself to be a parasite, a nonentity, an encumbrance to himself and all who knew him. It was the second time he had trudged to this place. It was thought his dedication to duty was admirable but, in truth, although never would he admit it, a shrewish wife had made the sharing of the matrimonial bed a torment. That he should feel like this after only three months of marriage intensified his sense of failure.

He had no idea when it was his life had started to fall apart. Perhaps it was when Mussolini had made his pact with Hitler and the first Identification Cards were issued. Under 'Description of Occupation', *'Contadino'* had been typed instead of *'Studente'*. He had been selected to attend Rome University to study languages, English and French, yet despite this achievement he continued to be categorised as 'Peasant'. All prospects he had of studying in the Eternal City had been scuppered by the outbreak of war. Unarguably, he was a handy man to have around a farm, but helping neighbours at harvest time, or periods of difficulty, did not warrant the title *'Contadino'* to be emblazoned on his documents for all to see and judge him by. Later, when conscripted into the Army he ceased to be identified as a peasant and was given a number. He became '308', the last three digits of a long Regimental number. He wondered if this new identity description was promotion, or demotion, from the rank of *'Contadino'*. After thought he decided it was demotion. To obtain an accurate description of self in Italian society seemed to be a matter of either bureaucratic chance or enigmatic coincidence.

All in all he had enjoyed Army life. It had introduced him to the intricate workings of the internal combustion engine. His learned skills granted him his first taste of significant identity and a rank of improved description. *'Meccanico'* was stamped on his papers, but the price of acquiring this social elevation had been prohibitive. Seldom did he see the azure of an Italian sky during the two years of his apprenticeship, buried as he was in the bowels of clanging workshops.

On the day it was announced the Battalion was to ready itself for duty in North Africa, he deserted. He simply walked out of the Barracks, never to return. Five miles from the Camp he shed his uniform, changed into civilian clothes – taken from a line of washing – and set out to walk home. It took him two months; one month to walk from Foggia to Reggio di Calabria and another to cross the Straits of Messina and make his way home to Raddusa. On arrival he explained to family and friends he had been discharged from the Army for medical reasons. 'Feet' he had said, pointing down at swollen and blistered appendages. The fact he had walked several hundred miles was never questioned as being the probable reason for the sorry condition of his feet.

First of the young men to return from war duty, Enrico was treated to a hero's welcome. Local dignitaries made speeches in his honour, proclaiming their high regard for duty bravely accomplished and, without embarrassment, continued to pontificate on how dedication to the burdens of civic duty had been the central plank of their own success in life. Old men in their shuffling years merely clapped his back in silent approval, no doubt, remembering their own past experiences of war and the indignities of military life. Motherly women in their determination to spoil him were undeviating in their attentions. Meals were delivered in such generous amounts that, after a short time, the un-eaten feasts began to endanger the immediate area of his shack being declared a hazard to health.

The reception he received from the younger women satisfied an appetite of a different form. Starved of male companionship *le ragazze* were voracious in their attentions. They enveloped him. He experienced the elation of being the honoured guest at a never-ending feast. Dishes of succulent variety decorated his life and he gorged mightily. For three months he wandered around in a state of sated delirium, but it was not to last. Intemperance has its price and always dawns the day when settlement is demanded.

A dumpy maiden called Francesca delivered the bill for his long debauch. In his menu of tastes he had categorised her as a soup course. She had been his little Miss Minestrone. The price she demanded was matrimony. She was pregnant, or so she protested. Honourably, he consented to marriage knowing the settlement would bankrupt his heart. He wed her the following week and by that deed immediately forfeited his position at the feasting board he had so omnivorously occupied. All the preferred sweetmeats he had sampled remained in daily view, each had a flavour of distinctive piquancy to torment the memory, but no longer were they available to assuage the hungers of his now under-nourished heart. Purgatory. It was little wonder he was depressed.

Following his impulsive decision to desert from the Army his self-esteem had plummeted. He had had enough. It was as simple as that. The Army had made him a creature of the night, a benign Dracula. He was a sunshine boy, not a mole. Besides, Africa was a no-no. There had been too many frightening stories of terrible hardships having to be suffered by the ordinary soldier. Tales of inexcusable incompetence, of non-existing supplies, of ill-preparedness for battle, of low morale, of disarray and disagreement at officer level, of desertions and field executions, of widespread disease and lack of medical provision to care for the wounded and dying; and always the concluding advice of those who had served, 'Don't go. Do anything to avoid being posted to a shambles that promises nothing but death and disgrace'. North Africa? Thank you, no! Rather to suffer the inconveniences of a fugitive life at home than perish, uselessly, in a foreign land for a cause that already was lost.

During his two months southwest trek across the boot of Italy

Freewill is Forfeit

Enrico had his first brush with men dedicated to Communism. Having to beg food at the end of each day's march often found him in the company of wandering malcontents, men who lived at the edges of society. Many of them were fellow deserters, or men who had fled their homes to avoid call-up, but unlike him, most had chosen their renegade existence motivated by the conviction that fascism was an evil that had to be opposed. Disciples of obscure political philosophies, believers in universal brotherhood, idealists, intellectuals, iconoclasts of every persuasion and social misfits of every kind gathered in out-of-the-way places to share food, clothing and whatever else was required to sustain the basic needs of their miserable lives. They shared a common stock of scavenged necessities. They knew him to be a deserter and assumed his transgression had been triggered by a conscientious objection brought on by political disillusionment. He became a familiar face within the esoteric circles of their brotherhood.

By association with men who provided him with shelter and sustenance, it was assumed, naturally, but incorrectly, that he was a committed anti-fascist who harboured a smouldering hate of the existing oligarchy. Had he admitted he had no interest in their political theories, or worse, he thought their incessant chatter merely a display of flummery, it would have deprived him of their succour. To be passed, day-by-day, and in relative safety, through a network of disillusioned politicos was reason enough to maintain a tolerant silence. After all, he was given sound advice on how to evade arrest, where and when it was safe to travel and above all, the trust and protection of staunch zealots. He would have lied to his grandmother for less.

Several weeks after his return home, despite his desire never to hear from, or have further contact with, any of their number, he had been approached and reminded of his debt to those who had saved him from the clutches of the Imperial executioners. He was informed he owed his life to the charity of the comrades and in return it would be expected of him, occasionally, to assist in acts of subversion against the evils of Plutocratic rule.

He wondered if it was cynicism that prevented him sympathising with his new comrades' political enthusiasms. He was convinced that Communism, both in practice and in theory, was a pipe dream envisioned by romantic fools. Never could it work. Humankind was too flawed, too lacking in altruistic sentiment for it ever to succeed. Greed, lust for power, ego, jealousy, all the myriad faults of mankind, would surface to destroy the ideal.

But since everything in life has to be paid for, with self-esteem if nothing else, he agreed to assist his unlawful comrades and promised to be available for whatever nefarious duty was required of him. What did it matter? As he was classified as a 'Fugitive from Law' he might just as well participate in fugitive activity.

He had come to this secluded spot once before and had waited in vain for the arrival of men who were to be dropped by parachute and escorted to a designated house in the adjacent valley. His instructions could not have been simpler. 'Wait, meet and escort the arrivals, then bugger-off home. Do it quietly and secretly. Understand?' His fellow conspirator then had enquired, 'I hear you got married recently, is this true?'

'Yes. It's true.'

'Your wife's curiosity might be aroused. . .'

'No,' he interrupted, 'I regularly go for walks at night. I don't seem able to break Army habits.'

'She doesn't know about your. . .?' He left the word 'desertion' unspoken.

'No. She knows nothing and will never know.'

'Not unless the *Fascisti* come looking for you, but as time passes this seems less likely to happen. There are too many of our kind for the authorities to know what to do, or even where to start, to solve the problem of desertion. It has become a fashionable activity, it seems.' As he turned to leave he had said, 'See to it, Enrico. 0300 hours, Thursday morning and for all our sakes, make certain nothing goes wrong.' At the time Enrico had wondered what he could have meant by the remark.

Enrico scanned the sky once more. Nothing. The night was soundless. He looked at his watch. It was 0310 hours. He decided to wait another twenty minutes then make tracks for home. He'd be there before Franscesca rose.

Had he been sent on another wild-goose-chase? Perhaps the

Freewill is Forfeit

Brothers merely were testing his reliability and obedience? Then Enrico saw a startling sight. Two hundred metres from where he sat a man and a woman appeared in the middle of the field. They stood up and hand in hand started to make their way towards the road more than two kilometres to the north. Lovers, he thought, lovers who had sought the sanctuary of isolation, and the luxury of rich pasture, for their nocturnal dalliance.

He looked at his wristwatch, once more. It was 0332 hours and time to go home. He rose and bent to rub the stiffened muscles in his legs. When he straightened he thought he heard the faint sound of distant thunder. He decided he would have to quicken his pace if he was to avoid the coming storm. Then he realised it was an aeroplane in the distance. This was not a test of obedience, after all. It was a *bona fide* duty. Enrico watched as an American DC3 took form in the night sky. Its approach was low and thunderous and, as suddenly as it had appeared, it was gone.

It was then he saw the parachutes. It was a beautiful, magical sight in the clear, moonlit, silent spaces of the heavens. It had all the solemnity, mystery and wonder of Gods being delivered to earth. He ran to the middle of the meadow to await their descent.

The first of the heavenly passengers landed fifty metres to his right. He sprinted through the long grass and stopped to watch a figure struggle with unruly, billowing silk. When he decided to step forward to assist he heard a voice from behind say, '*Sei Enrico?*' and he turned to face an armed man.

'*Si, signore, sono Enrico. Benvenuti in Sicilia,*' he replied.

The man ignored the welcome and walked past him to assist his struggling companion. Enrico heard him say in English, 'For Christ sake, get that bloody thing under control.'

They were British troops. What in the name of God had he got himself into? They were spies. They were the enemy. 'See to it that nothing goes wrong'. Well, already everything was wrong. Desertion was one thing, but actively to assist the enemy within spitting distance of his home was another matter entirely. He was unsure what to do. Probably he would be shot if he attempted to flee. He decided to co-operate until an opportunity arose when he could disappear in safety.

'*Rimini qui, ritorno fra poco. Capisci?*' the man said.

'I speak English,' Enrico blurted and immediately regretted the admission.

'Good. Well, you wait here, I'll be back in a minute.' The man repeated as he walked off to locate the third member of his group.

Enrico returned his attention to the bulky figure tidying a troublesome parachute into a manageable bundle. The figure looked over at him and smiled. Despite feeling aggrieved he smiled in return. A few moments later he heard a whistle and turned to see the Englishman beckon him with an over-arm gesture. When he responded to the summons he was handed a small spade. 'Dig' the man said. Enrico looked at him in disbelief. 'Dig a hole, man'. Enrico questioned the order by raising an eyebrow. 'The parachutes,' it was explained, 'they've to be buried'. It was a command, not a request. No sign of a 'please', or 'would you mind', nothing as civilised. It was the barked order of a superior addressing a peasant.

'You wish me to dig a hole with this?' Enrico held up the small military field spade and shaped a derisive smile. 'It will take all night.'

'They have to be got rid off'

'I understand,' Enrico soothed. 'They can be concealed for the moment. They can be buried at a later date, when it's safe.' He made a performance of looking at his watch. 'If we do not leave now it will be impossible for me to deliver you to your destination before dawn.'

'What you say makes sense,' the man admitted.

'If you gather your parachutes and follow me, I'll show you where they can be safely hidden.' After concealing the bundles of silk in the nearby wood, Enrico made a gesture he was to be followed and strode off. After a while he glanced over his shoulder and saw three figures in line following his lead.

Fifteen minutes later and still in line, they arrived at the spot where Enrico had left his tractor. He stopped and waited until they were grouped around him. 'There's a tarpaulin in the trailer. If you wish to remain hidden you can cover yourselves with it. We have a further ten kilometres to travel.'

'How long will it take in this contraption?' The Englishman, obviously, was dissatisfied with the transport.

'Half-an-hour, perhaps a little longer.' Enrico watched as they loaded their military equipment. He knew before the tractor journey was complete they would be cursing in discomfort. Without the luxury of suspension the trailer would rattle their snotty English bones to the point of breaking before they arrived at the destination. These foreign interlopers would experience the discomfort a Sicilian peasant feels at the end of each working day. Broken, used and abused.

Enrico settled to his drive. It would not be long before he was home. At his next meeting with the Brothers he would object to having been used for espionage purposes. He would announce that in the future he would refuse to become involved in traitorous activity. He did not object to participating in skulduggery, but to be placed in a position of having to help foreign spies was a treasonous act and an unacceptable insult to his patriotic sentiments. He may bear the stigma of possessing many dubious identities, 'peasant', '308', 'mechanic', 'husband', 'deserter', but never did he want to be categorised as 'traitor'. It was too disgraceful, too demeaning. He'd rather be hanged for rape than be accused of espionage. At present it was beyond comprehension he found himself trundling along a rutted road at four o'clock in the morning delivering an arrogant Englishman and his two minions into the protection of one of his own quisling neighbours. Was nothing in his life ever going to improve? Was he doomed forever to inhabit the gutter, a shameful victim of his own ineptitude?

In the early morning gloom he saw lights ahead. At first he presumed it was a labourer setting out for work. As the lights came nearer he began to pray the vehicle approaching was not travelling on the same lane. If they should meet it would entail the usual argument over who had right-of-way and whose duty it was to reverse. Enrico stopped the tractor. The tarpaulin folded back. He said, 'I think a vehicle is approaching and we're travelling on a single-track.' The reaction was immediate. He watched his passengers throw their weapons and equipment to the side of the road, leap from the trailer and take up concealed positions on each side of the track. Enrico heard a male voice calmly instruct, 'Drive forward fifty metres and stop. Avoid having to reverse if you can, but, if it becomes necessary, return to collect us when you're certain everything is clear.'

With a pounding heart Enrico drove forward and stopped. He could see what he feared was about to happen. The vehicle approaching was no more than two hundred metres away and heading directly towards him. He took several deep breaths and waited. He heard singing, then drunken voices. He felt relief. Drunks usually were easy to deal with. Returning from some celebration they would be good-humoured and incurious. The singing ceased and he heard the word *'Gastarbeiter'* being shouted. It was a word he had never heard. It was a German word. Jesus, Mary and Joseph, they were Germans. Were they demanding that he reverse?

A small four-seater, open-topped, military utility came to a halt ten paces in front of the tractor. The passenger threw a leg over the side of the vehicle and stepped out. He was wearing a German sergeant's uniform. The soldier sauntered forward and made a mock examination of the tractor and trailer. He looked back at his companion and laughed. The laughter was returned. The sergeant, still smiling, motioned to Enrico to dismount. In the grip of mental dysfunction and dry-mouthed terror, Enrico obeyed. The ability to think had deserted him. Nothing was real. Normal co-ordination and thought were impossible. Hypnotised, he watched the sergeant's scrambled attempts to board the tractor. When successful he beamed down at Enrico with a look of pride. His companion applauded the intoxicated achievement. The sergeant rose and made a bow. Enrico was spellbound. He watched as the German raised his arms as if making an appeal for the attention of some invisible audience. The gesture announced his next feat was to be a wonder of unbelievable dexterity. Slowly, with the exaggerated care of a drunk, he leaned forward, focused with difficulty and lowered his right arm in a theatrical sweep. He turned the ignition key. The engine started to rumble. The companion, dazzled by the brilliance of this performance, applauded once more and yelled his admiration by bursting into sudden Italian. *'Bravo, bravo.'* he screamed.

Encouraged by this reaction the sergeant was in a mood to surpass himself. He gestured with his hands his *pièce de résistance* would be to engage gear and drive the offending tractor and trailer off the road to its certain destruction. The companion German started to howl with pleasure in anticipation of what he was about to witness. He reversed his vehicle to give his sergeant room to manoeuvre and sat back to enjoy the promised finale.

Enrico found his voice, *'Per favore, non può fare questo'* he said. The companion dismounted and staggered towards him. He stopped in front of Enrico and gave him a glazed smile; then delivered a vicious uppercut. Enrico felt his head explode with pain. His legs buckled and he fell backwards. He became aware of being kicked. A burst of machinegun fire sounded and his assailant fell by his side. Enrico heard himself yelp with fear as he struggled to his feet. The sergeant on the tractor looked down at the scene in disbelief. He spun round to peer in the direction of the gunfire. He saw an armed man waiting. The figure spoke. *'Auf Wiedersehen, Fritz,'* the man said. It was the last thing the sergeant heard as a single bullet entered his heart.

Enrico was in shock and near to hysteria. In a haze of unreality he watched the executioner's companions walk towards the mayhem. For a while they stood in a group and looked down in silence at the result of the slaughter. He heard an accusing voice say, 'Was that necessary'? 'Yes', he heard being affirmed. A resigned sounding, 'I see', followed.

The executioner turned his attention to Enrico. 'Are you hurt?' he asked.

Never having felt worse, Enrico replied, 'I'm fine.'

'Good, in that case you can help me load these bodies on to the trailer.' While struggling with the corpses the executioner said to the watching soldiers, 'Don't just stand there, get rid of the blood. Mop it up with anything you can find. I want no trace left that these bastards were ever here. Do it,' he ordered. He turned to Enrico and barked, 'How far south of here is Lake dell' Ogliastro?'

'Not far,' was all Enrico managed to say.

'How far and in what direction?' The voice was abrupt.

Feeling he was about to vomit Enrico swallowed hard and tried to concentrate. 'About four kilometres south of here.'

'If I drove due south would I find it?'

'Yes, but there's no track from here.'

'Good,' the man replied. 'Are there obstructions of any kind?' Enrico looked blank. 'Are there cliffs, woods, or the like, between here and the lake?'

'No, just open land.'

'Perfect. This is what we'll do. I'll take the German vehicle and dispose of it, while you proceed to the destination with my friends. When that is accomplished you will return here by foot. You and I will meet,' he stopped to look around, 'there.' He pointed to a tree about thirty metres from where they stood. 'Understand?'

Enrico, panting with the effort of dragging his ex-assailant on to the trailer, dropped his burden and protested, 'You wish me to return here?'

'Just as soon as you can. I should be back here by daylight. How long will it take you to return?'

'I not want to return here in daylight.' Enrico pleaded. 'I do a favour for friends. I deliver your men, but I not come back.' Under stress his careful English was beginning to break up. He suffered the executioner's stare for several seconds.

When the man spoke, he said, 'You will do as I tell you, or be reported to the German authorities as a spy. Do you understand me?' He looked at his watch. 'You will meet me here at 0700 hours.'

The executioner vaulted from the trailer and bent to speak to his comrades. When he straightened, he strode towards the German utility, started the engine, turned the steering wheel and at pace catapulted over a bank and ditch to disappear from view. Without a word his two comrades mounted the trailer, made a final check to ascertain all was as it should be and slumped down beside the corpses. Enrico remounted the tractor to continue the journey.

Fifteen minutes later they arrived at the cottage. An old man was waiting at the door. He ran forward to meet the approaching tractor. One of the soldiers leapt from the trailer and ran towards him. Enrico watched as they embraced. Following a protracted conversation the old man walked forward, shook hands with the other soldier and mounted the trailer. He indicated to Enrico to drive forward. They left the road and bumped over rough ground. Several minutes later they came to a disused well. The old man dismounted and without assistance, dropped two bodies into the foul-smelling darkness of the long abandoned watering hole. When his task was finished he remounted the trailer and made a gesture they return to the cottage.

On arrival Enrico followed the old man into the house. When he entered what he saw would remain etched in his brain for a lifetime. Standing before him was a Madonna with glowing dark hair. He gazed at her in awe. She smiled over at him and said, '*Grasie, Enrico*, you have done much in our service.' Never had he encountered such beauty. He was entranced.

Another voice spoke. It said, 'Come, I will bathe your head.' He turned. Eyes of translucent green mesmerised his brain. Tresses of burnished gold filled his sight. The seraphic vision approached and took him by the hand. He allowed himself to be led to a chair. A basin of water was produced and laid on the table. He watched in a daze of wonder. He was to be anointed by angels. Water splashed on his head. He was being welcomed into their ethereal assembly by the rite of baptism. Goddesses were performing a ceremony of solemn sanctification. A strange sensation overwhelmed him. He had a mystical premonition that following the anointing his life would never again be exposed to unrewarding, unsatisfying, anonymous drudgery.

* * *

Jane and Anna were alone in the main area of the cottage. They sat at a table drinking what purported to be coffee and eating a simple breakfast of bread, cheese and olives. Enrico had departed to fetch David and Grandpa Michele had disappeared with the tractor and trailer to some place where he said it would never be found.

Jane put down her cup and blurted,

'He killed these soldiers in cold blood.' She was angry for harbouring the growing suspicion that David was not the person she had thought him to be.

Anna looked up from her plate. 'He had no choice. He had to do it. Think about it. By acting decisively he removed us from danger.'

'He's different,' Jane said, searching to find an explanation for her uncertain feelings.

'He's a soldier on active service. That's what soldiers do in war, they kill each other.'

'No, he took pleasure from it. I watched his face. He enjoyed the moment. There was triumph in his eyes.'

'What's troubling you? Is the romance cooling off?'

'It's not a romance, it's an affair.'

'You're not in love with David?'

'Love? Good God, no! I like him, but it goes no deeper.'

'You're using him.' It was an accusation.

'Don't be so dramatic. We all use each other in one way or another.'

'Not in that manner,' Anna chastised.

'The world might be a happier place if we did,' Jane teased.

'You'll never change. You're an amoral person,' Anna accused.

'I know. It's one of my better traits,' admitted Jane. They exchanged smiles. They were quiet for a moment. Jane spoke again. Her voice was thoughtful. As if quoting from some scripted passage, she said, 'And then I perceived he was capable of brutality.' She let the words hang in the air. In a lighter vein, she said, 'In all manner of ways he appears to be thoughtful and kind, but suddenly he can change and become unrecognisable, unknowable, a soulless stranger. I believe he is a deeply unhappy person who conceals his wretchedness behind a veneer of bonhomie.'

'Good heavens! I'd hate you to start analysing me.'

Jane jerked out of her thoughtful mood and laughed. 'You simpletons,' she said, 'are the most difficult to analyse.'

'Tell me what you think of grandpa?'

'That's unfair, we've only just met, but he appears to be exactly as I had imagined he would be, old, set in his ways and game for anything to break the monotony of his twilight years.'

'And our contact, Enrico?'

'He's magnificent. So Italian, wears his heart on his sleeve and reacts to everything with a sense of wonder.'

'And very good looking,' added Anna.

'Yes, I suppose you're right.'

'You mean you didn't notice?' Anna challenged.

Jane smiled and surrendered her pretence. 'Of course, I noticed.'

'Poor man, David treated him very badly. Did you see his face when he realised we were females? What a study!'

'He almost collapsed. I distinctly saw his knees buckle.'

'When you bathed his head to remove the blood he was swooning like a teenager.'

'If our instincts are correct I would say we have earned ourselves a trusty admirer.'

'I think you're right.' They lapsed into silence.

Jane was first to speak. 'How do you feel? Frightened?'

'No, not frightened. Apprehensive, and you?' Anna enquired.

'Frankly, I'm not sure. Without the Dexedrine I'd be terrified.' David had requested she not confess to the necessity of drug assistance until the end of the mission but, carelessly, she had let the truth slip out. She glanced hurriedly in Anna's direction to witness her look of surprise.

'Don't worry, as soon as we return home I'll resort to my old habit of smoking cannabis. Hallucinogens are more my cup of tea. I much prefer the mood of detachment to these induced feelings of confident fearlessness, believe me.' Jane forced herself to stop talking. She failed. 'Please, don't be disapproving, Anna. If I hadn't agreed to take the drug it would have been impossible for me to come on the mission. Over the years I've become a terrible coward, you see. At the mere threat of violence or danger I go to pieces. Please don't tell David you know about the Dexedrine, I promised I wouldn't tell you.'

'I should have been told.'

'I agree, but. . .' Jane shrugged her shoulders. 'I'm beginning to realise just how manipulative David can be. I don't know whether this trait is a plus or another minus in his baffling persona.'

'My God! You're lovers. Is it your usual habit to dissect and criticise the men in your life?'

'No, this is a new departure. Maybe as I become older I'm more difficult to please. Perhaps increased cynicism is a side effect of Dexedrine. The drug certainly heightens awareness.'

'Jane,' Anna scolded, 'are you suggesting awareness induces cynicism?'

'No. . . Yes. . . No. I'm not sure. Increased awareness could provoke heightened cynicism, I suppose. My own attitude has become more judgemental of late, I'm less patient, more argumentative and much more self-confident.' She looked across at Anna. In mutual affection they held each other's eye. Jane said, 'Why are we banging on like this?'

After a pause, Anna said, 'To keep terror at bay?'

'It's all so unreal.'

'I've never felt more alive.'

'Nor I.'

'And I'm as nervous as hell.'

'Me, too.'

'Don't be too hard on David. He may be complex, but he's decisive and has proved he's prepared to take extreme measures to protect us.'

'Yes, you're right. It's what I saw in his eye that disturbs me.'

* * *

Enrico arrived at the arranged meeting place to find David had not returned from his trip to Lake dell'Ogliastro. He slumped down with his back against the tree to wait. He looked at his watch. It was 0720 hours. By now his absence from home would be causing concern. Already Francesca would be broadcasting his truancy to all who could be bothered to listen. It no longer mattered. The decision was made. Nevermore would he return to live the parochial life of a downtrodden nobody. Marriage and insular life had to be abandoned if ever he was to experience more than impoverishment, the feeling of imprisonment and constant discontent. No longer was he prepared to tolerate the indignity of a peasant life. Never again would he have to endure Francesca's brain destroying company, or tolerate the torment of her unhygienic habits and unbearable slovenliness. He had run away once and would do it again, over and over, until he discovered his own somewhere Shangri-La. The adage was accurate, *'Vita è solo un attimo fuggitivo.'* (Life is only a fleeting moment.)

But now, his plight could hardly be worse. The Gestapo with their usual efficiency would make it their business to hunt him down. The Gestapo and the Italian State would pursue him for two unpardonable misdemeanours, desertion and murder. Eventual capture was inevitable. It was a bleak scenario. It left him with no other choice but to throw himself upon the mercy of his country's enemies.

He would plead with the Goddesses of War for their divine protection. He would beg to become a disciple in their holy cause. He would demand no reward for his services other than to be provided with food and shelter and, of course, the promise on their departure that he accompany them to wherever they were bound. To be elevated into a position of acolyte in their service would be the solution to all his problems. It would give his life new and significant purpose. Enrico looked at his watch. It was eight o'clock. He scanned the countryside. The Englishman was nowhere to be seen.

Seconds later he was tapped on the shoulder. He leapt to his feet in shock and turned to look into the steady, unsmiling eyes of the executioner.

'Shall we go?' the Englishman said in a matter-of-fact voice and gestured Enrico lead the way.

The journey to the cottage passed in silence. On arrival Enrico stood aside and watched his Italian neighbour stride forward to shake the Englishman's hand. They were invited into the cottage. The Goddesses were absent. It was explained they had retired to a bedroom, but before withdrawing had prepared a meal. Two plates of spaghetti and a flask of wine were laid on the table. Their host invited them to sit and announced if further services were required he would be sitting on the porch watching for unlikely movement.

Silence was sustained as they wolfed the food. When the plates were clean and the flask empty, the Englishman sat back in his chair, wiped his chin with the back of his hand and finally spoke. 'You can go now,' he announced.

The outrage of the command rendered Enrico speechless. All he could do was stare open-mouthed at an expressionless face.

'Report to your cell we arrived safely, but say nothing of our meeting with the Germans. Tell your superiors you delivered us to our destination without incident. Is that understood?'

'No, not understood,' Enrico blurted. 'I have no cell. I have no superiors. I do a favour for a friend. But, I tell you this. Now, you say I go. I go where? When the Germans they come looking for their soldiers I have no. . .' he stopped. He searched for the English word. His English went to pieces when excited. Vocabulary fragmented, pronouns became muddled and a stuttered mixture of tenses replaced fluency.

'Alibi,' said the gunman.

'Yes, alibi. If I go home what can I say? All night and all day, I am walking around looking for a lost tractor and trailer? I'm sorry Signor. . .' he stopped again, 'I do not know your name.'

'Call me David.'

'Well, Signor David, they will laugh and then shoot me.'

'Your farm machinery cannot be released to you for the simple reason it's saturated with German blood, but be assured, you will be handsomely recompensed for your loss.'

Enrico ignored the assurance. 'During the Gestapo's investigations it will be discovered I am a deserter.'

'You're an Army deserter?' David questioned.

'Yes.'

'Is that why you are mixed up in all this?'

'Yes, the Communists helped me, now they expect me to help them. I do this for them as a favour. I did not know it would be, how you say *pericoloso*?' They tell me nothing. Now, it is impossible for me to go home.'

'What about your family?'

'I have no family.'

'Are you married?'

Freewill is Forfeit

'To a woman I hate.'

'What do you plan to do?'

'I don't know. I'm too tired to think. First, I go to the barn to sleep. When I wake, perhaps then I know.'

* * *

It was early evening. Shafts of late sunshine streamed through the small windows of the cottage. The light created patches of vivid luminosity. Brilliant colours shone against the dark background of shadowed walls. The mixed glow spread an air of tranquillity; a mood of soporific relaxation. Jane, Anna and David were alone for the first time since their departure from an airstrip in Tripoli. Grandpa Michele, forever vigilant, was on the porch and Enrico was asleep somewhere in the barn. After arrival, Anna had slept, but Jane had not. Jane had been too agitated to sleep, but sensibly had forced herself to rest.

A normal sleeping routine was a luxury recently denied Jane. At first she thought being deprived the comfort of her own bed was the cause. Later it became evident Dexedrine was the root of the problem. The drug made sleep difficult to attain. Despite this irritating side effect she felt marvellous. She had told a white lie when she had confessed to Anna her dislike of Dexedrine. The truth would have caused Anna to worry. The effect of the drug was miraculous. It banished self-doubt, it bequeathed astonishing energy and never had she felt more confident and alive. It had been clever of David to recommend she try it. The drug was psychological dynamite.

Jane heard David clear his throat. He was ready to begin. Anna and she had been waiting while he had scratched notes on a pad. 'A problem has arisen that requires our immediate attention,' he commenced. 'It's a small matter, but inconvenient nevertheless. It's our Sicilian contact. He refuses to return to his home.' David stopped and tapped his pencil on his *aide-memoire*. 'After our little imbroglio with the enemy he's afraid of the possibility of being caught by the Gestapo.'

'And he's right,' Jane heard herself say.

David raised a hand to silence her. 'We're in a difficult position. I've come to the conclusion it would be foolish to release him.'

'It's not for us to decide,' Jane interrupted 'He should be free to go anywhere he chooses.'

David ignored Jane's belligerence and responded with patience. 'That's the trouble. He has nowhere to go and we dare not risk having him run around the countryside in his present state of terror.'

'Perhaps we could shoot him and throw him down a well?' Jane remarked with bitterness. It was out before she could stop. The vehemence of the remark made Anna gasp.

'Don't be upset, Anna,' David advised, 'This type of reaction is understandable. Her extreme dislike of violence is well documented.'

Jane glared at the floor. She hated when David used the grammatical third person as if she were absent. It was a type of rudeness she disliked, but rather than give voice to further expressions of discontent she decided to ignore the discourtesy. 'I'm sorry, Anna's right,' she admitted, 'the remark was uncalled for and I apologise.' She watched as relieved glances passed between Anna and David.

David, nonplussed, continued. 'Since it appears he has nowhere to go and already is on the run for the crime of desertion, it might be better during the short time we're here that we recruit him into our service. It would advantage us in two respects. One, we would have him under our control instead of having him wander who-knows-where being a danger to himself and the success of our mission; and two, he has knowledge of people in the area who can be trusted. Apparently he has a tenuous relationship with a group who sympathise with the Allied cause.' He paused. 'Naturally, I would like to know if my recommendation meets with unanimous approval?'

Anna was first to reply. 'Congratulations, David, I think that's a terrific idea. I'm sure he'll be a great help, especially to grandpa.' They looked at Jane.

Jane was delighted with the suggestion. She liked Enrico. She trusted him. He was the type of Italian she adored, a man of passionate nature who, despite the torments and iniquities of life, retained the demeanour of undefeated optimism. His eyes told everything you needed to know about him. He was a pet, a darling of a man. Yes, of course, she would agree. She looked at the waiting faces. 'Okay, by me,' she said, with feigned indifference, 'but only if he agrees.'

14

Tunisia

The nurse was blunt. 'You sit over there,' she said to Hank, pointing to a bench in the reception area, 'and you lot' she instructed, turning to examine each man with her clinical eye, 'can wait outside.' When Lance suggested due to the heat of the day it would be preferable they be allowed to use the waiting room, he was informed there was no waiting room and if one did exist it certainly was not for the likes of stud-booted, unwashed, microbe-ridden, sand-polluted, strangers such as they. Duly chastened they shrugged in Hank's direction and departed to the prospect of spending the next hour in the sweaty misery of the midday heat. Hank heard Robert snort in protest as they left the medical centre.

The sound of Robert's dissent evoked a pang of regret. It seemed to Hank he was cursed always to be the cause of his comrades' adversities. It had been his idea that Cowboy Thomson would be the correct officer to approach for assistance. He had convinced them Cowboy would listen to their plight and agree to help. He had argued an approach to an officer of lower rank would only entail them in further delay. Colonels and Battalion Commanders did not have the power to authorise special flights. These matters had to be referred to Divisional level for approval. Direct application through Cowboy was a manoeuvre to bypass a time-consuming process. It had been a mistake.

Cowboy's refusal to assist would not have prevented them from pursuing other of their discussed options, but his unexpected, direct instructions had obliterated the last hope of ever being able to resurrect the remnants of their operation.

Hank was furious that an American General, albeit of

Freewill is Forfeit

undistinguished record and dubious character, had refused to assist and in the process had scuppered all hope of continuing to Sicily. Cowboy's rudeness to Lance, a serving front-line officer, a decorated Major in the British Army, had been inexcusable. His military disinterest in what had been achieved by Robert's courage had been an example of crass professional indifference. Never once had Cowboy allowed his eye to alight upon the figure of Joe. To Cowboy the Joes of this world did not exist. Hank determined, one day, should the opportunity arise, he would extract a suitable punishment for the willful refusal to help them in their hour of need.

'Please follow me, Captain Remington, the doctor is ready to see you now,' a nurse instructed without a backward glance as she moved along the corridor. Hank rose and followed in her wake. The rubber soles of her shoes made a rhythmic squeak on the polished surface of the floor. He followed the noise while concentrating his attention on the attractive undulations of her figure. He had forgotten just how beautiful women could be. It was mesmerising.

'In here, please.' The nurse opened a door marked with a sign 'Private. Colonel Dr Hamish McPhee', and she stood back to allow him to enter.

Dr McPhee looked up from his desk and grinned. He stood and made a gesture of welcome. 'Come in, Captain, and take a seat.'

Hank moved forward and looked around the room. It was not what he had expected. Instead of a gleaming, sterile surgery, he had entered a dusty, sparsely furnished living-room-cum-office. Upon a floor of red linoleum stood a desk, three chairs and a raised, oblong examination table upholstered in black leather. The wall behind the desk was covered with faded photographs depicting pastoral scenes and groups of smiling men caught in the flush of some sporting triumph. In one corner of the room stood a brown canvas golf bag brimming with a variety of rusting clubs and in the other, propped at a precarious angle, was an oversized walking stick with a crooked bone handle. When Hank's eyes met the doctor's gaze he perceived his surreptitious examination of the room had been observed.

'Bits and pieces from home,' the doctor explained. 'Where I go, the clutter comes with me. It helps to remind me who I am.' He sat down, swirled in his chair and, with an open palm, invited Hank to sit. 'Well, young man you've been banged about a bit, I hear?'

'By whom?'

'What? Oh! General Thomson,' he explained. 'Quite concerned he is about you, laddie.'

'Without reason, I assure you, sir,' Hank said.

'Let's hope that's true.' He leaned forward and in a conspiratorial voice enquired, 'Satisfy my curiosity, will you and tell me, what is the garment you're wearing, Captain.'

'It's an Arab robe, sir. It's all I possess in the way of clothes.'

'We can soon sort that out.' He lifted the telephone and said into the mouthpiece, 'Tell the tailor to deliver a Captain's uniform,' he stopped and looked over at Hank, 'to fit a man of six feet weighing about one hundred and ninety pounds. Bring it to Dr McPhee's hidey-hole, at the double. Got that? Yes, the complete outfit. Thank you.' He replaced the receiver and sat back. Hank heard the springs of the seat groan under his weight. 'That was about right, was it?'

'Yes, very accurate, sir, thank you.' Hank decided he liked this man. He was another Robert; phlegmatic, direct and built like a bull. The accent was familiar, but not American. 'You're British?' Hank enquired, confused that the doctor was wearing the Army uniform of an American Colonel.

'Aye, at the outbreak of war I was doing some research at the Smithsonian and stayed a mite too long, so I joined you lot instead.'

'Any regrets?'

'Not a one. The pay, the uniform, the food and the general lack of bullshit just suits me fine.' He adjusted his position and cleared his throat. 'Shall we make a start? Take off your fancy gown and go and stretch out on that elongated pommel-horse over there.' He pointed at the examination table.

Hank stood, kicked off his sandals, uncoiled his waistband and allowed his body covering to fall to the floor. Naked he walked to the table and lay down. For several minutes he submitted to the indignity of concentrated physical scrutiny. When the sounding, peering, turning and probing ceased, he watched his medical examiner turn away, sigh and make an upward motion of his hand to indicate the examination was over. Hank sat up, dangled his legs over the side of the table and waited.

Dr McPhee returned to his desk and pointed at the door. 'There's a dressing-gown on the hook. Drape yourself with it. You'll find it more comfortable to wear than the rags you arrived in.' Hank complied and when 'draped', sat down.

'The lacerations you have suffered will heal in time and should cause you no further worry, but the injury to your right thigh may, in future, lead to the development of some clotting complication.' He paused. 'This is surmise only, you understand, so don't be in any way alarmed.' He stopped talking, swivelled his head from side to side and made a sudden lunge in the hope of swatting a fly. When satisfied the offending bug would offend no more, he returned his attention to Hank. 'Sorry, I just can't stand the little buggers,' he explained. He sat back and continued, 'As for the patches of heavy discolouration covering large areas of your torso, while I admit it looks disturbing, be assured, it is no more than evidence of last stage recovery from severe bruising.'

'These patches have just appeared,' explained Hank.

'Yes, it often takes a little time for bruised blood to show, but you'll be pleased to hear when the discolouration fades no further trouble will ensue. Your body has taken a battering, but you're young and healthy and well on the way to making complete recovery. Just give a mind to your right thigh, now and again. Any questions?'

'You're giving me a clean bill of health?'

Dr McPhee ignored the question. 'Tell me, how exactly did you sustain your wounds?' he asked.

'I was catapulted from a jeep and collided with a hill.'

'You were lucky not to have sustained several fractures. Can you remember the incident?'

'No. I remember riding the jeep, then nothing more until I woke up in a cave.'

'How long were you unconscious?'

'Two days, I think. I'm not sure.'

'Did you experience much pain?'

'Yes, but after several days it became bearable. I think I was lucky to have slept through the worst of it. I kept slipping in and out of consciousness for quite some time after the event.'

'Yes, you must have been badly concussed. Tell me, have you noticed any discernable side effects since your unsuccessful attempt to rearrange the desert scenery? Have you developed any sudden phobias; experienced any form of hallucination, either auditory or visual; noticed any unusual behavioural change; suffered from lack of concentration, been afflicted by mood swings, that sort of thing?'

'No. Not that I've noticed.'

There was a knock on the door and, when permission to enter was given, a Master Sergeant entered carrying an armful of clothes. 'I'll lay odds you've forgotten to bring socks,' the doctor barked at him.

'No, Colonel. Socks, shoes, underwear, tie, shirt, tunic, trousers and a cap. Will there be anything else, sir? Both men looked at Hank. Hank shook his head in response.

'May I?' Hank asked, pointing at the pile of clothes.

'Yes, of course. Try it on for size. If any of it doesn't fit we'll have it replaced.'

Hank rose from his seat and crossed the room. He ruffled through the garments and commenced to dress. 'What part of England do you come from, Colonel?' he enquired, in an effort to make polite conversation while dressing. The response was astonishing.

'What?' the Colonel exploded. 'Dae ye think a'm English? He demanded in an exaggerated vernacular. 'I'm a Scot. Surely that's obvious?'

'Of course,' said Hank in confusion, 'you said you were British and I assumed. . .'

'It's an easy mistake to make,' the doctor admitted. 'You're excused your *faux pas*.' His voice was normal again. 'No Scot likes to be mistaken for an Englishman. It can boil the blood. We're a

Freewill is Forfeit

fierce and complicated lot when it comes to protecting our national identity. It's a complex we Scots will have to rid ourselves of, but in the mean time, pathetic as it is, this cultural trait of taking affront will have to be endured by those who make the mistake of thinking we're English. However, to answer your question, I come from a wee place called Golspie.'

'Is that anywhere near Glasgow?' asked Hank, while bending to put on a sock.

'Nowhere near. Glasgow is in the southwest, Golspie lies on the northeast coast. Glasgow is an industrial metropolis, Golspie almost untouched wilderness.'

'Sounds wonderful,' Hank muttered, delighted to discover the shoes provided fitted perfectly.

'And that's where I'm going to live directly after this bastard war is over. You're a New York boy.' It was a statement, not a question.

'Yes, but I'm not sure where I'll settle after the dust subsides. I intend to marry a Glasgow girl, you see.' Hank said this without thought while examining a gap at the waistband of the trousers. He looked up at the Colonel and grimaced. 'I seem to have lost some weight. I'll need suspenders, I'm afraid.'

'Coming up,' said Dr McPhee and reached for the telephone. 'Braces,' he yelled down the line and immediately replaced the receiver. 'A Glasgow girl you say?' he enquired with interest.

'Yes. At present she's serving as a sergeant language instructor in Casablanca.' Hank found the shirt to be too big, but after a moment's thought, decided not to complain. 'She knows nothing of my interest, or of my intention, but. . .' He stopped and made a facial expression of hope by raising his eyebrows.

'Well, if it's your intention to marry a Glasgow girl you'll be sure to find she's a spirited filly. From my experience the lassies from Glasgow are forged in the steel works of the Clyde. Scotland is not a matriarchy by accident; it's a matriarchy by the egalitarian, Presbyterian force of its daughters. Your life will never be dull, that's assured. I know this from a lifetime of observation and experience. My Fiona's from Springburn, you see.'

Hank was having difficulty in associating Anna with steel works.

'She's the most beautiful creature I've ever seen,' he said in defence of the woman he loved.

'Oh! Aye! They're bonnie lassies, have no doubt,' the Colonel mused, again becoming more Scottish-sounding by the second, 'it's their personalities that make them unique.' He was prevented from pontificating further by a knock on the door. 'Enter,' he shouted.

'Suspenders,' the word was emphasised, 'and would Captain Remington please sign the documentation at reception when leaving.' The Colonel and Hank nodded in unison.

'There is one other formality that should be mentioned. In my report I intend to recommend you be considered for a military award. I read the *New York Times*, so I'm not entirely ignorant of your recent history. I can imagine what you have been through and the trauma you've had to suffer. If my recommendation is rejected, at the very least you will be awarded the Purple Heart.'

Hank was speechless. While the rest of the squad were in disgrace and accused of failure, he in turn was to be recommended for some military honour. Interpretation of the military mind was beyond ordinary understanding. 'My capture was reported in the *New York Times*?' Hank asked.

'Yes, in their 'Reports from the Fronts' column. It caused quite a furore, I believe.' Hank shook his head in bewilderment. 'I'm recommending also you be granted a period of leave.'

'Don't do that, if you don't mind, sir,' Hank interrupted, 'I don't want a period of leave. I'm sorry, but I would prefer the granting of leave to be left to my commanding officer, Major Bennett.'

'Take it easy, Captain,' Dr McPhee soothed. 'It will be a recommendation only. I've learned no one in this man's army ever pays a blind bit of attention to mere medics, so fear not.' He was smiling. He stood and stretched his hand over the desk. 'Well, laddie, good luck. Maybe we'll meet again one day and if you should marry your heart's desire, remember, when you're in Scotland you'll find me in Golspie.'

The handshake was genuine and firm.

* * *

Freewill is Forfeit

It took them a two-hour jeep ride to reach British Command Headquarters. They arrived layered in dust, sweating, hungry and weary. Their collective mood of discontent was further intensified by the reception they received at the main gate. A churlish duty corporal barred their entry and informed them without prior instruction, some relevant documentation, or written permission, he was not authorised to allow them to pass into the protected enclave. To break the deadlock Lance suggested the Officer-of-the-day be sent for and returned to sit with the others in the jeep to await his arrival.

'They're not interested, are they?' was Robert's unhelpful remark.

Lance glowered. He was not in a mood to banter with Robert. It was ridiculous they should be here in the first place. Their duty lay elsewhere, far from this arid outpost where they would encounter, at best, nothing more than minimal, perhaps even amused, interest for their plight. Operation Sleekit Beastie, it seemed, was cursed not to happen. From the outset it had been jinxed.

After fifteen minutes of impatient waiting a middle-aged lieutenant approached the jeep. Lance dismounted and took him aside to explain the purpose of their visit. His explanations were received with blank stares and shrugged shoulders. Lance had had enough. Tired of having their fidelity questioned he ordered the elderly soldier to find, if possible, a competent officer who enjoyed an IQ commensurate with his rank and while awaiting the appearance of this improbable individual whether it would be too much to ask if an exhausted group of combatants could be directed to a place of shade where they could sit, take refreshment and idle away the hours before the insult of yet more idiotic enquiry was made as to whether they should be regarded as *bona fide*, or not. The Officer-of-the-day blanched and turned to leave. Lance stopped him in his tracks. He reminded the astonished man it was normal military practice for junior officers when taking leave of ranking superiors to salute as a mark of respect. The incensed man saluted and turned heel.

Lance returned to the jeep to Robert's slow handclap. 'That's telling them, boss,' he said. 'Probably, now, we'll have to wait forever.'

'I disagree,' Hank said. 'I think curiosity will galvanise attention. I'll wager in five minutes we'll be sitting in shadow, eating caviar and quaffing expensive wine.'

'Wise up,' retorted Robert. 'You're in a British Army zone here, not an American boot camp.'

'*Stazitto,*' appealed Lance. They shut-up.

Within minutes a relaxed and smiling Major approached the jeep. His shoulder flashes announced he was a serving Officer in the Corps of Signals. He threw up a casual salute and, in one bound, leapt upon the spare tyre at the rear of the vehicle. He made a motion to Robert at the wheel to proceed and said, 'Drive straight ahead, Sergeant, pass the main building to the left and I'll tell you when to stop.' As Robert drove the instructed route the Major continued to talk.

'Where the hell have you guys been? London's been going loco attempting to trace you.' They turned and looked at him in astonishment. 'I'll explain everything in the office,' he said and, with surprising dexterity and balance, lit a cigarette.

They were led into a shaded room at the rear of a detached house three hundred yards from the main building. 'First things first,' the Major said. He produced a bottle of whisky from a cupboard, spread four glasses on the desk and splashed them full. He lifted the telephone to instruct the kitchen to have a meal for four hungry men delivered to his office. Hank grinned across at Robert. Robert shrugged.

'Now, gentlemen, allow me to introduce myself. My name is Evans, commonly known around these quarters as Taffy the Wire. I'm the communications chief. My job is to monitor everything coming in and out of this esteemed establishment. For the past fortnight regular requests have been made for information as to your possible whereabouts. Nobody seemed to know. London will be delighted to learn you're safe and well. Drink up, gentlemen,' he encouraged. 'You'll have time for another before the food arrives.' He lit another cigarette, threw the packet on the desk and waved his hand to indicate they were now common property.

'Where the hell have you been, anyway?' he asked in the obscure hope they might tell him.

'It's a long story,' Lance said. 'Major Evans. . .'

'Taffy, please,' the Welshman interrupted.

'Taffy, since we lost our radio early in events, would it be possible to use your transmission equipment to communicate with London?'

'Of course. The radio room is out of bounds to unauthorised personnel, of course, but just say the word and whatever you want to communicate will be transmitted.'

'Could you contact the SOE and inform them that following incarceration by Allied forces and other military elements, we are now ready to continue the operation and require only air transport be authorised for our mission to recommence? Could this be done immediately?'

'I'll do it now,' Taffy said, rising to leave. 'Finish the bottle, please gentlemen and there's another in the cupboard. Help yourselves, I'll be back as soon as I can.' He left the room.

They drank in silence and waited. After a while Robert rose, reached into the cupboard and opened the second bottle. He looked around to check if anyone wished to join him. They all sat forward and raised their glasses. 'Thought so,' he said and dispensed the whisky with unrestrained largesse.

When Major Evans reappeared two hours later his office was strewn with the debris of empty plates, full ashtrays, scattered glasses and two empty whisky bottles.

'I've a feeling you won't like this,' he announced, ' so I'll deliver it straight. You have been ordered to return to London for debriefing.'

'Holy shit!' exploded Hank.

'You are to be flown from here to Casablanca and from Casablanca to London.'

'Christ, what a time-wasting fucking palaver,' Lance said. 'Why can't the plane taking us to Casablanca be used to take us to Sicily? Did they tell you it was their intention to cancel the operation?

'No. What they told me was another squad had been sent to Sicily in your absence.'

* * *

Casablanca

In the corner of the room Joe was sprawled on a pile of cushions. His eyes were glazed, his hair ruffled and his face contorted into a shape the others had come to recognise as an expression of happiness. In his semi-comatose condition he stared out into a room of vivid colours while listening to the murmur of a male voice fill the air with sonorous sounds.

Lance, too, was in a state of euphoria. He was stripped to the waist, his bottom half covered with blue and white striped pantaloons. He lay in a horizontal position on a red plush *chaise longue a*nd stared at the ceiling. A deep silence surrounded his smiling presence. All distress, frustration and disappointment had been dispelled. He was at peace with himself and the world he inhabited.

Hank, garbed in a yellow robe, lay on a low couch. He was propped on one elbow attempting to maintain Robert's attention with the brilliance of his drug-induced insights.

Swathed in a red silk garment Robert sat upright and cross-legged upon a voluminous cushioned mattress stolen – he was informed by Abdullah as he had prepared the pipes – from the harem of a murdered Caliph. Robert had lost interest in Hank's monotone meanderings. At first he had listened with mild attention, but had become tired of clichéd reason being plied as wise pronouncement and had allowed his mind to wander. At odd intervals an autonomic reflex made him nod his head in response to Hank's endless monologue.

Robert was familiar with the effect opium had on the senses. Opium had its own magic. Some collapsed into dream-saturated stupor, others became imbued with a need to converse, to pontificate at length on insights revealed by drug-induced perception. A few, like himself, were granted a release from the inhibition of creative timidity. The drug bequeathed a lexical ability and banished the fear of creative impotence. No longer did blank paper intimidate the poised and hesitant pen. The drug realigned

Freewill is Forfeit

the barriers of comprehension and produced a desire to wed words to emotion without the stricture, or inhibition, of embarrassment. What seemed impossible to interpret became simple to unravel. The surreal became real: the intangible, tangible.

The pleas of his nocturnal ghosts, his constant dream companions, now could be heard and understood without difficulty. The sound of their torment was audible. The glass wall that stifled sound had been removed. Their urgent communications demanded attention. With lifted pen Robert fell into a cocooned trance of concentration.

Hank noticed Robert's interest had strayed. He assumed the drug had taken effect. He felt disappointed that his self-revealing, verbal thesis on adult responsibility, mostly, had gone unheard.

Earlier in the day Hank had felt wounded when told Anna had been transferred. His disappointment had been intense. Missing her by a few days was unendurable bad luck. An unhelpful orderly room staff had added to his despair. They had retained no details of her posting. He had been told information regarding her whereabouts could be obtained only by making application through Administration. Administration, in turn, had refused to disclose what was held on file. They, however, were prepared to admit Sgt McKay had been recalled to a training battalion for further military instruction. Where? They would not divulge. The reward for his afternoon's efforts had produced nothing more than the address of a department in Whitehall. The address of the department was the War Office. He felt devastated, but not disheartened. He would track her down. He would seek her out no matter where she was and, when successful, he would bend the knee and beg her hand in marriage. This was his resolve. If it demanded the patience of a stoic, so be it.

15

Sicily

Twenty-six year old Oberleutnant Oskar Steiner had a hangover. The previous evening he had attended the annual party to celebrate the seventh anniversary of Conscription Day in Austria. On the first day of April, 1936, he, and thousands of others, had flocked to join the ranks of Hitler's triumphal assembly. Each year a celebration was held for those who had enlisted on that glorious day. One hundred and forty-two men had turned-up at the get-together: all Austrian, all ranks, all in good voice and by the end of the evening, all very drunk. It had been the annual affirmation of eternal camaraderie, the event to mark the indestructible comradeship of those who were the most loyal of all the *Führer's* servants – the Waffen SS. As tradition demanded, it had been a boisterous evening.

The telephone rang on his desk. The noise made him wince. He stretched, listened for a moment and replaced the receiver with a grunt. Two of his men had not yet returned to their stations at Caltagirone. It was of little consequence. They would appear soon enough. A piffling matter, nevertheless, it had been correct of the staff to inform him. They knew, to their cost, his insistence he be kept informed of detail.

His hangover apart, this was proving to be a bad day. His desk was strewn with reports, each one a document of cheerless import. The recent despatches from Tunisia were desperate. The failure of Rommel's Afrika Korps to retake the southern town of Medenine had started the landslide. When the Commonwealth troops of the British Eighth Army could repulse the Divisions of Germany's finest fighting troops, then, truly, the writing was on the wall. It was rumoured the *Führer* had been livid when he had heard the news. It had been beyond his belief rookie New Zealand soldiers could rebuff, and better, the reequipped Axis Divisions. It was little wonder Rommel had been recalled to Berlin. His failure to oust the British had made it possible for Montgomery to advance, smash his way through the Mareth Line and join with the eastward advancing Americans. German troops now stood surrounded and squeezed from all sides. The Axis Armies in Tunisia either would be made prisoner, or driven into the sea. The loss of men and equipment would be incalculable. Rommel's inability to recapture Medenine had been a disaster, a disgrace. It deserved a punishment more than the humiliation of a ritual tongue-lashing, it demanded he be stripped of rank and publicly flogged.

Oskar hunched forward on his seat, stroked his brow and looked down at the sheet of paper before him. Once more he read its contents. When finished he picked up the document and, with a display of disgust, threw the letter into a bundle of papers at the side of his desk. He had heard the rumour at last night's party his formal application for transfer had been received at Command Headquarters with a degree of displeasure. The letter confirming the truth of the rumour had arrived and its manner of delivery ominous. It had been placed, pointedly, in the middle of his desk to await his attention. He had experienced a sense of foreboding when opening the envelope. He knew the refusal to his request would be couched in disapproving language. It seemed he was fated to spend the rest of his military career in the backwoods of a rural, nowhere land. He had thought after serving three years in Sicily it would have been regarded as reasonable to apply for a transfer. He had been wrong. His assumption had backfired. The application had tainted his otherwise pristine reputation and tarnished his good standing among the senior ranks of the battalion. The point of making the request had been to better himself, to indicate he was a man of ambition who wished to be given the opportunity of serving the Nazi cause in a more relevant, testing and productive manner. His application had been misconstrued. It merely had indicated to those in authority the request had been motivated by personal dissatisfaction.

Oskar had been careful to hide the fact that this interpretation was true. He was tired of Sicily. It was a dead-end, cultureless hole entirely inhabited by simpleton peasants and uneducated thugs. Sicily was a primitive enclave the modern world had left behind. It was an example of what life must have been like in the Middle Ages; a place of vulgar, brutish people held in thrall by the mythical claptrap of religion. The men had a tendency to violence and the women, suppressed by edicts of faith, had a mind washed attitude to sex akin to androphobia. Not the ideal society for a man who possessed an active libido.

Recently, more often than not, he had used the advantage of rank and uniform to force sexual compliance on unwilling women who, in the passing, had taken his fancy. It was distasteful, but all things considered, an understandable departure from normal behaviour. Their stoic unwillingness to submit did taint, to a degree, full satisfaction of the sexual act. An unyielding disposition sullied what he most desired: willing and simpering compliance to his domination.

Ideally, he required a stable of women, a harem of on call mistresses to be at his disposal, but Sicily, unfortunately, had abandoned its Pagan past and, instead, now embraced a religion of stultifying sexual oppression. It was no place for a man who had to suffer the agony of migraine if regular sexual satisfaction was denied him. Without the relief of constant sex he felt incapable of controlling his emotions. It increased his tendency to violence and blurred the boundaries of what was universally accepted as civilised behaviour. Living in a regimented culture had made him other than he had been brought up to be. Hitler Youth Camps, Party rallies, Army duty and Sicily had combined to eradicate the social constraints beaten into him during his childhood years. He no longer recognised the person he had become and no longer cared. Why should he? Was he not a first generation aspirant of a new order, a founder member within the ranks of an emerging Master Race? At the end of the day his function was to instil in the consciousness of inferior races the superiority of a blood-cleansed superpower. Everything he did was for the greater glory of Germany and Hitler's dream of creating a Thousand Year Reich.

At breakfast on the third day of their mission it was decided Enrico should lead Jane and David to the house of a known member of the local Cosa Nostra. They knew their journey would involve risk, but if contact was to be made with the *Capi*, some initial hazard had to be endured. It was agreed during the ten-mile hike that Enrico would lead, Jane would follow and David would bring up the rear. All open ground was to be crossed one person at a time and only while travelling under the cover of trees would they risk moving together. Jane and Enrico had already departed. They had set out to make their separate ways to the edge of the first copse three hundred metres to the south. David, as he prepared to leave, voiced his final instructions to Anna.

'Don't worry. You'll be safe here until we return,' he reassured. 'Should all go well, we'll be back by midnight. Sit tight, try not to be nervous and if by the odd chance someone should call don't become excited. Remember you're on vacation making an annual visit to your grandfather, nothing more. Be relaxed; strive to give the impression you're happy to be here.'

Anna pushed at his shoulder. 'Go, David,' she said. 'Don't worry, I'll be fine. Just make sure you look after Jane.'

'It seems Enrico has taken that responsibility out of my hands. His devotion to Jane becomes more embarrassing by the hour.' To Anna's relief she saw he was smiling as he spoke.

'I've noticed,' she said with care. She liked David and didn't wish to cause him hurt. She thought his relationship with Jane the most confusing aspect of the entire mission.

'What do you think? Is he trustworthy?' David enquired.

'I've the feeling he is. If not, we're soon to find out.'

'Well,' he sighed, 'I'd better be off if I'm to catch them up.' Without more ado he turned and left. Anna was alone, alone with nothing to fear but the sensation of fear itself.

Grandfather Michele had departed earlier. He had announced the previous evening he intended to make his regular visit to the market. He feared his absence would arouse unwanted curiosity.

David, impressed by the precautionary forethought, agreed all normal routines should be adhered to throughout the period of their visit. When they rose in the morning they discovered the old man had left before dawn.

Following David's departure Anna spent the morning in a flurry of domestic activity. She washed a small mountain of dishes, brought in wood for the stove, did some general dusting, made the beds and scrubbed every soiled garment she could find. The sun was high when she hung the clothing out to dry. There was a pleasant wind. It was a perfect day for drying clothes.

When she returned to the house she decided to make coffee. While filling the kettle she glanced out of the window at the billowing evidence of her labour. The simple, pleasurable sight of clothes flapping in the wind had a reassuring affect. It bestowed a feeling of homeliness.

She now felt more at ease in Sicily, less fearful. The calm of the past two days had helped her to settle. They had passed in a mood of quiet order, thanks mainly to David's steadying influence. She felt safe when David was around. Despite Jane's misgivings he was a first class leader, a natural motivator whose presence spread a glow of security.

With household chores concluded and with little to do, Anna decided to write her first letter to Hank. She would express herself simply, but sincerely; tell him of the heartbreak she suffered when she heard he was missing and of her subsequent sleepless nights of secret worry. It would be an introductory missive to indicate concern for his safety, a simple communication to make him aware of her affection. She dismissed the thought she might never be able to post the letter, or, if ever it became possible, where she should send it. She decided she would write the letter and post it, when possible, to the Headquarters of the US 7th Army. On the envelope she would put her home address in Glasgow.

Two hours later, defeated by what she thought would be a simple task, she threw a scrunched up pile of paper into the stove. Her efforts burned in a burst of flame. She continued to gaze at the black strips of ash until they vanished. The words she had managed to write had seemed trite and meaningless. They had

Freewill is Forfeit

failed to convey the correct depth of her feeling. She decided she would try again, soon.

It was mid-afternoon when she rose to collect the washing from the line. She lifted the clothesbasket and exited the back door of the cottage. In the distance she heard the sound of a distant vehicle. She stopped mid-stretch to listen. The sound became more distinct. It came closer. She held her breath and prayed whoever it was would pass. Her prayers went unanswered. She heard the vehicle stop at the front of the cottage. Her thoughts raced. Perhaps it was her grandfather? Perhaps he had taken the opportunity of a lift and had returned early? She walked forward and leaned against the back wall of the house. She inclined her head to look out on to the road. She saw empty countryside. She turned, walked to the other corner and bent her head forward. Her heart stopped. It was a German motorcycle and sidecar. The driver of the motorcycle sat straddled on his machine; the sidecar was empty. Panic flooded her senses. Paralysed with terror her mind ceased to function. She leaned back against the wall and gulped for air.

'Act as if you were on holiday', a voice screamed in her head. 'Be relaxed', 'be natural', the voice insisted. She knew what she had to do. With a concentrated effort she walked forward to the washing line and continued to gather the clothes. She put a fixed smile on her face and waited.

'*Buona sera, Signorina,*' a male voice addressed her.

She turned to confront the figure of a German officer. He was wearing the grey uniform of the Waffen-SS. His collar patch denoted the rank of Oberleutnant. '*Benvenuto, Signore. Che bella giornata!*' she said in greeting. She folded the garment she was holding, stooped to place it in the basket and walked towards him with a smile. As she approached him she wiped her hands down the sides of her dress as if prepared to shake his hand. He ignored her friendly gesture and examined her with a cold eye.

'Do you live here?' he asked, in a guttural Italian.

'Yes, sir. I live here with my grandfather.' She was confident the Tuscan accent she had developed would sound Sicilian to his ear.

'Where is he now?'

'At the market. He makes the journey once a week.' Anna reminded herself not to embellish answers, but to keep the information he demanded as sparse as she dare.

'And where is this market held?'

'At Castel di Ludica.'

'And does this absent grandfather of yours own a vehicle?'

Anna noted his Italian was better than passable. 'Yes, he owns a tractor, but makes his weekly visit by mule. If you'd care to wait he should be home at any minute.' She wondered if she should risk offering him some refreshment. It was a customary courtesy. 'I'm just about to prepare supper, if you would like to join us you'll be made welcome.'

He ignored the invitation and strode past her to examine the surrounding area. Anna watched his eyes absorb the scene. She knew he could search for a week and never find anything incriminating, thanks to the cunning of her grandfather.

'Does he keep his tractor in there?' he enquired, pointing at her Grandfather's shed.

'Yes.' Anna walked to the flimsy double doors and threw them wide. 'As you can see it's old, rusty and not much to look at, but it manages to serve its purpose.'

He made a sniffing sound to indicate he had no further interest in the contents of the shed. She swung the doors closed. When she turned to face him she found him staring at her breasts. Without moving his eyes, he said, 'You must be lonely living here?' It had overt sexual meaning. The atmosphere thickened with tension. Panic reddened her face. To conceal her discomfort she turned from him and walked forward to pick-up a stray clothes peg. The thought flashed in her mind, at least, she was on familiar ground. Another groping session was in the offing, but this time, when things got out of hand, there was no one she could call upon to come to her aid. She decided casual conversation was the best defence. 'I really enjoy my annual visit. I come for a fortnight each year. After the bustle of Messina I find the peace of the countryside very refreshing. Besides, there's usually so much to do I never have time to feel lonely.' Anna heard him grunt.

'You have employment in Messina?'

Freewill is Forfeit

'Yes, I teach. If you wish to examine my papers they're in the cottage?' To Anna's surprise he made a small bow and with his left hand gestured she should lead and he would follow.

As they walked towards the door of the cottage, he enquired, 'When did you arrive here?'

'A few days ago.' She knew it was too vague and quickly responded, 'This is my fourth day here. It's a pleasure to know I've another ten days to enjoy before I'm back in harness.' She struggled to force a smile.

When they entered the house she went to the bedroom to collect the forged papers. She prayed they would pass scrutiny. When she turned she found him standing in the open doorway. She feigned surprise and managed to say with humorous flair, 'This is my bedroom, sir. It's unseemly you should take such liberties.' Her humour had no effect. He closed the door and walked into the room. She knew then he intended to rape her. She decided should he attempt to penetrate her she would shoot him. The outrage of losing her virginity to an uncivilised philistine would give her the courage to pull the trigger. As a last resort she decided to change her demeanour. 'This is neither the time nor place for this sort of nonsense, believe me,' she challenged. 'If it's sex you have on your mind then your timing is terrible. I hate rough-and-tumble fucks, I loath being rushed and at the moment I happen to be menstruating.' He gaped at her in genuine surprise. 'And worst of all,' she continued, forcing herself to walk towards him, 'I don't even know your name. I have a rule, it's a small one, I know,' she announced, 'but I never make love to a gentleman whose name is unknown to me.' Anna withdrew slightly and smiled.

'Oskar, my name is Oskar.'

'Well, Oskar, what's the rush? Do you wish to submit me to the distasteful experience of unwilling intercourse, or wait until I can respond to you with pleasure?'

Oskar jerked forward and thrust his right hand between Anna's legs. She groaned, but made no move to resist him. With his left arm he encircled her neck and attempted to kiss her mouth. She felt her upper lip and nose being crushed. 'Please don't,' she moaned and sighed with annoyance. 'This is all so unnecessary, insultingly distasteful.' He withdrew his hand from between her legs and examined her distressed face. Anna saw the harsh set of his expression soften. He fell to his knees and clamped the lower half of her body with his arms. She felt his head press into her abdomen.

'Holy Jesus!' he gasped. 'Forgive me. I've forgotten how to behave in the presence of an educated woman.' He pressed harder into her body. She felt gripped by giant pincers. Had her act of deceit worked? Had her scarlet woman protests miraculously prevented her rape and his murder? She looked at the ceiling and gave thanks. She lifted her right hand and ruffled his hair. 'Oskar! Oskar!' she said in a tone of sympathetic chastisement, 'Women realise how difficult it must be for young men far from home. We accept, especially during war, men and women often abandon normal sexual behaviour to satisfy physical needs, but let's remember, we're not barbarians. Cultivated people bear the responsibility to maintain civilised standards of conduct.' She raised his head and peered down at him. 'Don't be distressed, Oskar, I quite understand and I forgive you. Your patience will be rewarded, I promise.' Anna forced herself to stop speaking. She felt she was beginning to believe her own words. She listened to him groan and heard him mutter a few words she didn't understand.

'I'm glad you came to your senses before you destroyed the hope of a future relationship,' Anna purred.

'You've given me something to look forward to.' She forced a chuckle to sound in her throat. 'Come,' she said, encouraging him to stand. He rose. He stood facing her in silence. Again she felt his hand slide between her legs. She placed her arms around his neck and hugged him with all the force she could muster. 'Please wait, Oskar,' she pleaded in a husky whisper. 'Not here, not in my grandfather's house. I would like to enjoy our lovemaking, but I can't, not here and especially not when I'm having my period. Can't you see, everything is wrong for me?' Anna took his hand from between her legs and placed it on her left breast. She whispered in his ear, 'Wait. Be patient, Oskar, and wait.'

He straightened and pushed Anna to arms length. 'Do you own silk stockings?' he asked.

Anna had to fight a sudden impulse to laugh. 'Of course, and garters too,' she said with a straight face. She knew, now, she was safe from being ravished. 'Do you think I don't know how to pleasure men?' She moved close to him and raised her right hand to tidy his hair. She examined his uniform and removed strands of her hair from his lapel. 'Shall we go through now?' she suggested. He nodded agreement and walked to the door. Anna took several deep breaths, picked up her documents and followed him out of the room.

She found him slumped in her grandfather's chair. She walked towards him and let her thigh rest against his shoulder. 'My papers, Oskar,' she reminded him. He stretched and took them from her hand. She watched him as he studied the documents.

'Anna. Your name is Anna?'

'Yes.'

'You are aptly named,' he said, as he returned the forgeries. In a sudden movement he swivelled and swung her on to his knee. Propped on his lap she wiggled into a comfortable position and asked, 'Why do you think that?'

'You possess the name of a great and tragic adulteress.'

'Do I?' Anna was genuinely baffled. 'Tell me?'

'No. You must guess. Being an educated woman you must know of her.'

'I can't think. Give me some clue.'

'Let me see.' He looked into the far corner of the room and returned his eyes to her face. 'She was portrayed in the cinema by Greta Garbo.'

Anna knew immediately. 'Anna Karenina,' she shouted. He hugged her and laughed. On the count of five she moved away from him and looked down at his features, 'Can we arrange to meet somewhere other than here? Sometime next week, let's say?'

'Of course. Where?'

'You decide, Oskar. Make it somewhere special, please, somewhere isolated and romantic, somewhere exciting and unusual. I'll make you a promise, you provide the ambiance and I'll provide your pleasure.' Anna thought her enthusiasm a little overdone.

'I have a small flat in Enna I think you would like.'

'A small flat? I like small flats; they're so private. That sounds perfect,' Anna enthused, with more control.

'I'll have you picked up. . .'

'No.' It was out too quickly. Anna rose from his lap and walked to the table. She turned to face him and said, 'I would prefer my grandfather knew nothing of this. You know how things are in country areas. Please understand. He's an old man who thinks his granddaughter is the Virgin Mary. It would cause him unhappiness to discover the truth of my libidinous inclinations.'

'Please,' he appealed, ' I understand better than you think.'

'Allow me to come to you, Oskar.'

'That would be pleasing, but how will you travel?'

'By bicycle, of course.' Anna watched him unbutton the left hand pocket of his tunic and produce a wallet. He selected a card and returned the wallet to his pocket. He rose from the chair, stood erect, made a stamping motion with his right leg, slapped his chest in a movement of self-satisfaction and smiled. Anna extended her hand to receive his card. 'Until the afternoon a week from today,' he said. He bowed, lifted her right hand to his lips and straightened. He turned and walked out of the house.

* * *

It was three o'clock in the morning. A single candle shed sufficient light to reveal weariness etched on each face. They had been active and without rest for twenty-one hours. The table at which they sat was strewn with evidence a meal had just been consumed. A silence had descended. No one wished to speak following Anna's description of her ordeal.

David was first to react. 'I've no wish to sound callous, Anna, but in this game all's well that ends well,' he said. Enrico snorted. Enrico was confident he now had earned the right to express opinion. David looked at him. 'Enrico?'

'Ends well?' Enrico questioned. 'What do you mean? An experience like that can scar a woman for life.' It was a valid protest.

'Okay, Enrico, we take your point,' David replied. 'No one is denying Anna will be traumatised for a period, but remember this is a military operation and scarred psyches come with the job. Understood?' David didn't wait for a response. 'All things considered we've had a successful day. No one is incapacitated, our cover holds fast and we have achieved our first objective, an arranged meeting with *il capo* tomorrow night. I realise we're all tired, but before we break up there are a few matters that require attention.' There was a communal groan. 'I promise it will take only a few minutes. First, let's tackle the matter of our visitor. You know, of course, why bastards like him are snooping around?'

'The missing men,' Enrico volunteered.

'Correct. This lieutenant will return. Perhaps not tomorrow, but he'll be back. I must remind you the Germans have a policy of reprisal and if we hope to keep the local population and especially grandpa, safe and free of threat, then we have no other choice but to vacate this house.' David ignored the gasps of surprise and continued. 'We will leave here directly following our meeting with the Cosa Nostra tomorrow night. We will attempt to depart by midnight and travel overnight to a new location. Before we execute this evacuation, however, it will be necessary to cover our tracks.' He stopped talking and turned to face Anna.

'Anna, I want you to write a note, put it in an envelope, seal it and write on the face of it, 'To Oskar'. The note will say how sorry you are to have been recalled to Messina and you look forward to a meeting whenever he can arrange to visit. You will conclude the letter with a plea he exercise a degree of discretion, hinting there might be a particular personage who would be displeased at his interest.'

'Someone else can write the note,' Anna interrupted. 'I'm still shaking. I don't think I could hold a pen.'

David looked at Jane. Jane agreed.

David turned his attention to the old man. 'Grandpa, on the other hand, will have quite a different tale to tell. When the German Lieutenant makes his appearance you will hand him the sealed envelope. When he has read the note you will explain, with suitable emotion, the proper reason for her departure. You had demanded she leave. You will tell him you discovered to be true what you had suspected for years, your granddaughter was a whore, a woman who consorted with men and lived an unchristian life. You were shocked to learn it had become common knowledge she was the current mistress of General Ernst von Kremer, the Garrison Commander in Messina.' David looked over at the old man, 'Get the picture, Grandpa?'

Grandpa responded by clapping his hands. David was unsure if he was being applauded, or Grandpa couldn't wait to perpetrate the deceit. David held the old man's eye and continued, 'Tomorrow our haste may deny me the opportunity, so allow me now, sir, to praise your bravery. You have been magnificent. Your advice and assistance have been invaluable and should this Operation achieve success it will be due, in no small part, to your courage and unstinting aid.'

David watched Grandpa's sun-scorched face slowly crumple. He saw the old man's head drop and, seconds later, tears splash on to his shirt. Quiet glances were exchanged. Enrico was first to break the tension.

'*Bravissimo,*' he said and commenced to clap his hands. Anna, Jane and David joined the applause. Grandpa rose from his chair and with awkward, self-conscious movements made a gesture of appreciation. Unable to hide his gratified senses and embarrassed by his show of emotion, he muttered, 'Now, I go to bed,' and left.

After a short silence David turned to face Jane. 'Well, Jane, what can I say? Did you realise your name still held such sway among the elite of the organisation?'

Jane smiled at David. 'You're the clever one, David, you should take the credit, not me. In London you put two and two together and came up with the right answer.'

'Modesty doesn't suit you, Jane,' sniped David.

'Christ! You were bloody marvellous today,' Jane enthused. 'This is your show, David. Without you none of this would be happening. I admit at the beginning I thought this little adventure was doomed to fail, but after today I really believe our efforts will not be in vain.'

'What we achieved today was due to your name, your celebrity and nothing else,' David insisted.

'Have it your own way, David,' Jane conceded. She sat forward in her seat and lit a cigarette from the candle. 'I thought it all went off rather well,' she said to conclude the conversation.

'I'd give it no more than five out of ten,' David said, to everyone's surprise

Jane sat back and stretched her legs. 'Why? Today went flawlessly.'

'You drank too much,' he accused and waited for her verbal explosion. It failed to materialise.

'Too much?' Her bafflement was genuine. 'Three glasses of Champagne, too much?' she questioned in disbelief.

'Too much,' he repeated, 'on top of your other medication.' David said this while tapping the side of his nose. Jane averted her eyes from his accusatory stare. 'They don't mix well,' he continued, 'and in future please be more abstemious.'

David turned his attention to Enrico. 'Well done, Enrico. You deserve a special vote of thanks. Your knowledge was invaluable, your assumptions correct and you are to be congratulated. Be assured, your loyalty will be rewarded.' David was about to address Anna when he heard Enrico say, 'I'm not doing this for money.'

David realised his words had been misconstrued. 'I'm sorry, Enrico, I didn't mean to imply you were a mercenary.'

'So long as this is understood,' Enrico stated. David wondered if his disapproval of Jane's drinking had angered him. He watched Enrico twist in his chair. He looked agitated. 'Two things I want,' he eventually announced, 'respect', this word was emphasised, 'and removal from Sicily.'

Relieved, David said, 'You'll have both, I promise you.' He made the vow with a solemn face. David sat back on his chair and stretched. He looked at his small team and nodded with open approval, 'Bloody well done, all of you. Now, go to bed and sleep well. Tomorrow is our big day.'

16

Sicily

'Three days,' he complained, 'three days and nothing.' Oskar was addressing the twenty men temporarily assigned to unravel the mystery of the two missing soldiers. 'They seemed to have vanished into thin air. It's a miracle,' he intoned, using wonderment as sarcasm. 'Miraculous! It's a phenomenon that confounds the senses. We know when they left, we know where they were going and we know they were driving a Kubel. What else do we know?' Oskar challenged.

'We know they were drunk, sir,' said a voice from the back of the group.

Oskar gave the man a disapproving look. 'But not so drunk they didn't know what they were doing. They were in boisterous good humour, gripped by the mood of the evening. Intoxicated, yes,' he conceded, 'but still alert and full of energy. So,' he sighed, 'where can they be?'

'Holed-up in some barn on a monumental piss-up.' It was the same soldier, a *Wehrmacht* sergeant. Oskar noted he was wearing the Iron Cross.

'That's your considered opinion, is it, sergeant?' Oskar asked, when the laughter had died down.

'Who knows, sir?' the Sergeant replied.

'You're suggesting our search is a waste of time; a useless exercise?' Oskar was struggling to control his temper. 'You are convinced all we need do is wait a few days and two drunks will appear to solve the mystery?' It was important to Oskar to be seen by his own men to be able to silence this battle-decorated incomer.

'It's the most probable explanation,' the man replied.

Freewill is Forfeit

'Why would two conscientious soldiers suddenly decide to desert?' asked Oskar, hoping his question would be the last of the old sweat's interruptions.

'Boredom,' the sergeant responded.

'I see,' Oskar declared. 'So I take it you have some secret knowledge of their mental states?' He was determined to better the man in the end.

'No,' replied the Sergeant, 'but I know they were bored. Boredom is the curse of all who serve in Sicily.' There was a communal rumble of agreement.

'Enough,' Oskar shouted. The Sergeant's opinion was true, but irrelevant. It was his behaviour. It was insubordinate. Only a year ago an assembled group would have sat in respectful silence while in the presence of an officer. Discipline was being forgotten. It was disgraceful. 'Stand up, Sergeant when you speak to a commissioned officer,' Oskar ordered, 'or has boredom stripped you of military courtesy?'

The Sergeant leapt to his feet. 'I'm sorry, sir, I meant no offence.'

'That's as maybe, Sergeant, but your remarks leave little to be desired in the company of other ranks.'

'I apologise again, sir. Forgive me?'

There was an awkward pause before Oskar spoke. 'Very well,' he said, once again disappointed he had had to resort to rank to achieve domination over an underling. 'Now you're on your feet you can depress us all with your report.'

'Of course, sir,' the chastened Sergeant said and cleared his throat. 'Sir, during the past three days the entire route from Enna to Caltagirone has been brought under scrutiny, every house has been visited and hundreds of Sicilians interrogated. In addition to the domestic properties visited, enquiries were made at police stations, hospitals and churches. Every garage, shed and out-building has been searched for the missing Kubel. It's my unfortunate duty to report no relevant evidence has been uncovered. All we know, sir, is after the men left the party they were never seen, or heard of, again.'

'Does this not strike you as being odd?' Oskar enquired.

'Yes, sir,' a few in the group chorused.

'Just think, two noisy, high-spirited soldiers returning home in the dead of night, when a dropped pin can sound like a felled tree and not one person can we find to admit sight or sound of them. What does this suggest to you?' There was no response. 'I'll tell you. It's the Sicilian code of *omerta* at work, the Sicilian's ingrained habit of silence. It is their tradition never to give authority assistance, never to help in the detection of crime. They believe vengeance is the right of the wronged family and all that tosh. Well, these missing men are part of *our* family. We'll play the Sicilians at their own game. We'll discover for ourselves by taking direct action.' Oskar, at last, was receiving the respectful attention he believed was his due. He was feeling more at ease. He looked at the standing figure of the Sergeant and indicated with a wave of his hand the delayed permission to sit. 'From 1700 hours today four roadblocks will be set-up within the search area. Each roadblock will be manned by two armed men on a duty sequence of eight hours on and eight hours off. This regime will continue until the mystery is solved.' The atmosphere became sullen. 'You will collect your individual duty assignments from the company orderly. In the meantime all leave is cancelled. It is my determination to have this matter brought to a satisfactory conclusion. Your full-hearted co-operation is essential. Do I make myself understood?' No one responded. 'Do I make myself understood?' Oskar repeated, raising his voice.

'Yes, sir,' the gathered men said in unison. The muted response caused Oskar to grimace. Their half-hearted attitude was yet another example of the increasing lack of enthusiasm beginning to plague the ranks of the *Wehrmacht*.

* * *

It was mid-afternoon when Grandpa Michele entered from the porch to warn David of an approaching car. He waved a finger in the air to indicate uncertainty. On isolated country roads traffic has its own rhythm and over the years grandpa had come to recognise the unchanging motion of the normal comings and goings. It was predictable and seldom changed. The approach of an unknown or unexpected car was an event to be treated, if not with suspicion, at least with caution. At present every unusual movement was treated with distrust. Grandpa's gesture was a warning to David he should take some precautionary action.

With a movement of his hand David directed Jane and Anna to their shared bedroom. He gestured to Enrico he withdraw to the small pantry and nodded to grandpa to resume his position on the porch. His silent instructions took less than five seconds.

When the room was empty David hitched up his smock and removed his revolver. It was an interesting weapon, a six shot .38 Galand, self-extracting, double action, revolver. He had won it in a poker game in France during his first abortive mission. Three Kings had beaten his fellow agent's hand of two pairs, Aces and Queens. Its ex-owner was now dead, executed by the SS when he had refused to divulge the names of comrades. The weapon was small, only eight inches long and had a polished walnut grip. David enjoyed its ownership, it was easy to conceal and delivered a firepower incommensurate to its size. However, his favourite weapon was his beloved John T Thompson submachine gun. The Tommy gun with its fifty round magazine could despatch Krauts a dozen at a time. But for assassination purposes his little .38 Galand could not be bettered. He liked its touch, its quality, its lethal effectiveness and above all, its history. He ran the fingers of his left hand over its surfaces and checked the chambers. The six bullets were in place. He returned the revolver to his belt and ran his eye over the visual areas of the room. When satisfied nothing was out of place he strode to a box concealed beneath the dining table and withdrew his submachine gun. He checked the ammunition drum and carried it to join Enrico in the pantry. Neither spoke.

When the vehicle stopped in front of the cottage David stretched to close the curtain across the door-sized gap between the rooms. He looked over at Enrico and whispered, 'Have you ever fired a pistol?' Enrico sneered. '*Si, signore,* during Army training.' David withdrew his Galand and thrust it at Enrico, butt first. To David's astonishment Enrico shook his head, shaped a slow smile, tapped his side and drew back his jacket. A sheathed knife hung at his side. David shrugged and returned the revolver to his waistband. The Italian mentality would forever be a mystery to him. They waited and listened.

At first they heard nothing, then they became aware of muffled voices, followed by the sound of the front door being opened. *'Prego. Si accomodi,'* they heard Grandpa say, before the curtain was hauled back to indicate no danger threatened. David lowered his weapon and let it hang by his side. He nodded to Enrico to follow and strode into the room.

A tall, muscular young man stood waiting. David laid his Tommy gun on the table and turned to face the stranger. Neither spoke. David inclined his head and raised an eyebrow. The young man responded in an educated Sicilian tongue. 'My name is Luigi,' he said, 'and I come at the behest of Don Giovanni Monteverdi. He sends his fraternal greetings together with a friendly warning. You are in danger and must leave this house at once.'

David raised his right hand to stop the young man speaking. He turned to Enrico and said, 'Go, fetch the others.'

When Jane and Anna entered the room the young man smiled, made a small bow of recognition and returned his attention to David. David nodded at the stranger to continue.

The young man looked directly at Jane. 'Don Giovanni Monteverdi sends his fondest regards to you *Bianca Neve* and has sent me to inform you of danger. He implores you to allow me to escort you to a place of safety.'

David looked over at Jane. Jane nodded the messenger was genuine. David returned his gaze to the visitor. 'Go on?' he instructed.

'We were informed last night of your presence in Sicily. Your invitation to meet here tonight was received by the Don with approval and pleasure.'

'Why should we leave?' David interrupted.

The young man turned to face him. 'A few of our men are employed at the German Headquarters building in Enna. This morning they overheard troops grumble about having to set up manned roadblocks throughout the region. The Germans intend to seal the area by 1700 hours.'

'And your instructions from the Don?'

'To deliver the Contessa to safety.'

'By what means?'

'By car.'

'Is it a four-seater?'

'It is, a small one.'

David turned to Grandpa Michele. 'How long will it take to retrieve Enrico's tractor and trailer?'

The old man scratched his head and said, 'Fifteen minutes, more or less.'

'Go now, Grandpa, and bring it here. Take Enrico with you.' David gave Enrico a nod of command. Grandpa and Enrico looked at each other in surprise. 'Now,' David ordered, 'and be as quick as you can.' They shrugged and left. David said to Luigi, 'You will take two passengers, the Contessa and her maid.' He watched the young man display consent with a nod. 'But before you depart we must know where you're going and where we can meet.'

'At the Don's home. It's in the outskirts of Piazza Armerina. During your journey to Piazza Amerina you will pass through a place called Aidone. When you reach there you will be met and escorted to safety.'

'Is it far?'

The young man shrugged. 'Twenty, twenty-five kilometres at the most.'

David turned to the women and said, 'In that case, ladies, you can prepare to leave.'

'There's the equipment, the radio, the weapons. . .' Anna started to complain.

'Be assured everything will be taken care of,' interrupted David. 'Strive to dress as two ladies out on an afternoon's drive. Take nothing with you except your papers. Now, move,' he barked.

Neither moved. 'Not before you tell us what *you* intend to do,' Jane demanded.

'I'll take a hay-ride with Enrico,' David announced.

'And all the incriminating equipment?'

'Under the hay.'

'And if stopped and searched.'

'That's something we'll deal with if we have to. Now, please will you go and prepare yourselves.' They left.

David reached under the table, lifted his weapon case and placed it on the table. He placed his Tommy gun in its case and left the lid open.

'Was it you who caused the disappearance of the German soldiers?' Luigi asked, as he walked across the room to examine the weapon.

'Yes,' replied David. 'Causing a bit of trouble, is it?'

'A little, not much,' Luigi said, unable to take his eyes off the Thompson machine gun. 'Until now, that is.'

'Do you get on well with them?'

'The Germans? Of course, couldn't be more chummy.'

'Do you like them?'

'They're much the same as everyone else. They're a mixture. The older ones aren't bad, the young ones are brainwashed idiots.' The machine gun still held his attention. 'Have you assassinated many men with this weapon?'

'One or two in my time, yes, and before I'm finished perhaps a few more. Who knows?'

'Are you paid well in Britain for this kind of work?'

The question sounded quaint in David's ears. 'Paid well? What do you mean?'

'Forgive me,' Luigi apologised, 'but you're the first foreign assassin I've had the pleasure to meet and I was curious about foreign rates of pay. I didn't mean to offend you. I'm just interested, you understand.'

'In our country it's not about rates of pay. I'm a soldier, an ordinary soldier doing his duty.'

'And that's all?' Luigi said with a mixture of admiration and confusion.

'Well, in my case, not quite. But that's another matter.'

'It's something personal? A vendetta?' Luigi sighed as if it had been a burden he had lived with for many years.

'Just let's say it's personal.'

'Of course. We Italians understand these things, *signore*.' Seldom was Luigi moved to be respectful, but while in the company

Freewill is Forfeit

of a man like David not to show respect would be inexcusable.

Jane was first to make an appearance. She wore a light blue summer dress with a broad white belt and, on her head, a matching white broad-rimmed hat. She looked chic, very Italian. David made a circle of inspection. 'Fine,' he said, 'the shoes are wrong, but fine.' They looked up as Anna appeared. She was wearing a yellow, low cut blouse, with a green knee-length skirt. She was hatless, her hair was pinned up and she was wearing make-up. Luigi made a sound in his throat when he saw her. David allowed himself an inward smile at the young man's reaction.

'What do you think, Luigi, does she pass muster?'

'*Incantevole,*' said Luigi, entranced.

'The clothing looks fine,' he said, 'but Anna looks too sophisticated to be a maid. Jane should wear the make-up and Anna be fresh faced. Go and wipe off the make-up, unpin your hair and while you're in the bedroom search your grandmother's wardrobe for something more suitable to wear on your feet. Ladies at leisure don't wear heavy walking shoes in the afternoon.' Jane wanted to scream at David's absurd precaution. Instead, she turned to Anna, gave her a nod and they returned to the bedroom.

David crossed to the window to look out. The road was empty. It was too soon to expect the return of grandpa and Enrico. He lectured himself to exercise patience.

'Is the Sicilian who left with Grandpa Michele your henchman, *signore*?' Luigi enquired.

'Henchman'? The word had a strange medieval quality. 'What do you mean by 'henchman'? Is that some sort of bodyguard? Why do you ask, do you think I'm in need of one?'

'No, *signore,*' Luigi chuckled. 'A henchman is a trusted aide. Maybe in your line of work you prefer to operate alone, I don't know, but if you need help I'd be honoured if you would think me worthy to assist?'

David admired the young man's fearlessness. High-octane adventure was catnip to this eager Sicilian leopard. 'I'm certain you're a fine young man, Luigi, but you must learn not to invite trouble into your life. Trouble will seek you out soon enough, but I'll keep your offer in mind. Good henchmen are difficult to find.

Should I ever feel I need your help I'll let you know.' Luigi beamed with pleasure. 'Now, come outside and point me in the direction to Piazza Armerina,' David instructed.

* * *

Luigi's car was a powder blue, two-door, 5-hp Fiat Topolino. It offered Anna and Jane little room in the rear. Before departing they had waited for Enrico and Grandpa Michele to return. Anna had been unhappy to leave without bidding her grandfather a correct farewell. When leaving, David assured them that Enrico and he would follow in their tracks as quickly as they could manage.

The first few minutes of the journey was travelled in silence. Jane was first to interrupt the reflective quiet.

'Is Don Giovanni in good health?' she asked Luigi.

Luigi snorted, 'Never better. He'll be sixty-five next month and still as strong as Hercules.' He looked in the mirror, but Jane was sitting out of his line of sight. She was behind him with her knees pressed hard into the rear of his seat.

Jane remembered Giovanni as a barrel-chested man of medium height. He and Carlo had been firm friends for many years. She had been told during Carlo's funeral he had been inconsolable. Her own distraught condition at the time had prevented observation of others, but Giovanni's grief, apparently, had surprised many of the mourners in attendance. Carlo's funeral was difficult to recall. It had passed in a mire of misery. There was one mystery, however, that had been a torment over the years. Had it been Giovanni who had sent flowers and parcels of Sicilian confections on the first of each month during the period of her imprisonment? She never did discover who her mysterious benefactor was, but always she had thought it might be Giovanni. She would ask him when they met. 'And his wife, Maria?' Jane enquired.

'Mother? Oh! She's fine. Still rules the roost, as ever,' Luigi replied.

Jane gripped Anna's knee. 'Are you Giovanni's son?' she asked in amazement.

'Yes, his younger boy. There are two boys and four girls in the family. You'll remember my elder brother, Roberto. He was the one chosen to sit beside you at table during your visit to us with Don Carlo.'

Anna wound down the back window and said, 'It's baking.'

Luigi was quick to respond. 'Small cars are hell on hot days. We'll take a break in a minute. My cousin Pietro has a small café not far from here. We'll stop to cool off and stretch our legs. We'll take a glass of wine, or perhaps you would like some tea?' Luigi thought it would be a splendid opportunity to engage Anna in conversation, a chance to interact with a stunning girl who had taken his fancy. He knew it would be safe at Pietro's, They would be surrounded by trusted acquaintances. 'So, what do you say, ladies?' asked Luigi smiling into the mirror.

'Will it be safe? Anna asked.

'As the Papal vaults.'

Jane looked at Anna. Anna shrugged. 'Okay, Luigi, but it's your treat.'

'My pleasure,' quipped Luigi. They fell silent.

'Here we are.' Luigi announced, as he pulled up at the roadside café.

Pietro's roadside establishment was not the small out-of-the-way café Luigi had led them to believe. It was palatial. Fronting a two-storied house, a raised terrace formed a sprawling semi-circular dining zone. Doric pillars, festooned with greenery, enclosed the customer area, giving it an al fresco ambience of order and taste. The tables were dressed with yellow and white chequered tablecloths. In the background the house walls were lime green. A terracotta and white striped awning stretched over the customer area.

'Like it?' Luigi asked, as they ascended the four steps leading on to the terrace.

'It's lovely,' said Anna, with a degree of apprehension when she observed most of the tables were occupied.

Luigi led them across to the front door of the main house. When Pietro appeared Anna and Jane were introduced as friends of the Don. Pietro, with usual Sicilian gesticulations, made a fuss of leading them out on to the terrace to a table reserved for special customers. It was at the shaded, far end of the balcony. As they passed to their table polite smiles of welcome greeted them on either side. When seated, Pietro announced they were to be his guests. Luigi beamed with pleasure and encouraged Anna and Jane to sample a selection of Pietro's famed sweetmeats. Jane ordered lemon tea, Anna *un vino locale* and Luigi a glass of beer. Disappointed with their choices Pietro disappeared to attend to his business.

Lulled by the tranquil atmosphere both Anna and Jane concluded 'Pietro's' was a place of safety. After a few minutes Jane relaxed and Anna's apprehensions evaporated.

Ten minutes later when refreshed and prepared to leave, Anna stiffened in her seat. At the far end of the terrace, in the full glare of the afternoon sun, she saw Oskar. He was sitting at a table in the company of a German Sergeant and two middle-aged men. They were engaged in conversation. In shock she turned to Jane and said, 'Give me your hat.' When the request was met with a confused frown, she reached out, snatched it from Jane's head and put it on at an angle covering her face. Luigi and Jane stared in surprise.

'It's Oskar,' Anna said, with bowed head. 'That's him sitting in the sunshine at the other end of the balcony. I'm certain he wasn't there when we arrived.' Jane and Luigi looked across. They saw a German Officer in his mid-twenties talking with three men.

'My God!' said Jane. Luigi looked confused. He was about to speak when Jane gripped his arm. He suppressed his bewilderment and took to fiddling with the contents of his glass. He had learned when to sit and be silent.

'Do you think we should leave?' Jane enquired.

'No we'll wait until they leave before we move,' Anna said in a whispered husk.

Somewhere in the background there was the sound of a violin. Jane recognised the music, it was a well-known Sicilian song. They looked over in the direction of the music to discover it came from the kitchen area of the house.

'Relax,' said Luigi, to ease the apprehension, 'it's just one of

Freewill is Forfeit

Pietro's business habits.' He lowered his voice, leaned forward and asked with concern, 'Is there anything I can do to help?'

'Please, do nothing,' Jane said *sotto voce*. They inclined their heads, once more, in the direction of the house.

They saw Pietro emerge from a door followed by the violinist and three male singers. They watched them stop, sort themselves into order and commence their walk towards the raised plateau of the terrace. As the group marched forward the three tenors burst into full-voiced song. Pietro was a dazzling sight in his newly donned kitchen whites as he walked into the glare of the afternoon sun. Before him he carried a silver tray at chest height. It was thrust out in front, held in a manner of practiced flourish. Behind him, dressed in a black suit and sporting a yellow cravat, the musician's body energetically bobbed up and down in time with the music. He was involved in a losing struggle against a force beyond his control; the erratic syncopation of his uninhibited choir. The tenors at his heel wore yellow sashes around their middles, separating the lime green of their shirts from the bottle green of their trousers. They were lost in song.

Everyone in the area stopped to watch the musical promenade. When the troubadours reached the terrace they were met with a ripple of applause. Curiosity about who was to be honoured stimulated conversation at the tables.

The procession was half way across the terrace before Jane realised Pietro was heading towards their table. 'He's coming here,' she squealed. 'Good God Almighty! He's coming to this table,' she repeated, unable to believe her eyes. She heard Anna moan with fright.

'He means no harm,' assured Luigi, in a useless attempt to calm the distress. 'It's his way of showing respect to friends of the Don.'

'Respect?' said Jane. 'The bloody man will get us arrested and shot with his palavers.'

'Do you want me to stop him?' asked Luigi.

'It's too late, he's almost here,' Jane protested. 'Leave this to me and for God's sake, Anna, try to keep your face hidden.'

Jane stood to receive the arrival of the group with a smile of welcome. She raised her hands in a flutter of feigned delight as Pietro placed a tray of delicacies on the table. The music makers formed a semi-circle to envelop them in sound. Pietro stood in a trance of satisfaction as the choir strained to end their performance with a flourished crescendo of close harmony. Suddenly, there was silence. The musician lowered his violin with relief and the tenors beamed with satisfaction, certain their efforts, once more, had transported an entranced audience. Pietro doffed his chef's hat and bowed. 'With Pietro's Pasticceria's compliments,' he proclaimed. His task completed, he signalled the choir to end their virtuoso performance with a few final bars of song. When the last notes were sung, he bowed once more and turned to retrace his steps across the terrace, followed by his musical troupe and the applause of appreciative customers. Jane slumped to her seat with a groan of exhaustion. 'Christ!' she exclaimed and turned to Luigi. 'Did that look ungracious?'

'No, you were perfect, very genial.'

'He saw me,' announced Anna. 'I watched him under the brim of the hat. I saw him recognise me.' Her statement was met with silence. 'He was uncertain for a while, then I saw him smile. He knows I am here.'

'Excuse me ladies,' Luigi said, 'the man you fear can cause you no harm. While you are with me you're in no danger. Please, trust my word.' He looked from one to the other. 'Do you understand what I'm saying? They nodded and forced weak smiles.

'We are in danger, Luigi,' Anna declared. 'The German officer is a Nazi sex fiend. Yesterday while inspecting Grandpa's house he attempted to ravish me. I got rid of him by making a promise of future sexual favours. He's here, he has recognised me and I'm afraid.' Anna was near to tears.

'As I thought,' Luigi said. 'You haven't been listening to me. Nothing bad is going to happen. So relax and don't be alarmed.'

'Buonjourno, Signorina Anna,' said a voice from behind. They turned and looked down from the terrace at Oskar's upraised head. 'I am checking outhouses in the vicinity, but what are you doing here?' His mood was playful, unthreatening. 'May I join you for a moment?'

'Of course,' croaked Anna. Luigi leapt to his feet and pointed Oskar to the nearest entry to the terrace. As Oskar walked round to ascend the steps, Luigi muttered, 'Be friendly,' and moved forward to meet the German. 'I'm Anna's cousin, Luigi,' he said to the advancing figure, 'and you are Oskar. Anna's been telling me about you.' He thrust out a hand in welcome. Oskar ignored Luigi's friendliness and, wearing an expression of contempt, strode past him. He sat beside Anna on the seat Luigi had vacated.

'So, you're a person of celebrity it seems?' Oskar said. He leaned forward and placed his right hand on her left thigh. 'You are looking particularly succulent today, if I may make so bold,' he declared. Anna was dumbstruck. He had insulted Luigi, ignored Jane and was groping her thigh within the first ten seconds of his appearance.

Luigi, still standing at the spot where Oskar had ignored him, called out, 'Hey, Corporal Klaus.' When the intended insult registered, Oskar's face contorted. He swung round to stare at the miscreant. The young Sicilian met his examination with a steady eye. 'Your manners leave a lot to be desired,' Luigi continued in a neutral voice. 'It seems you have forgotten you're a guest in this country and in the company of Sicilian ladies. We dislike the bad manners of uncultured foreigners and in your case we make no exception. So be a good little soldier boy, take your hand off Anna's leg and while you're about it, take your leave or take the consequences, the choice is yours.'

Oskar stood and strode round the table. His face was twisted with fury. That a peasant should deign to speak to him in such an impertinent manner and arrogant tone was beyond his comprehension. He raised his cane and struck. The blow cut Luigi across the cheek.

In the next instance Oskar's spine arched backwards in a curve, he stumbled, clutched at his heart, staggered to his rear, shuddered and collapsed on his back. He was dead. A knife handle protruded from his lower ribs. It had gone in at an upward angle and had punctured the heart. Luigi walked forward to remove the knife. He wiped the blade on the corpse. When satisfied it was clean he turned his attention to Anna and Jane and instructed, 'Walk slowly to the car. I'll join you in a few minutes. Use the side exit at the rear of the house.' In shock they left without speaking.

Luigi turned to confront the surrounding witnesses. Each face was etched with an expression of disbelief He strolled towards them with an air of regret. He shook his head and said, 'He was a Nazi rapist who ravished my sister.' He looked around the group and saw he was encircled with expressions of sympathy. 'I'm sorry if I've ruined the enjoyment of your afternoon, but it was my responsibility as a brother to revenge her dishonour. I'm sure you understand. Now, if you will excuse me, I'll go and report the unfortunate affair to the proprietor. My apologies to you all, once again.' As he turned to leave he heard murmurs of approval and several bystanders clapped his back.

He left the terrace and as he approached the house he heard a voice say, 'That's far enough.' Luigi turned to see a rifle pointing at his chest. 'Drop the knife and put your hands behind your head.' Having no other choice, Luigi obeyed.

When Jane and Anna were walking towards the car park they saw Enrico. He was sitting on his tractor not fifty metres from where they were. He was alone, waiting in a queue of traffic at the road junction. David was nowhere to be seen.

Freewill is Forfeit

17

Sicily

'Don't worry, Michele, you'll see Anna again soon enough,' David volunteered as the Topolino disappeared from view. 'She'll be back within the year, you mark my words.' David could see from Michele's face that words of sympathy were useless. Michele appeared drawn and grey. The distress of sudden separation from Anna had induced an unexpected emotional reaction. 'Go to the house and rest, Michele. Enrico and I will attend to everything,' David appealed.

'Just to have seen her was enough,' the old man said. He continued to stare in the direction of the car's departure. 'She has grown to be the image of her grandmother. When I married Lucia she had the same breathless beauty.' Michele shook his head as if to remove some unbearable memory and turned in a mood of dejection to walk to the house.

David waited until the door of the cottage was closed before he turned to Enrico and said, 'We have fifteen minutes. Position the trailer at the barn and load it with as much hay as you can fork.'

Things never change, thought Enrico. Once again he was the one selected to do the physical labour. 'And you?' asked Enrico. 'What will you be doing?'

David read Enrico's thoughts. 'Don't worry,' he replied, unable to keep a smile from his face, 'I'll be fully employed bringing the equipment to you piece by piece. Is that okay by you?'

'Sure, I just wondered,' Enrico said, suspecting somewhere he had been hoist on his own petard. 'But, before we do anything, do you mind telling me where we're going?'

'Piazza Amerina.'

'That's not safe.'

'Why not?'

'We'll have to pass through Aidone.'

'Yes, that's where we're heading. I've been told from there to Piazza Amerina we'll be under the protection of the Cosa Nostra.'

'The road to Aidone passes a few kilometres south of my home in Raddusa. I'll be recognised.'

'The route isn't negotiable, so don't let's argue. I'll drive and you can remain hidden until we're clear of Raddusa. How does that suit you?' David mounted the tractor before Enrico could answer.

Enrico shrugged and walked towards the barn muttering as he went. 'The tractor is sure to be identified,' he complained, as David fired the engine.

'We'll face that problem if and when we have to,' shouted David. He reversed the rig to the barn door.

When the trailer was loaded and prepared for the journey, David entered the cottage. He sat on a chair beside the slumped figure of Michele. He placed his hand on the old man's arm. 'We're ready to leave, Michele. Your property is free of evidence we've been here. You have my word on this, I've double checked to be certain.'

'It's odd,' the old man said, staring at the floor. 'Never once has my grandson's name been mentioned. Never once,' he repeated.

'Lance?' David enquired.

'Conrad.'

'Of course, Conrad.'

'When I asked Anna she said she didn't know.' He looked up and stared at David. 'She told me you would tell me, but you never did. Why?'

David lowered his head. He was thunderstruck. His concern for the mission had erased from memory that Lance was Michele's grandson. David removed his hand from Michele's arm. He wanted to make an apology, placate the old man with reassuring words, but embarrassment inhibited speech. 'He's missing, that's all I know.'

Freewill is Forfeit

'Are you afraid to tell me he's dead?'

'We think he has fallen into German hands.'

'You believe he's a prisoner of war?'

'Yes. I promise when the truth is known you'll be the first person I'll contact.'

'To your knowledge he's still alive?'

'Nothing we know contradicts this fact.'

The old man looked brighter. 'I'll be contacted through the usual channels, you say?'

'Immediately the truth is known,' David reassured.

'You must go,' said Michele. They rose together. Michele put out his hand, 'God bless you, Colonel, you're a good soldier and a fine man.'

'And you, sir, a gentleman.' David ignored the old man's hand and embraced him. As David strode towards the door he heard Michele shout '*buona fortuna*'. Without turning David raised his hand in acknowledgement and left the safe haven of the old man's home.

David strode to the tractor and said to Enrico, 'Jump aboard. Just keep the Tommy gun handy, that's all I ask. Keep your eyes open and while you're at it you can navigate. I know the general direction to Aidone, but that's all.'

'Keep driving on this road until you come to a junction, turn left and take no other turn until I tell you,' Enrico directed.

'Thank you, now you can have your afternoon nap.' He heard Enrico snort as he mounted the trailer.

The first ten kilometres of the journey passed in silence. Conversation between them tended to be communications of necessity. Their association was a liaison of convenience rather than a relationship based on mutual regard.

When Enrico spoke, he said, 'I'll take over now, if you want.'

'Okay,' said David, 'I'll drive to the end of this road and we can change over.'

When ensconced in the hay, David asked, 'How far now, Enrico?'

'Not far. Perhaps seven to ten kilometres,' came the reply.

David fumbled under the straw for his Tommy gun. It was in

position. He glanced around the trailer. Nothing was out of place. To the eye all was as it should be.

Several minutes later Enrico said, '*Signor David*'.

'Yes.'

'There is something you should see.'

David raised his head to look in the direction of Enrico's pointing arm. They had come over a rise and were at the beginning of a long decline. Half a mile away David saw three cars parked in line at the junction of an intersection.

'Could that be a road block?' asked Enrico.

'It could be, but there's no evidence of German troops. What's the building on the left?'

'It's a *Pasticceria*.'

'Is it a popular afternoon meeting place?'

'I think so, I'm not sure.'

'Okay, stop.' David fumbled amongst the straw for the binoculars. 'Damn it, Enrico, I can't find the glasses, where are they?'

Enrico turned and pointed. They were found at once. David steadied his arm on the side of the trailer and focused on the scene.

'Tell me what you can see,' pleaded Enrico.

'Everything appears normal. There's a parking area at the side of the building, but for some reason three vehicles have chosen to park on the road.'

'Is there sufficient room to pass with a trailer?'

'I'm not sure, it's difficult to judge from this range.'

In the distance they heard men start to sing. They looked at one another in puzzlement. David redirected his attention to focus on the terraced area adjoining the building.

'What's happening?' Enrico asked with impatience.

'I'm not sure, it's a little mystifying. It seems I'm looking at a party, a celebration of sorts. Luigi's Topolino is in the car park, Anna and Luigi are sitting at a table and Jane is standing. She appears to be making a speech. Is this Aidone?'

'Not quite. Aidone is about four kilometres west of the junction.'

252   Freewill is Forfeit

'You know, Enrico, I think we're home and dry,' David said. He scanned the scene once more and chuckled. 'It looks as if they've met up with Luigi's friends.'

'It's possible. The song is one of celebration.'

David ducked below the up-boards of the trailer to allow a car to pass. From his flattened position, he said, 'Drive forward to midway down the hill and stop.'

Four hundred metres from the junction Enrico came to a halt. David took a long look at the scene before him. When he spoke he said to Enrico, 'I've no time to explain, so listen with care. Drive forward at normal speed and when you arrive at the junction join the queue of cars. Stop the tractor a vehicle's length from the car in front and wait. Do nothing. Just sit and daydream. Do you understand?'

'Yes, I understand,' Enrico replied. At the next instant he saw David leap from the trailer. He was carrying his machine gun. He watched the Englishman sprint across a field towards a stand of trees. Within seconds he was gone from sight. Enrico hesitated and when certain he had no choice other than to obey David's terse instructions, he engaged gear and moved forward.

As David ran towards the wood he observed if entered from the south a downhill approach would bring him to within fifty metres of the building. He tried to make sense of what he had seen. Jane had been standing, *hatless*, smiling and the focus of attention. She was being serenaded and presented with tokens of welcome in full view of a German officer, a sergeant and two civilian companions. Judging by their headgear, the two men in suits looked as if they might be members of the Gestapo. Anna was wearing Jane's hat. Why? It clashed with her outfit. Was she wearing it for the reason she wished to remain anonymous? But, who would recognise her? She was unknown. Luigi had looked relaxed, but he would look placid during a volcanic eruption. The picture made no sense. It was a conundrum. Something was wrong.

David was halfway down the slope when he saw a Chef and four men enter the building. When at the bottom of the slope near to the north end of the wood, he stopped. He propped the machine gun against a tree, spread eagled on the ground and raised the binoculars. Only the south part of the terrace was visible. Luigi and the two women were hidden from view by the building. David noted the Germans had vacated their table. To advance further would require him to break cover. He perused the immediate area for places of concealment. There were none. The ground was flat all the way to the building. David decided to wait and observe.

He focused his attention on the people sitting on the terrace. All seemed normal. He scanned the rear of the building. It was clear. When he looked again at the terrace the people at the tables were standing. David focused on the face of a woman. She looked shocked. He moved the glasses from face to face. Everyone had the same look of consternation. He presumed some unseen event had arrested their attention. This was his time to move. He snatched up his weapon and commenced to run. He was midway across the clearing when he saw a figure appear from the back door of the house. David threw himself to the ground and peered through the grass. It was a German sergeant, the one who had been sitting at the table. David watched the soldier hurry to the corner of the building and detach the rifle from his shoulder. His movements appeared surreptitious, tense. It looked as if he was waiting for someone to appear. David felt foolish lying unprotected in the middle of open ground. He knew he had been lucky to escape being observed. He should have waited. He decided when the soldier moved he would retreat once more to the safety of the trees. He saw the soldier level his rifle and disappear. David rose and sprinted.

Once more concealed by trees, he dropped to the ground and raised his glasses. What he saw astonished him. From his fresh angle he saw Luigi being arrested at rifle point as Jane and Anna appeared at the rear of the building. It seemed they knew nothing of Luigi's plight. David guessed Anna and Jane were making their way to the car park. If his hunch was accurate he could move up the slope and exit the wood from its eastern edge. With luck he might be able to establish contact with the women. He peered again at the area in front of the house and saw Luigi being escorted through a door of the building. It was time to move.

A few minutes later David tapped Jane on the shoulder.

Freewill is Forfeit

David put a finger to his lips. 'Quickly, tell me what's happening?'

'Luigi has murdered a German officer. It was Anna's visitor, Oskar. He stabbed him in full view of everyone on the terrace.'

David decided not to enquire why they had been on the terrace. This information could be gleaned later. 'What are you doing in the car park?' he asked instead.

'Luigi told us to come here to wait for him.'

David noted Jane looked flushed and Anna distressed. 'Don't panic, ladies,' he said, 'events are not as bad as you think.' He resolved not to tell them of Luigi's arrest. It was better they didn't know. 'Listen to what I have to say. It's very important you do exactly as I instruct.' He glanced at both to be sure of their attention. 'Walk out of the car park and in a queue of cars you will see Enrico sitting on his tractor. Get on to the trailer and tell Enrico to barge his way through as best he can. You must leave the area, at once. Immediately, do you understand?' They nodded. 'He's to drive as fast as he can to Aidone. I want the three of you clear of the vicinity within the next five minutes.' David removed the Galand from his belt and handed it to Anna. 'Should any German attempt to interfere with your departure, shoot him.' He examined their faces. 'Are my instruction clear?' They both nodded. In a changed tone, he said, 'How many Germans have you seen in the area?'

'None, apart from Oskar and his Sergeant,' Jane said. Anna was examining the revolver.

'Conceal the weapon, Anna, please,' David implored. 'Hide it behind your hat if you don't know where to put it.' He looked from one to the other and said, 'Well, good luck, ladies, I'll see you later in Piazza Amerina.' With that he turned and left. Anna and Jane gazed after his retreating figure and commenced their nervous walk towards the road.

David strolled to the edge of the car park and crossed the field to re-enter the wood. He stopped to retrieve his machine gun from a ditch and scrambled down the slope to take up his original position overlooking the house. First, he focused his binoculars on the road. Vehicles were attempting to leave the car park. The hurried exodus from the *Pasticceria* had caused a minor traffic jam to form. Drivers were unable to exit the parking area until the queue of vehicles at the junction dispersed. David noticed an impatient motorist had taken over the duties of attempting to control the flow of traffic. He smiled when he saw Enrico had moved. The tractor was now second in line at the junction awaiting instructions to be released. He knew within minutes the tractor would be clear of the disorder and on its way.

David returned his attention to the house. The terrace was deserted. He swung his gaze round to concentrate on the area of ground surrounding the building. The property appeared abandoned. He gathered himself for his sprint and started to run. He stopped at the side of the back door and listened. Nothing could be heard. He gripped the handle with his left hand and pushed. The room was empty. He looked at a cement floor, tiled walls and a door leading to the interior of the house. David crossed the room and once more settled to listen. He heard German voices, followed by a shriek. Was Luigi being tortured? David tried to imagine where in the room Luigi might be. He attempted to isolate the noises. It was hopeless.

David heard Luigi make a liquid sounding moan. The sound could have come from anywhere in the room. Quickly he ran through the orthodox procedure for blind entry. Enter, count three, select target, or targets and fire. It was a routine he had practiced time and time again. He took a deep breath to steady himself, turned the handle and walked into the room. Three men looked up. Luigi was on a tiled floor, bound by rope to a chair lying on its side. His face looked grotesque. His head was badly swollen, misshapen and smeared with blood. The torturers had been taking it in turn to kick his head. On his left an unarmed Sergeant stood against a wall. He appeared to be watching the actions of his countrymen with distaste.

David released his first burst of bullets into the chest of the civilian facing him. In the confines of the room the noise of the weapon was deafening. He waited for the second torturer to turn. He saw the man's face contort with terror, then disappear into a mush of blood and bone as he pulled the trigger. David motioned to the sergeant to untie the unconscious figure of Luigi and crossed

Freewill is Forfeit

to the dead men to search for weapons. He removed two 9mm. Lugers, one from each corpse, and thrust them into his belt. He picked up the sergeant's rifle, unclipped the magazine and smashed the butt against the wall. He walked to the door on the far wall of the room, opened it and was confronted with expressions of fear on the faces of the kitchen staff.

'Luigi has been hurt,' David announced to the terrified group. 'No one is to leave these premises without permission.' David pointed at the Chef and summoned him with a forefinger. He turned to watch the German sergeant struggle to loosen the bindings securing Luigi to the chair. From his knees the sergeant looked up at him. It was a wordless appeal for assistance. David, again, motioned to the Chef. Pietro walked forward and entered the room. On crossing the threshold Pietro stopped, paralysed with shock at the scene facing him. Audible sobs of distress came from his throat. David prodded him forward with the barrel of the Tommy gun. 'Help lift him,' he ordered.

When Luigi was untied, Pietro retired to the wall and stared at the carnage. Two strangers lay dead on a blood-flooded floor, mutilated with wounds of unimaginable severity. Luigi, his friend, had been brutalised beyond recognition and it had all happened in his home, not more than a dozen steps from where he worked. It was too extreme to believe. His storeroom had become a slaughterhouse. He crouched into a foetal position and hid his face.

David walked to the kitchen door and said to an unseeing group of curious employees, 'Fetch a stretcher, or something flat to carry a wounded man.' He returned to the centre of the room and with a gesture instructed the German to retire to the far wall. He looked down at the young Sicilian to assess the extent of his injuries. Broken nose, probable shattered cheekbone, fractured jaw; the boy was in a mess. David bent to check Luigi's breathing. It seemed normal. He knew Luigi might drown in his blood if left lying on his back and bent to move him on to his side.

David rose, stared down at the unconscious figure and made a sound with his tongue. He looked over at the German and said in Italian, 'This is an act of barbarity.'

The sergeant came to attention and replied. 'I agree.'

David saw the sergeant was wearing the Iron Cross at his throat. This was a man of daring, a dangerous adversary. David walked over and placed the barrel of the Tommy gun at his throat. He jiggled the Nazi decoration with the muzzle and lifted an eyebrow.

'Russia,' the sergeant said.

'Huh! Huh!' sounded David and held the gun with renewed firmness. 'Tell me, sergeant, is there any reason why I should allow you live?'

'None,' the man replied.

'I agree. Now we've settled that matter, tell me, can you drive?'

'Yes.'

'Good,' said David and removed the weapon from the man's neck. 'Turn around, face the wall, sit down and don't move until instructed. Do you understand?' The soldier nodded. 'Of course you do, we understand each other perfectly, do we not?' The sergeant nodded once more. 'Good,' David repeated and strode towards the kitchen. 'A stretcher,' he yelled, into the adjoining room.

Four people appeared carrying a door. 'Will this do?' asked a woman in the carrying group.

'Yes. Put it down.' David examined a semi-circle of anxious faces. 'Do you have a staff room?' Some pointed, others nodded. 'Go there, all of you, and wait there until given permission to leave.' He watched them turn to comply. David walked over to the crouched figure of Pietro. 'Is this your establishment, Chef?' he asked.

Pietro peered up at him and said, 'Yes, it is. Who are you?'

'Don't be afraid. I'm a friend of Luigi's.'

'Who did that terrible thing to him?' Pietro asked.

'These bastards over there. Come, stand up, I need your help.' David turned from Pietro to face his prisoner. 'Hey, Fritz, time for a mission of mercy. You're going to drive to Aidone, but first, I want you both to place the injured man on this door and carry him to his car. Now,' ordered David.

The car park was deserted. David instructed Luigi be placed in the back seat. 'That's impossible,' protested Pietro. 'The car only has two doors, it's too small to put him in the back.'

'Get into the car and haul him in by the shoulders,' David barked, 'and while you're at it, search his pockets for the keys.'

When Pietro emerged from the car his Chef's uniform was smeared with Luigi's blood. He took several strides and vomited. David turned from the scene to motion the German to sit in the driver's seat. He walked toward Pietro and thrust out his hand. 'The keys,' David demanded. Pietro handed them over and vomited again. 'What's your name?' David asked the retching man.

'Pietro,' he managed to say between gasps.

'Do you own a telephone, Pietro?'

'Of course.'

'I want you to phone the Don's house. Tell him his messenger has been injured and will require medical treatment. Tell him, also, Luigi will be delivered to Piazza Amerina by *Bianca Neve's* bodyguard. Go. Do that at once'

'Luigi is the Don's son, not his messenger,' announced Pietro, while wiping his mouth with the sleeve of his jacket. David absorbed this information with mixed feelings.

'Please don't leave me with two slaughtered men in my storeroom,' pleaded Pietro.

'Get rid of the bodies in any way you can. Bury them somewhere in the wood. Have your staff hose down the walls and floor. The blood is fresh and won't be difficult to remove. Leave the German Officer's body lying where it is and when questioned, tell the investigators you know nothing except being told there had been a fight and an unknown Sicilian stabbed a German customer. Explain you think the melee had something to do with a girl. Tell them the assailant was arrested and removed from your premises by a German Sergeant and two German civilians. Keep it simple, avoid elaboration and make a fuss about loss of business.'

David turned to walk away and stopped. 'Tell your staff Don Giovanni will be grateful if nothing is said to the investigators about the fracas in the storeroom. They heard nothing and saw nothing.' David was conscious time was wasting.

'Now, pull yourself together, Pietro, no more questions, just go and follow my instruction.' David turned and approached the car. When settled in the passenger seat he threw the ignition keys to the German sergeant.

'Drive,' he ordered, 'and be careful with your responses should we be stopped by any of your countrymen. You're taking an injured man to the hospital following a road accident. Got it, Fritz? Any deviation and your head will be blown from your body. Okay, drive.'

At the outskirts of Aidone a car horn sounded and two cars emerged from a side street. One swerved in front to lead, the other fell into a position behind the Topolino. Ten minutes later they arrived at a two-storied house surrounded by other utility constructions. David saw Enrico's tractor and trailer parked at the side of one of the buildings.

'Stop the car, Fritz and hand me the keys,' David ordered. He put the ignition keys in his pocket and stepped out of the car. He placed his Tommy gun on the ground beside the offside back wheel and waited. Six men in black suits walked towards him. David pointed to Luigi in the back seat and stood back to watch the men struggle to extricate the young Sicilian. When Luigi was removed, David withdrew one of the confiscated Lugers from his belt, checked the mechanism and cartridge chamber, walked round to the rear of the car, raised the revolver and shot the German sergeant in the back of the head. A flock of roosting birds rose from the surrounding trees. He threw both Lugers into the interior of the car, replaced the keys in the ignition, retrieved his Tommy gun and walked towards the house.

When David entered the front door a man was waiting in the vestibule to greet him. David knew it was Luigi's brother. The family likeness was unmistakable. 'You won't need that here,' the man said, pointing at the Tommy gun. 'Besides, mother forbids weapons in the house. Put your weapon in there,' he said and pointed to a cupboard. David obeyed and turned to face a self-assured, smart-suited, Sicilian.

'I am Roberto Monteverdi, the Don's elder son,' the man said, confirming David's assumption.

'Lt Colonel David Hardie, British Army,' David responded.

'Come with me, Colonel Hardie. I've no doubt you'll be in need of some refreshment.' Roberto turned and walked into the interior of the house. David followed and was led into a spacious hallway with doors on each side. An elegant stairway curved around the walls. The stonework interior was hung with Italian tapestries. At the far end of the hall Roberto pushed open double doors and stood aside to allow David to pass.

The grandeur of the chamber he entered amazed him. It was palatial. Four elongated stained glass windows were positioned on either side of a huge fireplace. The surrounding soot-stained stone proclaimed regular feasting was not a forgotten ritual in the hinterlands of Sicily. In the middle of a white marble floor, dappled with coloured patches of reflected light, stood a medieval banqueting table. It bore the weight of four silver, multi-stemmed candelabra. It was the feasting hall of a Medici Prince.

'Take a seat, Colonel,' invited Roberto. David crossed the room to sit on one of the two high-backed chairs positioned at each side of the fire alcove. It gave him another view of the room. At the far end he saw a grand piano surrounded by a collection of other instruments on stands. A saxophone gleamed with an out-of-place lustre beside the severe black of an oboe.

'Whisky?' Roberto enquired. David nodded. When given the drink he drained the contents in one swallow and returned the glass to Roberto's hand. 'Another?' invited Roberto. David shook his head.

'Luigi?' David enquired.

'He's upstairs. The women are looking after him until the doctor arrives.'

'There's a dead German and two Lugers in Luigi's car. I think they should be got rid of.'

'Yes, you can relax, Colonel. My father's men are attending to the matter as we speak.' Roberto sat on the chair facing David. He placed David's empty glass on the occasional table at his side and said in English. 'In this neck of the woods it takes a man many years to establish a reputation, you seem to have managed it in less than a week.'

The remark, and the sudden switch to English, unsettled David. 'By your intonation I surmise you disapprove of my profession?' David enquired, reverting to his native tongue.

'It's merely an observation, Colonel. However, what I do admire is your easy familiarity with our language.'

'The result of a rounded education, nothing more,' David said.

'You were educated in Italy?'

'Milan and Paris, and you?'

'Oxford and New York. I studied International Law in both cities. My subject has little relevance in these straitened times, I'm afraid.'

'Your services will be required again soon enough,' David ventured.

'I trust your prediction contains the hope the present turmoil is soon to be resolved?'

'It's not a hope, rather a confident announcement. It is the singular purpose of our struggle.'

'And you come here in expectation my father will assist you in this singular purpose.'

'Precisely.'

Reverting to Italian, Roberto said, 'In that case allow me to introduce you to the man you have come to meet.' He stood and lifted his right arm to indicate the approach of his father. David leapt to his feet and turned to face Don Giovanni Monteverdi. The Don was of medium height, had the physique of a hammer thrower, was dressed in peasant attire and shod in slippers.

'This is Lt Colonel David Hardie, father,' said Roberto. The Don walked forward and clutched David's hand. 'My boy owes his life to your intervention. We Sicilians admire men of courage. Welcome to my home.' He gestured David should sit and turned to Roberto. 'A drink, please, Roberto,' he requested and sat on the chair vacated by his son. 'You have disturbed a hornet's nest, Colonel. The Gestapo will move heaven and earth to hunt you down.'

'Yes, they have a reputation of exercising energetic methods when annoyed.'

'If you remain in this area you will be found. As soon as Luigi can be moved I will arrange for you all to be taken to a safe retreat, but more of that later,' he said, dismissing the subject with a wave of a hand. 'In the meantime perhaps you can tell me why your

Freewill is Forfeit

military recruit women for dangerous missions?'

'For the simple reason more women than men volunteer for espionage service.'

'It's not a fit service for females.'

'I disagree. Some of our best agents are women.'

'Would you include the two women presently attending my son?'

'No. They're not ideal, I admit. They were last minute replacements.'

'I presume they were recruited for separate purposes. One to access a safe haven and the other to shield against possible unfriendly reaction?'

'Yes, you may disapprove, but that's the truth of it.'

'So, as I understand it, their presence in Sicily is no longer necessary?'

Roberto, who had been waiting for a pause in the conversation, leaned forward and handed a glass of wine to his father. He straightened and remained standing beside the chair.

'I don't understand the question,' David said.

The Don looked up at his son.

'My father is suggesting their purpose has been served,' Roberto said. 'If that's agreed, arrangements should be made to have them removed from the island as soon as possible?'

'Yes, I agree, but it will take time to arrange. Radio contact. . .'

'Colonel,' the Don interrupted, 'what we're suggesting is my family should arrange the method of their removal. Despite the German presence we Sicilians still conduct our daily affairs without too much interference.' He looked up at his son and smiled. 'These days of trust might soon be in jeopardy.' He turned again to David and continued, 'In the light of recent events I would advise the ladies be moved out of the country with a degree of haste.'

'Have you thought how this might be achieved?' David asked.

'Yes, by sea. A fishing boat can take them from the west coast port of Marsala to the port of Bizerta on the north coast of Tunisia.'

'To my knowledge Bizerta remains under enemy control.'

'You will be pleased to hear the Axis Armies in Tunisia have surrendered to the Allied forces. Bizerta is in the hands of the

British First Army. Perhaps you should also know Allied bombers have started to attack Sicilian harbours.' Don Giovanni stopped and sipped his drink. He stared at David. 'Do these events relate to your presence here in Sicily? I would appreciate an honest answer to this question, Colonel. All future trust between us could hang on the candour of your reply.'

'In short, the answer is yes. I am here to seek the Cosa Nostra's collaboration, and if successful, to initiate a programme of sabotage as a precursor to possible invasion.'

'So we have much to talk about, you and I?'

'I agree, and much to do.'

'In turn, let me reward your trust and tell you the co-operation you seek has already been pledged. With the connivance of the American Secret Service our American brothers, the Mafia, have been in active communication with us for several months. It would appear trusted communication between the Secret Services of the Allied Commands leaves much to be desired. Your presence would indicate the British know nothing of this clandestine collaboration.'

'Are you telling me our mission has been a waste of time and effort?'

'Not entirely.' He raised his glass and drank some wine. 'Despite many rumours to the contrary the Cosa Nostra is not a military organisation. If we are to co-operate to any effect we need the presence of an advisor with military know-how, a man who knows what's to be done and how to do it. In other words we need a trusted leader with balls enough to give the Bosch a run for his money.' The Don locked eyes with David.

'Look no further, Don Giovanni, you have your man,' David affirmed. The three men exchanged smiles.

'And is it agreed the ladies be despatched to the safety of Bizerta?' the Don enquired.

'The sooner the better,' David replied, 'but I'd like you to book a passage for three, not two. I promised Enrico safe conduct from the Island.'

'Enrico?' questioned the Don. He looked up at his son.

Roberto leaned forward and said, 'The tractor driver, father. He has been of service to us in the past. He's an Army deserter

Freewill is Forfeit

from Raddusa, marriage on the rocks and currently being hunted by the authorities. Yes, I think it wise he should go.'

'Agreed,' the Don said and returned his attention to David. 'I've despatched four men to assist Pietro to follow your instructions. Your orders were explicit and will be followed to the letter, I assure you. It will be hours before the Germans realise another two of their number have disappeared.'

'Three, father,' said Roberto. 'The Colonel executed his driver.'

The Don's face remained expressionless. 'You've had a busy day, Colonel and must begin to feel weary. A bath and a change of clothes will refresh you for the evening's merriment. Tonight is to be special. It's not everyday we have the pleasure of entertaining our beloved Contessa. But, before you retire let's go upstairs and pay Luigi a visit. His injuries, I'm told, are not as bad as first feared. He's conscious and has asked to see you. You've made quite an impression on the boy.'

* * *

There had been fourteen at the table, now only three were left in the room. Visiting guests had returned home, David and others had gone to bed and a group of four had retired to another room to play cards. Anna was lying stretched out on a Bokhara rug with her head supported by a pile of cushions. On her left Giovanni and Jane sat on the two high-backed chairs gazing into the embers of a dying fire. The murmur of their conversation gave the candle-lit room a peaceful ambience. Anna had been listening to the subdued exchanges, but her mind had drifted. She was peering into the shadowed recesses of the timbered roof in a forlorn attempt to discern the detail on the carved figures decorating the beams. Never had she dined in such opulent surroundings, or attended a dinner in the company of so many talented, relaxed and happy people. The icing on the cake had been when David had taken them aside to announce they were to be returned home under Enrico's protection.

Somewhere in the house she heard a clock chime. It was three o'clock, well past normal bedtime. She didn't mind, never did she want the pleasure of the evening to end. Following the traumas of the day, to be wallowing in a condition of complete safety was ecstasy. David had been first to retire. By the end of the evening he had looked grey with fatigue. Earlier in proceedings his company had been animated, but, as the night progressed, he had wilted. During dinner he had been sitting at the far end of the table between Giovanni's wife, Maria and the eldest daughter, Caterina. It had not gone unnoticed both women had been captivated by his company. Luigi, absent from the festivities, had already an admiration for David akin to hero worship and throughout the evening Caterina seldom had allowed her eyes to stray from his face. But, the evening had been Jane's. She had been the guest of honour and had responded to the compliment with style.

Anna couldn't imagine what type of person she would have been without Jane's humanising influence. Presbyterianised, rutted and settled to a life of dull predictability, no doubt. She wondered what Jane's assessment of Hank Remington would be if, in the future, they should meet. She knew it was unlikely to happen and foolish to entertain the thought.

* * *

It was eight o'clock when Don Giovanni rose from his bed. Although he had not retired until dawn, tired as he was, he had been unable to sleep. He found it relieving to be up and about and involved in the therapy of movement instead of restlessly turning and tossing in bed. He presumed it would be another hour or so before any of his family or guests would make an appearance. Unusually, this pleased him. He decided to make coffee and retire to the garden in the hope the morning sun would pacify his unquiet mind.

The rush of sudden and unexpected events had conspired to disturb the balance of his ordered life. It required less than common sense to conclude it would not be long before the Gestapo uncovered the truth of what had happened. Too many people saw and heard too much of what had taken place to believe it would remain a mystery for long.

266   Freewill is Forfeit

The German investigations would be thorough and, when the evidence was accumulated and the sequence of events pieced together, their reaction would be uncompromising. Anyone remotely involved would be marked for dire punishment. Harsh reprisals would ensue. To delay discovery of what had happened was the only feasible safeguard against assured retribution. Somehow the Gestapo investigators would have to be frustrated. Forthright deceits would have to be exercised until such time the Allied invasion was launched. When would that be, he wondered. Tomorrow? Next week? Next month? Whenever. It was sure to be soon. He would instruct Roberto to announce a 'meet' of the local lieutenants to have them organise a smokescreen of co-operative misinformation. A false alibi for Luigi would have to be concocted and Marsala and Siracusa alerted to expect the arrival of hunted fugitives.

When Giovanni was pouring his second cup of coffee he heard a voice call his name from the edge of the garden. It was the family medical retainer, Dr Alessandro Fratelli. Faced with a locked door, he had wandered round the house to seek some form of entry. Giovanni stood and beckoned him to approach.

'Come, have some coffee, Alessandro,' the Don invited.

'Coffee! Yes please!' the elderly man responded, rubbing his hands in anticipation. 'Real coffee is so hard to come by these days.'

Giovanni gestured his friend should sit. He allowed the doctor to savour a few sips before he asked, 'Well, Alessandro, what's the verdict?

'First of all let me say whoever assaulted your son intended to cause him serious injury. It appears some type of blunt instrument was used in the attack.'

'Gestapo boots,' announced Giovanni. The doctor absorbed the statement with an expressionless stare. 'I believe his German assailants intended to finish him off. Fortunately they were interrupted in the process.'

'I see,' said Alessandro. He made a shrugging movement with his shoulders to indicate distaste. 'In that case, Luigi has been very fortunate. A few more kicks and his attackers might have succeeded in their purpose. As things are, I'm pleased to say no great harm has been done. The injuries would indicate he was kicked three times; once to the parietal bone,' the doctor raised his arm and pointed to the top of his head, 'and this has caused an unsightly lump to appear; again to the zygomatic bone,' he placed his fingers on the upper part of his left cheek, 'and this blow was of sufficient force to cause the bone to fracture; and finally, to the mandible, the jaw,' and he trailed his hand down to point at the right side of his chin, 'which is severely bruised and will, I'm afraid, entail some future dental treatment.'

'Will the fractured bone require surgery?'

'No, it is a simple matter to reposition and set the zygomatic bone. It was the first thing I attended to when I arrived last night.' Alessandro reassured.

'On his arrival I feared he had been permanently disfigured.'

'Yes, the damage did appear alarming, but in a few weeks no trace of his present injuries will be visible to the eye. At the moment this sounds far fetched, but the skull is a marvellous construction and more flexible than it appears. You see the bones of the skull are connected by fibrous joints and these joints allow for a degree of movement, a modicum of elasticity. This elasticity, together with the convex shape of the skull's construction, enables the cranium to withstand blows of considerable force.'

'Can he be moved without causing further trauma?'

'It would be better, of course, he be allowed to rest for a couple of days, but should the journey be necessary,' he paused and made an expression of enquiry, the Don responded with a nod, 'then, in that case, supplied with advice and appropriate drugs there is nothing to prevent him setting off, providing the travel does not require him to be too energetic.'

'I was planning his departure for later today.'

'In that case I will prepare him as best I can. Eating will be his biggest problem for a day or two.' He finished his coffee, rose from his seat and walked towards the back door of the house.

Ten minutes later Roberto joined his father in the garden.

'Everyone still abed?' Giovanni enquired.

'No,' replied Roberto. 'They have all gathered in the kitchen.

Mother is about to serve them breakfast.'

'In that case we should join them to finalise plans for their departure.'

'Do you think it necessary they should leave so soon?' enquired Roberto.

'Necessary? I believe it's imperative they leave almost immediately. One should never under estimate German efficiency. With five of their military missing, plus the public murder of one of their officers, you can be certain the Gestapo investigation will be painstaking. To delay longer than is necessary would not only be stupid, but suicidal.'

'Perhaps you're right.' Roberto concurred. 'Do keep in mind Kurt and Wilhelm are coming here this afternoon to run through our concert programme.' Kurt and Wilhelm were *Wehrmacht* officers, musician friends of Roberto's. Kurt played the violin, Wilhelm the cello and Roberto the oboe. They regularly gave concerts in the surrounding area.

'What time do you expect them to arrive?'

'Two o'clock. The rehearsal should take about two hours.'

'While you're playing it should be an easy enough matter to smuggle them out of the house.'

'Vacate them under the noses of my German friends?'

'Good fortune always favours the brave.' They made rueful smiles.

'Do you think they should travel together as a group?'

'No, they should leave separately. The women and. . .' Giovanni hesitated and looked at his son for help.

'Enrico, father.' Roberto said.

'Yes, of course, Enrico,' he repeated. 'They should leave first for their journey to Marsala. The Colonel and Luigi can follow on behind to make their way to Siracusa. I suggest, to avoid roadblocks, the first part of both journeys should be south to Gela. From there they can travel east and west on their separate routes in the relative safety of the coastal highway.'

'Will Luigi be fit enough to travel?'

'According to Alessandro, yes. He is preparing him for the journey as we speak. Delegate one of our men to drive the women and Enrico to Marsala with the instruction to return immediately his passengers are safely delivered.'

'Which car should they use?'

'Luigi's Topolino.'

'And the others?'

'Give the Colonel the red Alfa. When they arrive in Siracusa Luigi can leave it with Pedro at the docks. There is one other important thing, let it be known I want all the lieutenants to attend a meeting here at eight o'clock tonight. Now, let's go and join our guests to inform them the remainder of the morning should be employed preparing for departure.'

* * *

As he approached the outskirts of the south coast town of Gela David glanced at his watch. It was almost four o'clock. So far, so good, he thought. He looked over at Luigi, silent since departure, and nodded assurance that the initial and dangerous part of the journey was now behind them. David wondered if he should make an effort to ease the boy's discomfort with sympathetic words of encouragement, but chose to reject the impulse. Luigi, he decided, would prefer to tolerate adversity without the further discomfort of being forced to listen to unhelpful platitudes. Luigi's features, although still showing signs of damage, looked less alarming.

With a hat to conceal the head wound and a scarf to mask the heavy patches of discolouration, he looked more like a man who had been on the wrong side of a violent argument than an individual who had been at the mercy of Nazi torturers. The grotesquery of the previous evening had been transformed, but while the damage appeared less horrifying, when examined, the wounds could still prompt a reaction of sympathy.

In a few moments he would turn the car left on to the safety of the main coast road to Siracusa. He estimated the remainder of the journey would take about two hours. With luck they would arrive at their destination in daylight.

The agitation of travelling unarmed through enemy territory was proving to be more nerve-racking than expected. At the

Freewill is Forfeit

morning meeting Giovanni had been adamant. 'No weapons, or any other form of incriminating luggage, should be carried while travelling to your separate destinations. Pack your bags with clothes, toilet necessities and other useful personal items, but nothing to arouse suspicion if stopped and searched.' He had continued, 'All the military equipment unloaded from the trailer, except the radio, which is damaged beyond repair, will be delivered to the Colonel in Siracusa by separate transport no later than two hours after his arrival. You are to adopt the guise of ordinary travellers going about your uneventful, unremarkable lives.'

Despite having agreed to travel unarmed David was struggling with intermittent attacks of nervous apprehension. Without the comfort of the Galand tucked into his belt, and separated from his trusty Thomson, made him feel naked. To dispel sensations of vulnerability he began to assess his current situation. Thanks to Don Giovanni he was now free of responsibility for two inexperienced women. He was travelling towards a safe house, far from fear of imminent capture and best of all, soon to be set loose in an area selected to be traumatised by the attentions of the British 8th Army.

The southeast sector of Sicily was the perfect region to perpetrate acts of sabotage. It was the geographical section of the island directly in the path of Montgomery's planned assault route. Operation Sleekit Beastie had evolved a new significance, taken a new direction. It was almost a fairy tale. Circumstances had conspired to transform what had been an almost abandoned Operation into a foray of unexpected, unimagined, providence. When bedded-in, with a regular supply of munitions, the opportunity to unleash havoc throughout the southeast area was assured. It was a dream come true, a chance to obliterate Germans by the dozen, with the added bonus of having the assistance of a trusted, fearless and dangerously angry 'henchman', the son of an influential Don, no less. Comforted by these thoughts he settled to his drive while observing and mentally noting for future purposes, the locations of industrial plants, barracks, defence installations and small power stations.

On their arrival at the suburbs of Siracusa Luigi began to give

David nodded directions. After several minutes of negotiating a maze of narrow streets they emerged into the open space of a small fishing harbour. A figure, loitering against the wall of a neglected warehouse, strolled over and smiled.

'Pedro', said Luigi and stepped out of the car. David watched the men shake hands and, following a short conversation, walk towards an abandoned, prefabricated construction at the side of the pier. They disappeared and a few moments later Luigi returned to the car.

'Come,' he instructed and turned to retrace his steps towards the hut. When David entered the pier-side hovel he found Luigi standing beside his fisherman friend. 'This is it,' Luigi managed to mumble through clenched teeth. 'What do you think?'

David examined the interior. The windowless, wooden walls were hung with fishing nets and coils of old rope. A large sea-stained mooring buoy, with a length of rusting chain still attached, lay in the middle of a generous floor area cluttered with abandoned, sea-faring detritus. Torn oilskins, damaged marlin-spikes, rusting shackles, old lengths of cable and other rejected items of sea-going equipment littered the interior in haphazard confusion. Two bails of hay were propped against the far wall, flanked by a selection of broken oars, empty paint tins and a small table with a missing leg. The hut was filthy, a neglected shambles and smelled heavily of tar and other scents associated with the sea.

'What is this?' David enquired.

'Our new home,' Luigi managed to croak.

'I've brought you candles,' Pedro encouraged, 'and there's a Cantina at the head of the pier. The food is good,' he enthused, 'nourishing and cheap and used only by local fishermen. You'll be safe here,' he finished.

'Like it?' Luigi enquired.

'Perfect,' David uttered, with obvious sincerity. 'It's absolutely perfect.'

* * *

It was two o'clock in the morning when Roberto was roused from sleep by a persistent hammering on the front door. He rose, put on his dressing gown and descended the stairs. When he opened the door two men leapt forward. He was lifted from his feet, propelled backwards against the wall and punched in the stomach. While recovering from the blow Roberto became aware of armed soldiers clattering through the vestibule to disappear into the house.

'Where is he?' demanded one of the strong-armed thugs.

A German officer, dressed in the black uniform of the Gestapo, entered the front door. 'Good evening,' the officer greeted, as he passed into the hall.

'Outrageous,' Roberto managed to wheeze, before he was gripped, slammed against the wall and punched, again. 'Be respectful to an officer,' he was advised.

'Bring him to me,' called the officer from the hall. Roberto was dragged into the house and released in front of a curled-lipped, cane-carrying figure. 'I have called to question a person by the name of Luigi Monteverdi, is he here?'

'Luigi's my brother. No he's not here, he's in Messina.' Roberto became aware of his father and mother, surrounded by other members of family and staff, standing on the stairs. Attired in different coloured dressing gowns they made a colourful sight. On a happier occasion it would have produced a pleasant photograph. The officer ignored their presence.

'A recent departure?' enquired the officer.

'He left two days ago on a business trip. May I ask why armed men are tramping all over my father's house in the middle of the night?'

'Certainly you may ask. We have come to arrest your brother.'

'On what charge?'

'Murder, the murder of a German officer, and if you are sensible I would strongly advise you speak only when invited. Do you understand?' Roberto nodded. 'Answer me, do you understand?'

'Yes, I understand,' Roberto replied.

'Good,' said the officer and glanced around the interior walls of the house. 'Perhaps this might be a convenient time to ask your father to descend from his viewing platform and join us.' He turned, raised his head and with ill-concealed impertinence, wiggled his cane to summon the presence of the Don.

Roberto watched his father detach from the group and begin his descent. As he approached across the floor of the hall an armed soldier appeared at the top of the stairs and called down, 'He's not here, sir. The house has been thoroughly searched, but there's no sign of him.'

'So, where is he?' was the first question the officer asked Giovanni.'

'My son has already told you, he's in Messina attending to the duties of my wine business.'

'And do you happen to know where he might be contacted?'

'Of course,' answered Giovanni.

The officer withdrew a small notebook from a pocket and handed it over. 'Write down the address,' he demanded. When Giovanni returned the notebook it was passed without examination into the hands of a waiting aide. 'Do you own a telephone?' the officer asked.

'Yes, there's one in my study.'

'And where in the house would that be?' Giovanni pointed to a door in the middle of the hall. The aide left the officer's side to march towards the study door and disappeared into the room. 'You say he left two days ago, well, we'll soon see.' The officer stretched to his full height and drew his cane sharply down to strike the side of his boot. 'A German officer was murdered yesterday in a café not far from here. When witnesses were questioned a few testified the man they thought to be the murderer was your son, Luigi Monteverdi. What do you say to that?'

'Impossible, they are mistaken. As you have been told, yesterday my son was in Messina. The truth of this can easily be verified.'

'How did he travel there?'

'By car.'

'What type of car?'

'I'm uncertain. He would choose one of the cars from our small fleet.'

'You own a fleet of cars?'

Freewill is Forfeit

'We have six available for business use.'

'Ah, yes! The business, of course.'

'My son Roberto would be able to tell you, if you would allow him to speak.'

The officer turned to Roberto, 'You may speak,' he said.

'Luigi took the Mercedes,' Roberto responded.

'You seem very sure.'

'I am. We argued over his choice. I wanted the Mercedes for my own use, but my brother chose to ignore my wants.'

The officer broke from the interrogation, crossed the floor of the hall and spoke into the ear of a waiting soldier. The soldier marched towards Giovanni's study. The officer returned to recommence the questioning. When he spoke his voice was belligerent, his manner confrontational. 'They inform me you are an important man in this quarter of the island. Let our visit serve to remind you that your power is puny when matched with the might of the German military. To me you are a pathetic nobody, a verminous parasite, the member of a thuggish fraternity whose existence can flourish only in societies deprived of the essential mechanisms of order. You are a hierarchical member of a class soon to be removed from existence with other categorised groups of inferior humanity. If you lie to me I will shoot you like a dog and have the rest of your family removed to camps especially prepared for the lumpen proletariat. Now our relative positions are clearly delineated, I will proceed, once more, to address the perplexing matter of murder.'

Don Giovanni had considerable difficulty concealing his contempt. He had been threatened many times in his life, but never by ineffectual insult and show-off words. He was used to more robust methods of interrogation, not outpourings of belligerent verbiage. Now he had the measure of this strutting egotist, he knew exactly how to act. He strove to adopt a respectful mien and said, 'We acknowledge your authority and assure you we will co-operate to the best of our collective abilities.'

This insincere statement seemed to placate the officer and again he slapped his cane against the leather of his boot. 'Very well,' he said, satisfied he had brought his victims to a state of malleable terror. 'Sicily is a country where rumour spreads with the speed of light and you pretend to have heard nothing of this murder?'

'With your permission,' Roberto interrupted. The officer nodded consent. 'I was told of the murder this afternoon.'

'And by whom were you informed?'

'Two *Wehrmacht* officers stationed at German Headquarters.'

'Where, and when, did this conversation take place?'

'In this house,' Roberto replied. 'They were here the entire afternoon rehearsing material for a concert performance. They also told me the arresting officers and culprit disappeared and are nowhere to be found.'

'You're proving to be a mine of information. Do these officers have names?'

'Major Kurt Schmit and Major Wilhelm Kruger.'

The officer shaped a sneer and turned his attention to watch a squad of men forming into ranks to be marched from the building. 'Permission to retire, sir,' requested a sergeant and, when answered with a nod, marched the armed soldiers out of the house.

'This absent brother of yours, when is he due to return?'

'Not for another two or three weeks. At this time of year he travels throughout Sicily meeting customers, opening new accounts, taking orders for the coming season and such like. When he leaves Messina he will proceed to Palermo. He travels on a planned route so at any given time we know where he can be contacted.'

'Following the afternoon meeting with your German friends, how did you spend your evening?'

'Uneventfully; a pre-prandial drink, a family meal with friends, a game of cards and bed.'

The aide appeared from Giovanni's study and marched towards the officer. He came to a halt and waited.

'Speak,' said the officer.

'Investigators in Messina visited the address supplied and they confirm yesterday afternoon Luigi Monteverdi was present in Messina, called on several customers and later in the evening departed for Palermo in a Mercedes.'

The officer's cane struck the leather of his boot. Without hesitation, or seeming loss of arrogance, the officer marched directly towards the vestibule and out of the house. The remainder of his entourage briskly followed his example.

18

'What type of aircraft is this?' Hank shouted at Robert a few minutes after take-off.

'A Halifax,' Robert yelled back.

Hank was not impressed. He glanced around the stripped-out fuselage and adjusted his sitting angle in an attempt to find a comfortable position on his parachute. He hunched his shoulders in a vain exercise to trap some warmth around his body and struggled to settle his mind to the tedium of the journey.

Leather, fleece-lined jackets and parachutes had been issued on boarding. 'For your comfort and safety' a corporal grinned as he had distributed the items. 'I hope you enjoy the flight' he said, making no effort to conceal his humour, or hypocrisy. The seven-man crew were Polish. They had been on a bombing mission somewhere in Europe and had landed in Casablanca to be refuelled for the return flight to the UK.

Why was it the manufacturers of military aircraft ignored the creature comforts of those forced to travel in their flying contraptions? The interiors had the appeal of long unemployed Siberian furniture vans. In Hank's experience they were nothing more than ear-piercing, refrigerated crate-carriers, designed by engineers imbued with a determination to deliver human cargo to destinations in a state of dysfunctional distress and frigid misery. Being a soldier in war was a dangerous enough occupation, but none of the perils could match the alarms of those who had to fly, and fight, in the bowels of airborne extermination chambers. It defined new horizons in the academic study of terror.

Hank glanced over at his companions. Robert was attempting to read, Lance was motionless, without expression, staring straight ahead as if in a trance and Joe seemed to be in a mood fluctuating

Freewill is Forfeit

between apprehension and childish excitement. The miracle of flight still held him transfixed. Hank was certain Joe's mood of enchantment would diminish to one of discomfort within the hour. They were splendid companions. The knowledge they were soon to be separated saddened him.

In the past he had met and parted from acquaintances without much thought, or care. His first year of Army service had tended to intensify this behavioural trait but over the time several scales had fallen from his eyes. The people encountered had transformed many of the attitudes and selfish traits, fashioned during his formative years. He had met Anna and fallen in love. She had introduced him to new emotional landscapes and changed the boorishness staining his previous attitude to women. Nightingale had taught him the enemy were men similar in almost every respect to those in the ranks of the Allied Armies and often were better educated and more refined.

Sensitivity had restrained many of the discussions he had had with Nightingale, nevertheless, their verbal exchanges had uncovered his friend's deep-seated loathing of war. War had become anathema to him. He could see no sense constantly having to kill unknown men for vague and inappropriate reasons. War had come to offend his philosophy. He had seen and experienced too much of war's unavoidable brutality and wanted no more of it.

Exposure to war had a habit of changing men. It forced a re-examination of self, demanded fresh assessments be made and asserted a need to confront ingrained attitudes, beliefs and behavioural patterns.

Nightingale had summed up war in neat and simple sentences. 'War,' he had proclaimed, 'was waged when one side believed the profits to be won outweighed the risks to be incurred, while those in opposition were prepared to face the danger of conflict rather than accept loss.' It was true. The Neo Destour fought for the righteous reason they wished to gain control of their territories from the French. The German ambition had been to initiate the policy of *Lebensraum,* to introduce a new era of economic and political stability for the Aryan races. To millions inhabiting the restless regions of mid-Europe *Lebensraum* was viewed as a progressive, albeit provocative, aspiration. The British, in turn, having subjected one fifth of the world to their political and administrative control, were required to protect a global reputation. Great Britain had international responsibilities and a threatened Empire to defend. When the aspirations of one group are interpreted as being a threat to the other, then strife ensues. None claim to be wrong. Each cleaves to a justifiable ideology, convinced of, and claiming, God's approval in their efforts to prevail. 'It always has been thus.' Nightingale had concluded.

Hank glanced at his comrades once more, half afraid if they could read his thoughts they might consider them unpatriotic. Fanciful theories had no place in their mental galaxies. Through their companionship an expensively educated, millionaire Yank had been taught a lesson in human affairs. Their influence had brought him to new levels of perception. During the time he had known them never once had social class, ethnic difference, rank, religion, or nationality, stained their comradeship, or been the cause of any dissent. Fellow combatants, unalike in education and social background, had merged seamlessly. As comparative strangers they had been prepared to risk mortal danger to secure his freedom. Without hesitation, or thought of safety, they had gambled their lives to relieve him from the misery of protracted incarceration. Also, an enemy, or a man perceived to be an enemy, driven by the edicts of Christian faith and the natural impulse to preserve life, had laboured to save him from death. All had responded to a fundamental inclination. They had acted, not for profit, not for glory or celebrity, but for something more rare, something almost divine. They had been impelled by the redeeming attributes of profound charity and merciful empathy. He would revere these men to the end of his days.

It was a well-worn cliché war revealed the best, and worst, in men, but he had been exposed only to men of the highest calibre. Comrade, captor and foe, each had contributed to his betterment. With that thought, despite his physical discomfort, he fell asleep.

'Ten minutes, gentlemen.' Hank heard the shout penetrate his head. 'We're due to land in ten minutes,' the call repeated.

Freewill is Forfeit

'Where about in the UK, corporal?' Hank heard Lance shout above the roar of the engines.

'Our home base, Harwell,' the Polish airman bellowed in reply. No one thought it odd a mid-European should refer to an English location as home. 'It's about seventy-five miles west of London,' a disembodied voice explained.

Hank stretched his limbs and attempted to rise. He fell back against the fuselage. 'Holy shit!' he cursed.

'Okay?' he heard Robert ask.

'Sure, I'll be fine in a minute. I fell asleep in an awkward position, that's all.' Recently, it appeared, all he had to do to claim unconsciousness was to sit. It was a trait usually associated with the elderly, but it seemed he had perfected the technique by his mid-twenties.

On landing, a waiting lorry delivered them to a hut marked 'Reception'. A middle-aged female lieutenant approached and, without any of the expected military courtesies, enquired if anyone in the party required medical attention. When her question was met with dull stares, she continued, 'No? Right, then sustenance first and after you're fed and watered you will be allocated sleeping quarters.' She glanced along the line of mixed ranks and announced, 'My staff will guide you to your various eating stations,' and left.

Robert smiled. They were back in England where class and rank distinctions were adhered to with an enthusiasm approaching religious fervour. Corporals did not eat with Sergeants and Sergeants were not expected to sit at table with Commissioned Officers, except on special and invited occasions. He once had heard a group of working-class pilot sergeants complain, with uncharacteristic bitterness, of the differences separating them from the benefits enjoyed by their public school-educated, commiss-ioned comrades. Despite the fact they were expected to perform identical duties in the air, when returned to *terra firma*, all equality and social intermingling ceased. 'And the interpretation of heroism', one disenchanted voice had echoed in protest.

The non-commissioned pilots came to realise an invisible wall separated them from their fighting comrades. They were sergeants and it was not accepted practice they be regarded as social equals. This dichotomy caused genuine dissatisfaction to fester among the mix of pilot volunteers constituting more than half of the fighting arm of His Majesty's Air Force.

Two hours later, when Hank and Lance were quaffing port and puffing at the forgotten luxury of cigars, the tannoy crackled and a voice announced, 'Captain Hancock Remington of the US Army please report immediately to the duty Officer-of-the-Day.' Fifty men turned to look at Hank and a muted cheer sounded from different parts of the room. Hank shrugged at Lance and strode from the Mess.

As Hank walked towards the orderly room he observed an American car similar to the model he owned in New York. It was a '38 Buick. Its Army colouring and shape looked out of place parked beside the blue/grey British vehicles. He stopped to reacquaint himself with its lines.

'Captain Hancock Remington,' he heard a voice call. Hank turned to watch the approach of an American Army Major.

'Yes, that's me,' Hank confirmed.

'Thank God for small mercies,' the man exclaimed. 'Pleased to meet you, Captain. Halliday's the name. I've bin lookin' to find you in this limey madhouse since heaven knows how long. The fact is I've bin ordered by General Simpson of 7th Army Command to collect you and escort you to HQ Bomber Command at High Wycombe.'

'I don't understand.'

'Neither do I, buddy, all I know is I should have had you there more than an hour ago, so if you don't mind, let's get goin'. Luggage?'

'Just take it easy, Major, slow down. Somewhere along the line there's been a mistake. I think you've got the wrong guy. Tomorrow I've to be. . .'

'Captain,' the Major interrupted, 'all I kin tell you is that General Simpson wants you at High Wycombe, tonight. His order to me was go and fetch Captain Hancock Remington at Harwell Air Base on a flight comin' in from Casablanca. That's you, ain't it?' Hank nodded. 'So don't be givin' me a hard time, just collect your kit and let's vamoose, okay?'

'I don't think you understand, Major, tomorrow. . .'

'Tomorrow is tomorrow, tonight is tonight. My orders are to deliver you to High Wycombe, *tonight*. Got it?'

'Where is High Wycombe?'

'Half way to London. Now, if you'd collect your luggage we'll get started. I've had enough of this airfield for one day.'

'You've no idea why General Simpson wishes to see me?'

'Nope, I'm just the messenger boy.'

'I see,' said Hank. 'In that case give me fifteen minutes, I've a sword to collect at reception and I'd like to tell my British Army friends where I'm going.'

'Sure. I'll come with you.'

'There's no need.'

'I'm comin' with you, Captain. It's taken me long enough to find you and now that I have, I'm stickin' to you like mother's molasses.'

'Be my guest, Major.'

'You bet!'

Hank returned to the Mess to discover Lance had vacated his seat at the table. He was nowhere to be seen. With Major Halliday in tow he made his way to the reception to collect his sword. It was delivered to his hand with smirks of amusement. He asked a clerk for paper and pen and scribbled a note to explain his sudden disappearance. He requested it be handed to Major Bennett when he reappeared. That done, he turned to his escort and said, 'It's the Buick, right?' The Major nodded. 'Okay, let's go,' sighed Hank.

The journey to High Wycombe took little over an hour. On arrival Hank was informed General Simpson had departed for the night, but had left a hand written message. Hank tore open the envelope and read, 'Collect uniform from American liaison officer and report to Flight Control for clearance to join special New York flight due for take-off at 0700 hours, tomorrow. Good luck.' It made no sense, but when had sanity ever been a feature of military life?

Hank turned to his minder and asked, 'After collecting a uniform and being assigned a bed for the night, is there anywhere around here where a man can get drunk without offending the sensitivities of the natives, or the sensibilities of the law?'

'I know just the place, Captain,' said Major Halliday, with obvious relish.

* * *

Hank's eyes blinked open. Disorientation became tinged with confusion. He was lying in a strange bed, in an unfamiliar room, gazing at an expanse of flesh. He was peering at a nameless back and had no memory of who it might be. He continued to study the geometry of its form. It was flawless, a landscape of physical perfection. The skin had a satin smooth sheen. He moved his hand to touch the entrancing surface. The flesh had a fiery quality. He made a hip movement and nudged in close. The warmth was exquisite. The voluptuous pleasure convinced him the sense of touch was the most unappreciated of the senses. His embrace disturbed the sleeping figure. She moved and wriggled closer to him. He was enchanted. 'What time is it, Hank?' she asked, in somnolent voice. 'Early,' he replied. 'Go back to sleep.' He looked across the room and remembered it was the accommodation allocated to him by the Duty Officer. He saw the issued dress uniform hanging on the back of the door where he had placed it before setting out on the town with watchdog Major 'Playboy' Halliday.

The events of the early evening returned in a rush. He knew the body beside him had to be a girl called Ruth. Holy shit! He had got drunk and landed in bed with one of the girls from the dancing troupe. He withdrew his hand from her back and looked at his watch. It was 0510 hours. He listened to her breathing. It was deep and regular. He turned away from her and listened again. She remained undisturbed. He lifted back the bedclothes and reached for his underwear.

While shaving he experienced a bout of self-accusation. The torment was fleeting. By the time his ablutions were complete he had thought of several excuses to explain away the actions of his improper behaviour. He hadn't slept with a woman for so long he

Freewill is Forfeit

couldn't remember. When mindless with drink he had succumbed to the natural impulses of his body. Stripped of inhibition and brain dead with booze, atavistic tendencies had triumphed over good sense and new-formed resolves. The tragedy was he couldn't remember. After leaving the Club his mind was a blank. What had transpired was wiped from memory. An interval of his life had disappeared beyond recall. In the past many friends had complained of amnesia following sessions of robust consumption, but they had been disbelieved. He had regarded their protested lack of recall as a convenient excuse to avoid admitting to inexcusable behaviour. He knew, now, their protestations had been sincere. The evening had been nothing more than a drunken escapade, an aberration, a thoughtless, inebriated folly. He was a casualty of over-indulgence. He comforted himself with the promise never would he allow it to happen again.

When dressed and ready to leave, he decided not to disturb the young lady's slumbers. As a final act he gathered items of soiled uniform from the floor and left the bundle heaped on top of a chest of drawers. When satisfied there was nothing more to do, he crossed the room, picked up his overnight bag and tucked his trophy sword under his arm. On passing a mirror at the door he stopped to check his appearance. He decided he looked like a hotel doorman. The dress uniform was the complete works, from gold lanyard to mirror polished shoes. He loathed its pretension, its ostentatious frippery.

It was 0630 hours when he approached the aircraft waiting to carry him home. A young woman in an American Air Force uniform walked forward and saluted. 'Captain Remington?' she enquired, squinting up at him in the early morning sun.

'That's me,' he replied.

'Good morning, sir. I'll take your items of luggage. They will be stored in the hold and returned when we land at Idlewild.' When Hank handed her the sword and overnight bag, she smiled. 'Nice cutlass,' she quipped.

'Will it be a direct flight home?' he asked.

'No,' she said. 'This is a B-24 Liberator. Our range is just a little over two thousand miles. First we travel to Reykjavic in

Iceland, then to Gander in Newfoundland and on to New York.'

'Many passengers? Or shouldn't I ask?'

'About eight top brass. You'll be travelling with the elite. They're travelling home to attend a conference,' she volunteered.

'And me?' Hank was about to ask, but suppressed the impulse. Why bother to ask? A crewmember on a Liberator would be the last person to know why he had been ordered home in unexplained haste. The only reason could be the Army was ashamed of the role he had played in the failure of an inter-Allied mission. His return was a stratagem to protect him from the disgrace of British Army criticism. The American Army wished to exercise its own right to inflict punishment. Perhaps he was fated to face Court-martial? It would explain the riddle why he had been ordered to wear the gold braid of a dress uniform. At Court-martial proceedings an accused soldier was obliged to face the ordeal in his finest uniform.

Several accusations could be levelled against him. 'Dereliction of Duty.' 'Making unwarranted donations to a hostile force.' 'Consorting with the enemy.' Whatever the charge, training camp bullshit would predominate and the 'silent insolence' trap, the ultimate catch-all clincher, for sure, would be much in evidence. When the Army wished to punish a soldier there was always a charge to be found to fit the accusation. In Army Regulations lurked a charge for every action, or inaction, known to man, no matter what. If one couldn't be found, one would be devised. The Army was an arbitrary power with its own flexible laws and interpretations. No! He didn't have to enquire why he was being protected from the ignominy of British interrogation, the reason was only too clear. He was being returned to face the wrath of his own military. He had been ordered home to confront humiliation. It was likely in punishment he would be sent to serve the remainder of his benighted Army career in some vast supply depot, staffed by Simon Slant clones, somewhere in the outer reaches of Alaska. He was going home to nightmare, so why ask?

But, he was wrong. Had he asked the young officer, she would have known. If she had told him, he would have been shocked.

* * *

As the car headed up the Finchley Road, Lance, sitting beside a WRAC chauffeuse, turned to Robert and Joe. 'Stir yourselves,' he said, 'we're here.' The journey from Harwell had passed in a mood of despond. Grey skies, drizzle and the bedraggled appearance of wartime southern England, had done little to lighten the melancholy.

When deposited at a block of offices in Baker Street, a reception clerk, obeying a telephoned instruction, redirected them to an adjacent building. It was Michael House, the corporate head office of Marks and Spencer. On arrival they found a middle-aged woman waiting to greet them. Above her brogue shoes, lisle stockings, tweed skirt and cardigan, a cigarette jutted from the corner of her mouth. Through clenched teeth and plumes of smoke, she requested Joe to wait in an anteroom and instructed Lance and Robert to follow her lead. They were taken to a top floor, back room. 'An afternoon cuppa?' she enquired, as she pushed open the door. They shook their heads.

'Come in, gentlemen,' they heard a male voice welcome.

They entered and were invited to sit. Lance and Robert looked over at an unrecognised Brigadier. He was in his mid-thirties. The uniform he wore announced he was an officer in the Hussars. His left arm was missing and a black patch covered his left eye. Among the array of ribbons above the pocket of his uniform was the red and blue-edged decoration of the Distinguished Service Order. Robert and Lance gaped at the improbable officer.

'El Alamein,' the Brigadier said in response to their stares. He smiled and leaned forward to select a folder.

'Although we've never met, the files inform me we were battle comrades in that endeavour. My name's Tony Grant, I was in 13th Corps with Horrocks, whilst you, Major Bennett,' he glanced at the file, 'were to our north in 30th Corps with Leese,' he fumbled with more paper, 'and you, Sergeant Lambert served with the Cherry Pickers, who were everyone's servants and everywhere when required.' He leaned back in his chair and smiled. 'I am pleased to meet you both. This evening we'll get together for a bit of a chinwag, but first, we have other matters to discuss. So, without further ado perhaps you'd care to begin, Major Bennett. I think a broad outline of events will suffice at this juncture.'

Lance cleared his throat and commenced to talk. It took him fifteen minutes to tell their tale of misfortune.

'So, you attach no blame to the American for the failure of your mission?' enquired the Brigadier.

'Of course not, sir,' said Robert, confused and offended by the question.

'Merely confirming a thought,' the Brigadier dismissed with a grin.

'Captain Remington's capture by the Neo Destour was occasioned by his attempt to extricate us from a situation I had allowed to develop,' confessed Lance.

'No,' interrupted Robert, 'had it not been for my interference and incorrect curiosity, the subsequent balls-up never would have happened.'

'So, what are you saying? Do you wish me to place on Report an admission of shared culpability?'

They responded together. 'Yes,' said Robert, 'No,' said Lance.

The Brigadier looked from one to the other. 'We botched it as a team,' Robert insisted.

'I was the senior officer,' protested Lance. 'It is proper procedure I accept responsibility for the failure.'

'I see,' said the Brigadier. 'Would it not be more accurate to say the mission's failure was due to misadventure?'

Robert nodded and Lance shook his head.

The Brigadier smiled. 'It's a negative exercise to apportion fault, but since the subject has been raised, it seems to me the Executive itself must bear some of the blame. In hindsight the Executive should have been less confident of American victory at Kasserine. Had your journey not been interrupted it is more than likely you would have fallen into German hands. When you were reported missing our assumption was you had been taken prisoner. The SOE failed your mission by not adhering to normal procedure, namely, the responsibility to deliver operatives to their zone of duty. In your case we failed in that regard. So, you see, gentlemen, shoddy administration and over-optimism contributed in large part to the failure of your mission. It has been decided no fault is to be apportioned to stain either of your peerless military records. You will also be pleased to hear the error made by the Executive was rectified when Operation Sleekit Beastie was relaunched.'

'Would it be improper to ask who were sent as our replacements?' Lance enquired.

'Lt Col David Hardie volunteered to go in your stead,' the Brigadier replied. 'He quickly assembled a new team as soon as he was informed of your non-arrival at Kasserine.'

'Did he have Sicilian back up?' Lance asked.

'Yes, a civilian volunteer and a serving sergeant in the Education Corps. Colonel Hardie was fortunate, he managed to seek out a Mafia heroine and together with. . .' he stopped and looked at Lance. 'I'm afraid you might find this difficult to believe, Major Bennett, but the third individual on the team is your cousin, Sergeant Anna McKay.'

'That's preposterous,' Lance exploded. 'He used her in my stead to establish the safe haven with my grandfather' Lance said, giving voice to his simple deduction.

'There were other reasons for her selection. I suspect Col Hardie used your cousin as a lure to encourage the Mafia heroine to volunteer.'

'Anna and a Mafia heroine? Forgive me, sir, I'm confused. Who is this exotic creature?'

'Her name is Jane McGregor.'

'Good God! Jane McGregor, Anna's Italian teacher?'

'The very person,' the Brigadier confirmed.

Lance was thunderstruck. 'I'm sorry, sir, this is unbelievable.' His mood changed. 'I fear I must protest and accuse the Executive of gross irresponsibility.'

'I'm inclined to agree with you, Major,' said the Brigadier. 'But that same accusation could apply to almost every operation we sanction. The Machiavellian deeds conspired within these walls never fails to convince me that in our desperation to beat the Hun we have abandoned the comfort of sane decision-making. Espionage is a rough and immoral trade. It is plied outside the normal parameters of decency and fair play. I suppose it is for that reason no one is forced to participate. As you know we only take volunteers.'

'I'm sure they never would have volunteered had they been made aware of the risks,' challenged Lance.

'On the contrary. You can rest assured they were briefed to the hilt. I admit, at the beginning there were one or two hiccups and questions raised as to their suitability, but they were soon ironed out.'

'Like what, sir, may I ask?'

'Parachute training presented a few difficulties, but was rectified by special coaching methods. The time available for training left much to be desired, but in the end they sailed through the programme with flying colours. By the relaunch of Sleekit Beastie all initial doubts were erased.'

'Do you know if they're safe and well, sir?' asked Robert.

'Yes, the reports received are encouraging. You must remember the military situation has improved beyond all projected expectation. Since the fall of Tunisia the Italian Army is in almost irrecoverable disarray. Disillusionment is rife and morale in a state of collapse. Recently, accusation and counter-accusation, has erupted between the Italian and German High Commands. At the moment they're at each other's throats. The friction between them is palpable and with very good reason. When Rommel was recalled to Germany to explain the defeat in North Africa he announced it was mainly due to the inept and meagre fighting qualities of the Italian soldier. He claimed the Italian reluctance to fight deprived the Axis armies of victory.' The Brigadier stopped speaking. He looked at Robert and said, 'Would you agree with Rommel's explanation, Sergeant Lambert?'

'I would not, sir. It's a blatant lie and an insult to the bravery of the Italian soldier. We men who opposed them in battle would tell a different story. The Allied Divisions confronting the Italians were better equipped and better armed and against these odds they wilted, but the courage they displayed and their tenacity of purpose, was admirable.'

'I heartily agree, sergeant. Unfortunately, Rommel's explanation of his North African defeat will be remembered. His assessment will remain in the historic memory, and I fear, in time, the accusation will gain in significance to become accepted myth.' There was silence. 'So, you can understand why the Italians feel aggrieved, and why their fealty to the Axis cause is beginning to fragment. Sicily now is a hotbed of discontent, a place of crumbling allegiances. It is into this happy situation the replacement operation has been dispatched. We're confident their reception will be friendly. Sicilian pragmatism will guarantee their welcome.' There was a knock on the door. 'Come in, Anthea,' the Brigadier called.

A young lady entered carrying a tray upon which was balanced a bottle of whisky, glasses, a jug of water, and a siphon. 'And this, gentlemen, is a small libation to welcome you home safe and well.' He rose, secured the bottle between his thighs, and removed the cork. He poured three small whiskies, and returned to his seat. 'To the cessation of war,' he said, and raised his glass to sip its contents. The short silence was broken by the sound of a far away siren.

'Our victory in Tunisia,' the Brigadier continued, 'has confronted us with a sizeable logistical problem. Allow me to explain. In the north of the country a large number of the defeated troops have withdrawn to the temporary safety of the Cape Bon peninsula, commonly known as the Tunisian Tip. They are surrounded and wait there in the hope of rescue. They wait in vain. Göring has withdrawn the German Air force from the North African airfields, and without the support of the Luftwaffe it would be irresponsible to attempt a Dunkirk-style rescue bid. In the south, following Montgomery's success at Mededine, thousands of men have abandoned their arms, and wait to be processed for internment. In total it is estimated a quarter of a million men will be made prisoner within the next few days.'

Brigadier Grant stood, picked up his glass and walked to the window to look down on the passing traffic. Lance and Robert looked over at each other. Lance shrugged. The Brigadier continued, 'Running around my mind is the vague idea that in the hustle and bustle of the confusion it would be a simple exercise to plant Italian-speaking *agents provocateur* among their number to agitate the present rancour existing between the two armies. Their duty would be to increase the Italian discontent, stir-up anti-fascist hatred, spread anti-German propaganda, encourage Communist sympathisers to participate in sabotage, that sort of thing. As I say, at present, it's only an idea. It requires more thought. During the next few days perhaps you could give the notion a little of your time. I would be pleased to hear the result of your deliberations.'

The Brigadier left his position at the window, and returned to his seat. 'And now to matters more pleasant. As we may need your services at a moment's notice we would prefer, for the present, you remain in London. As a small reward for your recent travails we have taken the liberty of booking three rooms at the Strand Palace Hotel. I trust you will enjoy the experience, and I implore you, please take full advantage of the services they have at hand.' He stopped. 'For your batman,' he looked down at his notes, 'Corporal Fazzi', he looked up for confirmation and Lance nodded, 'it will be a novel experience, I'm sure,' he smiled. 'Last, but not least, you will be directed to the lower floors where you will be fitted out with civilian clothes and issued with fresh uniforms. Anything else required will be supplied on request.' He stood, 'So, gentlemen, until this evening. I'll meet you in the ground-floor bar at 2000 hrs. That will give you plenty time to settle in.'

* * *

Robert sat in his hotel room and gazed at a sheet of paper. It had fallen to the floor as he had commenced to undress for bed. He recognised it was the unexamined notes he had scribbled during the period of his drug-induced transports in Casablanca. Intrigued by his find, he crossed the room and settled into an armchair to examine the scribbles.

At first viewing the pages of scrawl seemed to be nothing more than indecipherable twaddle. What he imagined the spectral voices had communicated seemed to make little sense. It was neither one thing, nor the other. It was a prosy concoction, a sequence of words in disconnected mood and metre. He squinted to read.

Freewill is Forfeit

The young men are gone, The young men are gone, again,
To fulfil an ancient folly, To feed the fatal flaw. When force
finds vigour to fulminate against its own extremity, Let
bugles blow, Let the field sport start.

He was unable to read the next line and allowed his eye to
move forward to where the script became legible.

The silence of women encourage the ear to hear the wind
whisper the outrage of unborn children.

Robert stopped reading. He sat back in the chair and lit a
cigarette. It was a Craven 'A'. He enjoyed an occasional cigarette.
'For your throat's sake' it proclaimed on the packet. On the strength
of this claim he had purchased a packet of twenty. The marketing
deceit brought a smile to his face.

He returned his eyes to peer again at the dishevelled writing.
It had a semblance of poetic form, although his erstwhile English
teacher would have been at pains to refute the assumption. What
followed was a blast, an accusatory outburst, an indictment against
an unexpected group of people. Robert recalled that passage of
reproach had been voiced by a man of unknown nationality. The
spectre had stood alone and had delivered the monologue as if
making an irrefutable declaration.

Generals, In Perfumed Tents, Jiggle lottery maps of misery,
Pin-pointing where eyes are to be gouged, and babies
bayoneted.
Bishops, In Cathedrals of cant, Juggle words in Memorial
worship,
Historians, In Halcyon Halls, Jangle jejune judgments,
Exculpating carnage by mythologising conflict.
'Til tyranny transmogrifies to testaments of celebration.
Parliamentarians, In Palaces of privilege, Joggle to protect
the Fascist Imperative, Saturating the systems of State with
elusive engineering,

The spectre then had bowed his head. On looking up, the stridency had moderated to tones of weariness.

Survivors, In traumatised streets, Struggle to demobilise memory, And bend to tax burdens for munitions to murder their sons.

Robert raised his eyes from the page. He remembered writing the lines. At the time the passage had seemed profound. Now, it seemed to be nothing more than inaccurate rhetoric, an unbalanced accusation against the entire establishment. Were the drug-induced messages no more than a sterile tirade of misplaced censure? Or had subconscious thoughts revealed a truth? He decided he was too tired, and much too drunk, to decide. He read on.

The young men are gone, The young men are gone, again, To have their bones implanted in regimental rows. Criss-crossing, White crosses, Patterning places with the debris of a desolate Deity.

Robert folded the paper and laid it aside. There was more, but it could wait. Most of the rest was indecipherable. He would attempt to unravel it when sober. He rose and continued to undress for bed.

* * *

Lance looked around the ground-floor lounge of the Strand Palace Hotel and was heartened to see most of the tables were occupied. In twenty minutes a deserted area had become a scene of bustle. It was reassuring to witness the strictures of war had done nothing to disrupt the English middle classes from their ingrained social ritual of taking afternoon tea. He remembered as a trainee, while attending OCTU, he would straddle his beloved BSA motorbike and travel the lanes and byways of Godalming and Virginia Water, in search of the perfect English Tea Shoppe. There had been so many he had been spoiled for choice. He suspected if he were to

Freewill is Forfeit

retrace old routes he would find them still in their chintzy, serene, timeless settings.

'With over two hundred thousand Italian prisoners waiting to be processed it's not difficult to guess we're Tunisia bound. The Army will need the help of every Italian-speaking soldier they can muster.' Robert was responding to Joe's attempts to solve the riddle of where next they may be ordered to serve King and Country.

Lance refocused his attention. 'I agree, but in what capacity?' he asked. 'The Brigadier almost told us we're Tunisia bound. He's not the type of man to waste our time by asking us to submit our thoughts without it having some relevance.'

'He's a clever operator. I think he's decided already what he wants us to do and the old fox is waiting to see if we come up with a better idea.' Robert turned in his chair to face Joe. 'What do you think, Joe, would you like to go back to desert climes?'

'Climes? Please, what is a climes?' Joe asked. Lance and Robert laughed. It was music to Joe's ear. The excitement of being in London and living in a hotel was a dream come true. Nothing but good fortune had graced his existence since befriending these men. Whatever they wished to do, wherever they decided to go, he would follow. He only had one concern. He gave it voice. 'If we go back to Tunisia we stay together, yes?'

'It's only a possibility, Joe,' said Lance. 'As things are in Tunisia it would be a simple matter to infiltrate the Italian prisoners. You and I would be perfect, but I'm not so sure Robert's Italian is quite up to standard.'

'You're right. I'd be exposed the first moment I spoke,' said Robert.

'You could be reassigned to 8th Army duty, or returned to Tunisia as an interrogator of sorts,' Lance suggested.

'That's not a bad idea,' Robert said. 'We could operate both sides of the same fence.' Joe and Lance looked confused. 'Mount a pincer movement,' Robert said in explanation. He continued to be met with blank stares. 'Okay,' he sighed, 'first let me say I think it would be a bad idea for you to pose as an Italian prisoner.' He said this to Lance. 'I think you'd look phoney, stick out like a sore thumb. The minute you started to rabble-rouse the Italians would sense something was wrong. Joe, on the other hand, is the genuine article. The first commandment of the deceiver is 'stick to the truth as much as you can'. On that premise what I suggest is, we, you and I, return as quasi-intelligence officers. The information gleaned from our interrogations would enable us to target the genuine malcontents.' Robert sat back in his seat and smiled. 'Then we can leave the rest to acting prisoner Joe to agitate to his heart's content with the foreknowledge that his manipulative grumbling was reaching receptive ears.'

'That's right,' Joe said to Lance, 'you not be good at being an Italian soldier. You speak Italian like an Englishman.'

'Well, you live and learn,' said Lance. Lance was upset. To have it confirmed his Italian retained an English inflection displeased him. For years he had been certain he had mastered the Sicilian dialect. Admitted, perhaps his speech was stained with a hint of Tuscan, but surely this was a common affectation among the educated classes of the island. However, he would bow to common opinion. Better to discover the truth now, than later. Mistakes of pride tended to be fatal in war. 'In that case only Joe can be used as a planted prisoner?' Lance conceded.

'While we operate as intelligence officers in the same detention centre,' added Robert.

'I'm sure our joint efforts would be fruitful, but to what purpose?

'We could harness the discontented into a Partisan battalion. In Turkey the Germans have turned around a complete Division of disenchanted Muslims to fight for the Nazi cause. The Germans even allow them to wear the fez as part of their uniform,' Robert enthused.

'That's not a bad idea, Robert,' Lance said. 'It would give each of us a separate task to perform. Joe on the inside posing as a prisoner, me to interrogate and identify the genuine malcontent and you Robert, to prepare and train the selected volunteer turncoats for future subversive action against the Nazis. Once a few companies were formed we could forage behind the Italian lines to real effect.'

'But, do you think it will appeal to the Brigadier?' asked Robert.

'I've a feeling it just might. We'll push the idea when we see him tomorrow.' Lance raised his arm to attract a waitress. It was time for tea.

19

Hank climbed aboard the aircraft to discover he was the first passenger to arrive. He examined the interior. It was furnished like no other military aircraft he had seen. The floor of the fuselage was covered with a red carpet patterned with the badges and insignia of American Army Divisions. Down each side of the central passage, at amply spaced intervals, was a line of five high-backed armchairs upholstered in tan leather. The compartment was walled in oak panelling. It was the miniature version of a New York Gentleman's Club. As Hank walked aft he passed two toilet compartments and entered a cabin furnished as a small reading area. The walls were racked with books, newspapers and magazines. He selected an English newspaper and continued his inspection.

The rear section was a smaller replica of the forward passenger area. It had two seats on each side of the passageway instead of five. He decided this was the over-spill area and the proper place to sit. He chose the rear seat on the port side. It was a position as far from the other passengers as he could manage.

Two hours later, when somewhere over the Hebridean islands off the west coast of Scotland, he was approached by the young lady who had greeted him on arrival. 'Is there anything you require, Captain Remington?' she enquired.

'Not unless you have a cure for a hangover,' Hank replied.

'A common complaint,' she said and left. Seconds later she returned with two pills and a glass of water. 'That should do the trick. If not, you'll feel better when you've had something to eat. A simple breakfast will be served in ten minutes. How would you like your coffee?'

'Black and sweet,' he answered. 'Could you supply me with writing paper and a pen?' he enquired. She nodded and left. Hank

Freewill is Forfeit

had been thinking of Gustav and remembered soon after arrival in New York he would have to arrange the transfer of money to the Neo Destour. To utilise time he would write a Note of Instruction; the method of transfer to be employed and the conditions appertaining to the final release of the promised money. Thereafter, it would be the simple matter of handing his note to the bank's Legal Department to implement. He wished the negotiation to remain confidential and by employing their services it would guarantee anonymity. It would also assure the transfer of funds be conducted with practiced efficiency.

Hank had been toying with the idea of inviting Gustav and Lisa to America at the end of the war. It would remove them from the hardships of struggling to live in a devastated country and from the ordeals and strictures of Allied occupation. As an architect Gustav would have little difficulty finding employment in New York. On the other hand, if he wished a change of profession, it would be a simple matter to find him a post somewhere within the banking regime. Gustav was a clever and adaptable man, upright and honourable in every respect.

At midday the aircraft touched down at Reykjavic. An informal buffet lunch was served to crew and passengers in the corner of a hanger at the edge of the landing runway. Food was consumed standing in huddled groups. While eating Hank mingled with the crew. They were an undistinguished mixture of individuals who, either through intimacy, or long association, had developed a style of communication that relied entirely upon the shaping of indecipherable gestures, or mouthing untranslatable grunts.

When Hank returned to his seat he was joined by a Canadian Brigadier dressed in combat fatigues. He looked unkempt, out of place, in the plush surroundings. He nodded at Hank, selected the forward seat on the starboard side and within minutes of settling, was asleep.

The monotony of the afternoon was made memorable by one event. He was summoned by a crewmember to a position where it was possible to view the north Atlantic seaway. Hank peered down at a cluster of icebergs drifting down from the Arctic. The magisterial beauty of the multi-coloured, gleaming towers, mystified his eye. He found it difficult to imagine anything more exquisite. The experience left him feeling haunted by his own insignificance.

When they landed at Gander it was raining. Passengers and crew were transported by bus to a local hotel to be served dinner. During the meal Hank was forced to share a table with three Generals. At first he felt exposed and self-conscious, until he realised their attentions were for one another and his presence was a matter of little significance.

On the last leg of the air journey Hank checked the notes he had written earlier in the day and, when satisfied with the accuracy and clarity of the contents, folded the sheets of paper and returned them to the top pocket of his uniform. Half an hour later, while midway through a magazine article proclaiming the beneficial effects of regular exercise, he succumbed to sleep.

He awoke when tapped on the shoulder by his faithful flight attendant. In fifteen minutes he would be home again. Eighteen months spent in uniform and he had yet to see an Oriental face. He had met people from every quarter of the globe, but never had he met a person from the ethnic group he had enlisted to fight. Not that he cared much now whether he ever did. All past anger had dissipated. The original feeling of fury was now only a memory; the memory of a righteous and naïve young man too eager to do what he thought was right. Now he wasn't so sure the taking up of arms and marching to war solved anything. War, it seemed, served no other purpose than to unleash a cataclysm to cull unnumbered, innocent human beings.

Hank felt the aircraft shudder as it hit the runway and as it taxied to its parking bay the flight attendant appeared at the cabin entrance.

'Everything okay?' she called. Hank reassured her with a nod. 'Would you mind waiting a few minutes while the Generals clear the forward cabin?' she asked. He shook his head. He had already decided to wait until they were clear before rising to leave. 'Good,' she responded. 'You'll be told when it's convenient to make your appearance.'

The words sounded ominous. 'Make your appearance'

Freewill is Forfeit

suggested his presence, if noticed, would be an embarrassment to his fellow passengers. Perhaps they were right to insist he wait. In America it was unhealthy to be seen with someone associated with failure. Americans treated failure like a contagious disease. He would sit, hidden and enclosed, without complaint and try not to ponder on the myriad injustices that plagued the lives of the ostracised millions of the world.

He felt the aircraft come to a halt. When the noise of the engines subsided he heard crowds of cheering people and a band playing the 'Stars and Stripes'. Enclosed, alone and unable to witness what was happening, Hank concluded the Generals were being treated to a ceremony of welcome. His wait might be longer than first anticipated.

After several minutes Hank became aware of someone approaching down the central aisle of the aircraft. He looked up and saw it was an American officer. The figure appeared familiar. The man who entered the cabin was Uncle Matty.

'Hello, Hancock,' he said. 'There's one helluva hullabaloo goin' on out there, I kin tell you.' Hank stared up at him in disbelief. This was not hallucination. Uncle Matty was stouter and now wore the badges of a full Colonel, but he was real. 'Never seen so many hysterical people. Public behaviour these days is appalling. They're all shoutin' and screamin' like crazed maniacs. It's terrible.'

Hank attempted to stand, but found his legs unwilling to bear the weight of his body. At least he was being welcomed home in typical family style. No polite preamble, no 'How are you, Hancock?', 'Good trip?', 'Glad to have you home safe and sound', no, just a torrent of complaint about the behaviour of excited people. This was Uncle Matty, no doubt.

'Well, are you ready to face the ordeal, m'boy?' Ordeal? Holy shit! Some form of punishment was in the offing, after all. 'I don't know if you deserve all this fuss, but there you are. To be honest, it wouldn't be happenin' if I had my way, but the press reports coverin' your capture and release has whipped up a frenzy of interest. The public's imagination has bin fired to fever pitch. To them you're a hero. So, stand up and make yourself ready to face your adorin' public. Every newsreel camera and tinhorn reporter east of the Rockies are out there waitin' to greet you, so get to your feet, straighten your spine and jut your jaw. Just remember durin' the playing of the Anthem to keep your face straight and your salute steady. Apart from that, you can try to look happy you're home.'

Hank remained rooted. 'I don't understand,' he managed to say.

Uncle Matty shook his head. 'Neither do I, believe me, neither to I. All I kin say is there's no accountin' for public reaction. Six months ago anti-war demonstrators were everywhere shoutin' their disapproval at anyone wearing a uniform, now these same people are out there cheerin' like mindless teenagers greetin' their favourite film star. It was our victory in Tunisia that changed the mood of the country. Now everyone is desperate for hero figures. The Army is under real pressure to react to their clamour and, of course, are only too willin' to stoke these new fires of patriotism with every method in the manual. New York has gone hysterical that, at last, they have one of their own boys to celebrate. Yes, New York is very proud of you, m'boy and needless to say the family, and especially your mother, are gratified beyond words.'

'I thought I had been summoned home to face disgrace?' Hank said, still unsure his ears were not deceiving him.

'Disgrace?' Uncle Matty enquired in genuine confusion. 'What in the name of God are you ravin' about?'

'I don't know what's been reported, but whatever's been written is wrong. There's been some terrible mistake. Real heroes do exist and deserve due acclaim, but I'm not one of them. I've done nothing to deserve the honour. I'm sorry, but I'm not a hero and refuse to go out there and pretend to be what I'm not. It would be immoral, quite unethical.'

'What?' Uncle Matt exploded.

'To receive undeserved acclaim would be dishonest,' Hank tried once more.

'What?' Uncle Matty yelled again.

'I think it would be wrong to perpetrate a deceit,' Hank persisted.

'Shut up,' Uncle Matty bellowed. He was having difficulty trying to understand what his nephew was attempting to imply. 'I don't know what you're tryin' to tell me and I don't give a damn,' he bawled, 'but I know one thing for certain, in two minutes time you'll be on parade in front of half of New York and if you refuse to comply the consequences will be catastrophic. The shit will hit the fan so hard the spray will reach all the way to the White House lawn. You'll be responsible for makin' the American Army appear duplicitous, the American public look gullible and worse, pulverise the morale of the entire nation.'

'I want. . .'

'Shut up,' Uncle Matty roared again. 'Don't dare to interrupt me when I'm talkin' and don't give me any more of your selfish, ethical, high-toned crap. Your principles are irrelevant. Do I make myself understood? No, don't answer. Just get one thing straight in your ungrateful, muddled brain, you could've spent your entire service in a Tunisian brothel for all anybody cares, but now you've bin made a hero, a hero you're goin' to be. Is that clear enough for your virtuous sensitivities?'

'But, it's all bullshit,' Hank managed to complain.

'The entire Army is built on bullshit,' Uncle Matty shrieked. 'If you don't know that by now you're a cretin.' Uncle Matty stepped back and straightened. His mood was ugly. 'Get to you feet, Captain.' He ordered. Hank obeyed. 'Check your uniform and put your cap on.' Hank obliged. 'You're now on official military duty and will act as instructed, understand?'

'Yes sir,' said Hank.

They walked to the door of the aircraft. At the opening Uncle Matty stood aside and gestured at Hank to proceed. Hank stepped out on to the exit platform.

The force of the welcome was overwhelming. The crowd erupted, flash bulbs blinded him and the band struck up 'Marching through Georgia'. Disorientated, Hank stood still and struggled to control his emotions. The unreality was paralysing. His world suddenly had become a nonsensical blur of noise, music and charged passion.

'Wave, for Christ sake, WAVE,' Uncle Matty roared from inside.

Hank responded like an automaton. He raised his right arm

and flapped it above his head. The crowd went berserk. Everywhere he looked banners and flags were being waved with unself-conscious vigour. The noise and spectacle pulverised him. A surge of absurdity coursed through his body. The force of it welled up in his throat. The sorcery of surrealism, collective passion, excitement and the happy cacophony of celebration, penetrated his core. He was captive in its power. Unwanted and unexpected, tears spurted from his eyes. He was out of control.

'Keep wavin', keep smilin' and begin to walk down the steps to the reception party,' Uncle Matty screeched from behind.

Hank withdrew a handkerchief to wipe his stained face. When the rejoicing assembly saw he had shed tears, they went wild. Their joy reached new levels of ebullience. The simple movement of a handkerchief revealed Hank to be a man worthy of worship, a man with the defining characteristics of a caring conqueror. New York, indeed, had a hero of distinction for the world to admire: a lion-hearted man with the sensitivity and compassionate spirit of a saint. The excitement was unrestrained.

'Walk down the fucking steps,' roared Uncle Matty, near to despair.

The next fifteen minutes of Hank's life passed in a state of dazed wonderment. His hand was shaken with furious energy. He was saluted and clapped, kissed and embraced by an endless succession of beaming admirers. By the time he reached the refuge of the airport building he was half blind with flashing cameras, bruised with bonhomie and beyond bewilderment. It was in this condition he was led to face the interrogation of his first press conference.

Uncle Matty cleared his throat to gain attention. 'Gentlemen,' he called and waited for the assembly to settle. 'Keep your questions short and succinct. You've got fifteen minutes, so go to it.' At once questions were fired from every quarter.

'What do you crave most, now you're home?'

'The address of a girl I met in Casablanca.' There was laughter.

'Is she a belly dancer, Hank?' There was more laughter.

'No. She's a British Army sergeant called Anna McKay and there's a reward for anyone who can discover her current where-

Freewill is Forfeit

abouts.' There were woops from the company.

'What's the first thing you want to do in New York?'

'Spend a few quiet nights in the Algonquin Hotel.'

'Is it true you were chosen to be part of a small Allied group selected to transgress enemy territory?'

Hank was unsure if he should respond to this question and looked over at his uncle. The Colonel was uncomfortable but nodded consent. 'Yes. I was wounded and taken prisoner on the eve of being parachuted into enemy territory.'

'Was that country Sicily?'

'It was.'

'Do you speak Italian?'

'British Intelligence put me through a crash course prior to departure.'

'Would you be willing to record a short interview for Radio Parliamo Italiano?' asked a pressman with a distinct Italian accent.

The Colonel rose and glared at the man. 'This is a press conference not a recruitment agency for foreign language broadcasters,' he barked.

'No need to get worked-up, Colonel,' the Italian journalist objected. 'It was an innocent request. A simple yes or no would answer my question.'

'Sit down, sir,' ordered the Colonel. The Italian remained standing and looked at Hank for an answer. 'Your request is out of order. Sit, or I'll have you ejected,' the Colonel shouted. The Italian sat. There was a rumble of complaint. An angry silence followed.

While resentment was fermenting a man at the back of the assembly stood and raised an arm. 'Yes,' said Uncle Matty, pointing at him. 'Proceed.'

'Hiya Hancock,' the man said. It was Hank's old friend Jack Dawson. With studied formality Jack announced his identity to the Colonel. 'Jack Dawson, *New York Times*,' His pedantic correctness evinced chuckles of appreciation.

'You'll never know just how good it is to see you, Jack,' Hank said. 'It's good to have you home, Hancock, but God man, what have they done to you, you look terrible?' There were gasps of surprise.

'Travelling is tiring. You know that,' Hank grinned.

'Huh! Huh! It's going to take more than a good night's sleep to put you back together again, Humpty Dumpty. What you need is a month's leave.' The applause was immediate.

'Do you have a question, Mr Dawson?' the Colonel demanded.

'So many it's difficult to know where to start,' Jack drawled.

'In that case you can sit down until your mind is made up,' the Colonel ordered.

Jack remained standing. 'With your permission I would like to proceed.' His repetition of the word 'proceed' was spoken in playful mimicry. The surrounding wordsmiths reacted in silent glee.

'Carry on,' conceded the Colonel. A murmur of anticipation greeted the permission. When Jack Dawson was on his feet the gathered group knew from experience to expect the unexpected.

'Thank you,' Jack said and returned his attention to Hank. 'You know nuthin' of what's bin goin' on in New York, do you Hancock?'

'Not a thing.'

'You didn't even know you were comin' home to public acclaim?'

'No, that's correct.'

'You were surprised, were you not?' The room was silent. Hank looked over at his uncle. His glance was met with a cold stare. 'No doubt, you were shocked?' Jack asked, again.

'Shocked would be a euphemism, Jack.'

'Can you find a suitable word to fit your reaction?'

'Disbelief comes easily to mind.'

'Incomprehensible?'

'Yeah, that would fit.'

'I thought so. What was your civilian occupation, Hank?'

'I worked as a banker in New York.'

'You were more than just a banker, you were Chairman Elect of the Remington Bartholemew Bank?'

'Yep!'

'When did you enlist?'

'On Christmas day, 1941.'

'Immediately following Pearl Harbour.' Hank nodded. 'You

joined an Infantry Battalion as a private soldier, why?'

'I wanted to fight the Japanese. I knew if I joined the infantry I would be certain to see action.'

'Exactly. You were a true patriot. You walked away from a secure position in a reserved occupation to fight for your country. Would it surprise you to know while incarcerated and recovering from near fatal wounds in the misery of an Arab cave, an attempt was made by a fellow Board member to oust you from your position in the bank?'

'What are you trying to tell me, Jack, I haven't a job to come home to?'

'No, the chicanery was exposed, but the underhand misuse of information, when exposed, outraged our readers. Ordinary people don't like to see a guy being done down when he's in no position to defend himself, especially when the victim is incapacitated, banged-up in a desert cave and being held for ransom by a bunch of fundamentalist Fellahin. The high profile you enjoy is due to the vigilance of my surrounding colleagues and their efforts to right a blatant wrong. We made a hero of you and you made heroes of us. Everyone in this room rejoices in your safe return. It's a happy and triumphant event for you, but also for the pressmen of New York. Welcome home, Hancock. You're a hero in spades; a military hero, a people's hero and you have made every scribbler in the room feel good about the work they do. So dispel disbelief, banish what you feel is incomprehensible and enjoy the limelight. Your acclaim is richly deserved.' Jack sat. Raucous cheers filled the room.

'That's enough,' shouted Colonel Mattheson, 'this press conference is at an end,' he shrieked. No one heard him.

* * *

Two days later Hank paid a visit to the offices of the *New York Times*. From the reception area he was taken to the third floor, through a large room crammed with desks and shown into an enclosed, glass-encaged, cubicle. Jack rose and strode forward to meet him. They embraced.

'Take a seat, soldier,' Jack invited. 'Well, what did you think of the performance. Was I good, or just sensational?'

'A bit heavy on self-congratulation, I'd say.'

'Ingrate. I was terrific. What a pompous shit, that Colonel guy.'

'He's an uncle of mine.'

'Is he? That figures.' They laughed.

'How's the Algonquin?'

'Good.'

'Mummy's not upset?'

'Nope. Saw her yesterday. Purgatory.'

'Gushing was she?'

'And some. I was treated like a prize show dog.'

'Did you get your leave?'

'Yeah, fifteen days.'

'Nice little touch of mine, for openers.'

'It was unnecessary blather. You knew leave was on the cards. You couldn't resist the opportunity of being rude to me in public.'

'The whole room agreed with me. You looked crap.'

'Yeah! Thanks a bunch.'

'Who's the chick?'

'What?'

'The Casablancan cutie?'

'Ah! Now she's special.'

'Good in bed, is she?'

'Don't know.'

'D'ya mean you can't make up your mind, or you really don't know?'

'I really don't know.'

'I don't believe I'm hearing this. You haven't come over all lovey-dovey, have you?'

'Must have. Tragic, ain't it, but what's a man to do?'

'And you don't know where she is?'

'Nope.'

'This office is pretty good at finding people, but the problem is she's in the Army. The paper's not so chummy with the military at the moment.'

'Why's that?'

Freewill is Forfeit

'Over us pokin' our noses where they weren't supposed to be. Of course, I was on to stinky Braithwaite like a shot. As soon as he made his move I knew he was up to no good. My suspicion was confirmed when the Army communiqué was issued stating you had been taken prisoner. That's when I got the rest of the guys interested. We were certain there had been a leak. All we had to do was find the source.'

'Cowboy Thomson?'

'That's the one. It would have been difficult to prove, but in the end we didn't need evidence. A few of us paid Braithwaite a visit and announced what we'd uncovered. It was enough. The terror of exposure prompted the old fart to resign the next day.'

'And Cowboy walks away unscathed, yet again.'

'Not quite. What we have on file will keep until the cessation of hostilities. We've unearthed enough dirt to bury him ten times over, but that can wait.'

'You're salivating, already.'

'I know, shameful, isn't it?'

'And, I suppose, from now on you'll expect my undying gratitude, a grovelling demeanour while in your saintly presence and to be showered with expensive knick-knacks?'

'It's only befitting you should want to reward me with tokens of eternal obligation. Perhaps I should have stressed your debt to me with more emphasis during my brilliant oration.'

'We're back to that, are we? Can't quite quell the sense of self-satisfaction, can you?

'Don't try to change the subject. Return, please, to this intriguing *femme fatale*. Does she have a name and what does she do apart from weaving love spells?'

'Her name is Anna McKay. She's Scottish and comes from Glasgow.'

'Ah! A wee blossom from the Gorbals.'

'Knock it off! She was my Italian teacher.'

'You make her sound like a blue-stocking.'

'Yeah, I think she is, a little.'

'Now I know you're kidding.'

'Could you trace her, do you think?'

'With the right connections all is possible, but what would be the point? If we did manage to trace her you wouldn't be able to see her until you were almost middle-aged. Wise up, there are thousands of chicks out there gagging for your body.'

'That scene's over for me, Jack. It's time to settle down. I want to be more like you and Grace, go to work, have a family, lead a normal life.'

'Christ Almighty! What did these fucking Arabs do to you, cut your balls off?'

'Who was the Italian guy?'

'Cesare Visconti. He runs a radio station. Clever guy! Knows a lot more thn he lets on. Want to meet him?'

'Not really,' Hank replied quickly. 'Is there any truth in the rumour?'

'About a medal, you mean?'

'No, about the Army's intention to parade me around the country as an example of perfect manhood?'

'That's the usual fate of American heroes. I noticed your answer was non-committal.'

'Had to be. The Army operates on reverse logic, the more interest you have in wanting to do a job, the less chance you have of getting to do it. Bakers become bricklayers and vice versa, if you see what I mean?'

'You'd like the job, then?'

'What? Traipsing around the country, staying in the best hotels, quaffing champagne, being pursued by knickerless women and having to submit to daily doses of adoration and acclaim. Mother would be pleased.' Hank's irony was obvious.

'It sounds horrendous.'

'Of course it does, unless it had some purpose.'

'You know the purpose. It's all about banging the drum, propaganda, fund raising, whipping-up. . .'

'Some personal purpose,' Hank interrupted.

'You've lost me.'

'A selfish reason to make the doing of it bearable.'

'Like what?'

'Like doing the rounds with a compatible partner.' Jack looked

Freewill is Forfeit

confused. 'We're not fighting this war alone. Don't you think America should be made aware of the sacrifices our British Allies are making? A joint allied tour would be a terrific idea. It would double the razz-a-ma-tazz, give the promotion added depth, flavour it with international appeal and make it more comprehensively triumphant.'

'And, of course, you would be on hand to provide a suggestion or two as to who might be suitable company?'

'Exactly.'

'Its neat, but it will never work. If the bigwigs agree to your idea, and I must admit it's a good one, they'll want to display the genuine article. They'll demand the real thing. If your young lady was a heroine, then it would be a different matter.'

'She's a stunner, I tell you. The Generals will love her. She'd be the best ambassadress. . .'

'Whoa! She's not a heroine. Got it?'

'I suppose you're right.' There was a short silence. 'Frankly, I don't give a two cent damn what I do, as long as I don't have to shoot bullets into strangers.'

'What's this? Cynicism, or maturity?'

'Neither. Sanity.'

'Holy Mother of God! You'll be joining Peace Marches next. That's sure to stimulate a few headlines. 'Extra, extra, read all about it, Hostage Hero in Pacifism Scandal'. What esoteric reason, or traumatic incident, has occasioned this sudden conversion?'

'Conversion?'

'The leap from hero to conscientious objector, or is this just another constituent part of the new enlightened man?'

'I suppose it was occasioned by consorting with the enemy.'

'What?' Jack exploded.

'It was a German who nursed me back to health. I wouldn't be here if it wasn't for him.'

'Don't tell me anymore, I don't want to be implicated. I'd be too tempted to write an exposé.'

'Join the queue. The *Boston Tribune* phoned me this morning. They want to buy my story.'

'Oh, yes! How much did they offer?'

'It didn't come to that, I turned them down at the first mention.'

'You turned down the offer to protect this German?'

'Yes.'

'You could have fictionalised that part of the story.'

'I couldn't do that.'

'Why not, for God's sake?'

'Because he's a great guy and it would be demeaning not to give him his real identity.'

'You like him that much?'

'He's a friend.'

'God! Hancock, I despair. You've gone all righteous and honourable. It's giving me a headache. I've seen these symptoms before. It's lack of sex. When did you last have nookie?'

'Four nights ago, I think.'

'You think?'

'I can't remember.'

'Hancock,' Jack announced, 'you know what?'

'No. Tell me.'

'You've gone seriously weird, that's what.'

20

London

'This is Enrico,' Anna said to Brigadier Grant, after she had introduced Jane and shaken his hand.

'*Benvenuto a Londra,*' the Brigadier said to Enrico and made a gesture they all be seated. When settled he looked across the desk and intoned, 'First of all allow me to say how relieved we are to see you home safe and sound. Your journey was interesting, I hear?'

'It was not without incident, sir,' Anna said.

Jane thought his question patronising. She knew Englishmen were adept at understatement, but to have their journey described as 'interesting' was almost dismissive. 'Petrifying' would have been a more accurate word to describe the horror of the homeward journey. When setting sail from Marsala it had not been known that every vessel leaving Sicily and approaching the Tunisian coast had been marked for destruction. An armada of Allied craft lay in wait to intercept, and destroy, all attempted bids to rescue the entrapped Axis forces from the 'Tunisian Tip'. After Dunkirk, fishing boats did not escape suspicion.

If Don Giovanni had been aware of this development never would he have suggested the escape route he did, nor would he have allowed them to board the rickety old fishing boat – laughably called *L'aquila* (The Eagle) – hastily selected for the voyage. When only twenty nautical miles from the Tunisian coast they were attacked by the minesweeper *Agamemnon*. To have survived being shelled, machine-gunned, sucked down by whirlpool and saved from drowning by the energetic efficiency of naval ratings, were experiences that demanded the use of a descriptive word more muscular than 'interesting'.

'How long were you at sea?' the Brigadier enquired.

'Three weeks,' answered Anna.

'Quite an adventure on its own,' the Brigadier remarked. 'I trust the temporary accommodation allocated is not too Spartan for your tastes?' he enquired. 'The usual quarters used to accommodate returning agents were made uninhabitable by German bombs, I fear. At the moment we're struggling to find alternative accommodation.'

'No, the rooms are adequate,' Anna lied.

Yes, adequate for troglodytes, Jane thought. They had been allocated a windowless, bare-floored cell, situated in the basement of the London School of Economics. It was furnished with two iron bedsteads, one tiny wardrobe and a couple of grime-encrusted Bentwood chairs. The cellar was damp and smelled of mildew. For ablution purposes the room boasted a cracked wash hand basin decorated with shit-coloured streaks formed by a constant drip from its single cold-water tap. Placed above this seldom used bowl, nailed above eye level to the bare plaster wall, was a six-inch mirror. Either it had been placed there by a previous inhabitant of gigantic size, or had been positioned for eye-arresting relief in a chamber otherwise devoid of ornament. In the centre of the high ceiling a 40-watt bulb dangled on a short flex.

'Other returning agents have found the quarters to be unsettling,' conceded the Brigadier.

Unsettling? Yet another gross understatement, Jane noted.

'Forgive my impatience, sir,' Anna said, 'but could you tell us what happened to the members of the original mission? It has concerned us and we're anxious to know.'

'Of course. You'll be delighted to learn they're safe and well.' Jane wondered if he was also adept in the use of hyperbole. If so, he was a man well-suited to his trade. To be in command of a variety of grammatical styles was a useful skill to possess when involved in the planning and execution of international foul play.

'It was assumed they had been taken prisoner by the advancing German Army?' Anna continued.

'No. Captain Remington was wounded and taken prisoner by Arab dissidents. Shortly after the others were apprehended and

Freewill is Forfeit

held by an American 7th Army battalion during the retreat from Kasserine.'

'Good heavens!' said Anna. 'Is Captain Remington still in Tunisia?'

'Do you know him?'

'Yes. I was his Italian teacher in Casablanca.'

'Oh! I see. Well,' he said, settling back in his chair, 'he was injured while attempting to avoid capture. During imprisonment he was nursed back to health. When Major Bennett and his team were released, they returned to the Arab stronghold to negotiate Captain Remington's freedom. You will be pleased to hear they were successful. They, then, were recalled to London. Upon arrival Captain Remington immediately was transferred to the States. I didn't meet him, but from all reports he appears to be fit and in good health.'

'Major Bennett and the others?' Anna asked.

'Major Bennett, Sergeant Lambert and Corporal Fazzi, following a short leave, volunteered to return to Tunisia. They intend to raise a rebel force from the ranks of disenchanted Italian prisoners to infiltrate behind Italian lines. So you see, all is well.'

'Have you received any news from Sicily? When we left Colonel Hardie and Don Giovanni's son, Luigi, were fleeing to avoid arrest. We've been on tenterhooks wondering if the Gestapo uncovered their secret lair?'

'I take it this Luigi person, the Don's son, is in league with David?'

'Yes, they became embroiled when David rescued him from the attentions of the Gestapo,' Anna explained.

'Indeed, it sounds an interesting story. As far as we understand they're still at large, but apart from that we know very little. We can only assume the radio has been damaged, or has developed some annoying malfunction, but my guess is, knowing David as I do, now he has established a secure base he is unwilling to break radio silence for fear of alerting attention.'

'Then it's only an assumption he and Luigi have evaded arrest?'

'No, we have learned from intercepted radio transmissions they're causing the Hun a great deal of unwanted grief. Fear not, we know for certain they're alive and active. I take it the young man recruited by David has the temperament required for tasks of an underhand nature?'

'Rest assured, sir, Luigi and the Colonel are two of a kind. Their partnership is sure to be a productive liaison,' Anna affirmed.

'That's good to hear, and his full name is?'

'Luigi Monteverdi,' answered Anna.

'I ask for compensation reasons only, you understand,' explained the Brigadier.

Jane decided to break her silence. 'Since the subject has been broached, perhaps this would be a good time to discuss the possibility of compensation for Enrico. By assisting us he has lost employment and possessions and, in consequence, is in a state of financial distress.'

The Brigadier looked over at Enrico. Taken aback by Jane's question he was uncertain what to say. 'We're certainly in your debt, Enrico, and we owe you more than just simple gratitude. Leave the matter with me and I'll see what can be done.'

Enrico was startled. Was this a manoeuvre to recompense him with money? He needed to be given opportunities to start a new life, not money. His needs were social, not financial. He required practical assistance to be integrated into the manners and habits of a new society. The offer of a few lira would do little to alleviate the torment of new anxieties. Over the past month, in the company of Jane and Anna, his English had improved by leaps and bounds. By observing officers aboard the *Agamemnon* his basic social skills had become more assured, more polished, but these important betterments had done little to erase the evidence of a gauche demeanour and rustic background. A sense of alienation remained. Self-consciousness and insecurity were the twin concerns of daily life. Everything was strange and overpowering. He existed in a state of wonder, mystified by the habits and sophistications of an unfamiliar environment. Everywhere around he saw people who were well dressed and had about them an air of refinement he was uncertain he could emulate. If this was the Shangri-La he sought, why was he plagued with the constant doubt he would be unable to survive in its advanced urban structure? Perhaps the

Freewill is Forfeit

Italian Civil Service had been correct when they had categorised him as a 'Peasant'. Integration and education were his immediate needs, not money.

When Enrico found his voice, he said, 'I made it clear from the start I wished no payment for my services. I asked only to be removed from Sicily and the promise has been honoured.'

'We cannot recompense you for the loss of assets, but what I can do is offer you employment. It would, I'm afraid, require you to go to Tunisia.'

Enrico was shocked. 'I don't understand,' he said, showing alarm. Had he not already deserted from the Italian Army to avoid being sent to Africa?

'You could join Major Bennett's squad. You'd be a perfect backup to his batman, Corporal Fazzi. He's a fellow-countryman of yours. Your duties would entail posing as an Italian prisoner-of-war and. . .'

Jane had heard enough. 'I have my own plans for Enrico,' she interrupted. 'If you wish to recompense Enrico for his services, you can arrange his transfer to America. As we all know Britain is not a safe haven for Italian nationals. In America Enrico would be free of suspicion and the fear of internment.'

'I'm afraid that would be impossible to organise.'

'Why do I find that difficult to believe, Brigadier?' Jane queried. 'You have the power to send men anywhere in the world just by the simple act of lifting the telephone.' There was silence. The atmosphere stiffened.

'Is there something troubling you, Miss McGregor?' the Brigadier asked. It was an attempt to nullify Jane's belligerent manner.

'Since you ask, a great deal troubles me, Brigadier. As a civilian volunteer I could complain about the Machiavellian methods adopted to recruit me into your service. I could object to the robust and hurried methods used to prepare me for surreptitious infiltration into enemy held territory. I could deprecate having been plied with drugs in order to comply with the ambitions of an over-enthusiastic military, but I won't. These complaints are merely personal dissatisfactions.'

'Many agents find the use of Dexedrine helpful when required to go for long periods without sleep,' the Brigadier interjected.

'I agree. When used on the odd occasion I'm certain Dexedrine can be beneficial, but when administered over a protracted period to the detriment of physical and psychological health, then, I think, the recipient should be warned of its deleterious effects and the danger of its addictive capability. After the drug was withdrawn I suffered a period of personal disintegration. I had to tolerate stomach cramps, attacks of acute anxiety, loss of appetite, inability to sleep and a host of other unpleasant symptoms. These unsavoury manifestations had to be endured during bombardment and subsequent arrest, by the British Navy. I realise my complaints must appear petty. When compared with the suffering and sacrifice of others my laments must sound like neurotic complaints unworthy of serious attention, but to return home and be offered accommodation unfit for livestock was, for me, one insult too many to tolerate.'

Brigadier Grant was about to speak when Jane continued. 'This catalogue of discontent, however, is irrelevant when set beside the central purpose of our mission. While entrenched in enemy territory I uncovered the surprising fact that our entire mission was a meaningless and unnecessary exercise. I discovered we had been despatched on a fool's errand. Allied co-operation with the Cosa Nostra was forged as early as December, 1941. What we were sent to achieve was already done-and-dusted.'

'The Americans?' guessed the Brigadier.

'Precisely. If there had been closer co-operation between members of your Executive and your counterparts in American Intelligence, you would have known our jaunt to Sicily was superfluous and an unnecessary risk of life.'

If the Brigadier was shocked he didn't show it. He leaned across his desk and said, 'No, not altogether. With your assistance we have been successful in placing one of our best operatives behind enemy lines with a infrastructure of support, but if what you say is true, then this information is of vital value and highly revealing.'

'Oh! It's true,' protested Jane, mortified her word was being doubted. The Brigadier looked over at Anna for confirmation.

'Sergeant McKay knows nothing of this revelation,' Jane snapped. 'I'm party to this knowledge only because of my trusted relationship with Don Giovanni Monteverdi.'

'And Colonel Hardie, was he told of this?'

'Yes. He was presented with the bare facts on his first meeting with the Don.'

'The bare facts?'

'He was told of the long-standing link between American Intelligence and the Cosa Nostra. He was told nothing more.'

'And you were?'

'Yes.'

'You intrigue me, Miss McGregor. Do continue,' he invited.

'Before I do, allow me to explain that the requested transfer to America was not for Enrico alone, it was for the three of us. The job you have given us to do is only half done. I would like to see it through to its finish.' The Brigadier looked confused, Anna puzzled and Enrico uncertain. 'A recent discovery of mine could be used to grant us employment at the heart of a transmission centre processing clandestine information passing between New York and Nazi-dominated Italy.'

'And how pray can your recent discovery work this miracle?'

'While in Sicily I discovered I hold substantial shareholdings in the New York radio station 'Parliamo Italiano'. This station was initiated, and is operated, by Cesare Visconte. Cesare is the son of Don Carlo Visconte, the man I lived with for several years. During Cesare's youth I had the responsibility for his daily welfare. We liked each other and became attached. We were a family in every sense of the word. Cesare was a gifted boy and proud of his father's achievements and status. He was also acutely aware of his privileged and princely position within the Brotherhood. Several months after his eighteenth birthday his father was murdered and, as you know, I was sent to prison for shooting the assassin. In consequence the Visconte family business empire collapsed. In order to protect certain assets from being seized by the confiscations demanded by the Italian Court, Cesare transferred as much liquidity as he could safely muster to a bank in New York. He then left Sicily and travelled to America to start a new life. I haven't spoken to, or seen, Cesare since. What was related to me by Roberto Monteverdi, however, was startling. During my imprisonment and subsequent secretive withdrawal to Scotland, unknowingly, I had amassed a fortune.' Jane had also discovered it had been Cesare who had sent the sweetmeats and flowers during the period of her incarceration.

'And who is Roberto Monteverdi?'

'He is the elder son of Don Giovanni and legal advisor to many of the Cosa Nostra families. He explained a proportion of the money Cesare had managed to save from the clutches of the State belonged to me. These were assets gifted to me by Cesare's father, money that I presumed had been confiscated. In my absence these unknown funds, together with Cesare's own inheritance, plus other additional money from Mafia friends, were used to launch the radio station 'Parliamo Italiano'. This station provides the Italian population of New York with their own language programme, but behind this façade, in reality, it is the hub of an intelligence network with direct links to occupied sectors of Europe. So, you see, Brigadier, when I requested we be transported to America it was not an idle suggestion. I'm sure the advantage of having patriotic employees at the heart of a radio network, partly owned by me, can hardly evade your interest.'

'I'm sorry you feel aggrieved by the way you have been treated while serving the Executive and I can only apologise for Colonel Hardie's over use of the drug Dexedrine, but there is little I can do now to reverse these complaints. I can, however, do something to correct your residential dissatisfactions. I agree the quarters you have been allocated are dismal and entirely inappropriate. Do you have a favourite hotel in London, Miss McGregor?'

Jane smiled at his English aplomb. 'I've heard the Savoy's not bad.'

Brigadier Grant allowed his amusement to register. He leaned forward to lift the telephone. 'Anthea, please telephone the Savoy Hotel and book three rooms. What? Yes, tonight until further notice.' He paused. 'Book the rooms in my alias and instruct the Booking Clerk to send the bill to Courtaulds. Yes, the firm Courtaulds, that's right.' He paused, again. 'Anthea, it will not be queried, just do as I ask, and Anthea, please send Julie to my office with tea for three. Yes, that's right, three, thank you.' He replaced the receiver. He rose, crossed the room to secure his cap and put it on. 'Please, excuse me,' he said. 'What I have to do might take an hour or two, however, after tea Julie will escort you to our basement where you will be provided with clothing and anything else you may require for your stay in London. I'll return as soon as I can.' He turned and left the room.

* * *

Later they returned to the Brigadier's office to be met by a middle-aged civilian and a young woman in naval uniform. The Brigadier was absent.

'My name is Bob Drummond,' the man announced, standing to greet them. He was a tall, tanned, American. He emanated self-assurance. 'I'm on the staff of the American Embassy here in London,' he explained. It was the only explanation they were given for his presence. When he had shaken hands with Jane and Anna, he turned to Enrico. 'Very smart,' he said, as he admired Enrico's single breasted, charcoal grey, hopsack suit, white shirt and red and black diagonal striped tie. 'A touch too English for my taste, but perfect for the Savoy. Is this your first visit to London, Mr Verga?' Enrico nodded. 'I thought it might be. I have taken the liberty to recruit Pamela,' he waved his hand in the direction of the Wren, 'to drive you around the sights while we struggle to dot some i's and cross some t's. Pamela, say hello to Mr Verga.'

'*Ciao,*' Pamela said.

'Good afternoon,' replied Enrico, with a smile of new confidence. Three hours of pampered attention had transformed his mood. He had showered, been shaved with an open razor, had hot towels wrapped around his face, had his haircut to a fashionable style, been subjected to a manicure and given assistance to select a wardrobe of clothes fit for a King. With the caress of fine clothes against his skin and the aromas of wealth in his nostrils, he had gazed at his transformed reflection in the downstairs' mirror and had smiled with genuine satisfaction. All previous uncertainties and anxieties had vanished at that moment. Truly, this was the beginning of his metamorphosis from peasant to gentleman.

'*Sei pronto?*' the young woman enquired.

'Ready when you are,' replied Enrico, determined to resist the use of his native tongue. He was dressed as an English gentleman and from now on he would disport himself as such. They left, leaving Anna and Jane uncertain of what was to follow.

Bob Drummond opened the conversation. 'First of all, ladies, allow me to compliment you on your appearance. You both look stunning in your new costumes. I apologise for the absence of Brigadier Grant. He has been summoned to the War Office and is unlikely to return for several hours. So, without further preamble let me kick off by addressing the central issue of concern, namely, the accusation that the American Intelligence Service has been guilty of concealing important information. When internal enquiries were made, the allegation was refuted with protests of angry denial. After further investigation, however, it was revealed by a Senator, who must remain nameless, that a tenuous link had been formed between, what he conveniently called, 'a non-budget sector of Intelligence and a closeted number of Mafia personnel'. The Senator explained this unofficial liaison was merely a link initiated as a watching brief. It amounted to nothing more than a precaution against the suspect activities of mistrusted aliens. I was told this 'extra-curricular co-operation' had to be denied. In other words, button-up, shut-up, it's not happening, end of story.' He stopped speaking and smiled 'You look confused, Miss McKay?' Drummond ventured.

'Why so hush-hush?'

'Can't you guess?' he enquired.

'I can,' said Jane. 'Ambitious politicians protecting their future careers. The Mafia in America is viewed as being a criminal organisation. Any hint of association with perceived lawbreakers would expose a politician to the risk of possible future, inconvenient accusation.'

'Exactly correct,' Drummond said, straining to prevent his eyes from straying to the shapely limbs assailing his eye. 'On the one

Freewill is Forfeit

hand there is military advantage, but on the other political embarrassment. That's the core of the dilemma. We Americans are a career-obsessed nation and success usually requires adherence to a code of virtuous behaviour. To be suspected of straying from the paths of righteousness can irretrievably blot the *curriculum vitae.*' He allowed himself a smile. 'Any deviation from the accepted norms of what is commonly thought to be decent has to be suppressed, hidden from the world and should any wrong-doing inconveniently emerge, denied with a straight eye. Cosying-up to the Mafia for military advantage is permissible, but politically it can never be admitted. Let it be done, by all means, but keep it hidden and should it ever come to light, deny, deny, deny. So you see, that a link exists is irrefutable, but to confess to the link, injudicious. This briefly explains the reason why the information failed to be passed on. The political arm of Army Intelligence doesn't wish the truth to be known and, of course, has never revealed the information to its own trusted agencies.'

Drummond looked at both women to judge if he had been successful in stifling discontent. Unsure, he decided to change the subject. 'And now, to more pleasant matters.' Looking at Jane, he said, 'Brigadier Grant told me you wished to go to America. Tell me, if permission is granted and you join the staff of Radio Parliamo Italiano, do I understand you would be willing to act as an undercover agent on our behalf?'

Jane was disturbed by his question. 'Not undercover. No. I'll keep you informed, but only with Cesare's knowledge and approval.' She watched Bob Drummond's face crease with concern. 'Don't be alarmed, when I explain to Cesare the political reticence to admit to the existing relationship, he will not be pleased. He has worked to establish an effective information service to be of assistance to the Allied cause and will be unhappy his efforts are being restricted at the whim of un-nameable apparatchiks. Information being unavailable to sectors that should be informed will anger him. Have no fear, Mr Drummond, you will receive regular reports, but it will not be outwith Cesare's knowledge. My actions will be overt.'

'Not too overt, I trust?'

'In the sense any information I believe should be passed on will be distributed to the correct and relevant agencies.'

'Excellent,' Drummond said, unwilling to remove his eyes from Jane's face. He thought her exquisite. She was intelligent, straightforward, frank and above all, beautiful to behold. He thought her a perfect specimen of mature womanhood. 'The day after tomorrow I'm flying home. I can arrange for you to accompany me, or would you rather return to Glasgow for a well deserved spot of leave before travelling?'

'Glasgow can wait. Two days time, you say? Do you mean all of us?'

'No, Sergeant McKay is a serving member of the British Army. It's beyond my remit to interfere with her movements.'

'I'm not going without Enrico.'

'Ah! Yes, Enrico. I can arrange Enrico's emigration, but Cesare Visconte would have to stand guarantor for his employment.'

'Done! We'll be able to find something for him to do in the station.'

'That's agreed then.' Drummond said, jubilant that the arrangements made would be an opportunity to further delight in Jane's company. 'My secretary will deliver the flight details to the Savoy. All the relevant paper work will be attended to by Embassy staff.'

Anna looked crestfallen. During a brief conversation her expectations had been dashed. Her life had suddenly fallen apart. She was losing the opportunity of going to Hank's homeland, losing the companionship of two friends and left to contemplate an uncertain future in the army. 'I was hoping I might be allowed to go too,' she complained, near to tears. She knew she sounded pathetic, but didn't care.

Drummond dragged his eyes from Jane and examined Anna. 'During my conversation with the Brigadier he told me you know young Remington.' he said.

Anna's heart pounded. 'Hank Remington?' she asked.

'Yes.'

'Do you know where I can contact him?' It was out before she could stop.

'Yes, he's on extended leave at home. He returned to the States about a month ago to a hero's welcome. The press coverage he received was enormous.'

'Hank's a hero?'

'That's right. He was an original squad member of the mission you were given to complete, yes?'

'Yes, correct. We met in Casablanca before the original mission's departure.'

'Perfect,' Drummond said and smiled. 'I'm sorry,' he said, 'let me explain. In the American mind there is no real perception of the sacrifices and hardships suffered by the British in this war.' Anna wondered what this statement had to do with Hank. 'In order to rectify this state of affairs it has been suggested certain military personnel be selected to participate in a joint American/British nationwide campaign. It will be an allied promotion to whip-up patriotic fervour, cement the importance of our present unique partnership. To be effective it has been estimated in order to cover America with minimal efficiency it will require the employment of four teams of four, two British and two Americans in each team. The eight Americans for this tour have been selected. One of the eight is Hank Remington. Of the corresponding eight Brits six already have been selected and a search is ongoing to find another two.' He stopped and waved a square of buff paper above his head. 'I have in my hand a 'Request for Transfer of Personnel' form. It is for a posting to Washington. All it requires is Brigadier Grant's signature, but before submitting it for approval I wanted to assess if you would be a suitable candidate for the posting. I'm delighted to say you would make a splendid recruit for inclusion.'

He stopped and waited for Anna's reaction. Her face flushed red and her mouth hung open. She was incapable of speech. 'Well,' he said, 'what do you say?' Anna continued to stare at him in disbelief. 'The Brigadier thought you would make a perfect partner to team up with young Remington and, now I've met you, I find it difficult to disagree.'

'Forgive me,' Anna said, in shock, 'do I understand I am being selected to travel on an American tour with Hank, in the company of two others?'

'Exactly,' he answered.

'When is this tour planned to commence?'

Drummond looked down at his papers. 'You will be flown to America with the other seven just as soon as the group selection is complete, but to answer your question, the British team is expected in Washington by this time next week.'

When Drummond looked up he saw two women standing in an embrace. The younger woman had tears in her eyes, the other was shrieking with laughter. The unorthodox behaviour surprised him. He concluded although men were capable of solving all the mysteries of the universe never would they achieve the profound comprehension required to unravel the enigmatic complexity of female behaviour. Man's feminine counterpart, the female of the species, would forever remain a mystery to the male psyche.

The accusation proclaimed by Sgt Robert Lambert's drug-induced ghost.

Generals,
In perfumed tents,
Jiggle
Lottery maps of misery,
Pinpointing where eyes are to be gouged
And babies bayoneted.

Bishops,
In cathedrals of cant,
Juggle
Words in memorial worship,
'Til tyranny transmogrifies
To testaments of celebration.

Historians,
In hallowed halls,
Jangle
Jejune judgements,
Making less the carnage
By mythologising conflict.

Parliamentarians,
In palaces of privilege,
Joggle
To protect the fascist imperative,
Saturating the systems of State
With elusive engineering.

Survivors,
In traumatised streets,
Struggle
To demobilise memory,
And bend to tax burdens
For munitions to murder their sons.

Other Books
from Argyll Publishing

The Machine Doctor
Peter Burnett
Thirsty Books ISBN:1 902831 33 0 pbk £9.99

Shortlisted **Scottish Book of the Year 2002**

'. . . an exhilarating and anarchic comedy shot through with a
withering social commentary'
Scotland on Sunday

'. . . an ambitious, multi-voiced satire on the soul-destroying
mind-numbing effects of the 21st century. . . hilarious' **The
List**

'. . . ingenious . . . it has energy and commitment, it is funny
and makes a serious point lightly' **The Herald**

The Wind in her Hands
Margaret Gillies Brown
ISBN: 1 902831 41 1 pbk £7.99

'an intriging picture of life early last century' **Caledonia**

'it never flags – the story of a strong woman'
Moray Firth Radio

'inspirational' **Press & Journal**

Selected Stories Brian McCabe
ISBN: 1 902831 62 4 £9.99 pbk 320 pages

'a writer whose craft is polished to the point of invisibility'
The Scotsman

'direct, economic and masterly' **New Statesman**

'spiky, observant, with a lethal wit' **Scotland on Sunday**
